OF DREAMS AND DRAGONS

KARPOV KINRADE

COPYRIGHT

EBOOK LICENSE NOTES

eBook License Notes

Disclaimer

DEDICATION

This book wouldn't be possible without the generosity shown by the Ukiah Valley Fire Authority in letting me tag along and ask a LOT of crazy questions, like "how would you treat a burn from a dragon?"

Special thanks to Mike Stewart, Captain, for answering a million and one questions, and to Hermano Moore, Engineer, Gabriella Bushway, Volunteer Firefighter, John Strangio, Captain, Robb Ramseier, Engineer and Kirk Thomspon, Chief, for inspiring me, answering questions, showing me around and letting me ride shotgun in the big red truck.

And to all the brave firefighters who work long hours, often without pay and without thanks, to keep us and our belongings safe when tragedy strikes. This book is for all of you.

This book was researched and written before the fires that have ravaged Northern California broke out. It will launch in midst of this tragedy. We will be donating a portion of the proceeds of this book to the local organizations helping support the first responders and those who have lost everything in these fires.

~KK

1

TWO WORDS

Everyone has a word. That one word that encapsulates and articulates so much of who you are, that on a Venn diagram there would only be a sliver that falls outside the scope of that word. Most people never learn their word, but it's out there, waiting to be found. Waiting to be called forth.

I... I have two words. My first word, only because I learned it first, is *hiraeth*. It's not even English—though the best words seldom are, so that should hardly be counted against it. I initially discovered *hiraeth* on social media, and it made me suck in my breath as something stirred deep within me. It's Welsh, and there's no direct translation into English, but it's defined as a kind of homesickness tinged with grief or sadness over a person or place that is lost to you. It carries with it a sense of longing, nostalgia and wistfulness, and it's an emotion that has weighed on me every day of my life that I can remember. Discovering there is a word for what I've always felt does help ease the sorrow some, but only in the way that identifying the monster helps ease the fear. It's still a monster. It still hunts you. But now you know its name.

My second word is so closely aligned with my first that it maybe doesn't count. *Saudade*—originating in Portuguese and Galician—

takes *hiraeth* another step, though. It is often defined as "the love that remains" after someone or someplace is gone—or even if that person or place is still in your life, but it has changed so much that you mourn the past or future.

These words are my ghosts. They haunt me, teasing at my mind as I go about my day. And they are directly tied to a life I can't remember, because I never lived it. A life that could have been.

If my father hadn't died before I was born.

If my mother hadn't married Pat.

If fate had taken a swing at someone else the day I was born, instead of setting its sights on me.

And today, my ghosts are more active than usual as I count the change for my groceries.

I usually shop early in the morning usually, when the crowds at Safeway are shorter, but today couldn't be helped. We're out of too many things and the kids are hungry, so I came after running other errands, when the lines are long and people are tired and impatient and ready to get home to their families.

Women are trained from childhood to be polite, accommodating and docile. To make others happy before themselves. To be self-sacrificing and humble. Which is why, as the line behind me lengthens, and tired shoppers check their phones for the time and sigh dramatically, I feel guilt. Guilt that I have to count out the quarters and nickels and pennies I found in the couch to pay for groceries for the three hungry children at home. Guilt that I have to keep putting back items that push my total too high. Guilt that I couldn't do all the math and taxes and weights of produce in my head, thus saving everyone the hassle of waiting on me. Guilt that I have to use food stamps to cover what my couch change can't.

Guilt.

Because I'm making the people behind me wait too long.

The cashier, Martha, is a middle-aged woman who's worked here as long as I can remember. She's always been kind, and fast, and I try to pick her line whenever I can. She doesn't shame me with silent looks and frowns that others sometimes do, even without realizing it.

She gives me a small, sympathetic smile as I help bag my groceries in reusable bags that have seen better days. One is so frayed I'm not sure it will survive this trip.

"You sure you don't need another bag?" Martha asks.

"Gotta make these work till payday," I say, loading up my cart.

She nods in understanding. "Hang in there, Sky. You know what they say... this too shall pass."

I give her the best smile I can muster and nod. "Thanks, Martha. Sorry about this."

She's already scanning the next customer's food though, so I leave quickly, hoping to get home before the kids.

Fall has settled into the bones of the little city of Ukiah, and today is colder than usual. Winter is indeed coming, though we feel less of a sting two hours north of San Francisco than most of the country. The wind whips around my face, freezing my nose and ears, as I push my cart through the expansive parking lot to my car.

I can smell the rain before it falls, but I have no way of covering myself or my groceries, and the deluge of water soaks me to the skin by the time I pop open the trunk. I make quick work of getting the groceries into the car, but the last bag doesn't survive the experience and rips apart in my hand, depositing my food onto the wet asphalt.

At least the rain is cover for the tears threatening to fall. I'm exhausted, overwhelmed and so very tempted to leave the food there and get home, but some of it's still salvageable. And this was our grocery budget for the week.

A few eggs are still in one piece, and the fruit is only slightly bruised. If I cut it up for a salad, the kids will eat it without complaint. Probably.

I grab whatever looks edible and deposit it on top of the remaining bags, then finally slide into my car, where I'm marginally more sheltered from the rain. When the engine starts on the first try, I offer a prayer of thanks to whoever's listening. The car's an old beater I got off Craigslist. It's missing a window, the heater doesn't work, and the engine looks like someone tried to repair it by blasting it with fire and hoping for the best. I taped now-soggy cardboard over the missing window, and that was the extent of my repair budget. Now I use the powers of manifestation and luck to keep the thing running.

One perk of living in a city that's only about five square miles, despite it being the largest city in Mendocino County, is everything is under ten minutes away.

I drive past the 101 onramp, past the Starbucks I can never afford but always look at with longing, and turn at the corner gas station. Our house is across the street from a park, near an elementary school. On the outside, it looks like every other house on the block. Remarkable only in how ordinary it is. The lower middle class dream, minus the white picket fence.

It's when I unlock the door and walk inside that the truth of my home life hits the hardest. That's where the shadows live, behind the closed doors and draped windows of houses that look like everyone else's. Skulk past the white-washed exterior and you'll find the rot fast enough. But most don't care to dig even that deep. They may smell the decay, but they don't want to deal with the reality.

The groceries are nearly put away when Caleb sprints down the stairs at full speed, nearly breaking his neck as he trips over the last step.

I don't know how I get from the kitchen to the living room so fast. Sometimes it's like I blink and am standing where I want to be.

I catch the six-year-old mayhem-maker before he kills himself, and nearly sob from relief when he looks up wide-eyed, and then grins like a little idiot. "That was amazing, Sky! Let's do it again."

I grip him harder before he escapes my arms, his black hair flopping over eyes almost as dark. "Oh no, kiddo. Not again. I need your help in the kitchen. Where's Pat?"

Caleb shrugs and runs back upstairs before I can stop him. I sigh and stand, my body feeling a lot older than its twenty-four years. I trudge upstairs and check Caleb's room. He's sitting on his disheveled bed playing with his toy fire truck and another toy car flipped over on its side. The fire truck races across pillows and blankets as Caleb shrieks in a high pitched squeal meant to mimic the sound of a siren.

"Look, Sky, it's you and Blake saving people," he says as the fire truck arrives to help the turned over car. He pulls out two dolls dressed in nursing outfits and mimics them helping another doll that was thrown out of the truck. "This one's you," he says, holding up a female doll with brown hair.

I ruffle his head. "She looks just like me."

Caleb grins, putting his attention back on his truck as I look around the room.

Caleb shares the room with his teen brother, Kyle, and little sister Kara. I expected to see her in the crib under Kyle's bunk bed, but it's empty. "Caleb, where's Kara? And where's Pat?"

Caleb looks up from his truck. "Gone."

"What? Where? When?" I'm trying to stay calm, but my voice is rising in pitch and volume. How long was Caleb left alone? And why did Pat take Kara?

"I dunno. Just gone. They left when I got home from school."

I grip the doorframe so hard my fingers turn white, then take a calming breath. "Thanks, buddy." I ruffle his hair and leave him to his toys as I run downstairs.

The living room is a mess. Pat left empty beer cans on the coffee table, and cigarette butts on the ground. The litter box in the corner stinks to high heaven and the cat's food and water bowl are empty. "Marshmallow? You around, kitty?" I pull out a toy and dangle it, hoping the bell will entice the white fur ball from her hiding place, but nope. She's not interested in humans right now. I give up and clean out her litter box, refill her food and water, then grab a trash bag to clean up after the man who calls himself head of this family.

The kids are his.

I'm not part of this family.

Not really.

Pat makes that abundantly clear.

I rub at a bruise on my arm and stretch my sore back.

The dishes are done and the house is as clean as I can make it by the time Pat returns with Kara. Kyle trails behind them and drops his backpack by the front door.

I don't bother telling him to put it away. Not today.

I storm over to Pat. "Where were you? How could you leave Caleb alone?" The anger has been boiling in me for hours, and I can't contain it anymore.

"Back off, you free-loader." Pat slurs the drunken words, but I don't need to hear him speak to know he's been hitting the bottle. Hard. His dark eyes are glazed over and there's a vagueness about his expression that is familiar. He sneers at me, his lip curling. "I knew you'd be home soon. He's old enough to look after himself."

"He's six, Pat! That's not old enough, that's child endangerment. And where did you take Kara?" When she hears her name she reaches for me, and I take the toddler from her father. She has snot all over her face, her cheeks are red from the cold, and she's not wearing a coat.

"She's helping me make a little cash. At least someone does." Spittle flies out of his mouth, hitting me in the face. "I swear, the only reason I still let you live here is because of the debt I owe your mother, God rest her soul. But the dead aren't much good to the living, are they?"

I hand Kara to Kyle and tell him to take her upstairs. Kara's face crinkles into a cry as she calls my name, her arms held out to me. Kyle frowns, wanting to stay and help, but I shoo him away with Caleb following behind. I don't want them around when Pat's like this.

"You let me live here because without me running this house and raising these kids, you'd lose everything, including the extra money you get from your social security for them."

I should have kept my mouth shut. I know better, especially when he's like this. Hard liquor rather than beer was his poison of choice today. I can smell it on him. And I know what that means.

But knowing changes nothing. I seem pathologically incapable of biting my tongue. A character flaw I would be happier without.

Sometimes, the anticipation of pain is worse than the pain itself.

When his fist flies at me, I feel the pain of its impact on my jaw before it lands. And then my whole face is on fire.

I fall to the ground, hitting my head on the sharp edge of the staircase as I fall. But I don't cry or scream. I've learned not to. The last time I did, Kyle heard and came to help, and ended up in the ER due to a 'terrible fall' that broke two bones. I won't let that happen again.

When I was a child, I always wondered why I never saw stars when I was hit. In cartoons they always saw stars, but I only ever saw darkness as my vision blurred and shrunk in on itself until there was nothing.

I always wished for the stars.

Pat stands over me, waiting. He knows I'll get up, despite conventional wisdom telling me I should stay put and wait for him to grow bored and walk away.

Another character flaw.

I get up.

And in that moment, something happens.

A light ignites in me, burning my skin from the inside out. Energy rushes through my body.

Pat takes an unstable step backwards. "What the—"

I take advantage of the moment and step forward. He dwarfs me in girth and height, but somehow I feel bigger, stronger, taller right now. "You will never hit me again," I say, my voice sounding foreign, distant, like someone else talking through me.

Pat stumbles back. "Get away, you freak. You creature. You're not of my blood. You're not of my kin." His face turns ashen, all color draining from him as he stares at me in horror. I know what he's seeing behind my eyes. I have seen it in his too often.

I point to the front door. "Get out. Now."

And to my utter shock, he listens. His drunk ass flees the house, the door slamming so hard behind him it rattles the walls. When it's clear he's not coming back anytime soon, I slump to the ground, hugging myself. I think of the power that just overcame me, and I tremble. Not because I don't know what happened.

But because I do.

2

FROM THE GRAVE

The surge of adrenaline I had is gone, leaving in its wake a shaken shell of a girl with a crushing headache. Viscous liquid drips into my eyes, stinging, and I wipe at it, leaving a crimson stain on the brown leather wristband I always wear on my left arm. I rub at it with my shirt, but the stain persists, the crevices of the engraved vine soaking up the blood. This had been a gift. A reminder. Protection, of a kind.

My eyes fill with tears, whether from the pain, the confrontation with Pat, or long buried grief, I don't know, and I'm too weary at a deep soul level to parse it out just now.

Kyle creeps down the stairs holding a washcloth. "Is he gone?" he asks in a whisper.

I nod, and Kyle speeds up, taking the stairs two at a time with his long, gangly teen legs until he's next to me, pressing the wet cloth against my head. "You might need stitches this time," he says softly.

"Grab my bag," I say.

He nods and runs back up the stairs to my bedroom where I keep the first aid kit.

He opens the canvas bag and rummages around. "What do you need?"

"I have to wash it first," I say, trying to stand, but a wave of dizziness lands me back on my ass, and I groan at the impact.

Kyle puts a hand on my arm. "Let me help you."

I hate that he has to do this, but he's right, it's bad this time. I could walk him through the steps, but I don't want more on his shoulders than there already is. Instead, I pull out my phone and text the one person I know will help without question.

Can you come home? Urgent. Bring med supplies.

Blood is stinging my eyes, and I don't bother waiting for a response. I know he'll come. He always comes.

I touch Kyle's shoulder. "Thank you for your help, but I'll be fine. Blake will be here soon."

At the mention of Blake, Kyle relaxes, though the stress around his brown eyes doesn't ease. I must look even worse than I feel. "Remember, head wounds always bleed more. There are a lot of blood vessels close to the surface, so it looks worse than it is. I promise." My words seem to reassure him some. "Where are the littles? Are they okay?"

He frowns. "They're in the closet."

I close my eyes and sigh. "I'll check on them soon. Go do your homework."

He's about to argue, but the front door opens and Kyle runs to greet Blake.

"How's our girl?" I hear Blake ask.

"Not good," Kyle says, his voice so broken I feel my heart break a little too.

"I'll take good care of her."

I open my eyes enough to look at Blake, and he whistles as he takes the washcloth from me and examines the cut on my head. "Sky Knightly, you are a mess. This will leave a scar. Stitches would help."

"I can't afford the ER bill."

There's pain etched on his perfect face as he nods. "I'll do what I can."

He makes quick work of it, cleaning it first, then applying pressure to stop the bleeding. "I'll give it 15 minutes. If we can't get the bleeding to stop, I'm taking you in whether you like it or not."

He lifts my head gently and sits on the couch, then places my head on his lap as he holds sterile bandages against my wound. "What happened this time?" he asks.

"The usual. Just Pat being Pat."

"This isn't normal, Sky," he says softly and without judgment. Only love. Compassion. Kindness. All the things that make me feel weak right now.

"I know," I say. "But I can't leave the kids alone with him."

"There has to be a better way. You could still try to get custody."

"A single 24-year old who couldn't even make rent without her best friend paying half the bills and has the kind of work schedule we do? In what universe would a judge give me custody of three kids? Steve barely got custody of his own. Forty-eight hour work shifts that often become longer don't impress in custody cases. And Pat doesn't have a record, he's just an asshole."

"An abusive asshole," Blake says.

"Yes," I agree.

"Maybe the kids, and you, would be better off if you report—"

"Don't say it," I say. "They have no one else. No other family. With Pat gone, they'd be separated. Kyle would end up in a group home for teens. It would ruin them. Who knows what kind of abuse they would endure if the system got ahold of them. At least here I can protect them. *We* can protect them."

We've had this conversation before. Many times. The facts never change.

"And who will protect you?" Blake asks softly, as he strokes my long hair.

I don't have an answer for him. I will have to protect myself. That's always been my life, especially since my mother died giving birth to Kara.

"He's escalating," Blake says.

"I know."

And I do. I know Pat is getting worse. I know it's only a matter of time before this gets really bad. We get a lot of domestic violence calls at the station. And they're often the ugliest. I've seen my future with Pat, and it isn't pretty. So I know the risk. What I don't know is what to do about it. How to fix it. How to stop him. How to keep our family together and keep these kids safe. And stay alive.

After fifteen minutes, Blake checks my head. "Looking better. I'm putting butterfly bandages on it... though you really should get stitches. You'll need to ice it when I'm done."

"Yeah, I know the drill." Blake and I have known each other since we were kids. Fun fact, he was my first husband. Of course, we were in kindergarten at the time, so it wasn't legally binding. Then around puberty he realized he was gay, and all romantic notions between us ended. Now he's like a brother. A ridiculously gorgeous brother with perfect black hair and a perfect physique. And he's my roommate and surrogate uncle to the three kids I call my own. I don't know how we'd make it without him.

Blake hands me two pills and I pop them in my mouth without asking what they are. Pain relief of some kind, and that's all I care about.

When I can finally sit up, I realize he's dressed for work. "Our shift isn't until Saturday," I say, hoping I didn't screw up my schedule somehow. I don't have childcare lined up until the weekend.

"Steve called in," he says.

"Kid sick again?"

Blake nods.

"Poor guy. Single parenting sucks."

Blake laughs. "You would know. But I'm going to call and tell them to find someone else. I need to stay here with you, in case you have a concussion."

"No, I'm fine. Kyle's here if anything happens. You go."

He stands reluctantly, grabbing his bag. "You sure?"

I nod, but regret the movement as pain lances through my head. "I'm sure."

He doesn't look convinced, but I know he needs the money and there aren't many who can cover the shift. We're too understaffed and dependent on volunteers as it is. So I stand and walk him to the door. "See? I'm fine. Just a headache. I'll be right as rain tomorrow."

He snickers at that. "Tomorrow you'll have a black eye and feel like something that exited the back end of a sick dog."

"Thanks for the optimistic prognosis, doc."

He kisses the side of my head that isn't a bloody mess. "Be careful. Don't let that drunk asshole back in. And call if you need me. I'll be home in minutes. With backup."

"Thanks, Blake. For everything."

He nods and steps out to the porch. "I'll come straight home after my shift."

Once he's gone, I shut the front door and lean against it, closing my eyes as I collect my thoughts. I need a better plan than wait and hope I don't die at Pat's hands. But right now, I need to check on the kids.

I find Caleb huddled in the back of the closet in their bedroom, with Kara sleeping next to him on a pile of dirty laundry, her black hair stuck to her head with sweat. This used to be my room, so I know every nook and cranny and hiding place. I crawl in with them and he snuggles into my arms, his nose dripping snot onto my shirt as his tears swell his big brown eyes.

"He hurt you," he says.

I don't want to lie to him, so I say nothing for a while, and just hold him. Minutes later, his tears dry up and he sighs deeply into the crook of my arm.

I lean down, whispering in his ear. "Did you know this was my closet before you were born?" I ask him.

He shakes his head no.

I smile. "It was. And did you know there's a secret to this closet?"

Now his eyes widen, all fears forgotten as his young mind is gripped with the mystery. "A secret?"

I nod. "A hidden treasure. Want to see?"

He bobs his head eagerly, and I grin as I move clothes, toys and old shoes away from the corner. I pull up the edge of the carpet and show Caleb how to loosen the board to access the secret hiding place. "Go ahead and see what's in there," I tell him.

With all the eagerness of a curious six-year-old he reaches in and pulls out everything he finds. There's a box of dusty crayons that smell like childhood and summers and wax and imagination. A coloring book that's mostly colored in, but there are still some blank pages left. A metal box full of odds and ends I collected as a child: dried leaves, stones, loose change, a matchbook, some old Halloween candy that could probably survive the apocalypse, and a journal.

I take the journal from him and open it, my hands shaking. It's pink and green, with a dragon on the cover that used to be covered in glitter that's mostly faded now. Inside is my childhood scrawl filling up page after page with dates, times and the exact things that happened in the most boring and mundane detail. What I ate, what I wore, what so-and-so said that was completely awful and ruined our friendship. But somewhere in the middle my hands pause, and I slow my breathing as I try to make sense of what I'm seeing.

There's a shift in my writing. Not just a different pen or different hand, but a different language. Words turn to symbols. Glyphs. I don't recognize them, but seeing them sends shivers through my body, because as foreign as they are, they feel familiar. Like I should know what they mean. And it brings me back to my words. *Hiraeth. Saudade.* The homesickness and loss and nostalgia hit me hard, rocking me back until I'm pressed against the wall.

I slam the book closed and clutch it in my hands. Caleb has forgotten all about me as he scribbles in the coloring book. Kara is just about to wake from her nap and will need changed and fed. I ruffle his hair and plaster a fake smile on my face. "Now you'll always have something to do when you're in here," I say.

He nods, content with the small treasure of a child.

I pick up Kara and crawl out of the closet, still clutching my old journal, my head pounding from the movement. "What do you want for dinner tonight? Fish sticks or... fish sticks?" I try to hide my pain under a smile.

He looks up at me, a goofy grin splashed across his face, one that isn't fake or forced. Children are so resilient. It's the only explanation for how any of them survive to adulthood.

"Pasgetti!" he says.

I frown dramatically and put a finger to my mouth as if thinking about it. "That didn't sound like fish sticks. But I'll see if we have any noodles and pasta sauce, okay?"

He nods. "Okay!"

"Will you settle for fish sticks if that's all we have?" As if he has a choice. But he's a good boy and he knows how this game works, so he nods.

I'm about to walk away, when I pause, remembering the cat. "Have you seen Marshmallow around?" I ask.

Caleb doesn't look up from his drawing; he just shakes his head no.

I leave him to his closet and crayons and take Kara to the couch downstairs to change her. She looks up at me with large dark eyes, blinking slowly, as if she's trying to figure out the human words for all the deep thoughts she holds in her mind. I wonder if babies come to this world knowing all the secrets, but forget them when they learn how to speak.

I kiss her forehead and she smiles and wraps her pudgy fingers around my index finger. "Sky!" she says in her baby voice. The fact that my name was her first word still makes me weepy. She may not be my child biologically, but I've been raising her since she was born, and couldn't love her more.

Once she's changed, I put her in a high chair with a sippy cup and some cut grapes to snack on while I set about making dinner.

We do indeed have the makings for 'pasgetti', and a few hours later the littles are fed and happy and in bed, and the kitchen is cleaned up of Kara's attempts at using spaghetti as art. Only Kyle remains awake, watching me with worried eyes. "Some day he'll go too far," Kyle says, not looking up from the math book he's pretending to study.

"I'll be okay," I assure him.

Now he looks up, setting his book aside. "What happens when you and Blake aren't here anymore? What will happen to us?"

My heart breaks a little as I walk over to him and kneel so that we're eye to eye. "I'm not going anywhere. You're my kids and I'll always be here to protect you."

I can tell he's about to cry, and that he doesn't want to do it in front of me, so I let him go without a word as he runs upstairs to get ready for bed.

I stay downstairs, enjoying the peace and quiet. While Pat technically lives here on paper, he spends most nights elsewhere. With women. At bars. Drunk in alleys. When it's just me, Blake and the kids, it feels like a real home. Pat could be gone for the night, or for the week. We won't know until he comes back. So I've learned to take advantage of the moments without him whenever possible.

I get comfy on the living room couch and turn on the TV, flipping through channels until I find something semi-decent. Some kind of soap opera western fantasy thing. When I finally fall asleep, dreams haunt me. Dreams of faceless men taking the children away.

I wake in a cold sweat on the couch, the TV still on, my head pounding from a horrid headache. I check the time: 3:48 a.m. Too early to be up, too late to try to go back to sleep.

So I put on a pot of coffee, pop a few more pills Blake left me, and prepare a breakfast of oatmeal for the kids. As I sip my coffee and stir the oatmeal, I hear a thump at the front door. Probably Blake coming home after his shift. He really needs to work on being quieter in the middle of the night, though.

It's still dark out, and when I open the door, the cold mist of morning washes over me. The porch is empty—no Blake. Maybe it was the cat. I'm just about to go back inside when something catches my eye. A stained leather bag—cracked and old—sits at my feet. There is something unnatural to its shape. Something wrong. I lean down, and a rancid smell hits my nose. My stomach turns. I try not gag as I use the edge of my shirt to cover my hand and pull the bag closer. There is something. A piece of paper sticking out. I clutch it and read.

"I TOLD you there will be consequences. This is but the first."

AND THEN I see what's in the bag. And my stomach cramps and vomit spews from my mouth. I try to aim it at the potted plant to my right, but only half meet my mark.

I just found Marshmallow. Or part of her, at least.

3

A POUND OF FLESH

My eyes fill with tears, and I force myself to look around, to look for the person who did this in case they haven't disappeared. I find something, some*one,* in the shadows. A man steps forward. A man in a dark cloak wearing a dark hat. His cane clicking against the concrete path. His short, gray beard neat against his chin. Thick silver buttons run down the front of his coat, and black boots cleaned to a shine cover his feet. When he speaks, his voice is old and thin like withered paper. "Hello, Ms. Knightly. It appears you have found my message."

My throat goes dry and I clench my fists, assessing the man standing before me. His composed expression hides whatever he might be feeling or thinking. His dark tailored suit and finely stitched trench coat speak of wealth. His tone is that of a man accustomed to getting his way.

But there's something more about him. Something that gives me pause, and prevents me from responding as I might otherwise. He just killed my cat and seems entirely unconcerned. He could be armed, and likely is. I'm not. Pat's gun is locked upstairs, with the bullets secured in a separate locked case—at my insistence if he was going to persist in his desire to have the weapon in the house with children. All I have on me is an old cell phone, hardly a worthy weapon, my lightsaber app notwithstanding.

I need more information. I need to know what—and who—I'm dealing with before I let myself react. I need to stay calm as I think of a plan. If he attacks me, I'll run into the house and bar the door and call 911.

"How do you know me?" I ask, my voice only wavering a small amount.

His gray eyes bore into me as he speaks. "I know your family. There is a long history there. I am... an old friend, you might say. Call me Mr. Pike." He tips his short top hat towards me while partially bowing, a conciliatory smile on his aged face.

My voice remains steady as I slowly move my hand towards my pocket, to reach my phone. "Nice to meet you, Mr. Pike. I'm curious, why are you visiting?"

"It was time," he says. "This meeting was scheduled long ago, you see, between Pat and myself. Yet, he is not here and you are." He smiles warmly. "Oh and you needn't bother about hiding your phone. You may use it, but I'm afraid it won't perform as you wish."

I'm baffled by his remarks, but I pull my phone out of my pocket slowly as he nods in approval. I look down, seeing the numbers that I need to dial. I move my finger over the nine, but it slips off the phone screen. I try again, but it's as if I'm trying to climb a wall of ice. My finger can't connect. It slips off each time I attempt to dial.

Panic wells in my gut, and Mr. Pike clears his throat. "As I said, it won't do as you wish tonight. So let us continue as we were."

My voice is no longer calm, as fear settles into my bones. "What do you want?" Whatever game he's playing, or trick he's managing, it's preventing me from calling for help. I need another plan. Maybe I can scream. Get a neighbor's attention. Or maybe I can run back into the house before he can stop me.

Or maybe... I glance down at my wristband as I weigh the cost of such a choice. No. I can't. It's too high a risk. Even for this. Not yet, at any rate.

"Pat and I made an agreement," Mr. Pike says, " a long time ago. I have honored my side of the bargain, but he has yet to honor his."

"So you killed my cat?" I ask, too harshly. With too much anger. I cringe, expecting him to attack me for my insolence.

But he doesn't look the least bit aggravated. If anything, his eyes turn sad. "Yes. Yes, I did. You see, I arrived in this town a week ago. It was a week ago that the deal should have been honored. It was not, and so I am back here again, as Pat knew I would be, with a reminder." He pauses. "I am truly sorry it was you who found my message. It was meant for Pat and no one else."

He seems sorry I found the cat, but not sorry he killed an innocent animal; I need to get away from this man. He's most likely a sociopath, perhaps even a psychopath, and if so he would have no qualms about taking another life... maybe even a human one.

Perhaps if I can get him talking—distract him with the sound of his own voice—I can creep back into the house. Get the kids somewhere safe. Call the police, if my phone will work.

"What deal did you and Pat make?" I ask, as a feeling of rage for my bastard step-father surges in me. Of course this would be his doing.

"That is between Pat and myself," Mr. Pike says. "But, in essence, I helped him with a problem, and now he must help me with mine."

My eyes narrow. "What kind of problem? Pat isn't very good at helping himself out of trouble, let alone anyone else."

He cocks his head. "It is not a problem you would understand. Not yet, at any rate. Oh, and don't bother trying to creep back into the house while distracting me. You may leave at any time. It is Pat I came for, not you. But perhaps you could help me find him? As a friendly courtesy?"

Beads of sweat break out on my forehead despite the frost in the air. I nod, willing to say anything this man wants to hear to get him off my porch. "Yes. I'll let him know you were here."

"Very well. I will return once again tomorrow at this hour. And if Pat has not honored his side of the bargain, then I will bring another message. One far more personally painful."

He turns to leave, the moonlight glinting off the opal tip of his walking cane. As soon as his eyes are off me, I dash into the house, slamming the door shut behind me. I latch the deadbolt, my hands shaking in terror. My thin cotton shirt is soaked in cold sweat, and I can't stop the tears that flood my eyes.

I take a deep breath and once again attempt to dial 911. This time, my fingers don't slip off the phone.

4

A SLAB OF GRAY

I wait by the window, watching my breath fog the glass. My palms are slick with sweat. My chest is heavy. Every second, I imagine the man with the cane walking back down the street, returning before the police arrive. Every second, I imagine what I may have to do to protect my family. I think of Pat's gun again. I don't want to use it. But I will if I must.

A minute goes by. Another. And after what feels like forever, a police car pulls up by the sidewalk. I recognize the officer who gets out. Dean Lancaster, a tall blond with a guy next door look. We met before—on the job. The fire department was called in to offer back up on a car accident with suspected fatalities. It involved a messy body extraction and the Jaws of Life. He was on duty at the time, and we all went out for drinks after our shifts ended. One thing led to another, and there was kissing involved, but it never went further than that. My choice. Not his. And I've been trying to walk the line of friends with him ever since.

He's been trying to erase that line all together.

When he walks up to the porch, I open the door and invite him in. We sit on the couch as I explain all that's happened.

"Can you describe him again?" asks Dean, putting a hand on my knee.

I scoot to the edge of the couch, slipping away from his unwanted advance, and go through the very detailed description I already gave. Tall—at least 6'2", graying short beard and hair, cold gray eyes. I describe Mr. Pike's face in exacting detail, down to the mole on the lower right corner of his jaw, and everything he was wearing, down to the tri-colored wood of his walking staff.

Dean frowns. "That's not much to go on. It could be almost anyone. But we'll do what we can."

"What do you mean? I gave you so many details a sketch artist should have no trouble capturing his likeness."

He pats my leg as he stands. "I just... I just don't see how this will be enough."

I stand to face him, and notice there's something about Dean's eyes, about his expression, that makes me think of how my fingers slipped off my phone. Something's not right.

"Look," he says, "I'll come by again tonight to check on you. Maybe we can get some coffee or a late dinner, talk more about this."

His words barely register. My mind is on one thing and one thing only. Protecting my kids. "You need to find him," I say. "And until you do, we need protection."

Dean rubs his stubbled chin, then nods. "We'll leave a patrol outside the house. Let me know if you learn anything more about this Mr. Pike."

I sigh and nod. "I will." Though I doubt it will help. Whatever voodoo this man works, it's good at protecting him.

"You need to find Pat," Dean says. "Ask him about this. I'll check around town too." He glances at my head, the bandage there, and his voice turns soft. "You know, if... if you file a report—"

"This wasn't him," I say, covering my cut self-consciously. "I fell down the stairs carrying laundry. It looks worse than it is." A lie. Always a lie. But if it's a lie you've told yourself so many times you've started to believe it, does it still count as a lie?

"Right. Well, if you remember that happening differently, give me a call." Dean grins, his tone shifting. "So... what do you say to that dinner?"

His words pull me away from the things that matter. I meet his gaze, my face serious. "Dean. I'm not interested. I told you so before, and I'm telling you again. Back off."

His jaw stiffens. "Look, Sky, things will go a lot more smoothly if you just... co-operate. Remember, this investigation can go easily, or—"

"Or I call your boss, Nick, and let him know your impeding this investigation and sexually harassing a victim. I suppose it could go that way, if you'd like." I raise an eyebrow.

He frowns, then turns sharply and heads to the door just as Blake runs in.

"What happened? What's going on?" he asks, pushing the black hair out of his eyes and glaring at Dean.

"I'll let you two talk," says Dean. He checks his watch, then leaves the house, closing the door behind him.

Blake turns to me. "What's going on? Why was he here?"

I push thoughts of Dean away and explain everything that happened for the second time tonight. When I reach the part where I described Mr. Pike to Dean, I sigh in exasperation. "Can you believe he thought my description wasn't good enough?"

Blake's eyes glaze over a bit and he frowns. "Well, to be honest... he's right. That's not much to go on."

I flinch. "What'd you say?"

"Hmm? Oh, I know you don't want to hear this, but I agree. That's not much to go on."

That's not much to go on.

Dean used the same words. The *exact* same words.

"Wait," I say, my whole body shaking with stress. "What did you hear, exactly? How did you hear me describe Pike?"

He shrugs. "Average height. Average build. Like I said, that's not much to go on."

I remember my phone. The way my fingers slipped off.

"But don't worry," says Blake. "We'll find him. Nothing like this will happen again."

For the first time in a long time, I don't believe my best friend.

DESPITE MY BEST efforts to describe Pike, Blake doesn't hear what I want. When I tell him this, he just shrugs. "I'll grab some coffee," he says. "Something tells me we're both gonna need it today."

He runs to Black Oak Coffee Roasters—a locally owned coffee house with the best lattes in town and great latte art—and when he returns, we spend an hour digging a hole in the backyard in which to burry Marshmallow. We wake the kids and get them breakfast before breaking the news to them, and through tears and sorrow, we have a mini funeral for the faithful Marshmallow. He got hit by a car, we say. It is a small lie, but a big kindness.

Then I manufacture a fake smile and go about making the day as normal as possible for the littles: Lunches packed, backpacks ready, hugs and kisses exchanged. And after the kids are all dropped off at school and daycare—with warnings to the offices that the kids need to be watched extra carefully and not leave with anyone not on the list—I make a quick stop at Home Depot and head back home. With a fresh pot of coffee brewing—nothing as good as Black Oak but it'll have to do—I get to work changing all the locks in the house and making sure the windows are secure. I'd love to get an alarm system put in, but that's not happening right now, so I make do the best I can. Satisfied that neither Pat nor Mr. Pike can just waltz back in here, I lock up the house and climb back into my car, sagging against the steering wheel as I try to keep my wits about me.

Before I try starting the engine, I pull out my phone and call Pat, knowing he would have been passed out somewhere earlier. The call goes to voicemail and I leave a stern message. He needs to call me back now. We have something to discuss. Then, I drive.

It doesn't take me long to reach my destination, and a light trickle of rain splashes against my face as I walk through the expanse of grass with gray granite slabs marking the end of a life every few feet. With head bent, eyes to the ground and my coat pulled tightly around me, I make my way to the one grave I care about in a sea of them.

The rain obscures my tears as I kneel in the grass and rub a hand over the headstone I came for. Laura Knightly. Beloved wife and mother. She died too young, leaving behind too many who needed her. I lay a flower next to her name and speak in a hushed voice, though I see no one around me.

"I miss you, Mum. Things were different when you were here." And they truly were, because Laura Knightly was a good mother. She protected us all from Pat's wrath and alcoholism as best she could. I don't know why she never left him. Maybe her religious beliefs prevailed. Maybe she, like me, worried what would happen to the kids if she did. Maybe she was charmed by his good days, because he did have them. Days when he taught me how to shoot his gun. Days when we would work on repairs around the house or put together cheap furniture. But the day she died changed everything.

We lost a mother. Pat lost his wife. And then he lost himself completely in drink and anger. There were no more good days. And he blamed me. He blamed me for stealing her attention from him when she was alive, and he blamed me for her death, though it was complications from birthing Kara that ended her life. But then, he blames me for everything wrong in his life. I am his scapegoat, whether it's poor weather or stock market changes, I'm responsible.

Nearly two years ago, I lost the most important person in my life. Since then I've made it a habit of coming here once a week, and though on hard days like this I'm tempted to forgo the ritual, in truth, it's on hard days like this that I need to visit the most. Because I find a kind of peace here, even if only for a while.

"Is today the day, mum?"

Like always, there is no response, and like always, I am left wondering. "What did you mean that day?" I ask again, remembering the day Kyle and I played outside many years ago. How he ran out onto the road without a care. How a car came speeding, me too far away to do anything, and then how in an instant I was across the street, holding Kyle in my arms, safe. My mother found us only moments later, and through tears she said some things I barely remember. But what she said last, I remember still. "One day, little feather, your true self will be revealed, and even though those closest to you will turn against you, you must promise me something. Promise me, that when that day comes, you will remember what's in your heart. Promise me, you will never forget who you are."

I asked her what she meant, but she said no more. And now every day I wonder, is today the day?

Is Pike's arrival simply the precursor to something more? Something my mother tried to warn me about?

I don't know, and I don't bother worrying more. I swore to my mother I would take care of the littles. Keep them safe. Make sure they had a chance at a good life, and that is what I intend to do. First, I need to find that bastard, Pat, and force him to tell me what evil deal he's made. Then, I make him pay up, no matter the cost.

The smell of rain and freshly cut grass invigorates me, and I stand, ignoring the tickling numbness in my legs as my blood gets moving again. I clutch my jacket around my chest and walk back through the cemetery, the rain fizzling into barely a drizzle. It takes several moments before I realize I'm no longer alone. A man sits nearby, leaning over a grave, a silver flask clutched in his hand that he takes long swigs of. His coat is black and long and whips in the wind, revealing pants and a shirt that are just as dark. Even his short hair is raven black. The only bit of color he wears is a blood red scarf... a streak of fire in the windy rain.

"Those we love don't go away; they walk beside us every day," a deep voice says, startling me. It's the man with the scarf, but I can't tell if he's speaking to me or to the grave. His voice is resonant, and his accent sounds British. "Unseen, unheard, but always near. Still loved, still missed, and very dear."

My eyes mist as I pause to look at him. "That's... that's beautiful. Who said it?"

He shrugs. "Not sure," he says, still facing away from me. "I saw it on Etsy once."

I can't help but smile at his unexpected answer, and it feels good. It's the first real smile I've had in a while, so unlike the fake ones I put on for the kids and Blake.

"Thank you," I say to the back of the man's head.

"For what?" He stands and turns towards me, his piercing blue eyes taking me in with one look.

"For reminding me there are still things to smile about," I say.

He tilts his head towards the graves we are surrounded by. "Lose someone recently?"

"No... not recently. But I don't think time makes as much of a difference as people say."

He nods, his face flickering with a glimpse of his own grief so fast I almost think I imagine it. "I don't suppose it does," he says. "For what is time, but a measure of things that have already happened or have not happened yet? What is time, but a measure of nothing."

"Another Etsy quote?" I ask, trying to lighten my voice, but failing.

"Actually, I made that one up."

A smile plays at my lips. "A philosopher, are you?"

"More a collector of philosophy and purveyor of fine ideas." He winks at me, and I grin.

"Is that a lucrative career? High demand?" I tease.

He chuckles and reaches to shake my hand. "I'm Kaden, by the way. Kaden Varis."

"Sky," I reply, slipping my hand into his. "Sky Knightly." His grip is firm, but reserved. Controlled.

After too long a moment, I drop my hand back to my side reluctantly. His warmth beat out the cold of the day for just a moment. "I lost my mum," I say suddenly. "It's been a couple years, but it feels like yesterday." I don't know why, but I feel like I can share with this man. Perhaps because he is a stranger. He doesn't know my history. My problems with Pat and the kids. I can hold my grief close to me a little longer, in my own private space.

"I'm sorry," he says. "Though words such as those are never suffi-cient, are they? I too lost someone dear. An old friend. Like a brother."

I glance at the gravestone he's standing over. Chadwin Morrison, it says. He died at twenty-six years old, just one year ago today. So young. So tragic.

"It's never easy, is it?" I say.

"No, it never is."

My eyes focus back on him. "Are you from Ukiah?" This is not a big city, and he doesn't look familiar. I'd remember a face like his.

"No," he says. "But I was in the area on business and I came to pay my respects. Did you know, the French don't really say, 'I miss you'? They actually say, '*tu me manques*,' which translates to, 'you are missing from me.' He pauses, searching my face for something I don't understand. "I think they may have the right of it, because when I'm here, with him... or his spirit or memory... whatever you want to call it... I feel more complete than anywhere else."

"Complete. That's a good word for it," I say, thinking of my own feelings. "Like you don't want to leave, because the world out there is wrong somehow. And sometimes... sometimes you just wish you could forget the person who is gone, because then it might be easier to live without them."

He nods, his eyes losing focus as he thinks of something—or someone—far away. "It is true, what you say. But I read another quote, one that has stuck with me, particularly in times of grief. 'If you can't get someone out of your head, maybe they are supposed to be there'." Kaden pulls a hat out of his jacket, a sleek black beret, and puts it on. "It was a pleasure meeting you, Sky. I hope one day you'll find peace in the world of the living, and not just the world of the dead." With that, he walks away, and the sky turns darker once again, pouring down on me as I walk back to my car.

I'm about to start the engine when my phone buzzes. I check the screen, hoping it's Pat.

It's Blake. His voice is hurried. "All hands on deck at the station. We've got a fire and need you here immediately."

5

EYES IN THE FLAME

There are technically four firehouses in Ukiah, but only two are staffed full time. Even only running two, we are constantly short staffed, and rely heavily on volunteers to keep our department going, which is why it's not surprising to get called in on a day off. What's surprising is the time of year. This isn't fire season, but that doesn't mean fires don't happen.

I primarily work the South Station, which I prefer. The North is more plush. It's a house with a kitchen and living room: big screen television, bedrooms and a real home feel. The running joke is that it's Club North. The South Station is where all the personnel offices are located, so it's not just the two to three firefighters on duty, but also the fire chief and everyone else. It's more political, but you also get to know more about what's going on. I like being in the know.

However, on weekends, the South Station feels empty, cold, and sterile. It doesn't have the home-like feel of the North Station, which I don't like. But today there's a larger group than normal when I arrive, as everyone prepares to assist on this fire.

Blake arrives at the same time as me and frowns when he sees me. "How's the head?"

"Hard as ever," I say, smiling through the headache I still have.

"I'll take a look at it later," he says as we enter the garage. "Make sure it's healing."

Blake, with his dark hair, blue eyes, and aristocratic features, is more like a movie star firefighter than a real life one. When we went through training together, he was worried his sexuality would be an issue at the station. You work so closely with your crew, sleeping and living together three or more days a week, covering for each other, protecting each other on the job. We both quickly saw that as long as he did his job—and Blake is an amazing paramedic and firefighter—he'd be treated with the same dark humor and respect everyone else is. That is to say, he gets teased as much as anyone. No one cares that he's gay. But he gets ribbed a lot for his excessive use of hair gel.

It was always Blake's dream to be a firefighter. For me, it was a way out of the life I'm stuck in. A way to help others and a way to do good. But also, it's a way to stay close to Blake, to the only adult family I really have. Our crew is a second family for me, and one that treats me a lot better than my real family. And... there's something about the fire that has always called to me. It draws me in. It's a living, breathing thing that must consume in order to live. Fire has always fascinated me. The secret truth is, you won't find a firefighter anywhere who isn't at least a little bit of a pyromaniac too. The love of fire seduced us to this job, not the desire to kill it.

I head to my locker to grab my gear. Steve sees me first and laughs. "Well, folks. Dragon Girl is here. So today should be eventful."

I roll my eyes at him. "Don't be stupid, Steve."

Steve's been in the department a long time and is a staple here, which is why he gets so much support from the chief when his kids interfere with his shifts. He swings an arm over my shoulder and squeezes. "Everyone loves being on shift when you're here, DG. What firefighter doesn't want a good fire now and then? Especially this time of year."

"I think tales of my fire-attracting nature are highly exaggerated," I say.

The chief walks over to us and smiles. "Actually, I ran the

numbers on a lark. Statistically we have 60% more fire calls when you're working."

My jaw drops. "You ran the numbers? That can't be true. That's impossible."

We get called out for just about anything. Car accidents, support for paramedics, support for police... you name it, we're there. But fires are what we all live for. It's kind of messed up, when you think about it. Any of us who work in emergency response basically depend on tragedy to strike for us to practice our skills and do our jobs. We don't wish for bad stuff to happen, not really. We just hope that if it's going to happen, it happens on our watch. There's nothing worse than a firefighter who's gone too long without fighting a fire. We start to get bitchy and restless.

But there will be no rest today.

I pull on my pants and boots, then my jacket and climb into the fire engine. Connected to the back of my seat is a tank—a Self Contained Breathing Apparatus—that I'll strap on as we drive, so I'm ready to roll the moment we get to our destination.

I'm sitting in the back, with Blake—who's our engineer—driving, and Steve navigating. Once we get there, Steve will call the shots. Blake will work the engine. I'll assess and be ready to respond.

But we'll have to wait for the North Station to arrive before we can go in. There needs to be four firefighters present at all times, two to enter the building, two to stay outside.

My heart pounds against my ribs as the sirens blare into traffic, clearing our way. We get as much information as we can before we arrive at an apartment complex on North State Street. The building is four stories tall. Possible casualties.

When we arrive, there's no visible fire, but we can see smoke pouring out of a corner window. When you work an area like Ukiah you have to get to know the buildings, houses, structures, so you know what to look for when tragedy strikes.

This building has four units on each floor, for a total of sixteen. We need to isolate the unit that's at risk and protect the others, plus make sure the whole structure has been evacuated. The rain has completely subsided, and the day has turned warm and sunny—not an advantage for us.

Fires are living things. They hunt. They feed. They move through space with intention. A good firefighter understands the fire. Respects the fire, even. And learns to anticipate the fire's next move.

"Time to fight the dragon," Steve says to us, a gleam of that familiar excitement I know we all have reflecting in his eyes.

We share a smile, then get busy. Blake works the engine, getting the hose ready, while I walk the periphery to assess any risks. I've determined the point of origin and am about to holler to Steve, when something catches my eye. A man lurks in the shadows near the building. He's dressed in black and I can't see his face. "Sir, I need you to come with me," I yell.

He doesn't respond.

I run forward. "Sir—"

He steps back. Into the shadows. And he's gone.

Dark smoke hangs in the air. The fire's spreading.

I walk forward, searching for the man, but finding nothing.

Then I hear a scream on the second floor. It sounds like a young girl.

"Steve! We've got a child in the building. I'm going in."

This is risky. And dangerous. And the only time we're allowed to break the rules and go in before there are four firefighters present.

I know Steve will join me soon, but I don't wait. I can't. There's a girl up there, and I need to get her out. With ax in hand I push through a door and take the most direct path to get to the second floor. The mission is simple and direct. Get the girl and get out. We're not trying to stop the fire right now, just rescue the child. The fire will come later.

Flames envelop the space in front of me and I step back to avoid the blast. My suit will protect me, to a degree, but still I feel like I'm boiling alive.

The flames rise up and I avoid them to find the stairs. I move carefully, checking the stability of each stair, each door and wall, before inching forward. One mistake could be fatal.

When I get to the second floor and locate the unit, I use the ax to break the door in.

"Sky?" Steve yells.

"Up here! Second floor!"

I do a quick search of the living room. The flames are licking at my feet as sweat trickles down my back, arms, face. "Hello? Anyone here?"

I hear a sob, but it's fading, which isn't a good sign. I think it's coming from one of the doors in the hall, likely a bedroom. I rush forward with more speed, and miscalculate the structural integrity of the unit.

The floor breaks under my right foot. I fall hard against the ground, my ax flying from my hand as I use my arms to break my landing. I try to stand, but my foot is stuck in the hardwood floorboards. "Steve!" I call for my backup, but don't hear him. I know the girl is in that bedroom, and that she's likely running out of air. I pull at my foot, desperate to get unstuck. The wood groans and burns around me.

Panic fills me, but I push it aside. You can't afford to let fear take over with a job like this; it would be paralyzing and deadly. I can still hear the girl cry if I strain, but it's so faint.

And then... it stops. Nothing. "Hello! If you can hear me, yell. I'm coming for you. Don't give up."

Fun fact, most people don't die in fires from the fire itself, but from smoke inhalation.

It's not really that fun of a fact, now that I think about it.

The fire is progressing in such a way that I know I have to find her or leave, and soon. I don't have the equipment to contain or control what this is becoming.

All I hear is the crackle of flames eating into the apartment and the tearing of wood as it falls apart. My radio comes to life, Blake's voice on the other end. "Sky, get out of there. Steve can't get in. We're using the ladder, but the structure isn't sound. Get out now!"

I reach for the ax. It's just out of reach and I push myself to stretch further until it's just barely in my grasp. Carefully, I pull it towards me until I can hold it securely.

With measured blows, I break apart the wood keeping my foot trapped and pull myself out, then stumble towards the bedroom door and push it open.

I see her there, on the other side of a wall of flames. She's unconscious, doesn't have much time left.

So I rush forward.

And the ceiling collapses.

Beams of wood crash down between me and the girl, and I fall back just in time to avoid getting buried under the bulk of the debris. A large piece of stone ricochets off the wall and hits my mask with a loud crack. I scream in pain and suck in a lungful of smoke. The mask is broken, obstructing my view, so I tear it off and try to avoid taking deep breaths.

There's a window on the other side of the room, near the girl. If I can get there, I can get us out and use the ladder to get down.

Smoke fills my lungs. The room is a burning inferno, the wood turning to ash. A rush of dizziness sweeps over me. The smell of fire fills my nostrils. From the corner of the room, something moves. A flicker of a shadow, then the silhouette of a person. A man, I think. He faces the flames and I look to where he's looking, into the fire. And there... there I see the impossible. I see eyes in the flames. Red and burning. A set of teeth. A pair of claws. The world around me narrows in, growing darker, and I fall...

Arms pull at me.

My body is lifted.

Fire above me.

Smoke.

I'm choking.

I can't breathe.

And then.

Light.

Sky.

Wind.

I suck in air, but it feels as if my lungs are full and can't take it all in.

Someone sticks a mask over my face, and oxygen forces itself into my reluctant lungs. Blake? I try to speak, but I can't.

"Gotta get you to an ambulance... "

I'm fading. My mind blinks out. And in the darkness, I see the beast writhing in the flames. Hungry. Waiting. Hunting.

And then I remember her... and my eyes pop open, and I pull the mask off my face, choking out words as I do. "There's a girl in there. Save her."

Blake stands over me, his eyes downcast. "I'm sorry, Sky. We can't go back in. Not until we put out the fire. The foundation is collapsing. It's... It's too late."

6

PAIN IN THE PAST

The fire takes hours to put out. I stay, but only as support. I'm not allowed back in, and my condition is monitored. In the end, amidst the ash and ruin of the apartment complex, they find the remains of a girl trapped on the second floor, her body as charred as the house. An autopsy will be done, but it's likely she died from smoke inhalation before the flames ever touched her.

The fire will be investigated as to cause, but likely it was carelessness. Someone left a candle burning or the stovetop on. Or a cigarette fell from a drunken hand.

The hardest part is when a middle-aged couple arrives on the scene, their faces filled with fear and shock. They live here, they tell us. Their daughter, she was home alone working on a school assignment while they were out of town for the day. A trip to Santa Rosa. She was old enough to be alone for the afternoon. They never imagined anything would go wrong.

Blake is the one to break the news, while I stand by his side, knowing how he feels. I've been in his shoes.

The man breaks first, falling to his knees, tears streaming down his face. The woman grabs her husband's shoulders, her face frozen in shock.

I wince at the ferocity of emotion I bear witness to. I am to blame. I should have gotten to her in time. They didn't deserve to have their lives ruined like this. That girl didn't deserve to die today. What did any of them do to deserve this?

I walk away as Blake goes into the details, trudging my feet along the grass, reliving my time amongst the flames, and what I saw within. My mind loses itself in a haze, and I don't know how much time goes by until Blake pats me on the shoulder. "Head home. We'll finish up at the station."

I nod, still dazed. It takes about fifteen minutes to reach the station, grab my things, and leave to pick the kids up. By the time I arrive at Mrs. Ruby's, the kind old lady next door who sometimes watches the kids while I work, the sun has already set. The day has felt eternal and never ending, and I still have to find Pat. My twenty-four hours is almost up, and I don't know what the man who calls himself Mr. Pike will do when he shows up and Pat isn't here.

I move in a haze as I lock Kara and Caleb into their car seats, my mind torn between my personal problems and the fire that took a young life today. I look at Kyle, who sits next to his siblings with earbuds in his ears, lost in his own world. The girl was about his age. I try to imagine myself in the position those parents were in today. I shudder at the thought and push it from my mind. These are my kids and I will do whatever it takes to keep them safe. Losing them would kill me.

Blake arrives home shortly after me and makes dinner—bless his heart—while I call every place Pat might be. Every dive bar in town. But no one has seen him.

Which means he likely hit a liquor store and is hanging somewhere with the homeless to avoid detection. The homeless are invisible to most, their plight swallowed up by the self-enforced blindness of a people unwilling to look that kind of fate in the eyes.

Once the littles are in bed and Kyle is upstairs playing video games, Blake brings out a bottle of something strong and pours us both a glass, then holds his up. "May her family find healing, and may her spirit find peace."

I can't keep the tears in anymore, and the taste of them bleeds into the alcohol as it burns down my throat and numbs me just a little.

After a few drinks, I can see the sorrow on Blake's face, the sadness trapped behind his tough exterior. He does it for me, I think. Staying composed.

"It's okay to cry," I say to him, finally, the drink making the world a bit fuzzy around the edges. "You don't have to be strong for me. We have the right to grieve together," I say, reaching for him.

He wraps an arm around me, and I lay my head on his chest, and together we let our pain out.

We must have both fallen asleep at one point, though it's not that late, only eight by the time I wake up and head to the bathroom. I'm washing my face and changing the bandage on my head when I hear glass breaking. A far too common noise in a house full of kids. "Kyle? What happened? I won't be mad, but speak up."

I follow the sound, walking into the kitchen, and I see the middle window is shattered, broken glass splayed over the tile. Pat crawls through the opening, huffing and puffing until he sprawls onto the floor. He's shirtless, smells of drink, and I notice he wrapped his shirt around his fist to break the glass.

"You bastard," I scream. I look around for something hard to hit him with and find Kyle's baseball bat lying by the door. I grab it and hold it up.

Pat throws his arms in front of his face. "Now come on. I just wanted to get some food."

"So you broke into the house?" I'm livid. I can't afford to replace that window. And I've been trying to reach him all day, but instead of contacting me, he breaks in like a thief to steal food I need for the kids. Food *I* paid for.

"Well, I know you don't want me around. Figured I'd sneak in and grab some grub. But hey, since we're all here, wanna share a meal with good ol' step-dad?" His voice is slurred and his footing unstable as he tries to stand. I'm surprised he made it through the window without injury.

"You want food, Pat? Then tell me something. A man came to the house early this morning looking for you. Calls himself Mr. Pike." I pause and watch his face for any signs of recognition.

His eyes go wide and he reaches for the window. I get there first, slamming my bat down on the window sill. I'm not trying to hit Pat, but his hand gets in the way and the bat smashes into his fingers. He falls back cradling his knuckles. "What'd you do that for?" his voice is a shrill whine.

"Sky? What's going on?" Kyle stands in the doorway of the kitchen. "Everything's fine," I say. "We're just having a grown up talk. Go get ready for bed. It's getting late."

"It's only eight," Kyle says. "I'm allowed to stay up till nine, you said."

I sigh. "Fine, but you have to stay in your room reading a book, remember?"

He looks at me, then Pat, then me again. "Why's Blake sleeping on the couch?"

"Kyle, go to bed. Please." I'm trying not to let my frustration show, but this has been the day from hell already, and I'm afraid it's just going to get worse.

"Okay, fine." He finally leaves, and I hope he's not spying in the other room. There are some things a kid his age doesn't need to know.

I turn back to Pat, lowering my voice. "Tell me everything. Now. Or I swear to god I will beat you with this bat and not think twice." He flinches at the threat and I press my advantage, remembering his fear of me yesterday. "Who is Pike? What deal did you make?"

Pat looks ready to run again, but seeing my resolution, he reconsiders and slumps into a kitchen chair. "It was... just a favor."

"What kind of favor?" I ask, raising the bat a little higher.

"I was in trouble, all right? Bad trouble." He sighs, acting the consummate victim. "Some people wanted money from me. Said I owed them for a deal gone bad, but they knew there was a chance of that from the start—"

"Stop making excuses for once in your miserable life!"

"Look... these people, they were trouble. And Mr. Pike, he made the trouble go away."

I scowl at him. "How?"

"I don't know," he says. "You don't ask questions. That's his way. He fixes it, and that's all you need to know."

"And what did you offer in return?"

"I... " he pauses, biting down on his lips.

"What?" My voice is cold, low, scary.

He doesn't answer. He looks away, avoiding eye contact.

"What!" I raise my voice and the bat.

Spittle flies out of his mouth as he talks. "You gotta understand. I would have been killed. They would have killed me, and then where would we all be? What would have happened to the kids? To Laura? I had to think of the family!"

Right, like his motives have ever been that self-sacrificing. But his words send a chill down my back. Whatever he did, it's bad. And not bad for him, because Pat never makes deals that would be bad for him if he can help it. "Pat, shut the hell up and tell me what you did."

His head falls forward. "I offered one of the kids, okay? In exchange for Pike making the problem go away, he could come and take one of the kids at his chosen time."

The bat falls to the ground and I fight the urge to vomit as all the blood drains from my face. My voice is barely a whisper now. "You offered... I... I can't believe it... how could you?"

"It's the only offer he takes, okay? He makes your problems go away, and then, when the time is right or his need is great or what-ever, he comes to take a kid."

"For what? Why does he want kids?" A dozen reasons flood my mind, each worse than the next. What kind of child slavery ring is this bastard running?

"I don't know, I swear!" He's sweating now, and his eyes dart around the kitchen, likely looking for something to drink. "To be part of their cult, or something. That's how they recruit, I think."

My knees are shaking and I sit down in a chair across from him.

"This can't happen, Pat. Pike is going to go away, and you're going to make sure he does. He's not taking one of *my* kids."

"You can't stop him," Pat says, his voice defeated. "He can do things no normal man has any right doing."

I think back to how I couldn't call 911 on my phone, and how Dean and Blake couldn't register my description of him. "Which one?" I ask. "Which of the kids does he want?"

"The youngest," he says. "He likes them young, impressionable, I think. So they take to the training better."

Kara. He's coming for the baby. My baby. The baby my mother died to give birth to. She was told she shouldn't carry to term, but she insisted. She knew she was too weak, but she didn't care. As she lay in the hospital bed hooked up to machines, her skin so pale and translucent I could see her veins, she held my hand and looked into my eyes. She was delusional. Calling me by another name. *"Elliana."* Grasping for me. *"Elliana."* Screaming at me. *"Elliana. I am scared, my friend. I am scared."* I could see the terror in her eyes. I swore then and there I would take care of the littles no matter what.

When the machines started to beep faster, and the doctors and nurses came to rush me out, I knew it was over. Hours later they handed me a baby so pink she looked like a tomato, and I held her in my arms and whispered in her ear even as tears still poured down my face. "It's a big scary world out there, I know, but I'll protect you, okay? I promise." She seemed to smile then—though the nurse said it was just gas—and I don't know if I've ever been as happy and as sad in the same moment since.

Strength returns to my limbs and I stand, emboldened by a new determination as Pat sits there and weeps his tears of self-pity. He reaches out and tries to touch my hand but I push him away. "I don't want your tears. You sold one of your own children to save your skin. One of *my* children. The child Laura gave her life to save." He flinches at the name of my mother.

"Please," he begs. "Please find a way to save her. The place she'd go. The things she'd have to do... "

"What things? What place? What do you know of it?"

"I wasn't always a useless drunk," he says, surprising me with this brief moment of self-honesty. "I used to work for people... people with power. I knew things. Too many things. I was a liability when their system of power crumbled. This man, this Mr. Pike and his ilk, they enslave children into a life you can't imagine. She'll be brainwashed or worse."

A knot forms in my gut and I pace the kitchen floor. I need to find Mr. Pike before he comes back for Kara. Whatever this child trafficking ring is, it needs to end now.

My phone buzzes, and I check the message. What I read makes me curse under my breath. I hoped something like this wouldn't happen, but of course it was a fool's hope.

"How would you find him?" I ask, clenching my jaw, my knuckles turning white around the bat, an idea—probably a very stupid idea—forming in my mind.

Pat rubs at his nose. "Well, he's looking for kids, right? If any are missing, that's where to start."

I was thinking the same.

I look down at my phone again, rereading the message from the station.

Calling all available personnel for an immediate search and rescue. A child has gone missing in Low Gap Park.

7

GHOST IN THE FOREST

I grab my pack, check to make sure it has all my supplies—water, power bars, a headlamp, change of socks, a GPS and my radio —and slip on a thick coat. I turn to Pat. "Stay here. Keep an eye on the kids. There's a patrol car outside for protection. I'm going to try to find Pike before he finds us."

Pat nods, and I wake Blake and show him the text.

We get to the staging area at the parking lot outside the park as others from the fire and police department show up to help. There's about twenty people total, which isn't a great head count but not our worst either.

It only takes a few minutes to get the basics. Teenage boy went hiking alone, never came home. This was his last known whereabouts. He's not answering his phone and the GPS tracker for the phone isn't working. We all take a map and a partner—Blake and I choose each other— and head out.

It's a new moon, which means limited natural lighting. We both wear our headlamps to keep our hands free as we hike through the woods. It's late, dark, and the only sounds are the crunching of twigs under our feet and the calls of creatures in the night.

I explain to Blake what I learned from Pat and tell him my plan. Then I show him what else I brought in my pack.

"A gun? Are you nuts?"

Blake doesn't like guns.

"I'm going to find this guy. Before he takes my baby." Just the thought of losing Kara kills me inside.

Blake shakes his head. "That's insane. We need to let the police handle this."

"Like Dean?" I ask, knowing his answer.

"Well, not like Dean, but someone else in the department surely."

"Blake, something weird is going on. I can't explain it, and even when I do you don't seem to understand, but this isn't a normal guy we're talking about. I can't risk leaving this in someone else's hands. I'm running out of time. I only have a few hours before Pike said he'd return."

I stumble over a rock, catching myself against a tree. My limbs are too tired to be hiking tonight—I've already dealt with a head injury, a fire call, and loss of consciousness due to smoke inhalation. I should be resting, letting my lungs and body recover. Instead, I'm trekking through a dark hiking trail, hoping the kid we're looking for is okay, and hoping I can catch Pike before he comes to collect my baby.

We've been walking for an hour when Blake stops, takes a swig of water, and excuses himself to find a tree to relieve himself.

I look down at the picture of the missing kid on my phone. Mat Parson. He's thirteen with a shock of bright red hair and a face full of freckles. He's from the same school as Kyle, and I think I may have seen them hanging out together. I try not to imagine what my little brother will have to go through if his friend is never found. I try to look for—

A twig snaps nearby.

I turn to the right, pointing my headlamp at the source of the sound. Nothing but trees and darkness. But... Wait. A sound. Whispering.

"Blake? That you?"

I look around but don't see anyone, so I creep forward in the woods, following the whispers. "Blake? Hello?"

It occurs to me it could be the boy we're looking for, and I yell his name as well. Maybe he's hurt and calling for help, but his voice is too weak to talk. I walk faster, suddenly certain he's close by. I pull out my gun, just in case I find Pike, and hold it securely as I pick up my pace.

The cold metal feels foreign in my hands. I've trained at a shooting range and have a license to carry a concealed weapon—not uncommon in the fire department—but I've never actually pointed a gun at another human. I hope I don't have to pull the trigger tonight, but I will if it means saving a life.

The path I'm on divides into two, and I travel right, where a dried-up stream used to live before the draughts and heat wave. Another whisper. A bitter wind.

I step onto a short cliff overlooking a clearing. I scan the area, my headlamp illuminating the broken trees and large rocks and—

There. Something

A body.

A boy.

Splayed unnaturally over a fallen tree. Limbs at odd angles. Someone stands over him. A man dressed in black.

I raise my gun.

And then I see it.

The wind catches his red scarf.

"Kaden?"

"Step away from the boy!" I yell, pointing my gun at him.

Kaden turns towards me, his blue eyes shining against the beam of my headlamp. "I didn't harm him," he says instantly, bending down over the body.

"Don't move!" My arms are steady, but my heart pounds against my rib cage. Sweat beads down my forehead. I release the safety on the gun and slow my breathing.

"Please," he says, his voice urgent. "I must finish cleansing the body."

"Don't move, or I will shoot!" My mind is frantic, trying to piece together what is going on. Pike isn't here. Kaden is. Is Kaden working with Pike? Is Pike at my house already?

"If I don't finish what I started, we will all be in danger," he says.

What is he even talking about? "Don't touch him!" I walk down the cliff, closing the distance between us. The reality of pulling the trigger is even harder than I thought; I try to push the thoughts away, but I can't stop my mind from recoiling at the thought of hurting another person. A person I know. A person I was actually attracted to. I went into my career to save people, not kill them.

Kaden pulls back from the body and lifts his gloved hands in the air. "I know what this looks like, but you have to trust me. The boy's body must be purified, otherwise—"

A strong wind hits us. A stray lock of hair comes loose from my ponytail and flies around my face. His scarf flails about, but... it doesn't drift in the same direction as the wind. It's moving against it, to the west. This makes no sense. My eyes follow the direction his scarf is blowing and... I see it. In the woods.

A pair of eyes wreathed in flame.

Nostrils filled with smoke.

A razor sharp mouth.

Just like my vision in the fire. But I was hallucinating then. A side effect from lack of oxygen.

Am I hallucinating again? Am I more injured than I realized? Nothing about my life in the last twenty-four hours makes sense.

The creature glides out of the trees, its large red body half mist, half physical form. Its head is that of a wolf, its body that of a serpent.

I blink, expecting it to disappear.

It doesn't. It draws near instead.

My gun wavers in my hand. I shouldn't be holding a weapon if I can't even decipher fantasy from reality. What if I shoot someone innocent? What if none of this is happening and I'm just losing my mind?

My mum never said much about my father, but she did say he wasn't right in the head before his death. What if I inherited something from him? What if I'm totally losing it? Where's Blake? I need him right now. I need him to tell me what's real and what's not. Because I don't even know anymore.

And then Kaden speaks, in a voice so low, I almost don't hear him. And I realize he's not looking at me anymore. He's looking in the direction of the monster. *He sees it too.*

"Run," he says. "Run now!"

I hear his words, but they become jumbled in my mind. I can't think. Can't move. I'm paralyzed by self-doubt.

And then the creature lunges forward.

And I act on animal instinct.

I fire my gun, aiming directly for the vision before me.

But the bullets do nothing. They fly through the creature as if it were a ghost. A spirit. As if it didn't exist at all. But this all feels entirely too real. And I don't think I'm imagining the body of the boy, or Kaden standing before me.

I brace for death, hoping that when it comes I'll wake up and realize this was all a nightmare.

Death doesn't come. I don't wake.

Instead, the creature passes me by. And heads straight for Mat Parson.

Kaden yells something I don't understand and jumps in front of the boy's body, but the spirit whips around him.

And slams into the corpse.

The creature vanishes, and for a moment, everything turns quiet. Even the wind dies down to nothing, the air so still it's stifling.

Then the boy gasps for breath. His chest rises and falls. Impossible.

I rush forward to help.

"Stop!" yells Kaden.

I follow his gaze.

And I see the boy's eyes. I see them roll back into his head until only the whites show. I watch as his hands and legs crack and move at odd angles, rearranging themselves to work again.

"It's too late," Kaden says. "It possessed him." He pulls something from his coat.

Something metal that glints against the light of my headlamp.

It takes my mind a moment to process what I see. A sword. The largest sword I've ever seen. I wonder how he even manages to hold it. The hilt is simple, wrapped in leather strips, made for large hands. The blade is bare, no markings or embellishments, the steel black as night.

"I'll hold if off," Kaden says, positioning himself between me and the moving corpse. "It will follow you, Sky. It will follow you until it kills you. Run. Run now!"

The boy stands, but his movements are awkward, as if someone wears him like an ill-fitting outfit. His eyes turn red as if they burn with flame. The boy roars, but the sound he makes is not human. It is guttural and monstrous, and it makes every instinct in me terrified. His young teen muscles expand, getting larger and larger, growing until his skin rips open, revealing raw, unnatural flesh. His jaw comes unhinged, then tears his face apart as a new head explodes from his throat, its giant mouth full of layers of sharp teeth, its tiny eyes at the top of its head like a deep sea fish. What was once a boy has grown twice the size of any man I've ever known. It lashes out with a giant pink tongue forked like a snake's. Trying to grab something. Trying to kill something.

My body takes over as my brain freezes.

And I run like never before.

8

BROKEN ONE

Lungs burning.
Feet pounding.
Heart racing.
I push my body to the limit.
I'm not fast enough.
The serpent-like tongue lashes out, grabbing at my ankle, pulling me to my knees.

Steel flashes through the air and Kaden cuts the tongue in half, freeing me from its clutches, but the severed part lives on. It jumps and wiggles and tries to wrap itself around my leg.

I kick it away and stand up, forcing myself to keep running.

Through the darkness I run, over stone and bush and under-brush, zigzagging through trees, twigs snapping underfoot, my body covered in cold sweat, the world around me a blur of blacks and grays.

Behind me, the creature cries out in pain from the blow Kaden dealt. The sound is like a dying deer, a blend of child and animal and fear and pain, and it chills my soul.

I have no idea where I'm going—the map I committed to memory long forgotten—but I know I'll reach the end of the woods soon. Will that mean safety? Or will I be leading this monster towards a populated area, putting more people at risk?

I make a split-second decision and change directions, knowing I'm heading deeper into the woods, but away from anyone else who might be harmed. This new path is less traveled and the terrain more wild. I trip on the root of a tree and stumble. Something in my foot snaps as I fall forward, and pain shoots through my body. I bite my tongue until it bleeds, and tears well in my eyes as I cradle my right foot.

Despite the pain, I force myself to stand. My foot can barely handle my weight, likely broken somewhere. I look around, trying to figure out what to do next, and I see the creature and Kaden behind me.

The beast strikes with claws in a savage flurry of destruction, no pattern to its assault. And yet, Kaden evades each attack. He's fast, unnaturally so, but something about his movement is wrong. His left side is more agile than his right. His shoulder is stiff. Was he injured? Did the beast wound him?

Kaden told me to run. He said he had to purify the body. Did he know this would happen? That this monstrous thing would take the boy's corpse for itself?

If he knew... if he's here to help, then he wasn't the one who killed Mat Parson. And if Kaden is innocent, and he's in danger... I need to help him.

The creature appears more corporeal than before. Less smoke, more mass. I can use that to my advantage. I raise my gun and aim, hoping to get a good shot, but Kaden's too close. He's blocking my line of vision. I need a different angle.

I circle around the two of them, limping through the pain in my ankle, as I ignore my survival instincts. I've grown used to fighting my flight instincts as a firefighter. We run into the kind of danger most normal people flee from.

And so I do the same now. I take position against a tree—where I can remove all pressure from my foot, and I raise my gun and aim, my line of sight clear, my finger on the trigger.

The creature turns towards me, as if it knows my thoughts. My intentions.

And it charges.

I fire as many bullets as I can.

Some of them strike true, taking the creature in the arm, the chest, the head.

Dark black blood splatters into the air. But the creature does not slow. The night sky fills with the unnatural sounds of the beast's agony, but it does not pause. It does not show any other sign that it feels pain in the least.

It closes the distance between us so quickly, I barely have time to think. To move. To react.

Kaden lands at my side, as if he flew or leaped to reach me. How he got here before the beast, I have no idea.

He pulls me into his arms, and he jumps.

We fly into the air, higher than many of the trees around us, moving so quickly the wind whips at my face, forcing my eyes closed. My stomach lurches at the change in motion, and I cling to Kaden for my life.

We seem to hover forever, and then we land.

The impact reverberates throughout my entire body, rattling my bones, shaking my vision, sending shoots of pain into my already injured foot.

Kaden doesn't slow at all. He carries me as if I weigh nothing, navigating through trees and rocky terrain, his boots barely touching the ground.

The beast gives chase, filled with a bloodlust that seems unstoppable. What remains of its tongue lashes out, cutting into the flesh of my arm, my blood mixing with its own, creating a crimson mist around us. I hold in my cries of pain, knowing I dare not distract Kaden right now; He is the only thing keeping either of us alive.

I hold my trembling hand over Kaden's shoulder and fire more shots into the night. Whether my bullets make contact or not I cannot tell, but the beast is unfazed regardless. I need to find a weak spot, something that will stop it in its tracks.

The eyes. I need to hit the eyes.

I take aim, steadying my hold with both hands, as Kaden jostles us over rocky terrain.

My bullet errs to the right

The creature gains on us.

My next shot is too far left.

The creature continues gaining on us.

I close my eyes and slow my breathing. I remember my mother's words as she would guide me in meditation, as she helped me control my heart rate. *"The physical form is controlled by the mind and the mind is controlled by the spirit. Center yourself in your truth, Sky. Center yourself in your truth, and you control all things."*

I steady my breath, heed her words, and fire.

The beast recoils, clutching at its head with its monstrous hands. One of its eyes runs black with blood.

We begin to pull away, but the creature leaps forward, one eyeball dangling from its socket. It almost lands atop us.

Then Kaden drops, sliding through a stretch of mud, me still in his arms. We propel into darkness, and I realize we are passing under a bridge. Kaden moves one of his arms, gripping me with the other, and reaches into his jacket. He tosses something to the ground... a golden coin covered in symbols I can't decipher. It hits the ground at the edge of the bridge, and a wall of golden smoke fills the space between us and the monster.

The beast smashes into the smoke, then jumps back as if electrocuted, letting out a wail of pain and anger as the wall bursts with white light. Moving quickly, Kaden tosses another coin at the other side of the bridge. The beast leaps over us, searching for an opening, but it's too late. It hits the second wall and lightning flashes in the golden smoke.

Kaden falls back against a wooden pillar under the bridge. His breath is heavy and his body is covered in sweat. And then... he laughs. "Thought we were dead."

I slide out of his arms and sit down in the mud, keeping weight off my right foot. "What is that thing?" I whisper.

"A Fenrial Spirit," he says. "A corrupted one."

"A spirit... "

He looks at me, his blue eyes piercing. "It wants you. Your body, to be more exact."

My eyes widen. "What? Why?"

Kaden sucks in a breath, and his body calms as he replies. "There are people... people like you who draw spirits to them. You're like a conduit. You're not an empty shell, but you have an opening—a crack in your spirit. And your power, it leaks out, attracting them."

"What are you talking about?" Spirits, conduits, empty shells... My mind is spinning and I'm trying to grab hold of something that makes sense, but nothing does. Not the beast. Not the golden walls of smoke. Not the powers Pike displayed when I tried to use my phone or describe his appearance.

Kaden continues, his voice calm. "Spirits can't affect the physical world by themselves. They need a body. But they can't take one already occupied. They need one that's empty. They need someone dead."

"Like Mat," I say, things begin to click in my mind.

"Yes." He holds my gaze, his blue eyes pleading with me to believe him. "I swear to you, Sky, I found him already dead. I think he stumbled down the cavern and fell on the broken tree. One of the branches tore through his gut. He was stuck there, on the tree, bleeding out until he died."

I can't imagine his pain. His agony. His helplessness, as he tried to call for help. As his words were whisked away by an uncaring wind. As his life bled out of him. He must have been terrified. So alone. What were his last thoughts? Were they of fear? Of sadness? My heart breaks for the boy who died alone, and bile rises in my throat. I turn away, emptying my gut into the mud.

When I finish vomiting, Kaden continues. "Usually, bodies stay dead," he says. "But I knew Spirits were in the area. So I sought the boy out. I tried to purify his body before it could be possessed, but, well, you showed, and you know the rest."

"Purify? How?"

"With this," he says, pulling another coin out of his coat, this one silver, the symbols on it just as strange but different. "This is a talisman," Kaden says, shuffling the coin across his knuckles. "This one purifies a body to protect it from corruption. The ones I threw earlier form barriers against unwanted spirits. They don't last forever, though."

He pushes himself off the pillar and hisses in pain, falling back down.

"You're injured!" I limp towards him. "Let me see." I have enough medic training to know what to look for, how to handle it.

He nods and pulls off his coat to reveal his shoulder. The cloth from his shirt is burned through, and his flesh is a seared red blister. "It's from earlier. Nothing I can't take."

"This is a third degree burn," I say. And then it hits me. "The fire! You were there, at the fire. You were the man I saw."

He rolls his shoulder, flinching so quickly I barely notice. "Yes," he says. "When the girl died amidst the smoke, I knew the Fenrial would come for her. I was too late, though. I fought the possessed body as best I could. Almost won, even. But... the house collapsed. I got out with the burn. The Fenrial got out too. They do that, leave a body if they must."

At mention of the girl, I am overwhelmed with fury. "If you were there, why didn't you save her? Why did you let the beast take her?" I expect him to strike back with words.

But his voice remains calm. "I didn't let her die. I wouldn't do that, but I have no way of finding those in danger." If anything, he sounds sad. Helpless. "I can only find those who are already dead. Or very near it. Only those who have opened themselves to the spirits."

"I see." Though I don't see at all. I don't understand any of this. I shake my head, looking around for anything I can use to help Kaden, but I don't have a med kit with me. I slump back down, shivering in the cold wind, pulling my jacket close. Around us, the wall of gold holds strong, but I hear the beast, the Fenrial, behind it, pacing along the bridge. The night is dark, and getting even darker.

"You said the Spirits want my body. Why?" I ask.

"You are what some call a Broken One," Kaden says. "You draw spirits even though you live, because some part of your own spirit has fractured. It's not something you were born with, not usually. It manifests later, from trauma. Even then, it begins as a small crack in your spirit. A crack that grows over the years. Eventually, that crack spreads into a gaping hole that leaks enough of your own spirit to reveal a chasm that needs filled. Spirits are drawn to that empty space. And so are those like me."

Pieces of a convoluted and mysterious puzzle begin to fit together. A puzzle I didn't even realize I'd been trying to solve since I was a child. Ever since my mum gave me my leather cufflink. "That's the business you're in, isn't it? You're here because of me."

He nods without saying a word.

"So what? You protect me? And then you fix this crack in my spirit?"

He sighs. "Not exactly. I protect you, yes. But there is no way to fix the break. There is only a way to fill it."

"Fill it?"

He nods, a lock of dark hair falling into his eyes. "With another spirit."

"But... I thought the point was to not let spirits get those like me?" My eyes dart to the wailing beast and I shudder. Is that what he wants to do to me?

Seeing my fear and revulsion, he reaches for my hand. The contact shocks me. I'm so cold. So chilled to the bone and scared beyond anything I've ever felt. But the feel of his hand, of his warmth, of the reassurance his touch provides, sends a calm wave through my body.

"There are two basic kinds of spirits, Sky," he says. "Those that are corrupted, like the one outside this wall. And those that are not. Corrupted spirits wish to cause chaos and destruction in the world. They seek out dead bodies, hoping to possess them. They seek out Broken Ones even more, hoping to overtake them. With dead bodies their time is limited. Decay and rot set in. If they can possess a Broken One, they can live forever. Over the years, because of the leak in your spirit, your body has grown closer to the spirit realm. And thus, you would make for a much more powerful vessel. If a Fenrial inhabited you, even I would have a hard time stopping it."

I squeeze his hand gently and glance at the fading barrier, the dissipating smoke. "Seems like you're having a hard time already," I say, my voice hopeless.

He nods. "Fair enough. But it's my shoulder. It's slowing me down. If I'd had a way to keep the spirit still for a moment, I could have ended it, but it's too fast. Well, too fast for me in this condition, at any rate."

I raise an eyebrow at that. "You seemed unnaturally quick. And the way you jumped, how is that even possible?"

He chuckles. "That's where the second kind of spirit comes in. The Pure Ones. They can bond with a Broken One, but they will not take over your will. At least, not if you keep them in line. Instead, they seek to establish a symbiotic bond with their host. That bond is the only way to make a Broken One whole again."

"So you have one of these spirits?" I ask. "A Pure One?"

He nods. "I do." He pauses, staring at the golden smoke, a thin wisp now. "How about I tell you more about this when we get out of here. That wall won't last forever."

"When? You're sure it's not if?" I eye the Fenrial prowling on the other side of the golden light.

"Come now," he says, grinning with such confidence I wonder about his sanity. "Pessimism never won any battles. I believe Eisenhower said that."

I shrug. "I wouldn't know. Public education around here isn't what it used to be."

He chuckles.

I can't help but smile too.

For a moment, we grin and snicker at our own foolishness, forgetting our impending doom. Perhaps that is why we laugh. To drown out our own despair.

Kaden's face grows dark. "I will admit, we aren't in the best of positions. The Talisman's weakening, and I don't have any more of their kind. In about two minutes the Fenrial will be upon us."

My heart races again at his words. We need a plan. "So these Pure Spirits. They give you powers? Abilities?"

"Yes," he says slowly. "If you know how to control them."

"They let you do things... things that should not be possible?"

He narrows his eyes at me. "Not what most consider possible, true."

I try to deny it, but the pieces have been coming together in my mind for some time, filling in so many gaps of my childhood. "I... I can help us," I say, holding out my arm.

He shakes his head, his eyes widening. "No. Before the barrier falls, we must run. I'm in no shape to fight off the Fenrial. It will consume you and kill me."

"No. It won't." I pull the leather cuff off my wrist, exposing the symbol beneath. The creature jerks its head towards me, its red eyes glowing.

"What are you doing?" Kaden asks, voice raised.

"I'm saving us," I say. And I hold my hand forward, revealing the secret my mother kept hidden for as long as I can remember. Adrenaline surges through me, and though I don't know what I'm doing, or how to channel what I've always known I have, I focus my thoughts and my feelings and my fears into one purpose. And as the golden hues that carved out the smoke walls fade, I walk forward towards the beast. My body convulses.

And I change into my true form.

9

TWIN SPIRIT

Ever since I can remember, I've worn the leather band around my left wrist. If I ever took it off, my mother would scold me. If Pat ever saw me without it, he would fly into a rage that often ended in bruises. But in my most private of moments, I studied the mark on my skin that the band hid. The mark that made me different. The mark that made me move from one place to another in a blink, made water boil or freeze around me. The mark that made me powerful.

The mark that made me dangerous.

I don't know why the band is special. But I finally understand what my mark means.

Spirits are real.

And one lives within me.

A white glow explodes from the symbol on my wrist, consuming my body. My skin turns ivory, my hair turns silver and whips around my head in the wind. I feel lighter on my feet, as if I'm barely touching the ground. All the pain in my body is replaced by a euphoric feeling of endless power.

With the barrier down, we are vulnerable, but the Fenrial sees me glowing in the darkness of night, and it jumps back, hissing, as if realizing I'm not the host it was hoping for. I'm not a Broken One. I already have a Spirit. Now it's time to see what I can do with it.

I whisper something, then. Words I do not understand, but which feel part of my very soul. And the light from my body pushes outward, taking shape before me. Claws. Wings. Scales. Eyes of silver, glowing, like me. My spirit, in its own form. A silver, winged serpent, ready to defend me. Ready to fight.

It crashes into the Fenrial, biting down on the monster's neck and knocking it to the ground, pinning it with sharp claws.

Kaden rushes forward, leaping past me, and impales his sword into the Fenrial's neck. There is a bone crunching sound as Kaden saws through the creature's neck, cleaving off its head. It rolls away from us, with eyes still moving, tongue still lashing out. But then, as if realizing it's no longer connected to its body, it gives one last gasp and falls still. Its headless body squirms and shakes, the muscle and skin melting away, burning like a pile of steaming sludge, until only the boy's body remains, fully intact, and just as fully dead.

Kaden pulls two silver coins from his coat and lays one on each of the boy's eyes, then whispers words in another language.

"*Alar argaris.*" A hissing sound rises from the body, then it goes quiet and Kaden sighs. "It is done. The spirit is purified. We will not see the corrupted Fenrial again."

The silver serpent that saved us vanishes, and the glowing of my skin fades to my normal cream. My hair darkens to its ordinary brown, and I fall forward, exhausted, and land on my knees on the cool earth.

Kaden kneels next to me, his eyes studying me. "You're a Twin Spirit. But how?"

I lean back onto my feet to face him, and for the first time I realize my ankle no longer hurts. "I don't know," I say. "Ever since I was little, I knew something was different about me. But I never knew what, not until you told me about the spirits. Not until you showed me what you could do. I knew, somehow, I could do the same thing."

"Not the same. Not yet. Not without practice." He frowns. "This is strange. I could sense strength in you, but it was barely a sliver. The sign of a Broken One. And yet now I can clearly see the spirit within you. A Dracus, or Dragon, in your tongue."

"A... dragon?"

"It is said, all spirits were once living creatures. That Fenrial once hunted in the northern mountains. That dragons... well, dragons are another matter. You will see, in time." He pauses, and picks up the wrist band I wear. "I wonder... "

He hands it to me and I put it back on, a reflex so ingrained in me I don't even think about it.

Kaden nods, as if I've just answered a question. "I see. It appears this leather cuff keeps your spirit hidden, but not completely. It's leaking out some of your power, making you look to others like a Broken One."

"Do you have a mark like mine?" I ask.

He rolls up his sleeve, revealing a black horned serpent caged within a circle of flame. "It is the seal that makes a Broken One whole again," he says. "It's what makes one Arayel, or a Twin Spirit. Of the two worlds. That of the seen and the unseen." He pauses. "In simpler terms, it means that once you bear the mark, you are of the physical and the spiritual. Both together. At once. Never apart."

That doesn't really make it sound much simpler. It sounds unreal. Impossible. Fantastical. And for a moment I wonder if this is all a dream... a terrible game played by my imagination. But then I look at the boy, dead so young, a tool for the Fenrial to get to me, and my eyes burn with guilt and grief. "Tell me truthfully," I say through a thick throat. "Did he die because of me?"

Kaden frowns. "Corrupted spirits have little power in the physical realm without a body. But the more ancient ones do have some sway. Enough to make a log roll out of a fireplace. Or to make a boy trip in the woods."

The tears I've been holding in are released, and I bury my face in my hands and cry. I'm the reason that girl died in the fire. The reason this boy bled out in the woods.

Kaden scoots closer to me, putting his arm around my shoulders. "You did what you could. More than I expected," he says softly. "You knew nothing of this world, of corrupted spirits, or the true nature of your mark. Their deaths are not on you, they are on me."

I can hear the pain in his voice and I look into his eyes, into the heartache etched on his face. "It is my duty, the duty of the Ashlord, to protect those who need protecting. To defend them from the spirits who seek to take their life. And twice today I have failed."

He swipes at his eyes and as suddenly as his sorrow appeared, it is gone, replaced by a cold determination. "Thank you," he says, "for using your spirit to help stop the Fenrial. But you must not summon your dragon again. Not until you learn to control it. You were lucky that your mother knew how to bind your spirit. Most of us suffer a painful fate when first we discover our powers."

"Why must I keep it hidden? My spirit did as I willed it to. I wanted to stop the Fenrial and I did." I've never felt that kind of power before. That kind of freedom. I realized in that moment as my spirit was unleashed that I've been living my whole life imprisoned by this wristband, a part of my soul chained by whatever my mother did to bind my spirit and hide it. I know she did it to protect me, but I don't think she realized that in protecting me she was also killing me little by little. Sometimes a person needs a taste of freedom to realize they have never been free. After, they can never go back to being who they once were. They are forever changed by what could be.

"While it's true that your spirit did as your instincts commanded, it will not always be so. You were lucky. We were on a mountain, in the woods, with no one else who could have been caught in the collateral damage. But it will not always be so. You have power, Sky. I believe you are the second strongest untrained person I have ever met, and though that is a gift, it is a curse as well."

"I would never hurt anyone," I say. "Not unless I had to."

His eyes soften, but his voice is still firm. "I know that's not your intention, but intention is not enough. You need training." He holds his hand out to me. "Come with me, Sky. Let me train you. Let me show you how to control the spirit within. If you don't, it will only be a matter of time until you hurt the children you so desperately seek to protect."

I freeze, the blood draining out of my face. The children. "How do you know about my kids? I never mentioned them to you."

I back away from him, suddenly suspicious.

"Like you guessed," he says, dropping his hand, "I'm here because of you. At least, I am now. And it would have been foolish not to do research."

I feel violated. Lied to. And... panicked. How much does he know about me? About my kids?

This unease feels all too familiar, and I wonder... is he working with Pike? Was this a distraction to keep me away so Pike could go after Kara? I hoped to catch him out here, but... Pike must have a spirit as well. That's how he did so many crazy things that made no sense. And if he does, the police will be no match for him. "I have to get home," I say, my mind focused only on my kids. "Now!"

"Sky, wait! I need to--"

His words hang in the wind, a distant echo, and I realize I'm no longer in the woods. I'm on a cold, dark sidewalk, one lone street-lamp flickering as if it's about to die at any moment. Across from me, shrouded in ominous shadows, is my house.

My vision spins, and I suck in the cold air as I attempt to still the dizziness threatening to overwhelm me. How did I get here? I was just with Kaden, on the mountain. This has happened in the past, where I find myself moving from one place to another in a blink, but never this far. Never to a place I couldn't have even walked. Something inside me is changing. I look down at my wrist, and see the leather cuff still in place. Either the power in me is growing, or whatever magic my mother gave me is fading.

I shake my head. I don't have time to figure this out right now. I check my phone to make sure I'm not late, then run to the police car parked across from my house. I gesture at the two officers inside. "We need to leave! Now! Help me get the kids out of the house and--"

I stop at the rolled down passenger window. The streetlight illuminates their faces. A red line across each of their necks, and a water-fall of blood spilling from their throats, their skin pale, their eyes open and glossy, unseeing. Dead.

My heart beats a frenzy against my chest and my gut twists as I dash across the street to my house. I can't be too late. I can't--

The front door is cracked open. I barge through it, into the living room. It's dark. Light from the street casts everything in a sickly pale hue.

From the kitchen I hear a whimpering. I take a step, then two, until I see a maddening sight.

Pat slumps on the cracked linoleum floor, his teeth shaking, his eyes bulging in fear and pain, his arm outstretched, pulled up so unnaturally his shoulder looks dislocated.

Pike stands over him, cloaked in black and wearing his hat. He holds Pat's arm against the kitchen table, and moves an object back and forth in the darkness. A long, thin saw, thin enough to hide in a cane. It grinds against Pat's arm, cutting through flesh and bone.

Pike looks up when I enter, a banal smile on his face. "Good evening Ms. Knightly. How good to see you again."

10

REAPER

"The screaming stopped five minutes ago," Pike says. His words are calm. Smooth. As if he exerts no effort hacking through a man's arm. "He is only tentatively hanging onto consciousness now."

"Let him go!" I roar, my voice tearing through the room. It shakes the glasses in the sink, but Pike doesn't even blink.

He looks back down at his handiwork. "In a moment. Once the deed is done. You see, Pat would not give up a child. He had forgotten about his bargain, it would seem. But pain can be a potent reminder." He pauses, his expression thoughtful, as if mulling over a complex math problem. "About halfway through the process, he finally surrendered, finally owned up to his end of the deal. But, I'm afraid it would be wrong to stop cutting now. The reminder would feel unfinished, and I despise leaving things half-done."

He resumes sawing at Pat's arm, the bone crunching sound reverberating through the small space. My stepfather drools, his eyes halfclosed, his body limp, his arm held up by the force of Pike and nothing more.

The sheer horror of it all dulls my mind for a moment, but then his words fall into me one by one, until they form a complete thought. He finally surrendered, Pike said. Finally owned up to his end of the deal. The deal to give up one of his kids. One of *my* kids.

There are no more rational options left to me. I cannot talk my way of out this. The police cannot help. I have but one choice. I reach for the leather cuff around my wrist, and I pull--

Pike throws up his hand, and a screech fills the air. It drums in my ears, pounding into my skull, into my blood and bones, pulsing in my heart, like a hammer beating down on me. I fall to my knees and try to cover my ears, but I can't move my arms. The sound is too loud, too encompassing. I can't reach over to pull off my wrist band. It's like trying to move the earth.

Pike smiles, completely unaffected by the sound ripping apart my insides. This is how it all ends, I'm convinced. This sound is the end of it all. But Pike, he continues his gruesome task of sawing Pat's hand off. "Do not worry, the children will not wake. I have made sure their night is restful."

My eyes widen and Pike chuckles. "Oh, they are not harmed, have no fear. Only sleeping." Pike looks down and smiles a satisfied smile. "Ah, there." He pulls the saw across Pat's arm once more and Pat falls to the ground, his body limp and draining of blood on the tattered linoleum floor. Pike holds the severed hand up triumphantly like a crimson trophy from a macabre game. He examines it briefly, a clinical expression on his face, then tosses it aside. "Now, it is time I had what I came for."

He wipes down his saw with a kitchen towel, then sheathes it back into the cane until it once again looks innocuous. He walks around the puddle of blood pooling around Pat, and passes me. "I am sorry you had to see that. It was not necessary. You should have stayed away. It was none of your concern after all."

None of my concern? *None of my concern!*

He heads upstairs, to the children's bedroom. To take one of my kids.

I will not let this happen. I will protect them with everything I am. I swore this to my mother. To myself. To them.

With all the strength I have left in me, I fight this force that's paralyzed me. Despite the crushing weight pinning me in place, I stand. Slowly. Painfully. It feels as if every bone in my body cracks from the effort. Every muscle tears at the strain. But I push through it.

And I manage to get to my feet. I grab the kitchen counter for support as I push my legs to move. One step. Then another. One more.

But I'm taking too long.

The stairs creek and Pike descends, a bundle of blankets in his arms.

No.

"What beautiful eyes she has," he whispers, smiling at me.

And then he leaves out the front door. And the screeching sound in my head is nothing compared to my own pain exploding from within.

My baby. He took my baby.

Kara!

I try to scream her name, but no words leave my mouth. Instead, there is the roar of a beast, the roar of my spirit fighting to be free.

And with all I have, I charge outside, following him into the dark street. He's already down the road. "Give her back!" I yell, my voice carrying far, the power of my spirit strong.

He stops and turns to face me. He looks impressed despite himself. "You resisted my power. How interesting."

Branches snap to the left of me, and I see a man running towards us, from the park, a red scarf waving behind him.

Kaden.

But... how?

He notices me, then shifts his eyes to Pike, but I don't have time to think about him, or what he's doing here.

I grab my wrist band, knowing I must end this now.

"No!" yells Kaden. "He's not like us. You can't fight him."

It doesn't matter. Nothing he says matters. Because I have no choice. Even if he's right and this is a fool's hope, it's the only hope I have.

Pike raises his cane, and then... he changes.

His eyes turn red. His face sinks into itself, his lips pulling away to show teeth and gum and bone. His cheeks become stretched tight over his skull. Even his clothing changes, his robes turning to torn rags, as if he is decomposing in front of me.

His walking stick extends, pulsing. The crystal orb at the top explodes into pieces and red steel pushes through, turning the cane into a scythe. He's using his spirit, changing like I did, but this seems different. Wrong.

His ragged robes reveal his pale skin. Crystals jut out from his chest, his arms, his shoulders. Red gems that look as if they've been impaled into his body.

They glow, and that glow spreads through his flesh, beneath his eyes, throughout his whole body.

I'm mesmerized by his transformation, by the power he wields over me. It all happens in a blink, a moment severed by a split consciousness as I register what's about to happen, unable to prevent it.

In an instant, Pike stands before me, moving through the air as if he's one with it.

I don't even feel his scythe as it slices upwards.

He missed, I think.

But even as I think this, I collapse to the ground, my body catching up much faster than my mind as my feet buckle under me. My jaw hits the hard concrete. My body rattles from the impact.

A spray of crimson rain splashes around me, and it takes another moment to realize it is my blood in the air.

Then the pain hits.

Brutally. Fully. Completely. I scream, and it is the sound a deer makes when it's being attacked by a mountain lion. The primal scream of prey helpless against the predator.

My eyes search my body for the source of all this blood, and I see it. He's cut through my Achilles tendons, cut them open. Cut through muscle and bone. One ankle barely remains attached to my body. The other is half torn off.

I reach for my foot, my mind frozen, my body in shock. And I scream again. My fingers are gone, my hands now just bloody stumps.

I'm done. I never stood a chance. He will take Kara, and she will be in the clutches of this monster, and I will have failed her. Failed my mum. Failed myself.

I know the killing blow is about to come.

And then I hear the crash of steel behind me. Kaden stands between me and Pike, his sword locked with the scythe.

"We meet again, Ashlord," Pike says with icy calm in his voice. "Let's see if you've learned anything since our last encounter." He pulls away and strikes.

Kaden throws up his arm and something black and thick, like dark steel, grows over his hand, down to his elbow. The scythe hits the hardened skin and ricochets off.

I need to help, but I'm losing blood so fast. Pike doesn't need to strike me again to kill me, I can already feel myself dying. But I still have power in me. Power untapped. Unused. Raw and untrained, but still... it's all I have left.

Through agony, through the most pain I could have ever imagined, I lift my severed hand and hold my wrist to my mouth. With shaking teeth, I tear at the leather strap around my wrist, then pull it free, revealing the symbol beneath, unleashing my power.

Kaden said it could be dangerous, using my spirit form again, but I don't care. I need to save Kara.

My body fills with light, my skin turning ivory, my hair turning silver. I feel my muscles knitting back together, healing. No less painful than when they were severed, but some strength returns, and I roar with all the fierceness I've left buried in my soul. I roar with all the pain, all the fear, all the outrage of this unjust world. I roar as a body forms around me... scales, claws, wings, teeth. I see my spirit materialize, roaring along with my rage. Sparks fill the air... lightning, not from the sky, I realize, but from me. From my spirit. It strikes out left and right, tearing apart the earth wherever it lands, ripping jagged wounds into anything it strikes. When it hits near Pike and Kaden, they break apart.

It is only then that I hear the voice. A whisper on the wind. "Sky... " Too late, I turn and see him. Kyle stands outside the house, his face drowsy. He looks at me with worry. With fear at the horrible sight before him.

And I see the lightning, now out of my control, unwieldy in its wildness, turn on him.

No. No! Noooo!

I will it to stop. To end.

But even I cannot contain what I have unleashed.

The lightning strikes towards Kyle. The darkness of night fills with unnatural light.

And then he is there.

Kaden.

He rushes forward, faster than I've ever seen him, and somehow... somehow he outruns the lightning. He grabs Kyle, pushing him out of the way just as the lightning strikes them both.

I hear Kyle scream in pain.

And Pike escapes into the shadows, holding Kara close to him.

My baby.

Is gone.

I REMEMBER her baby breath on my face as I held her close to me.

The way her tiny hand squeezed my finger.

The weight of her against my chest at night while we slept, in between midnight feedings and diaper changes.

How exhausted I was those first few months, dealing with the loss of my mother, a newborn baby to care for, and Caleb and Kyle, in their own grief and anger.

The joy I felt at her first word, her first tooth, her first attempts at walking.

And I remember my very first words to her after our mother died. My promise to her. "I'll protect you."

KARA IS MINE.

And this bastard isn't getting my daughter.

I will not break that promise.

Kaden has Kyle.

I need to get to Pike before he's gone.

My feet and hands have healed themselves, and though pain still floats in me like an ever-present houseguest, I push myself to stand and force myself forward.

I run through the shadows, through the dark streets, as fast as I can. Faster than I have ever moved. So fast everything around me is a blur.

I don't have a weapon, but I think back to what Kaden did, how his body transformed. I concentrate, and my arm changes, my hand extending, turning into a crystal claw. I stare at it a moment, in awe of what I'm doing with these new powers, flexing and moving this weapon that I now wear as a second skin.

Pike won't get away.

I catch up to him, surprising both of us I think, as he turns to see me, shock in his eyes.

I strike, ready to kill him with my crystal claw, preparing myself to grab Kara before she falls, but Pike is too fast.

He slashes up with his scythe, a trail of fire in its wake.

It takes me at my legs, slashing my body in two.

The scythe cuts through my neck.

And everything goes black.

11

SANCTUARY

The shock of coming to consciousness is not one I can easily describe. I thrash about trying to feel if my whole body is still complete. It is. Was I having a nightmare? Am I dreaming now? The pain of my evisceration is still heavy in my mind, but as the seconds pass, the memory flees, as if it was only an imagined thing. My eyes spring open, and I search around, looking for something familiar.

I am surrounded by a field of grass so green it looks painted. Of trees so lush and bark so thick and rich that it is more real than anything I've ever seen, so real it seems fake in its aliveness. Nothing in my life has ever held so much life, so much presence, so much *realness*. Flowers bloom around me in pinks and purples and reds and blues. A vibrant garden that renders me unable to imagine anything more beautiful or visceral. The fragrance of flowers overwhelms my senses with honeysuckle and lavender and the scent of roses so pure my mind is spinning.

I can practically taste the smells carried on the warm breeze. I look down at my body and see it is healed, the blood gone, though the memory of being severed in pieces still lingers, like a bad odor. In the distance, a grassy hill rises to the too-blue sky, and on it grows a silver tree, with branches and leaves that glisten their metallic beauty in a sun I don't see but still feel the warmth of.

In all of this beauty and wonder, in all this majesty, it takes me a moment to notice the slab of gray beside me. A grave stone, so like the one I visit regularly to commune with my dead mother. But this one does not bear the name of Laura Knightly. This one bears a name much more familiar.

My own.

And there are two, side by side. Both with my name.

"I'm sorry I couldn't stop him." The deep voice surprises me and I turn to see a familiar face.

Kaden is standing, his silhouette against the light of the invisible sun.

"Am I... dead?" I ask. I can think of no other explanation for this discombobulated experience.

"Yes," he says, tilting his head, his black hair falling once again into his too-blue eyes. "And no." He walks forward, leaves crunching under his boots, until he stops before my headstone. "Remember what I said earlier? You are of two worlds now. The seen and the unseen. Even with your body gone, your spirit remains."

"What is this place?" I ask, though some part of me surely knows. I've been here before, after all, but my memory eludes me.

"The spirit realm. Well, a part of it, at least. Your part. Your unique space, made by your mind alone." He looks around, smiling. "You have a gentle soul. A kind and protective one. You'd be surprised to see what others form for their realm. Some call it a sanctuary. Others a dream. It is a place Ashlords can go at will. And a place we all go in death."

I died, I think, though the memory is separate from me. I was sliced in half by Pike, even as he held my baby Kara in his hands. My heart breaks and I fall to my knees. She's gone. My baby is gone with that monster. The tears come, then. Unbidden but full of fury and rage. I dig my nails into the earth, squeezing my hands until they hurt. "It's over then, isn't it? Pike took her."

"He did." Kaden walks towards me and kneels before me, his

hands on mine. "But there wasn't anything you could do. Anything either of us could do."

I look up into his eyes, the blue of them even brighter in this realm. "Are you even real? Or just some phantom conjured to make me feel better?" If I am dead, the thought occurred to me that this could all be in my mind. An endless cycle of pain and false comfort.

"I'm as real as you," he says, smiling with a hint of his dimple showing. "With enough practice, Ashlords can visit each other's sanctuaries, at least while in close proximity, and while the sanctuary is being manifested. I saw you come here upon death, and so I followed. I thought you could use the guidance. You could try to get rid of me, of course. Each person is quite strong within their own sanctuary, and each visitor quite weaker."

I try to process all he says, but my mind is on one thing. "Is there a way back?" I ask. "A way back to the real world?" I have to find Kara. I have to save her, and protect Kyle and Caleb.

"Yes," he says, but he pauses, his voice hesitant. "In time, your body will recuperate, but it will be weak for days, at least for someone as untrained as you."

"How long?" There's an urgency to me, now. A hope. A burning need to set things right.

"A while here, but not long in the physical realm. Time moves differently here, you see. Slower. Every world, every dimension has its own way of gauging time, which is, after all, just an illusion. Time itself doesn't really exist. It's a construct we use to measure the unmeasurable."

I can't process everything he's saying, but one thing sticks out. I will recover. I will get my life back. "So... I can't be killed?"

He cocks his head, thinking. "If only it were so... All Ashlords can be killed. First, you must destroy their body. Then you enter their sanctuary and kill their spirit."

"But... if I'm stronger here, and you're weaker, how does that work?"

"You are stronger," he agrees, "which would make it difficult. But I can assure you, Pike would have no trouble destroying you."

My bravado fades at the mention of Pike. He bested me so quickly. So easily. And he took my baby. "Is he coming? Here?"

Kaden looks to the trees, a frown on his face. "I doubt it. He seems to be leaving us alive. I don't know why. Perhaps it's part of his code."

"What code?"

"Whatever code he abides by. Think about it, he must have one. You've seen how powerful he is, and yet he only takes children as part of a bargain. He could, theoretically, just steal them. No one would be able to stop him, and yet, he insists a contract be made and honored. That the debtor pay voluntarily, though how voluntarily is debatable given his methods. Still, it's curious, isn't it?"

"Not exactly the word I'd use for it," I say, as I remember Pat's hand being cut off... as I remember how my cat looked in that bag, dead. And how Kara looked in that monster's hands as he killed me without remorse.

Kaden nods his head. "Of course. Apologies. You see, I've been hunting Pike for many years now, and yet his ways seem more and more mysterious."

"Hunting him? Is that why you were really here, for him?"

Kaden is still. Quiet. I hear only the sound of a gentle breeze blowing through the flowers as he contemplates his answer. "Yes. I was tracking him. But then I found you, a Broken One, or so I thought, and suddenly I had two matters to deal with. I did my best to keep you safe. Perhaps I focused on you too much." Kaden frowns and rubs his face with his hand. "Enough to let Pike get away."

"You could have stopped him?"

"No." He frowns. "I couldn't have stopped him. Not alone. If I find Pike, my orders are not to engage. Instead, I'm to call for reinforcements and attempt to set a trap."

"And yet, you helped me. Me and Kyle."

He folds his hand into a fist. "I wasn't about to stand there while he hurt you and the children," he says.

My voice softens and I reach for his hand, laying mine on top. "Thank you," I say, my mind spinning with all the new information.

"You said you've been hunting, Pike, right? Then there must be a way to find him. A way to find Kara."

"Maybe, but tell me... even if you could catch Pike, how would you defeat him?"

"I..." I pause, stumped for a proper answer. I don't know how I'd stop him. I gave all I had, and Pike killed me in one blow, as if breaking a toy...

Kaden puts a hand on top of mine, squeezing gently, his eyes pleading with me. "Come with me," he says "to the place where Ashlords are trained, and I will teach you how to fight."

I hesitate, not sure how to react to this offer. "You said even you can't beat him."

"Not alone, but maybe we can together."

I can't leave, I can't leave the children... but I can't abandon Kara either...

"You know," says Kaden, his eyes intensely holding mine. "I take back what I said. You *are* the strongest untrained person I have ever met. And if you don't take control of your abilities, it's only a matter of time before you hurt someone again. Maybe kill them."

"Kyle..." My hands fall away from Kaden's as I remember the lightning striking my brother. Kaden pushed him out of the way... risking himself. But Kyle didn't escape unscathed. The lightning hit his arm. Burning him. He yelled. Screamed in pain.

"I need to help him!" I pull myself up, and realize I feel no pain. My foot is truly healed, my body mended.

Kaden stands before me, holding his hand out in caution. "You will, soon. Your body has almost regenerated."

I look around at this beautiful world and realize how empty it feels without those I love. I nearly killed Kyle, but only because I unleashed whatever spirit is inside me. "I'll go back. I'll wear the leather band my mother gave me. I'll keep the kids safe."

"But for how long?" asks Kaden. "Your power keeps growing. Right now, you seem a Broken One while wearing the band. How long until you seem a full Ashlord?"

"What will you do," I ask, "if I don't join you?"

He holds my eyes with his, his face chiseled from stone. "Traditionally, I would have to kill you, but I won't do that. Not to you. However, consider what will happen if you don't come with me. Even if by some miracle you don't lose control of your powers, it will only be a matter of time before another Ashlord finds you. And I promise, they will not be as considerate as I am."

I bite my lip and frown. "Maybe I'll fight them off."

"You wouldn't even know how to enter their sanctuary. You would never be able to kill them."

"So what then? My only choice is to die or go with you? To train somewhere to be this thing you call an Ashlord?"

"Put simply, yes. Come with me to the Cliff, and train to be an Ashlord. It's your only chance of saving Kara someday. Or don't, and wait here to die, hoping you don't hurt anyone before you do."

This choice seems like no choice at all, but I must consider everything. What will happen to Caleb and Kyle if I leave? How do I keep them safe then?

I look to the gravestone... a sick reminder of the lives that hang in the balance of my decisions. "If this is my sanctuary, why do I have two gravestones here?"

"It's not uncommon. Usually, they represent the number of times your physical body has died."

That takes a moment to sink in, and I step back, shocked. "So you mean, I've died twice?"

He shrugs, as if this is all very normal. "It appears so. The first time must have been when you were young, if you can't remember, that is. And if that's true... you must have had your spirit for a long time. Rare, but not impossible. Some people are born Broken Ones, you know. Kara was one. I suspect it's why Pike wanted her."

"Kara... how?" And then I remember her traumatic birth... how the effort ended up killing my mother.

"Of course," continues Kaden. "As I said before, a Broken One has not yet bonded with a spirit. Often doesn't until they reach adulthood. But there are a few exceptions. Like you, apparently."

"What does Pike want with her?" I ask. "What does Pike want with my baby?"

"I don't know," he says. "We've never found a child he's taken. But he always takes them alive. One would assume he's keeping them somewhere, but for what purpose, I do not know. You could help us find out. If you came with me."

He's good at the bait, I'll give him that. "All these things you don't know. How am I ever supposed to get Kara back, even with your help?"

"Just because something hasn't been done yet, doesn't mean it can't be done. I'm not one for giving up, and I suspect you aren't either."

No... My entire life I've kept going, even when some days all I've wanted to do is give up... but I keep going... for them... for Kyle and Caleb and Kara. For my mum.

I sigh, knowing I have very little choice in this. "Tell me what I have to do. How do I get out of here?"

Kaden rolls a silver coin over his knuckles, the metal glinting in the sun. "It's a lot like waking up, actually. You just have to decide to do it."

I close my eyes and imagine this place a dream. I think of home... of days cuddled up on the couch with Caleb, Kara in my arms, Kyle sitting next to us on the floor as we watch an old movie together and eat buttered popcorn.

I open my eyes... and nothing has changed. The trees still sway around me, the gravestones cast their shadows.

I sigh, letting my head fall, and then I see my hand... breaking apart like burning paper... specks drifting off in the wind.

"Good," says Kaden, a smile in his voice. "You're learning. When you get back, remember my offer. I must leave soon, and if you wish to have a chance of saving Kara, you must leave with me."

I nod, and then my body turns to nothing.

12

DEATH BE NOT PROUD

I wake up on wet asphalt still covered with my blood. I check my body for severed parts, but it seems that once again I am whole. Everything is healed... physically at least. My heart is still bleeding out. My daughter is gone.

I call for her, but I know Pike took her somewhere I can't hope to reach on my own. Somewhere not of this world. And then I remember Kyle, and I jump up and run back to the house.

It's as if no time has passed. He is laying on the grass with Kaden, who stretches to help him up. There's an angry burn covering Kyle's right arm, and tears stream down his face. He clenches his jaw, groaning in pain. "It'll be okay," I tell him, as I lead him into the house. I examine the wound, and it's not as bad as I first thought. "We need to run it under cold water, then put clean bandages on it."

I tell Kaden where to get my first aid kit as I take care of Kyle. "Where's Caleb?" I ask, trying to distract him from the pain as the cold water wakes up all the nerves in his arm.

"Sleeping," he hisses through his teeth. "Sky, what happened?"

He glances at the blood in the kitchen. At Pat passed out and missing a hand.

"Don't look." I say. "Let's just take this a moment at a time. Keep your arm under water. I'm calling this in, okay?"

He nods and I step away and use my phone to first call 911, then Blake. I make a tourniquet for Pat's arm, to stem the blood flow. I find his hand and put it in one of the kids' lunch coolers with some ice, hoping it's not too late to save it. I have no idea how much time has passed through all this. There's too much to do and only one of me. I don't know how to help everyone. I don't know what to do about Kara. I'm lost.

Kaden returns in a flash with clean bandages, and I dress Kyle's wounds and lay him on the couch with an ice pack on his forehead and some pain pills to take the edge off. "Stay here. Don't move. Don't look at anything. We'll get through this."

He grunts, and I know when he's recovered from this he'll have questions, but for now, he's too out of it to notice that his baby sister is missing. That Pat could be dying. That I did die, but somehow didn't.

Death be not proud... the first line of an old sonnet by John Donne flits through my mind, and I can't recall why I know it—likely from an old English class, but the words settle into me, helping me process what I just went through in a way my own words can't. *"Die not, poore death, nor yet canst thou kill me."* Death. The one thing you can't walk away from. And yet I did. I walked away from death. Death cannot kill me.

A strange euphoria stirs in me, and I'm torn between this indestructible power I feel, and the pain and grief of losing my child. What is happening? Nothing makes any sense in my mind, but somehow, I still have to operate in the human world, with human rules and human laws.

The paramedics arrive with the police. They triage my stepfather and brother, getting them settled into the vans as Blake arrives.

"I have to go with Kyle," I tell the police, who have questions I can't answer. Kaden stays, surprising me. His hand rests on my back, his eyes unreadable. Blake looks to me, then him, his face full of confusion.

"What's happening, Sky? Who's he?" There are questions beneath those questions, and I know it. He knows it.

"I can't explain everything now. Will you go with Kyle? Keep him safe? Caleb is still sleeping."

He nods, then kisses my forehead. He side-eyes Kaden again, then leaves with Kyle in the ambulance.

The police question me and Kaden. He answers more than I do, and seems to know how to navigate human procedures. A missing person's report is filed. An ABP put out for a man matching Pike's description.

All the things that a cop in this town can do are done, and none of them will be enough. They're wasting their time, but I can't tell them that.

Dean, of course, is one of the officers taking my statement, and he can't seem to stop himself from glaring at Kaden. "Who are you again?" he asked, several times.

Each time Kaden patiently explained he was a 'good friend' of mine in from out of town. Surprisingly, he was able to provide proper identification and an address located in Swords, England. I raised an eyebrow at that, but said nothing.

Eventually they left, though I could tell Dean didn't want to leave me alone with Kaden. I would have laughed, if my heart hadn't been so broken.

And so here we are. The two of us. I've checked on Caleb at least six times, but he's sleeping peacefully. I woke him once to make sure he wasn't in a coma, and he moaned about being tired and fell back into bed. I kissed his cool forehead and pulled the blankets more snugly around him, tucking him in for what would likely be the last time.

The sun is starting to rise, and I can't believe how long I've been awake, and how much has happened.

I died.

And now I live.

And Kara is gone.

My mother knew this would happen. Or at least, something like this. But how? Why? I need to know.

Kaden picks up his coat and slides it on and says he has to leave. "I have a few things to handle. But tonight, we must leave. Meet me at this address," he says, handing me a slip of paper with the name of a winery in Healdsurg. "By the fountain. I'll wait as long as I can. If you don't come, worse things could happen to you and your family."

"Are you threatening me?"

He frowns. "No. Some might say I've lost my edge around you, that I'm failing at my job by giving you an option. But I believe people are capable of making the right choice, and in so doing, they have more power on their path." He looks deeply into my eyes. "I hope I'm not wrong about you."

I watch him walk away, and I pull my sweater around me as a sharp wind digs into my skin. "You're not," I whisper, though I know he can't hear. But still, his head tilts, and he looks back, just once, and just for a moment, and I wonder if maybe he did hear, because there's a small smile on his face, before he turns away once again.

I HAVE NO CHOICE. Not really. My only chance of finding out what happened to Kara, is by going with Kaden. I will save her if I can, avenge her if I can't. And I will learn to control my powers.

If Kaden hadn't been here last night... I shudder to think what would have happened to Kyle. He would not have come back from the dead as easily as I.

I spend the next several hours scrubbing blood out of our floors, trying to make the house as comfortable as possible for my little family.

I try not to cry. I try not to think about what I'm about to do. About what I'm losing by making this choice.

Everything.

Everything I have ever cared for. Everything I have ever known.

When Blake and Kyle return from the hospital, I hug them both, my eyes swollen from tears that refuse to stay contained.

Kyle pulls back eventually, his eyes tired, his face gaunt. "What was that... outside?" he asks. "I saw you... glowing." He whispers the last word as if scared I will tell him he's crazy, and he takes a strand of my brown hair in his fingers, looking at it, studying it, wondering—very likely—how he saw my hair turn silver.

"It's not something I can explain," I tell him.

He scowls. "Why? Because it's grown up stuff?"

I almost laugh at that, because what I wouldn't give for a normal grown up problem right now. "No, not at all," I say, looking him straight in the eyes. "It's because I don't understand it either. But once I do, I'll tell you everything, okay? Pinky promise."

His eyebrows shoot up in surprise, but he holds out his pinky and nods, and we lock fingers.

I ruffle his hair with affection. "It's time for bed now."

He's about to do as I say, but then I see his face change. I see him remember everything else that happened. "Where's Kara?"

I glance at Blake, who looks as gutted as I feel. "She's... " I don't know how to say this. "She's... gone, Kyle."

"Gone where?" His eyes roam the house and fall on the blood stains I'm still struggling to get out of the floor. "Did that man take her?"

I can't shield him from this. If it were Caleb, I could frame it differently. But Kyle is a teenager. He's not stupid. He knows what he saw. So I tell him as much of the truth as I can. "Yes, he did."

Kyle's eyes widen. "How do we get her back?"

"Not we. I." I let my words sink in, as I frame my next thought carefully. "I don't know where she is. But I swear to you, I will find her. One way or another, I will find her." I don't promise to bring her back, because I can't. I'm not sure I'll find her alive. But I will find out what happened to her. And I will make Pike pay for what he's done. That I promise.

Kyle nods. "So you're leaving?"

"I wish I didn't have to, but yes. I'm the only one who has a chance at this."

Kyle hugs me again, harder. When he pulls away, his face is older. This night has aged him. "Go. Do what you have to do. But catch the bastard who did this to my sister. Promise me, Sky?"

I nod, swallowing my tears. "Blake will take care of you two while I'm gone, okay?"

He nods again, his eyes filling with tears. "Will I see you again soon?"

"I..."

His voice breaks. "Will I ever see you again?"

He feels the weight of what I'm doing. We all do.

"I hope so, kiddo. If I have anything to say about it, you will. We will be together again."

After getting him to bed, Blake and I sit on the front porch as I get ready to explain everything to him.

But before I can say a word, Blake looks down at my wrist. "You're not wearing your band."

"Then you understand," I say, realizing I don't have to explain it all. Not to him.

"So it's like we always thought, then? You're not the only one."

"No..."

He nods. "Well, that explains what Kyle told me he saw."

He puts his arm around me and holds me close. I know Blake will take care of my kids. I know he'll keep Pat in line. I know he'll keep my secret.

Because when we were kids, we made a vow to look out for each other. And when we sat alone in Blake's treehouse, behind his parent's home, I took off my bracelet, and I showed him what I could do.

Back then it wasn't much, but it was enough to astonish him, and convince him I had power. He was the only one I ever told. The only one who ever saw my true self.

We each held each other's secrets, when the world would have turned on us. When his parents turned on him for being gay. When

Pat turned on me for being different. We were each other's safe harbors.

Leaving him is almost harder than leaving my whole life.

"I'll take care of them, Sky. Don't worry about the boys. I got them. You find our girl."

The tears flow, and I wrap him in a hug. "You've been a brother to me, you know that, right?"

"I know that, sis. We're family. Now and forever."

Before the kids wake up, I kiss them each, saying silent goodbyes. It's better this way. Caleb is too young to understand what's happening, and Kyle already knows. Even still, Caleb's eyes pop open as I adjust his stuffed bunny next to him. "Why you cry?"

"I've got to leave for a bit, little guy. To help Kara. But Kyle and Blake will be here to take care of you, okay?"

He doesn't understand what I'm saying, but he snuggles closer to me. "Love you, Sky."

"I love you too, Caleb."

With one last hug for Blake, I turn away from my home, from everything I've tried to build in my life, from my work as a firefighter, from my kids, from my best friend, from a step dad who made my life hell... I say goodbye to it all.

I know what this decision means: I will be a suspect in Kara's abduction if I disappear. I'll be replaced at work. The kids will miss me. Maybe hate me.

But it's the right choice.

The only choice.

I can't keep living as if I'm an ordinary girl.

I'm not.

It's time to claim my power and save my daughter.

13

THE ELDER DRAGONS

It is dark by the time I reach the winery. People have long since gone to their beds, leaving the night to the crickets and frogs and foxes. Even the roads are near empty, missing the hum of engines. I drive through a gravel path until I can park my car on a gravel lot. Then I text Blake with my location, in case he needs to find me, and so he can pick up my beat-up car. There's a dirt road that leads deep into fields of grass. The man I seek is at the end of the path.

Kaden sits under an olive tree, sharpening his blade with a whetstone. His skin is pale in the moonlight and his eyes bright blue. His coat is crumpled off to the side. I see the vest he wears unbuttoned, revealing his bare arms and chest. His muscles coil and stretch as he grinds stone against steel. The burn mark on his shoulder doesn't appear to bother him anymore. He seems more sculpture than man. A relic from a time long past. When warriors and monsters did battle.

His voice is soft when he speaks. "I will be honest with you, Sky. There is a chance you may never see your daughter again. Even if you master all there is for you to learn. Even if you find your enemy and end him. It may already be too late."

My hand curls into a fist. "I know Kara may be dead already. But even if I can't save her, I won't stop fighting until Pike is stopped. Until he can never take a child again." I take a step forward toward Kaden. "You held your own against Pike. Teach me how to do the same."

He grins. "Usually, you would begin with a more basic teacher—"

"I need to be the best. Better than you, even, if I'm to defeat Pike." I lock eyes with him, studying his reaction.

For a moment, he seems to contemplate my words, then he smiles again. "Very well. I will begin your training. But, once we reach the Cliff, we shall have to go our separate ways. I will have my duties to uphold, and you will have lessons to attend."

I take another step closer. "The Cliff? I've heard you mention it before." *Back in my Sanctuary.*

"It is the place where Ashlords are trained. Where you will be trained."

"And what happens if I change my mind? If I want to leave?"

He grinds the stone once more against his blade, and the sharp edge glints in the moonlight. "You cannot. Those who give up on training, or those who fail, are made Charred. They remain at the Cliff, serving to its every need."

"So they are made slaves?"

His eyes look far away. "We are all slaves in a way. Our duty is simply different." He pauses. "It is too dangerous to let Twin Spirits run amok. So one way or another, they serve the Cliff. Willingly, or not."

I look around at the dark rolling hills that surround us, at the fields of olive trees and their leaves swaying in the wind. "So where is this Cliff?"

"Like me, it is not of this world."

I step closer again, sitting next to him by the tree. "What do you mean?"

"I grew up in a land far away, a land much different than yours. A land you will soon see. It is a place of harsh winds and magnificent beasts. A place of windswept ruins and towering castles. A place of spirits and serpents. A place of dragons."

I glance at him, my gaze intense. "Dragons? Like my spirit?"

"They say spirits come from the dead. I speak of dragons that yet live." He points to the night sky. "Once the stars are aligned, I will take you to my world. To the world of the Cliff and the Wall of Light. The world they call Nirandel."

"Nirandel... " I repeat, trying to commit the name to memory.

Kaden flips his sword over in his hand and begins to work on the side yet dull. "I recommend you leave any electronics behind. They will not serve you in my world."

I pull my cheap cellphone from my pocket. "Why not?"

He shrugs. "Each world has its own rules, laws of nature, as it were. Your technology does not work in Nirandel, nor can it even be made if one tried."

"Why?"

He raises an eyebrow. "Why does gravity pull us down? Why does time move forward? It's just the way things are, whether we like it or not." He pauses. "For example, your world, this world, Gia as we call it, has no limit on technology, and yet it is weakest when it comes to any forms of magic. In Nirandel magic is strong, but technology weak. There is no reason, as far as anyone knows, though some scholars do have a theory: that a world has only so much space for technology and magic. If it has much of one, it must have little of the other. A balance can also be struck, some say, if both magic and technology were to be of middling levels, but I have yet to see such a world."

"I see..." I say, my thoughts spinning. "So it's like a person. You can be lithe and agile and small. Or huge and muscled and strong. You could even be something in-between, but you can't really be both."

Kaden nods. "Interesting perspective. I shall have to tell the scholars." He puts the whetstone away, and with the tip of his sword, draws a triangle in the dirt.

"What is this?" I ask.

"You're first lesson." He points to each corner of the triangle. "These are the three pillars of Spirit. Transmuting, Imbuing, and Beckoning. Beckoning you have already done twice. Once in the forest against the Fenrial. Once against Pike. It is when you summon your Spirit into physical form. Transmuting you have also done, when you changed your hand into a claw. Transmuting, you see, is the art of blending your body and that of your Spirit's into one. Imbuing, you have yet to try." He pulls a silver coin from his pocket and runs it across his knuckles. "For it is the art of infusing other objects with Spirit in order to give them power." He flicks the coin to me, and I catch it.

"So Imbuing is how you make talismans," I say. "Like the one you used to create a barrier around us under the bridge."

Kaden nods. "Talismans may not have great power, in the literal sense, but their strength lies in their versatility. They have far more varied uses than Beckoning or Transmuting."

I grin, excited by the wealth of new knowledge I have access to. "How do I make one?"

"You start as we all start. By learning the glyphs." He points at the talisman in my hands. "That is the glyph for purify. One day, you will need to use it to vanquish corrupted spirits as I did with the Fenrial. Memorize it. Know it as well as you know your name."

He hands me a stick. "Draw the symbol into the sand. Over and over until you can draw it without looking. Until you can draw it without thinking."

I begin the exercise, remembering Kara. With every stroke I draw in the sand, I imagine a world in which I could have saved her. A world in which I could have used my abilities to stop Pike. A world in which Kyle and Caleb and Kara and I sit together on the couch eating 'pasgetti' and laughing at the silly things in life.

"Are you sure you wish to come with me?" asks Kaden. "If you do not, another Ashlord will come for you, but you may have more time with your brothers. Once we leave, you may not see them again for years. You may not see them again ever."

I have considered all the options, and this is still my choice. "Like you said, I need to learn to control my powers. If I don't, I'll harm the very people I care about."

He nods, then looks to the sky. "The stars are almost aligned.

Before we go, let me tell you a story. A story of how the nine worlds came to be."

My eyes go wide. "Nine?"

"Don't get too excited. They are not all inhabitable, much like the planets around earth. But yes, there are nine. Keep drawing the glyph and listen. For here is the legend of Nir and the creation of the Nine Worlds.

OUT OF DARKNESS was born the first dragon, Alandel, and she had nine children. Nir and Gai, Ava and Inf, Heln and Spri, Var and Min and Undi. When their mother died, the elder dragons divided her body amongst themselves. Var took her flame. Min took her blood. Undi her eyes, and Spri her wings. Inf took her scales and Gai her bones. Ava took her heart and Heln her spirit. And last Nir took her mind. And with what they took, each elder dragon formed a world for themselves, and so the Nine Worlds were born.

Nir, however, was not content with simply land. Why have land but no one to share it with, he asked? And so, using the last pieces of Alandel's mind, he created mankind. He treated them as his children, and taught them how to master fire, how to tame water, how to grow crops and build homes. Nir enjoyed people so much, he took their form often for himself, and one day, even fell in love with a woman. They bore three children together, the first High Dragons, blood of both dragon and man.

It was not long until the other elder dragons grew jealous of Nir and his children. They too wanted the company of people, and so they approached Nir, asking for people of their own. The elder dragon Nir said he would let his children decide whether they wanted to live in other worlds or not.

Gai, who had taken her mother's bones, had built a large world full of mountains and seas and rivers and lakes, and some people said they would go to her world. Ava had built a world of flying islands and deep caves, and some people too said they would go there to live.

Other people preferred other worlds. But Var had built a world of fire, and Min a world of ice, and no people chose to join them there. The two elder dragons grew furious. If they could not have mankind on their worlds, they said, then they would take the other worlds for themselves. And so, a great war began.

For millennium, the elder dragons battled each other, until it is said only Nir, the smartest, and Var, the strongest, remained. The two were equal on the field of battle, and so Nir devised a plan. We can continue for another millennium, said Nir, and accomplish nothing, or we can divide the worlds between us and have peace. But there are Nine Worlds, said Var. How do we divide them fairly?

We split one world in half, said Nir, and each take one side. Var agreed.

And so the elder dragons met on the world of Ava, and together they prepared to cast a powerful spell to split the world in two. We stand on different sides of this river, said Nir, for this river is in the middle of this world, and this way it will be fair. Var agreed. And so they cast the spell. A giant blade of light fell from the sky to tear the world in two, but it did not fall upon the river, for you see, Nir had lied. The river did not split the world in half, instead it was the field that Var now stood upon. And thus the blade of light fell upon Var himself, tearing his body, instead of the world, in two.

What Nir did not know however, was that Var was pregnant, and when Var died, from his stomach spilled a thousand dragons. They spread throughout the worlds, killing mankind and feeding off their Spirits. In days, almost all the people were dead, and so Nir did the only thing he could. He used all his strength to draw the dragons together and cast a wall of light around them, cutting them off from Spirit and man. So powerful was the spell, that Nir gave his own life to cast it. And so, the final elder dragon died to save his children, and the age of the Ancients ended. But some say Nir is not dead, just asleep, regaining his strength, and when mankind needs him once more, the elder dragon will awaken.

KADEN PAUSES, letting his words sink in.

His mythology is so different from the ones I grew up hearing. It reminds me of a children's fable more than real history, and it would be easy to call it trivial. But I've seen too much to dismiss the fantastical anymore. And I have a feeling I'm about to see a lot more.

Kaden stands and throws on his long black coat. "I can see the questions in your eyes," he says, "but it is time. The stars are aligned." He holds out his hand to me, and I take it, and he guides me to a fountain amidst the olive trees. The shallow water shimmers in the light, casting our pale reflections back at us. Kaden pulls a coin from his pocket and flips it in the fountain, and the surface of the waves changes. Where once the water seemed shallow, it now seems of infinite depth. Where once it seemed chaotic, it now seems as still as a mirror. And where once the stars seemed but a reflection, they now seem to shine from beyond the waves.

"Are you ready?" asks Kaden.

I nod.

And together we jump into the fountain.

14

NIRANDEL

I brace myself for the cold shock of water, but instead emerge into a sea of stars. A night sky never ending. I float through the darkness, as if there is nothing but space around me. No air. No water. Only cold. Only night. And the stars and planets and moons shimmering in the unspeakable distance.

There is the sound of water breaking. I look up and see Kaden appear from nothingness. His scarf and coat and hair drift up slowly, as if he were sinking, and he moves through the space as if swimming, until his arm is touching mine.

I want to speak, but I dare not let the air out from my lungs. I do not know if I can breathe in this strange place. Kaden gestures for me to follow him, then swims forward, toward a ring of golden light. A nebula, I think I've heard it called. I follow Kaden, paddling through the sky, and find that moving here is much like moving through water, but easier and faster, as if there is no friction of any kind. It's like my dreams, where I would fly as if swimming. I wonder if I am really in space, but I cannot be. I would freeze to death.

The nebula grows larger before us, until it covers all my vision with gold. Up close now, I realize it's not a multitude of stars as much as a wall of light. Or perhaps it changed as I grew closer. Kaden swims past me, disappearing behind the golden hue. For a moment, I hesitate to follow, but there is no turning back now. I reach out with my hand, touching the light. It feels soft and smooth and warm. With one final push, I plunge forward, letting the sea of stars engulf me in its warm embrace.

My head breaks through the surface, and I emerge as if from a deep dive, gasping for air. I stand in a shallow pool of crystal clear water, my feet touching sand that was not there before. The air is thinner here. The wind weaker. And the heat stronger.

It is bright. Night has turned to day, the sky a clear blue. Lush green bushes that look like the tops of palm trees circle the pond we just stepped out of, and thick vines fall from taller trees. Dense emerald grass covers the ground, and small purple flowers that sprout in clusters dot the landscape. Far above, I hear a shrill bird call, then a chorus of responses from the nearby trees, a beautiful song reverberating through the air.

Past the trees and the grass, past this little oasis we have landed in, is an endless horizon of silver sand shining too brightly in the sun. An endless stretch of desert with no signs of life, at least above the surface.

"Something is wrong," says Kaden, walking out of the water, his clothes dripping onto the grass. "We were supposed to arrive closer to the Cliff. This place..." His words trail off, and he stands silent, looking at the sky.

I walk onto dry land, my wet clothes rubbing against my skin. At least it's warm. I'd be freezing in the wind. "What happened? Your fountain portal broke or something?"

"They're not portals," he says, "not really. It's more about the stars. When the stars align over certain bodies of water, that water can be used to travel between worlds. All one needs is a travel talisman and the knowledge of which stars align where and when. It changes from month to month, year to year. It's not a simple science, but I was certain we should have arrived miles north of here." He pauses, frowning. "I heard whispers... talk of the stars fading, the light dying..."

I raise an eyebrow. "Care to explain what you're mumbling about?"

He turns to me. "Some say this world is ending. That soon our magic will fade away and the light will vanish. That darkness will come. Of course, there are always those who speak of the apocalypse and there always will be. I gave no credence to it, but the stars..." He shakes his head. "I must have made a mistake is all. Simple as that."

He glances around. "Now where was... ah. Here." He runs up to a tree with emerald vines and large, multi-faceted crystals that grow in place of fruit. He brushes away a pile of sand and stone, revealing a symbol underneath: two black swords crossed over each other in an X. "One of our hidden caches," he explains, grabbing a handle obscured in the ground and pulling. The symbol opens like a hatch, revealing a small space stuffed full of objects: clothing, a pair of daggers, something that might be food.

Kaden passes me a blue cloak and robes and a towel. "Dry off, then put these on. They will keep you warm in the night. And they'll help you fit in with the locals."

He grabs a pair of black robes for himself, then pulls off his shirt. He starts unbuckling his pants and—

"What are you doing?" I ask.

He pauses. "Apologies. I forget myself. Modesty is much less important on Nirandel than in your world. I'll find a more private location." He walks away, disappearing behind a tree.

I take the moment to undress and dry off, then put on the new robes. They are thin and light and seem made of silk, and it isn't long until I start to feel cooler in the heat. I throw a hood over my head to shade my face, and adjust the blue cloak on my back, then check my reflection in the lake. I look as if I've stepped out of a fairytale, one about knights and princesses and wizards.

Kaden emerges from the trees, dressed all in black once again, except for his red scarf. He grabs a bag from the cache and packs our old clothing. "This look suits you," he says.

"Is this how everyone dresses here?"

"More or less. This world is much like your medieval age in some ways, and yet quite different in others." He pulls a scroll of leather from the cache and unrolls it on the sand, revealing pictures of mountains and trees and cities and borders. A map. Kaden points to the bottom left of the scroll. "We are here, in the Silver Desert. We need to get here." He points to a picture of a fortress to the north.

I read the script next to the drawing. "Dragoncliff."

Kaden nods. "The place where you will train. We call it the Cliff for short." He points to a line on the map near our location. "We will follow this river until we reach a village. Then we can hire a carriage. I'd say we should be at Dragoncliff in three weeks."

That's much longer than I expected, and I feel anger burning inside me for the delay. Every moment I'm not training is a moment I waste. The faster I master my abilities, the faster I can stop Pike. But this rage is foolish. I was stupid to think this journey would be a quick one. I will need to train, but I will also need to eat and sleep and rest. I will need to learn about this new world: the laws, the manners, the customs, just so I can survive long enough to defeat my enemy. This journey may take months, I realize, even years. I will need to steel myself for what is to come.

A small creature flutters down from the trees and hovers before me, pulling me from my stupor. I almost think it a bird, but it's unlike any bird I have ever seen. Its skin is smooth, featherless, and glows a pale blue. Though it has wings, they are more like fins, and the creature appears to swim through air rather than fly. I raise a hand, and it twirls around my finger, gently touching it with its wispy long tail. The creature hums, a sort of ethereal purr, and rubs against my palm. It has no beak, more a toothless mouth, and it seems to smile.

"Starcatchers," says Kaden, as he grabs two water skins from the cache and fills them in the oasis. "This one seems to like you."

I pet the little Starcatcher in my hand, half wondering if this is all a dream. "Where did the name come from?" I ask.

"They are born as little Pods." He holds his index finger above his thumb. "Little bitty things, that can't fly or glow. But when they're old enough, the old tales say Pods go on a quest, a voyage amongst the stars. And when they find a star of their own, they eat it up, and let it engulf their bodies in warmth. The star becomes a part of them, and so they glow from within and forever get the power of flight. And thus a Pod becomes a Starcatcher."

The little bird squeals in delight, then zips up, disappearing amongst the trees. I chuckle, and realize my sadness has been swept away by the little creature, at least for a while. There is so much to see here, so much to learn. Perhaps I can lose myself in this new knowledge, and make learning, and not despair, my guide.

"Tell me more about your world," I say, gesturing to the map. "Show me your capitols and borders. Your cities and towns."

Kaden begins. "As I said, we are in the Silver Desert. Just north of us is the city of Al'Kalesh, and deep within, lies the Palace of Storms. It is where the Emperor, Titus, rules."

"How much land does he control?" I ask.

Kaden gestures at the map. "He is Titus, the Unbroken, the Slayer of Dragons, the Emperor of Nirandel."

"Of Nirandel... so you mean... all of it? The whole world?"

Kaden nods. "Yes. The whole world. Though of course, there are places where his laws are... difficult... to enforce. The Ashlands, for one. The Frozen Mountains, for another." He points to the locations. The Ashlands at the center of the map. The Frozen Mountains to the north. Then he points to the east. "Here are the Sunstar Isles, where people ride giant beasts amongst the waves and study the ancient arts of Kargara, a form of martial arts." He points to the west. "And here is La'Moko, a giant island with a proud and wise people, who believe in peace above all." Kaden leans back, sighing. "Once, long ago, these lands were ruled by the High Dragons."

"The ones in the story? Half man? Half dragon?"

Kaden stares into the distance, at the silver sand, his eyes dark. "They were real. Magnificent beings with a connection to Spirits unlike any other. They could do things with Beckoning, Transmuting and Imbuing that I can only dream of. Their Spirits were like giants, titans, forces of nature capable of shaping the very earth." There is awe in his eyes now, wonder in his words. "I dreamed of being one of them, wished for it with all my being. But..." the thrill leaves him. "But it was not meant to be. And the High Dragons were not meant to live on."

There is a sorrow in him now, and I touch his hand with mine, seeking to ease the pain. "What happened to them?"

"First, they turned on each other," he says. "They divided the lands amongst themselves, but like Alandel's children, they were not content with a small piece of the world. They had to have it all, and so civil war after civil war ravaged the land. There were times of peace, of course, but they were always short lived. And then the High Dragons made a terrible mistake. They burned the wife of Titus Al'Beckus." He pauses. "Titus was a man of the middle class, a group of people who had grown in wealth and power yet still had to heed every High Dragon's order no matter how mad. They were tired of wars they cared nothing for, tired of rules that did nothing but rob them, and so, under Titus Al'Beckus, they rose up. Like a tidal wave, the rebellion swept through the land, killing every High Dragon in its path, until none remained."

He takes a swig from his water skin, and says no more.

"But if the High Dragons were so powerful," I ask, "how were they defeated in battle?"

"The Emperor's Shadows," Kaden says, his brow furrowed. "Little is known of them, other than they were Titus's most loyal servants, and underwent rituals best forgotten. They are... more beast than man. Unnatural things. I pray you will never come across one."

He turns back to the map, his mood shifting, turning lighter, as if to brush away the darkness of the past. He points to a large circle at the center of the map. "And here is the Wall of Light."

I trace my hand over the lines on the map. "The Wall of Light? Like the one in the story?"

He nods. "It *is* the one in the story. The one Nir created to keep the dragons at bay. It is an Ashlord's sacred duty to defend the Wall, for if it were to fall, the Nine Worlds would be covered in death and ash."

I point at the picture of Dragoncliff. "But if this drawing represents a fortress, then the Wall of Light is huge. Longer than all your rivers, and larger than any city. This map can't be to scale... can it?"

Kaden sighs. "The Wall of Light is vast. It can be seen from nearly all of Nirandel. Especially in the night, when the skies are dark."

"So it's enormous."

"Thousands of dragons live within. Maybe hundreds of thousands. The Ashlands past the wall stretch on for hundreds of miles. We do not even possess an accurate map of them. Every couple hundred years, an Ashlord with great ambitions will set out to make one, but none have ever returned from the center alive."

Kaden glances at the sun. "It's past midday now. We should travel while we can. Before it gets dark. Then we'll make camp." He rolls up the map, stuffs it in a bag, and throws the pack over his shoulder. "Once I get a better look at our surrounding area, I should be able to pinpoint our exact location," Kaden says. "Then it should be easy to find the river."

"You seem to know these lands quite well," I say.

He smiles. "There is a library at Dragoncliff full of books and scrolls. As a child, I would pour over all the maps, dreaming of adventure. I wanted to uncover new lands and discover new creatures, but as my teacher once said, such things are not for those of Ash." He looks down. "It saddens me, sometimes."

This world may be old to him, but it will all be new to me, and for the first time since jumping into the fountain I'm filled with something akin to excitement. Then a thought occurs to me. "You were at Dragoncliff as a child?"

Kaden doesn't look at me. "We do not choose when we become Broken Ones, nor when we become a Twin Spirit, and my training began when I was very young." He walks away before I can say more.

I follow him through the brush and emerge onto a desert of silver sand, a vastness of rolling dunes as far as the eye can see. Kaden stares at something in the distance, his smile fading. I follow his gaze to a ruin amongst the sands. Structures and pillars half buried in the earth, withered by time and wind and weather.

"What's wrong?" I ask.

"That place..." Kaden clenches his fist. "That place is where my best friend was murdered."

15

DRAGONSTONE

"How did it happen?" I ask, staring at the ruins. There are burn marks along pieces of fallen stone, and deep grooves that look like giant claw marks.

"There were rumors of a Corrupted One," says Kaden, his gaze fixed on the rubble. "A Broken One taken by a Corrupted Spirit. Reports said it attacked a caravan by the ruins, slaughtering all but two woman who escaped, feeding off the souls of the dead. My friend, Alec, and I, were ordered to investigate the matter and slay the beast. We found the creature at night. A Scabrial who had taken a strong host. It stood the size of three men. Had pincers for a mouth and four arms covered in razor sharp spikes. A hard blue shell protected most of its body, and a hundred eyes sprouted from its head. It was a challenging fight, but nothing we couldn't handle. I took the beast head on. Alec circled around to strike from behind. We were winning, until..."

His fist hardens, vein pulsing on his neck. "Until *she* appeared. A woman. Clad in white armor, her face covered in a featureless mask, her hair crimson red. She had been sitting on top of the ruins, hiding in the shadows. She moved in an instant. Above us one moment. Then behind Alec the next. She stabbed him through the back, her sword exploding from his stomach. I entered his Sanctuary, to help him fight, but he was already dead there too. She stood over his corpse, the world around us disintegrating into ashes. The Sanctuary burned, and my friend burned with it."

Kaden's eyes glisten in the sun. "I tried to chase her. But she just vanished. One moment she was there. The next gone. As if she faded into shadow. It was as if... as if she had been waiting for us. As if the whole mission was a trap. But how? How could she bring a Corrupted One to the ruins? Or maybe... maybe she knew where we would be, and so she decided to strike. Maybe..."

His words turn to erratic murmurs, and I take his hand, stilling his trembling fingers. He looks at me then, eyes full of rage and sorrow and heartache. "He always wanted to return home. So I took his body back to Ukiah, the place he grew up. I made sure he was buried at the cemetery near his father and mother." He says no more, though his tense body sends off waves of anger, like an energy pulse I can practically feel.

I let the silence linger before asking, "What happened to the woman?"

Kaden shrugs. "Some see her, now and again, clad in that white armor. They say she burned a manor in Al'Kalesh. Sunk a ship in the Frozen Sea. No one knows who she is. Only that she appears as if from nowhere, bringing chaos and death in her wake, and disappears just as quickly. They call her the Outcast now. A ghost on the wind." He turns his eyes to mine, and they are hard and unyielding. His body is still, focused. A warrior bent on one thing. "I've been tracking her for three years now. Someday, I will find her and make her pay for what she did."

"She's your Pike," I say softly.

He nods his head briefly, then begins walking, into the desert.

After hours of hiking over sand, we arrive at the river that will take us to Al'Kalesh. Kaden says we will have to pass through the city on our way to the Cliff, or waste days going around. By the time we wade into the river to refill our waterskins, tall grass sprouting all around us, my legs are tired, my lungs are dried husks, and the water I sip on tastes strange.

When I say as much to Kaden, he chuckles. "You're used to plastic or glass." He holds up the waterskins. "These are made from the bladders of Boxen."

I wrinkle my nose at that. "What's a Boxen?"

He points past my shoulder, and I turn, following his gaze to the horizon. In the distance, against the backdrop of the blazing sun, a caravan travels over the sands. Two giant beasts, covered in fur, carry large packs upon their backs. Two more pull a huge cart. The animals remind me of bison, but far larger, at least four times the size. Their horns are massive, elaborate things, splitting off at the tips like branches to make intricate shapes. There are symbols and lines and drawings etched into the white horns, difficult to make out, but beautiful.

Kaden walks up to my side. "The Akari—the people of the desert—carve their history into the horns of their Boxen. Tales of many generations. For you see, Boxens live for hundreds of years, passed down from mother to daughter. They are gentle, loyal creatures, used all over Nirandel, but never respected as much as here in the desert."

"They're beautiful," I say, as the caravan tracks across a sand dune. "Are they hunted?" I ask, holding up the waterskin.

"Yes, though such things are frowned upon. These waterskins were made in the natural way. When a Boxen dies, its family makes use of its entire body, letting nothing go to waste. They make tools from the horns. Clothing from the furs. Food from the meat. And of course, these waterskins from the bladder. They were a gift, from a family I once helped."

I smile. "So is that why the water tastes funny? Boxen bladder is the special ingredient?"

"Yes, partly. Our water also has a lot more mineralization. Your water is rather... " he pauses, trying to think of the word. "Bland. Lifeless."

"It's water," I say. "It's not supposed to taste like anything."

He just shakes his head. "You've really grown up with such deprivation. It's hard to imagine. But alas, now you will see all you've been missing." His tone is lighter, and it feels good to engage in some gentle banter after hours of tortured silence.

"Sorry if I don't find animal bladder to be a delicacy," I say as we both use the river to wash the dust off our faces and hands. "At the risk of sounding like one of my kids, how much farther until we reach Al'Kalesh?"

"We should be there in two days." He refills his waterskin and I do the same. "Perhaps sooner, if we catch a ride." He grins at me, then turns and runs towards the caravan we saw traveling over the dunes.

By the time I catch up, Kaden is already speaking with a small man wrapped in white robes, his skin dark, eyebrows large and expressive. Kaden passes the man three coins—talismans, I realize upon closer inspection—then gestures to me. "Sky, this is Massani. He and his family have agreed to allow us to travel with them."

I look at Massani, then at the cart behind him, at the woman with raven hair sitting there, three young boys scrambling around her and a little girl no older than four on her lap. "Thank you," I say to all of them.

Massani walks up to me, grabbing my hands. "*Olkesh amish, Shashami. Orta enhu.*" He leads me forward, toward the giant Boxen in front of the cart. "*Artu, Shishami. Artu.*"

"What is he saying?" I ask, smiling to cover my nervousness.

"He wants you to touch the Boxen," says Kaden. "The Akari say the animals have the ability to read a stranger's heart."

"Alright then," I say. I step forward toward the Boxen. Its head is huge, about the size of my entire body, its nostrils near the size of my head. I raise a hand slowly and gently place it above the Boxen's dark lips. The beast groans, exhaling sharply, kicking up dust.

"*Ikashi. Ikashi,*" calls Massani, grabbing the Boxen by its harness, calming it down.

I back away. "I'm sorry. I didn't—"

Kaden laughs. "No. It's good. The Boxen likes you."

My hand falls on my chest, and I sigh in relief. "Oh... okay."

"*Artu, Shishami. Artu,*" says Massani, taking my hand and guiding me onto the cart. I sit next to the woman with black hair and yellow robes, Kaden on my other side.

"*Anavri et tuu ah,*" says Kaden, and the woman says something back, smiling.

Kaden glances at me. "She is Etu. Massani's wife. And these are their four children. Gatack. Alep. Etoon. And the little girl is Kenta."

I wave hello to all of them as the cart begins to move, catching up to the rest of the caravan. The little girl pulls on my hair, and I barely escape her grasp, laughing. We chat for a while, Kaden translating my words, until the sun begins to set, and the children become drowsy.

I turn to Kaden, whispering in his ear. "They called me *Shishami*. What does it mean?"

He turns his head to the side, squinting. "I believe it means traveler... in Akari."

"Traveler," I repeat, grinning, as the caravan stops for the night. We make camp under the shadow of a great ruin, a black tower jutting from the sand. As we help Massani and his family set up tents, Kaden tells me it was once a fortress of the High Dragons, shattered in the uprising, and now withered by time. A great fire is made at the center of the camp, using wood carried by the Boxen, and the entire caravan huddles around, dozens of people all related in some manner. I sit with Kaden and Etu, her children playing a game in front of us, making symbols with their fingers. As the sun sets, three moons rise in the desert sky, and I marvel at the wonder of it, so different from my own world. Kaden notices and winks at me. "Magnificent, aren't they? Legends say the moons represent the mother dragon and her children, for only one is ever full at one time. The other two are always growing, trying to become as great as the mother."

My focus is pulled away from the sky as the elders begin to tell stories. Kaden translates the main details, but mostly I enjoy the flow of the language, the poetry in its beats and rhythms even when I don't know the exact translation.

The younger men and women pull large drums from the carts, and play loudly into the night, chanting as the thunderous thumps of their instruments reverberate across the sand dunes. Their voices blend together, a rising cry both primal and beautiful, filling my body with euphoria.

A young girl runs up to me, presenting me with a necklace. Black beads with a small black horn as the pendant. "Is this for me?" I ask.

The girl nods, and I take the necklace, smiling and thanking her. She runs back to Massani, and I catch his gaze. He nods thoughtfully, and I think the gift may have been his idea.

Kaden leans closer, his voice soft. "That is dragonstone, Shishami. A great gift, taken from the horn of a dragon. They say the High Dragons could shatter such stones to infuse themselves with great power."

I trace my hands over the necklace, feeling the weighty pendant. "Why would they give this to me?"

"Because they know who you are," says Kaden. "A Twin Spirit. In their culture, our kind is revered, our connection to the Spirits honored. They know we keep them safe, and this gift is but a small thank you."

I raise my shoulders, mouth agape. "But... I haven't done anything."

"Perhaps not yet. But you will. One day. It will be your duty to defend the worlds of men and women." He pauses, taking a piece of bread from a plate. "The Akari have a special sense when it comes to the Spirits. An understanding most could only hope to achieve. Perhaps they know things we don't. Perhaps they see something in you that even I do not."

He says no more, and I turn back to the fire, to the pulsing drums and chanting voices. Some of the men and women begin to dance, their bodies writhing around the flame, their figures casting strange shadows on the sand. The rhythm of the music grows louder, syncing with my heartbeat, echoing within my very chest. My skin grows hot, my palms sweaty. The dragonstone seems to throb in my hand, matching the drums. Thump. Thump. Thump. The music grows louder. My vision begins to spin. The fire and stars and moons and people blending into a chaotic painting. Dots cover my eyes. My head feels light. The dragonstone pulses. Thump. Thump. Thump. I notice my wrist then. I notice the bare symbol there. Stripped of the brace I left behind. The dragon gazes back at me, pushing against its circlular cage. Thump. Thump. Thump.

The world spins.

And I fall back.

Into darkness.

16

UMI

I wake on a slab of gray. A field of stone. The sky above me is blue and clear, but at the edge of the horizon fierce winds blow and lightning thunders in dark clouds. I am in the eye of the storm, on an island of peace within a sea of chaos.

I pull myself up until I am standing. My feet are bare. My blue robes have been replaced by a white dress drifting in the cold wind. I look around and see that I am on the peak of a mountain jutting from the ocean, fierce waves crashing against the rocks below. There is no life here. No grass. No trees. No bird in the air or lizard on the earth. Nothing. Nothing but me.

And him.

He sits on a thin ledge protruding forward from the mountain and overlooking the water, his turquoise cape dancing in the fitful wind. I am not sure how I know he is a *he,* but I do know, and I walk forward and then sit next to him, crossing my legs as he has done.

The man turns to me. A ragged hood covers his head, hiding his hair, and a smooth, featureless mask the color of pearls covers his face. There are no hints of eyes or a nose or a mouth. Nothing. Just white. Just... empty.

"I tried reaching you sooner," he says, his voice light and delicate.

"But alas, you were cut off from your Spirit, and in turn cut off from me. We... do not have much time left, I am afraid."

"Who are you?" I ask.

He tilts his head to the side as if considering the question. "I have been called many things. Father of Time. Mother of Earth. The wise. The just. But I am none of these things. Not really."

He fidgets with his fingers. "The Sundering is upon us. Val's children will break free. You must stop this."

His tone is plain, clinical, like he is reciting a math problem. "There are things you must do. Things you must accomplish before you are ready."

I shake my head, frowning. "Ready for what? What do you mean?"

"I... I am not what I once was," says the man. "I cannot stop Val's children alone. You will be my champion. And this time... this time you will not fail."

"What do you mean, this time?"

He gestures below, to the raging water, to a maelstrom swirling beneath us. A dark pit swallowing the ocean. "Did you know," he says, "when waves travel through water, is not so much the water moving, as energy passing through it. Time, the way you see it, is much like a wave. It moves forward, and you believe it moves the entire ocean. But it is but one wave, one stroke of energy, and there are many more. You see the wave. I see the ocean."

He points at the endless storm before us. "There is no beginning. No end. Just time. And the waves that pass through." He pauses. "I... I do not know if these are the right words to explain. For how do I describe a color you have never seen? How do I describe a sound you have never heard? This... this is difficult."

He goes quiet, and I try to remember why I am here, where I was before, but I cannot. My mind is blank. Empty. Like his mask. Like this world.

"This explanation will have to suffice," he says finally, nodding, as if content. He rubs his fingers on the stone, tracing a symbol I do not recognize. "To begin, you must do three things. First, you must unlock your Spirit. Second, you must find the Dream that Cannot be Dreamt. And third... third..." He rubs his chin with a gloved hand, as if trying to remember something. "Apologies. The instructions change each time. The last ones did not work. These... these must work. Yes. Third... Third you must die."

He pushes me from behind.

And I fall.

Through the air, screaming, the wind ripping into my skin.

I fall.

Into the maelstrom, into the water, the impact crushing my flesh.

I fall.

Below the waves, into a deep blue darkness.

There I drift, in the endless ocean. My body broken. My mind weak. My air runs out, but I do not gulp for more. I do not try to live. Those instincts are gone. I just... am. Nothing. Everything.

I do not know how long I am in the water. Forever. Never. Time has lost meaning. All I do is sink.

Sink.

Sink.

Sink.

And then I see it.

In the darkness.

A colossus.

A silver serpent slumbering in the deep.

It is the ocean. It is the storm. It is everything. Nothing.

I find its face. Eyes closed. Still.

Something pulses in the water. A word.

Umi.

Umi.

Umi.

I feel it. I know it. It is me. Not me. Something else. Something more.

The ocean groans. The earth roars. Heavy eyelids move.

I look at the colossus, the serpent, the dragon.

And then...

Then it looks at me.

I WAKE GASPING FOR BREATH, covered in cold sweat. Wet blankets cling to my body. The earth moves below me. No. Not the earth. Wood. A cart.

I push myself to my elbows so I can look around. I am on the back of a cart, laying on a bed of furs, blankets atop me, bundled packages around me. The sun is up. People are talking. Wheels churning.

An animal grunts. A Boxen.

Something rattles to my side. A necklace. A dragonstone.

And I remember where I am.

The caravan. Massani. His wife, Etu. Their children. Kaden.

I try to speak. To call out, but my voice is hoarse, barely a whisper. I try to tap my hand against the wood, but the sound I make is feeble. So I just lay there, for hours, until a little boy climbs over the front of the cart. He notices me and freezes, eyes wide. Then he yells. *"Erata, Shishami. Ana erata."*

Kaden appears from behind him, scrambling to my side. "I couldn't wake you," he says frantically.

"What... what..." I clear my throat, finding it stronger than when I first woke. "What happened?"

"You fell unconscious at the feast, but why, I do not know."

I sit up, my joints aching and popping. "I had a dream... a dream of a silver sea and a white serpent. A dragon below the waves."

Kaden nods. "Such dreams are common when one first becomes aware of their Spirit, but they don't usually cause one to faint."

"I felt something last night," I say, studying my wrist. "I felt as if my mark was... trying to break free."

Kaden rubs the stubble on his chin, frowning. "It seems without your wrist brace, your Spirit has been given room to grow. Having locked your true self away for so long, you may now be going through an accelerated growth process. Perhaps that is why you feinted."

"There was a man," I say. "In my dream."

"A man? Odd. Usually it's just you and your Spirit. Did he say anything?"

I touch my temples, trying to remember. "He said... he said I had to unlock my Spirit." He also said other things, but I cannot remember them.

Kaden nods, but doesn't speak.

"How long was I out?" I ask.

"The night and about half a day." He shakes his head, clenching his fist. "We should have taken things slower. You are still weak from regenerating your body. Your flesh may feel healed, but your Spirit is not."

"I'm fine," I say, feeling better by the moment. "There is something else. Something else I remember from the dream." I hold out my wrist with the mark as Kaden watches intently. And then I whisper.

"Umi."

The air before me blurs.

My skin grows hot.

And then he appears in my hand, a vision becoming real.

He is no larger than my palm.

His scales are silver.

His wings a pale blue.

My gaze meets his sapphire eyes.

"Hello, Umi."

He roars in response. My dragon. My Spirit.

"Umi," echoes Kaden. He grabs my arm. His eyes wide. His voice shaking. "How... how do you know that name?"

17

AL'KALESH

"I heard it in my dream," I say.

Kaden relaxes his hand and pulls away, letting go of my arm. "I'm sorry. I... I shouldn't have said anything." He sits down, clutching his head. "Umi is your Spirit." It's not a question. A hard statement.

The small dragon coils around my arm, wrapping his tail around my wrist. "Can you see him?" I ask.

"Yes," says Kaden, his head down, eyes staring at the wood. "Faintly. Because I'm a Twin Spirit. Most will see nothing, not unless you want them to."

The dragon crawls up my arm until he sits on my shoulder, purring into my ear. "He's so much... smaller... than before," I say.

"He will grow larger when needed," says Kaden, gaze still down. "The more you improve at Beckoning, the more control and power will you have over his physical form." Kaden turns away, toward the sun. He hasn't looked at me or Umi since I said his name.

"What's wrong?" I ask. "What does the name Umi mean to you?"

Kaden sighs. "Umi is the reason I am an Ashlord. Umi is the dragon I slayed." He turns to me, finally, and sucks in a deep breath. "The Wall of Light is not perfect. From time to time, a part of it cracks, shattering open. The Light repairs over the course of a few hours. But it's enough time for a nearby dragon to slip out. Many years ago, a silver one did so. It was a colossus. The largest dragon seen in ages. As it left the Wall, it grew even more powerful, consuming the Spirits around it as dragons do. It gained abilities. Fire so hot it was white. Scales that could blend into its environment. A roar that could bring even the strongest Ashlords to their knees.

"The dragon burned all villages in its path. Massacred hundreds of lives. It's path of carnage was straight for Al'Kalesh. The largest city in all of Nirandel, where the serpent would have killed thousands. Most people believe when a dragon escapes, the world will end. That their kind will sweep across the Nine Worlds and turn all to darkness and death. But it is not so sudden. It is a war. A battle. Between dragons and people. There are tactics. Strategies. Those of Ash were dispatched to stop the dragon before it could reach the capitol. I was but an Ashknight then. Me and my two friends, Alec and Phoenix, were the last of our group. We arrived at the Golden River, meeting dozens of our order there, knowing the dragon would pass our way. When it arrived...

"We were unprepared. The beast killed three of my comrades instantly. Three more a second later. It didn't try to fly by us. No. It wanted to fight. Wanted to kill. And I... I was frozen.

"Screams filled my ears. Death and terror spread before my eyes. The land along the river burned, a flame so bright it lit up the night, so deep it still leaves a scar over the earth to this day.

"I was a coward. A fool. My friends were not. Alec and Phoenix attacked. They did their best, but it was not enough. The dragon knocked them to the ground, burned their limbs. My friends... my friends were going to die and it would be because of me. Because I could not find the strength to fight.

"As the dragon landed, preparing a final strike against my friends, it did not even seem to notice me. So inconsequential was I. So weak was I.

"But I could see it. So close. Its giant sapphire eyes not far. And as the dragon prepared to breathe fire a final time, to turn my friends to ash, I charged. I summoned all my strength. Used all my knowledge of Spirit. Before the mighty leviathan could react, I Transmuted my body, growing scales over skin, growing claws over hands, and I tore out the dragon's eye.

"It reeled back in pain, but I did not slow my assault. I ripped out its other eye, and then... then I went inside... past the flesh... past the skull... I slashed into the dragon's brain, and it fell. When it hit the river, the very earth shook. Its dying roar tore at the very air.

"As its life faded, I heard something then. One word. Umi. Umi. Umi. And I knew it was the dragon's name. It communicated with me somehow, touched my Spirit. The last thing it could do in the world, and it chose to speak to me."

Kaden pauses, his gaze vacant, lost in the past. "I was made an Ashlord the next day. The people of Al'Kalesh proclaimed me their savior. They called me Darkflame, Iron Dragon, and more names than I can even remember. Outrageous rumors spread throughout the Cliff. I tore the dragon's head off with one blow. I had gone to the battle alone. Preposterous, but I was a hero.

"Yet I did not feel like one. Because inside, I knew I was a coward. I knew I only won because of luck. Because as my comrades were killed, I did nothing, and that made me invisible to the enemy.

"They say Spirits come from the dead. But I have never met a Spirit I recognized. Until now. Until Umi. I am sorry for how I reacted. But his name brought me back to another time. A darker time."

I scoot forward, closing the distance between us, and take his hand in my own. "I know what it is like to be paralyzed by fear," I say. "I've seen it on the job, when fighting the fire. I've frozen myself. What matters is pushing through. And you did. You fought the dragon, and you won."

His lips curl, a hint of a smile, and then he turns to the horizon. "We are here, Shishami. Welcome to Al'Kalesh."

THE CAPITOL of Nirandel sprawls over the desert. One side surrounded by the Golden River, the other by silver sand. Where everything south of the city was nearly barren, here the land is lush and rich and green, and emerald trees and bushes grow in the shadows of the giant yellow stone walls of Al'Kalesh. The air is humid and thick. The scent sweet and powerful drifting from purple flowers as large as a man. Birds whistle songs from above. Lizards the colors of opals scuttle about the shrubbery. Starcatchers glide around the vines, singing secret messages to each other. A proper road leads into the city, built of solid white stone, and wide enough for dozens of people. They move in masses, one side heading into the city through the steel gate, the other side leaving the city with Boxen-pulled carts and goods in tow. The chatter of many voices, many languages, fills the air, a cacophony of sound both chaotic and exciting. The people wear an eclectic array of clothing styles. Thin and delicate silks. Thick wool robes. Jewelry made of gold and gems. Jewelry made of bones and vines. Many cultures have come together here. Many lives.

Past the gate, the wonders of the city unfold. Golden buildings built of sandstone. Stalls full of marvelous rugs and trinkets. Street performers playing flutes, juggling swords, eating fire. Children running amok, laughing and singing and playing games in the side streets. And above it all looms the Palace of Storms, a giant citadel built on a hill in the center of Al'Kalesh, casting a shadow over a quarter of the city. Two stone towers grow from its golden dome roof, reaching so high in to the sky, pale blue clouds drift around them. Thousands of windows adorn the white walls, made of colorful glass depicting stories and portraits. The door must be four stories tall and looks made of pure gold. The whole structure seems to speak: *You are beneath me. You are nothing.*

And perhaps this great structure is right.

For inside lives the Emperor, ruler of all Nirandel.

WE PART WAYS with Massani and his family at the gates, as city guards clad in white and red armor inspect the goods within their cart, checking for illegal items and hidden criminals. I thank our companions for their help and their gift, then Kaden leads me to a stable where he buys a pair of horses with a bag of coin. "The city is too large to walk through," he explains as he checks the saddle on his black stallion. I've never really ridden a horse before, pony rides as a child aside, so Kaden guides me through the process. He helps me mount my steed, a beautiful white mare with a black star in the center of her forehead, who I name Moon.

"These horses are well trained," Kaden says. "Move your reins in the direction you wish to go, and they will follow. If you wish to go faster, squeeze your thighs and feet against the horse. However, I recommend we go slow at first."

I nod, and together we ride at a leisurely pace through the city of Al'Kalesh, Umi perching on my shoulder, my steed following Kaden's, head to tail. I notice a wooden sign carved to look like a flame, the words "The Dousers" engraved onto it. It hangs over a small building with piles of buckets stacked before the door. Tools of a firefighter in this world, I imagine. It would be near impossible to keep a fire contained here. So many buildings, so squeezed together, such narrow side streets, most made of quite flammable wood. And I wonder if The Dousers are a group of volunteers, or if putting out flames is their job—their calling.

I wonder a lot of things. And as we make our way past the docks, where giant wooden ships sway in the water, I ask Kaden the questions that have been on my mind. "Why do people on Earth not know about the Nine Worlds? Why don't we trade goods, information?"

Kaden shuffles a coin across his knuckles as he rides. "Most people here don't know about your Earth, either. To them the Nine Worlds are a myth, nothing more. Only Nirandel is real."

"Why the deception?" I ask.

"As my mentor once said, 'There are always three truths. The physical, the emotional, and the spiritual.' Always three reasons... well, or more. Physically, it is difficult to travel between the worlds. With few exceptions, only Broken Ones or Twin Spirits can, thus most people could never make that journey. Establishing trade would be difficult, and almost useless, since your technology would not work here, and much of our magic is weaker there. Emotionally, there are challenges as well. People already have much to worry about. To tell them about other worlds... worlds that could pose threats or disrupt their worldview, could create greater chaos and stress, and to no good end. Thus the truth is a closely guarded secret, at least here in Nirandel. Those of Ash and the Emperor know of course. But the common people do not."

He pauses, considering his next words. "Finally, there is the spiritual reason. You could call it ethics as well. Once, thousands of years ago, a group of Ashlords made themselves known on your world. They took advantage of their abilities, winning battles singlehandedly, destroying villages when their tempers flared. Tales of their powers soon spread, many becoming myths about creatures or gods, and the Ashlords grew in influence and strength. They had forsaken their duties in order to raise themselves up as kings and queens. They enslaved the people of your world, and massacred those not enslaved. As you can imagine, there were many problems with this. The Masters of Dragoncliff did not approve, and so they sent a force to assassinate the outcasts. Terrible battles ensued, causing much destruction, but they spared Earth from even greater chaos. After the outcasts were all killed, and their time on Earth forgotten, stricter rules were enforced. Those of Ash would forsake the kingdoms of men and women, allowing them to rule themselves. We would only protect from Spirits and dragons, nothing more."

"I see..." I say, understanding the decision to keep the secret, but not certain I agree. "And you didn't care to tell me earlier? What if I spilled the information?"

He smiles. "No one would have believed you. No one who didn't already know."

I nod. It makes sense, I suppose. If I started telling people on Earth about Nine Worlds and dragons and Spirits, they wouldn't believe me either.

I ask the second question on my mind. "Kaden... how old are

you?" I've heard him talk of ancient events as if he were there, and I wonder...

"Many centuries," says Kaden, "too many for you to comprehend."

My eyes go wide. "But... how? Because you're a Twin Spirit?"

He shakes his head. "Because I am an Ashlord. I... I cannot say more. It would not be proper. But once you finish your training, you will understand." He pauses. "There is something you don't yet know about this world. Something you should understand." He points to a wagon forged from steel pulled by a Boxen, surrounded by a dozen guards clad in silver armor, a red flame upon their white capes. They look around constantly, and keep their hands on the swords at their hips, prepared for an attack, ready to protect whatever it is they are guarding.

"They are transporting dragonstone," says Kaden. "Blue stone, most likely. There are many kinds, but blue is the most valued here. It can be ground into a powder and taken in a drink. It extends one's life. Indefinitely, if they keep taking the powder regularly. The nobles here purchase the stones in bulk from the Cliff for exorbitant prices. It is the way we fund the protection of the Wall of Light." He seems sad as he says this, but I do not know why.

"The blue stone, is that how you live so long?"

"No," says Kaden. "As I said, I cannot speak of that. The blue stone is how nobles live forever, how the Emperor will live forever." He lowers his voice. "Unless of course, he is murdered."

"You mentioned Masters..."

"Nine Ashlords chosen to lead the rest. Since they don't age, they are rarely replaced."

I nod. It doesn't seem the best leadership system. But—

I hear the screams first.

Terrible cries of pain and despair.

My heart jumps in my chest. My breath catches. "What's going on?" I yell.

And then, as we emerge into a plaza at the base of the palace, I see. The crowds of howling people.

The pyres.

Nine of them. A person tied to each one. Burning.

Umi hisses at the display.

I clutch my reigns tightly, my knuckles turning white. "What is this?"

"An execution," says Kaden, his jaw tensing. "This is how it's done here."

The smell of ash and smoke and wood fills the air. And...

I turn to the side, trying to keep myself from vomiting.

"It's strange, isn't it?" asks Kaden. "When human flesh burns, it smells much like any animal."

My gut convulses uncontrollably, and I dry heave, my stomach already empty. Food rations have been low since we started our journey. Only bits of bread and dry meat.

Once the nausea begins to pass, I sit up straight, taking in more of my surroundings. The plaza is large, fitting hundreds of people. They circle the pyres, yelling and cheering and throwing food. They pack together, close to the fire, yet maintain a strange perimeter, about a dozen feet from each execution. I wonder why, and then I see the man... no... the *thing* standing at the center of the plaza.

It is huge, twice my size, made of thick muscle coiling under pale skin. And it has no eyes.

Two black pits stare from its skull instead.

Dark spikes run down its spine.

A scaled tail grows from its back, slithering in the air.

Long claws grow in place of nails.

It wears no shirt, only black leather pants and sturdy plain boots. Black tattoos cover its body, even its head, which is shaved clean. They spiral like flames. And though the creature has no eyes, I feel it sees me. Stares straight at me.

"A Shadow," whispers Kaden.

The Emperor's Shadow. "Why... why does it have no eyes?" I ask, trembling.

"They say the eyes are a distraction. You see the spikes down its back? They are made of dragonstone. Impaled into the Shadow's body. You see the tattoos, they are glyphs. Flesh Imbuing it is called. The practice is... forbidden. At least, it was until the Emperor created his Shadows. He used them to win the Rising, to kill all High Dragons. Now Shadows may use Flesh Imbuing, but no one else. The practice twists their body, gives them the tail, the claws, and abilities, strength, a second sight, more things as well perhaps... the art, you see, is a well-kept secret by the Emperor. Even the Masters of Ash do not understand the details of Flesh Imbuing."

The Shadow turns its head in our direction. Its tongue, long and forked like a snake's, sticks out and retreats in an instant, tasting the air. The creature steps forward, the crowd parting before it as if out of instinct. And I realize, the Shadow is heading for us.

"Darkflame," it hisses, in a voice low and oozing, stopping before Kaden. Though we are mounted on horses, the Shadow stands as tall as us.

"Sylus," replies Kaden, and I realize he recognizes the Shadow.

Sylus smiles, revealing sharp white teeth. "The Emperor has been looking for you, Darkflame. He has a matter he wishes to... discuss," he holds the s unnaturally long, turning his head to me. "And who is this?"

Umi crouches on my shoulder, growling, eyes fixed on the Shadow. I straighten my back and force myself to stare at the pits Sylus has for eyes. "I am—"

"No one of importance," says Kaden. "Just a—"

"I am Sky Knightly," I finish, not allowing myself to be cut off.

Kaden sighs, but says nothing. His eyes beg me to be quiet.

Sylus walks up to my horse, patting her head, the tile shaking under his boots. "I will remember you, Sky Knightly of no importance." He tilts his head, dark pits looking past my shoulder, until I realize he is looking *at* my shoulder. At Umi.

"Your Spirit is powerful," says Sylus. "But young and untrained. Tell me, have you considered the Emperor's service?"

"I..." I realize what he's asking. At least, I think I do. He wants me to join the Shadows. And it makes sense. Because if Shadows use a form of imbuing, they must be Twin Spirits.

Kaden stares at me, his eyes dark, body tense.

"I..." I never realized there may be an option other than the Cliff. Kaden never told me. But then I look at the Shadow once more, at his twisted and deformed body, and it brings back a memory. A man changing before my very eyes. His skin growing thin, gemstones growing from his body, at least I thought they were gemstones, but what if they were dragonstone? "I... I'm looking for someone," I finally say. "Someone who calls himself Pike."

The Shadow's smile returns. "Then you best keep looking. And if you find him, let me know. The Emperor takes interest in such matters."

If Sylus knows something of Pike, he will not tell me. There is no reason to join the Shadows, at least no reason I see. "Why are these people burning?" I ask, shifting the conversation.

Sylus tastes the air once more. "One of the men killed a woman who refused him. One of the women stole food for her children."

"And the punishment for both is burning?" I ask, my blood boiling at the thought of the woman.

The Shadow shrugs. "I do not make the rules. Only enforce them." He turns his head back to Kaden. "Now Darkflame... it is time you come with me."

"No," says Kaden.

Sylus smiles. "Then perhaps Sky Knightly of no importance will accompany me to the palace." His giant hand clutches my reigns, tugging at them.

Kaden clenches his fist. His eyes turn dark. The wind picks up around us, howling, whipping my cloak and Kaden's crimson scarf. The shadows on the ground seem to grow longer. Darker.

"You will not touch her," say Kaden, voice low, primal.

The Shadow hisses.

The wind picks up.

Kaden's jaw tenses.

A vein pulses on Sylus's neck. And then...

Then the Shadow smiles, releasing my reigns. "Very well, Darkflame. Another time."

The wind stills.

The shadows retreat.

And the crimson scarf falls.

Sylus turns, walking away. "See you soon, Darkflame. The Outcast is becoming a problem. A problem the Emperor wishes to discuss."

I turn to Kaden. "Perhaps he has information."

"No," says the Ashlord, face still hard. "The Emperor does not release those he takes into his service. He plays games, pulls strings, gains leverage over them. Alec once had dealings with him and... and it did not go well. I almost lost my friend then, before the Outcast killed him."

He guides his horse forward, out of the plaza, and I follow.

I want to ask about the darkness, about the wind and the scarf, but I can see the hardness in Kaden's body, the cold in his eyes, and so I say nothing, as we ride in silence, away from the fire and smoke and screams.

18

DARKFLAME

As the sun begins to set, we arrive at the other edge of the city. Here the buildings are small, the streets full of mud and nearly empty. Kaden leads us to an inn for the night called *The Lucky Coin*. I hear the music first. A upbeat jig reverberating through the air as Kaden ties his horse outside, then shows me how to do mine. I see the lights second. An orange glow filling the windows and cracks of the wooden building. In a part of town dark and quiet and hollow, *The Lucky Coin* seems bustling with life and song and laughter. Once we step inside, the smells hit me. Sweet cherry pie. Hot soup. Roasted beef. Dozens of men and women gather around the tables, some sitting on chairs, some standing because the chairs are taken, others finding unique places to rest: a windowsill, an upside down bucket, the floor. A pair of men play cards in the corner. Another group tosses dice at the center of the room, crowds making bets around them. A woman plays a lyre near the fire place, singing a fast song, the words hard to make out over the roaring and laughter. Waitresses walk around, dressed in red and white, carrying tankards the size of my head and foaming at the brim. This part of town was empty it seems, because well, the entire town appears to be here!

Kaden guides me past the mass of bodies to the counter, where a red-headed bartender dries a glass with a white napkin. He has a long, kind face. Freckles dot his cheeks, and a short red beard covers his jaw. His eyes are small, fast things, full of joy and laughter. When he sees Kaden, his lips part in excitement. "Kaden Varis! I haven't seen ye in ages. How ya been, lad?" He wraps an arm around Kaden, then ruffles his hair. "What's the occasion?"

Kaden motions to me. "Bringing a new one to the Cliff. Sky Knightly, meet Skip, my dear old friend. Skip, meet Sky Knightly."

I hold up my hand, but instead of shaking it, Skip gently takes my fingers in his, then kisses the top of my knuckles. "A pleasure to meet ye, lass."

"The pleasure is mine," I say, surprised by his manners.

Skip grins, then gestures to a boy sitting on a stool, his feet up on another chair. "Ay, boy. Break's over. Get back to the kitchens. Make room for Darkflame and his friend."

The boy looks up at Kaden, eyes wide. Then, without a word, he runs off, disappearing behind a door, the sound of clattering pots follows in his wake. Skip chuckles. "Boy doesn't know whether to be like ye, or be terrified of ye."

"Both sound about right," says Kaden, as we sit down on the stools by the bar.

"What shall I get ye?" asks Skip, placing hands on hips.

"Starpie," says Kaden.

"Drinks?"

"The usual."

Skip grabs of bottle of something blue and mixes it with a bottle of something red. He pours the concoction in two glasses filled with ice, then adds a dash of white cream. He slides my drink toward me. "The Dragon's Kiss. Be careful lass, it has a bite."

I stare at the fizzy purple drink, the liquid turning to smoke at the top. It smells divine. Carefully, I take a sip. The liquid burns my throat, but it tastes sweet and smooth and cool at the same time. A mashup of flavor that sets my senses alight and makes my skin tingle.

"Yum," I say.

Skip nods as if to say, 'I know.'

I notice the painting behind him, the only one in the inn. "Who's that?" I ask.

Skip glances back, then chuckles. "That be our Emperor, Titus Al'Beckus, may he reign forever."

Titus Al'Beckus makes a stunning figure in the portrait. His face is hard, withered, a scar on one of his cheeks. Despite it, or perhaps because of it, he is devilishly handsome, the kind of man who looks better with age. Silver streaks line his black hair, which comes together in a ponytail at the back. His uniform is black, with gold buttons and gold clasps holding his cape in place. He holds the hilt of a sword at his side. This man is a warrior. A lion.

Skip shrugs. "It keeps the loyalist happy, if ye know what I mean. Gets me better tips, too."

Kaden gulps down his drink and asks for a refill. "We'll need two rooms," he adds.

"Only one left," says Skip, making the second Dragon's Kiss. "Sorry, friends."

"One will do," I say, glancing at Kaden.

He gives me a look as if to say, 'are you sure' and I nod.

"One room then," says Skip, grinning. He gives Kaden his second drink and leans in conspiratorially. "So tell me. What have ye been up to?"

Kaden sips his drink. "I have business in town. A few leads to follow up on."

Skip raises a thick red eyebrow. "The Outcast?"

Kaden nods, glancing at me. "Sky will stay here. I'll return before dawn."

"We're separating?" I ask, the thought of being on my own in this strange world unsettling.

"Don't worry," says Kaden. "Skip will keep an eye on you."

The innkeeper winks. "Don't fret lass. This here is the safest place in all of Al'Kalesh, I swear to ye."

"I'd rather go with the Ashlord, thank you very much," I say.

"Not these places," Kaden says firmly. "If I run into the Outcast there will be trouble. Trouble you are unprepared for." He drops three coins on the counter and stands, adjusting his scarf. "I'll see you tomorrow." Without another word, he walks off, disappearing behind the door.

"Don't take it personal, lass," says Skip, shaking his head. "Kaden can be of one mind, sometimes. Like a force of nature. Sometimes, ye get caught up in the storm, but there be no one else I'd rather have on me side."

"You seem to know him well?" I ask, seeing an opportunity to learn things about Kaden he won't tell me himself.

"Aye. We go way back, Kaden and I. Back to when he was a wee little Ashling, still training at the Cliff."

"What's with the scarf? He wears it everywhere?"

Skip nods thoughtfully. "Aye. They say his mother gave him the cloth, before he came to the Cliff, though no one knows for sure. What be certain however, is that be no ordinary scarf. They say it blows against the wind, blows toward Corrupted Spirits. Warns of danger. Or leads him to it. I thought it mad, until I saw it me self."

I remember the Fenrial. I remember the crimson scarf blowing against the wind. "I saw it too," I say, taking another sip of my drink.

"Aye. Best be careful around him, lass. He be a good man, for certain, but he has a way of drawing things to him. Bad things. Dark things."

"What do you mean?" I ask.

Skip leans closer, lowering his voice. "They call him Darkflame for a reason, lass. He be the greatest dragonslayer around. Killed a thousand of them they say. More. While others cower in terror of the beasts, Kaden faces them head on, carving a trail of death in his path. It wasn't always so... not in the early days... but after the silver dragon, after that kill, something changed in the man. As if he walked with death from that day forward."

I look down at my drink, at the dark purple ooze swirling there. "He hardened," I say. The alcohol is starting to affect me, loosening my tongue, relaxing my nerves. I take another sip. "It happened to me too. When I... When I met the one they call Pike."

The bartender freezes at that, little eyes going still, lips in a tight line. "What do ye know of him, lass?" he asks, words quiet and quick.

"He took my daughter," I say, gripping my cup harder.

"I'm sorry. I..." His face turns sad for the first time. "I too lost someone to Pike."

Kaden didn't mention that, but, seeing the grief on Skip's face now, perhaps he had good reason. I feel sad. Then angry. "You traded away your—"

"No. No," he says frantically. "Never. It was my niece, Anny. Wee little lass with a mop of red hair like her mother's. Kindest thing in all the worlds. It was me brother, gambling pig, who sold her away to clear his debts. I... I tried to stop him. To stop Pike. But I could do nothing. I am no great warrior." He sits down, sighing. Then tears begin to fill his eyes, and he clutches his head, sobbing.

It feels strange, finding someone who has undergone a pain I once thought mine alone. But of course Pike has taken other children, left other families grieving. How many are there, I wonder. How many like me and Skip who feel powerless to protect their loved ones?

"I'm sorry," I say. "I shouldn't have presumed." He didn't do the same to me, and now I feel like a heartless fool. This new hardness within me, this new rage, is not one I'm accustomed to.

I take Skip's hand, pulling it away from his head and holding it close. "I will find Pike," I say. "I will free my daughter and your niece. And then I will end him."

The tears stop. Skip pulls away, his face going pale. "Ye don't know, do ye?"

"Know what?"

He takes a deep breath. "There be no one to save, lass. They're dead, ye hear? Dead."

My drink sits half-full, forgotten. My lips tremble. My fingers shake. "That... that can't be. No one knows what happens to the children—"

"Aye, they don't know truly. But this summer, I found a package in my room," says Skip, pouring himself a drink. "A pile of little bones lay within. And..." he takes another deep breath, trying to keep the tears at bay. "And a red ribbon. The one Anny used to wear all places. I knew then. I knew... she was gone. Forever."

"But Kaden said—"

"Kaden don't know yet," says Skip. "I have yet to tell him." He pauses, his voice growing deeper. "Ye package will come too. Maybe not today, maybe not tomorrow. But it will come. And then ye will know, once and for all."

Anger and shock and sorrow twist within me. This can't be possible. It's a lie. A mistake. "I need to go," I say, asking him for the room.

"But ye're meal—"

"I need to go."

He gives me directions, and I run upstairs. I find the room and fall into the bed, letting my tears out as I scream into the pillow.

She's not dead.

She's not dead.

She's not dead.

My dreams are dark things. A creature with a thousand arms tugs at my hair, my clothes, my nails. It rips me apart, into a million tiny shards, then pieces me back together and does it over and over and over again. *You failed her*, it whispers. *You let her go. Now she is mine. Mine. Forever.*

I wake gasping, my eyes stuck together, my throat thick. Last night, I didn't even look around my room, but today I take it in: the furniture is simple, just a bed and a dresser. The sheets are white and coarse, wet from tears and sweat. The air smells of dust. The only light source is the window, and it hurts my tired eyes.

The small room is empty except for me. Kaden hasn't returned. I walk downstairs, finding the inn nearly empty: a man smoking a pipe in the corner, Skip wiping the counter clean. No sign of Kaden.

"He's not back, if that's what ye are wondering," says Skip, not looking at me, eyes fixed on his task. "Ye are welcome to take a seat. Breakfast will be ready soon."

I take the same stool as last night. "I'm sorry for the way I left."

"It should be I who am sorry, lass. Not ye. I was indelicate. Mention of Pike, it brings the worst out of me, ye know? I'm sorry."

A moment later he brings me a bowl of warm porridge and bread. I eat slowly, mechanically. An hour passes. Another.

Kaden doesn't return.

"Do you know where he is?" I ask.

Skip shrugs. "Sorry, lass. Haven't a clue."

Another hour.

And then several more.

The sun begins to set, casting hues of purple over the inn.

People bustle in more frequently, preparing for a night of revelry.

"I should go look for him," I say, clutching the counter.

"Where?" asks Skip. "It would take ye weeks to go over all of Al'Kalesh, and he may not even be in the city." He notices my nervous eyes, then brightens his tone. "There be nothing to worry about, lass. He's pulled this move before, not showing up like he should, but he always comes back. Few things can kill an Ashlord, and Kaden be the toughest Ashlord there be."

The door opens, and my heart skips a beat as I turn to see who it is.

It is *not* Kaden.

The Shadow hunches over as he enters the inn, his massive body too big for the building. His tongue licks at the air. He does not move his head to scan the room, and yet I am certain he sees everything inside.

Another Shadow walks in behind him. This one is different from the first. He has horns, two massive ones sprouting from the front of his bald head. His tattoos are slightly different as well. The first Shadow has no horns, tattoos familiar, and I realize how Kaden recognized Sylus.

The innkeeper's lips stretch into a tight smile that doesn't reach his eyes. "Lord Sylus. How can I help ye?"

"We come to collect the sum you owe to our gracious Emperor, may he never burn."

"I've already paid my taxes," Skip says, then quickly adds, "my lord."

Sylus steps forward, wooden floor creaking under his heals. "The records say you did not."

"There must be some mistake—"

"The Emperor's servants make no mistakes."

Skip swallows once. "Of course. Forgive me. I... I must be confused. I can gather the sum, but it will take some time."

"We require the sum now," says Sylus, clenching his fist.

The horned Shadow behind him grins, and I see what is happening. They're trying to earn more coin, perhaps for the Emperor, perhaps for themselves, by double taxing, counting on no one standing up to them. Not counting on me.

I stand up, Umi appearing on my shoulder. "Leave him alone. He's already paid your sum and you know it."

Sylus tilts his head. "Sky Knightly of no importance. What a pleasure. I believe you are new to these lands, so I will warn you only once. Impeding me is punishable by death. Challenge me again and you will find yourself upon the pyre." He smiles, showing his sharp teeth, and looks past me. "Now, shall we proceed."

A man and woman sneak out of the inn, behind the Shadows. Those who remain keep their heads down, trying not to draw attention. Skip trembles, teeth chattering. "Like I said, I don't have the funds for ye just yet. But if ye come back in a fortnight."

Sylus tsks. "That will not do. Shall we begin the punishment?" He takes a quick step forward, his body flexed and threatening, and I, out of instinct, out of fear, react, my Spirit gathering power, and launching a small streak of lightning at the Shadow's feet.

The bolt misses, hitting the floor just in front of him, leaving a black mark on the wood.

"No," murmurs Skip.

Sylus smiles. "To the pyres, then."

He steps forward again, and Umi roars, and my heart punches against my chest, and I have no control, lightning exploding from me, this time in all directions. The bolts miss the Shadows. One zips behind me. "No!" I yell but I can do nothing.

The bolt hits Skip in the arm, and he falls back, yelling, his wrist burned. Another bolt hits the curtains and they set aflame.

People scream. More flee the inn.

The lightning stops. The terror at what I have done seems to have reigned in my Spirit.

A terrible laugh echoes around me. "You are your own undoing," says Sylus. Then he rushes for the exit, his partner in tow. He slams the door shut behind them, and I hear something large being moved. "Goodbye, Sky Knightly of no importance," he yells from outside.

As I realize what he has done, I run to the door, but I am too late. They have barricaded it somehow, trapping us inside. Me, Skip, four men, two women, and a child, a little boy.

The fire spreads.

The inn will burn.

All of us with it.

Because of me.

No.

I channel all my strength, all my Spirit, pushing against the door. It groans and cracks beneath my weight, but does not open. I look to the windows, but they are covered in flame. There will be water in the kitchen. Not enough to put out the fire, but perhaps enough to clear an exit. No. It would take too long to fill the buckets. The fire would spread too far then. Maybe we can soak blankets in water. Use them as cover as we jump out the windows. Maybe. But it's dangerous. There must be another way. Another path. Upstairs!

The windows.

"Everyone," I yell. "Run upstairs. Jump out a window." The building is only two stories. They should land safely. A broken leg in the worst case.

No one responds. They are frozen, coughing at the smoke.

"Now," I yell. "Upstairs if you want to live." I grab the closest man to me, the largest, his beard and hair braided, and using my enhanced strength, pull him with me to the stairs. His eyes go wide, seemingly surprised I can move him.

Skip glances at me. He nods, then turns to the other guests. "Upstairs. Now. Listen to the woman."

They break their stillness then, following me up the stairs.

"Fire. Fire!" I yell, knocking on the walls, letting the guests in their rooms know they need to escape. "The path downstairs is blocked. Open your window. Climb down."

I get to the first room, where a middle aged woman sits in a haze. I run past her and open the window. "Out. Now!" I roar.

She doesn't seem to hear me, and I notice a pipe laying by her side, the scent of something odd in the air. I turn to the big man by my side. "You go out first. Then catch her."

He nods, then crawls out the window. He hangs down first, then let's go, landing safely.

"Ready?" I call out.

"Ready," he says in a deep voice.

I pick up the woman who still seems unaware of my presence, then toss her out the window. The man catches her.

I move out of the way, letting those behind me go. The other man. The two women. "Where's the boy?" I ask.

The man shrugs.

I grit my jaw and lunge past them, taking the stairs down in two leaps. The bottom floor is an inferno. Tables and chairs burned to a blackened crisp. The air dark with smoke.

"Hello," I yell, searching for the boy. No response. No sight of him. There. A cough. I hear him. He sits under a table, one of the few unburned, hiding, surrounded by fire.

I need to get to him. How? I turn to the kitchen, hoping to cover myself in a wet blanket, but that path is blocked now, the hallway rug covered in flame. What about the bar? I find a pitcher of water, then pour it all over myself, no time left to grab a blanket. Then, my hair and shirt soaking, I run through the flames. I leap over a streak of fire, landing at the table. I lean down and grab the boy, who is crying and yelling and coughing. Holding him close, I run back for the stairs, trying to shield him as best as possible with my body. I cough as I move, the smoke filling my lungs, my head turning dizzy. I stumble at the stairs, but grab onto the railing. Just one at a time. Just one at a time. I make it up, the second floor now covered in smoke, the hallway dark and hazy. I rush to the window and stick my head out, gasping for clean air. "I have the boy. Somebody needs to catch him."

"I will," yells the big man, stepping forward from a crowd of people.

I nod, then look at the boy. "You'll be safe. I promise," and with that, I throw him out the window.

The man catches him, and returns him to a crying woman I haven't seen before.

"You next," says Skip from down below.

"I need to check the room," I call back. "Make sure everyone is out." I turn before he can respond, rushing through the hallway, pushing open each door.

I make it about hallway when I collapse.

The smoke is thick in my lugs, burning them. I cough, try to breath, but there is no fresh air left. The floor feels hot beneath me. Flames flicker at the top of the stairs.

I need to finish. To check every room. But the longer I lay there, the less important it seems. The less important everything seems.

Kara.

Kyle.

Caleb.

They slip from my mind. A distant memory. And my eyes feel heavy and my head feels strange.

I just need to rest is all. Rest, and then I will be better.

I start to close my eyes.

And then the roof explodes.

Beams of wood tear away, revealing an open night sky. And there, in the darkness, is a dragon.

Its scales are black and glint like steel. Red lines cover its body.

Two sharp horns sprout from its terrible head. The beast lunges down, grabbing me in a huge claw. It lifts me up into the sky, and I leave the fire behind, cool air whipping at my skin, filling my lungs. The beating of wings pounds against my ears. Yells and screams rise from below. I do not fully process what is happening. I cannot. My brain is still reawakening.

The beating stops, and the claw opens, and I tumble down, landing in cold mud. The dragon steps back, eyes glowing red, nostrils exhaling steam. The beast sits down, and though I think I'm imagining it, the dragon grows smaller, and then I realize I'm not imagining it, and the serpent has turned my size. The black scales fade. The wings pop and cracks and disappear into its back. The claws retract. Until only a man remains, his skin a pale blue in the moonlight. His hair black and messy. He grabs me, lifts me up against his hard body, and I realize he is naked. "Are you injured?" asks Kaden, his voice gentle.

I nod, leaning my weary head against his chest. For a moment, I just want to rest here and forget the problems of the world. But there is still work to do.

I pull out of his arms and face the people gathered around the inn. "We have to stop the fire!" I yell through a hoarse and dry throat. "If we don't, it will spread to the nearby buildings. Grab buckets, bowls, pans, anything that can hold water, and bring it here. Anyone know of The Dousers?"

A young man nods.

"Good. Take my horse. Find them. Bring them here. Everyone, let's move." I run to the nearby house, looking for a bucket.

In no time at all, we have more than a dozen, and I show the villagers how to make lines to the nearest wells. We pass buckets down from the wells to the inn, and throw them over the fire. Nearby buildings are evacuated, the denizens joining in to help. The Dousers arrive, bringing more tools. I stand at the front, closest to the inferno, throwing bucket after bucket of water on the flame.

I do not think.

I do not feel.

I do not let the memory of Kara slow or distract me.

I just act. I just *be*.

And then the tears come, though I think of nothing. Not the life I left behind, the daughter I failed, my two brothers who I abandoned. Nothing.

Nothing.

Nothing.

Nothing.

I do not think. I just do. Big wet sobs are ripped from me, as I toss bucket after bucket, quenching the fire, both without and within. I fight the flame. I fight the pain. The sorrow and heartache that has been building within me these past few days. I put it out. I beat it.

I toss buckets of water, and I think of nothing.

Eventually, the fire is out, and I am on my knees in the mud, covered in filth and tears. Nothing but a black skeleton remains of *The Lucky Coin*. The surrounding buildings never caught fire. The people have gone.

Kaden steps beside me, now dressed, red scarf billowing in the wind, and puts a thick cloak over my shoulders.

"She's gone," I murmur.

He says nothing. Just sits by my side, shares the warmth of his body with mine.

"She's gone," I say again, a little louder.

Kaden holds me, my head on his shoulder.

"She's gone," I yell, a sob racking my body.

Still, Kaden says nothing. I do not know how much time passes. Minutes. Hours. But there, in the darkness, in the cold night, Kaden Varis holds me, until the grief has left my body, and my tears have dried. He holds me.

And yet, he does so much more than I can explain. So much more than I can ever repay.

———

When the sun comes up, I leave Kaden's firm grip, and walk around the burned corpse of the inn. I find a purple flower behind the remnants of the building, a piece of beauty that survived the carnage. Kaden tells me the flower is called a Moon Tear, and I think the name fitting. I pick the flower and pull a medium sized stone from the earth. I stick the rock into a patch of grass by the city's wall and lay the flower against the makeshift grave. With a stick, I scratch the word *Kara* into the stone. "I'm sorry I couldn't save you," I whisper. "I'm sorry I can't go back to your brothers, for fear of hurting them. I'm sorry I failed my promise to keep you safe." My jaw hardens. My tone hardens. "But today I make a new promise. I will find Pike. And I will avenge you."

19

DRAGONCLIFF

Kaden finds us a new inn in the city. We could theoretically continue our journey to the Cliff, but we are both exhausted from a night of putting out fires. The inn is called *The Weeping Willow*, a poetic name, I suppose, and while *The Lucky Coin* was full of life and laughter, this place is but a hollow shell in comparison. Kaden gets us each our own rooms this time, and pays for a weeks' worth of lodgings for Skip. "Ye don't have to, friend," he argues, but Kaden just shakes his head.

"I want to," says the Ashlord.

As we head up the stairs to our rooms, I walk at the back with Skip, who has bandaged his burned wrist. "I'm sorry," I say. "For hurting you."

"Don't fret, lass," he says. "I've suffered much worse, on account of being Darkflame's friend and all." He pats my shoulder. "Not many people would stand up to a Shadow like that. Ye might be as crazy as your traveling companion. But I'm grateful to you and know you didn't mean to cause injury."

I walk him to his room, then go to find my own. My hand brushes against the handle, and I pull back, wincing in pain.

"What's wrong?" asks Kaden, running to my side. He studies my palms and arms. They are burned in multiple places. I must have touched something hot in the blazing building. "I'll get bandages," says Kaden. Before I can protest or say I'll be fine, he leaps down the stairs in one jump, disappearing.

I enter the room and sit on the plain bed, the exhaustion of the last twenty-four hours catching up to me. A moment later, Kaden returns carrying bandages and a jar full of some kind of ointment. He sits down next to me and carefully applies the sticky substance to my burns.

"Thank you," I say as he works.

He nods, reaching for a burn on my upper arm that spreads to my shoulder. "You'll need to pull up your robe," he says. "If you'd like, I can step out and—"

I take off my robe and pull off my tunic, leaving only my breast binding.

Kaden clears his throat. "Very well then."

I eye him coyly. "I thought modesty wasn't important in Nirandel."

"It's not," he says, his fingers gently massaging my shoulder. He is close to me, our legs touching, his breath warm on my skin.

And perhaps because of all the sorrow and loss I have felt, perhaps because of the pain and emptiness that has consumed me, I just want to feel *close* to another human being again. Perhaps because of this, or perhaps because of whatever's been lingering between us since we met, I lean forward, into Kaden, and catch his blue eyes with my own. I draw my lips closer to his, my breath heavy, my eyes closed, and then I wait.

For a moment, we are both still, a raw, primal energy hanging in the air between us. And then Kaden leans forward, his lips meeting mine. He tastes of earth and salt and wilderness. His scent is of pines and fresh grass and the wind. He takes my face in his hands, gently caressing my cheek with his rough and callused fingers, pulling me closer, deeper into the kiss, and I lose myself in his arms.

The door slams open, pulling me out of my thoughts, as Kaden and I draw apart. "I thought the two of ye would like some lunch—"

Skip stands in the doorway, holding a tray with two large bowls of stew and tankards full of mead, his mouth frozen in an O. "I... um... I'm sorry if be interrupting something."

"You're not," says Kaden quickly. "Come on in."

I study the Ashlord, frustration creeping in at how easily he dismisses our kiss. His face is focused, the passion that was there a moment ago swept away.

Skip hands Kaden the tray. "I'll leave ye two to it, then."

"Stay," says Kaden.

"I'd rather not, friend," he says uneasily, disappearing into the hall as the door closes quietly behind him.

Kaden places the food and drink between us and begins to eat his.

I do the same.

A moment later, Kaden speaks, his voice clinical. "The kiss was a mistake."

My lip tightens in a line. "I'm beginning to agree."

"I don't mean to offend, it's just..." Kaden sighs, rubbing his temples. "It is forbidden for those of Ash to have intimate relation-ships. Pleasures of the flesh are allowed, but nothing more."

"Who said I wanted something more?" I ask, taking a big spoonful of stew.

Kaden looks away, his eyes sad. "Yes. I suppose you don't." Before I can reply, he stands up and walks to the door. "We should get some rest. There's a long journey ahead of us."

I SLEEP through most of the day and night. At sunrise, Kaden wakes me and asks me to join him downstairs. He has hired a carriage to take us the rest of the way. Skip greets me at the door, and gives me a hug as we are about to depart.

"I have given up on little Anny," he says somberly. "But I see there be some fire in you yet, lass. So I will tell ye what I know. Look for Pike in The Dream that Cannot be Dreamt."

Something tugs at my mind. The memory of a dream I cannot recall. "What does it mean?" I ask.

He shrugs. "All I know is the name. Heard whispers of it from folks who came and went at the inn." His face turns even sadder at mention of *The Lucky Coin*, and I wonder how his life will go, now that he has lost his livelihood and home. I feel a kinship with him over this tragedy. All of life is transient, no matter how permanent and unyielding we like to imagine it. Everything we think matters can be swept away in a moment. From fire. Death. Floods. War. Life. Which begs the question: What really matters in the end? If all that we cling to is just illusion, what is the truth? What is real? What will last?

"Thank you for the information," I say. "I swear to you, I will find Pike one day, for Anny and Kara."

He nods, though I see there is no hope in his eyes, as he bids farewell to Kaden and retreats inside *The Weeping Willow*.

The carriage driver tells us to hurry, as she spits something that reminds me of tobacco, and Kaden guides me into the carriage. Our two horses are tied to the back, to come with us, but Kaden thought a carriage would be easier than riding after our ordeal. We begin the bumpy track up north. It will take at least three weeks to reach the Cliff. We stop each night to eat and sleep at inns or camp out on the roads when we aren't near enough to a town. Kaden and I don't speak about the kiss, or anything remotely personal, but at night, around campfires, he shows me a few new glyphs to practice drawing. After a week, he begins giving me basic instruction in hand-to-hand combat, and it's the most intimacy this long trip affords us. Eventually, I grow bored of the long silences that punctuate even longer days, and I ask him about the day of the fire. "I saw you change from a dragon," I say. "How?"

He looks out the window of the carriage as he speaks. "As you know, Transmuting allows a Twin Spirit to change parts of their body to those of their Spirit. I am capable of changing my *entire* body."

I glance at Umi, who sleeps on my shoulder. Sometimes he is

there, at other times gone, keeping to a schedule I do not understand. "Is that something I will be able to do?" I ask.

"Perhaps," says Kaden. "It is technically possible, but I know of none alive who have developed the skill except me. Most never push their Transmuting skills that far. They focus on Beckoning instead. Why turn into your Spirit when you can summon your Spirit more easily, they wonder?"

I wonder this too.

Kaden continues. "But there are reasons. You have more control over your own body. And... you are more powerful. There is something, when you and your Spirit are one, that surpasses the both of you individually."

We speak little after that, the carriage bumping along, jostling my bones and my nerves in equal measure. Days pass, and our talk turns to local gossip, weather patterns and he regales me with more deep thoughts of philosophers from both our worlds. The awkwardness of our kiss that still lingers between us, like the scent of perfume after a woman leaves the room. But it's becoming easier to ignore.

We're on the road nearly three weeks when we travel through the center of a small town. Children play outside, running around our carriage, while their parents carry large baskets and shop at a small outdoor market set up with stands for produce, meats, grains, fabrics and tools. Some pause to glance at our carriage as we pass, but then return to their day unfazed.

The sun is setting, casting purple and pinks over the land, when Kaden gestures me over to his window. "We are nearly there," he says. "Look."

I scoot closer to him, my leg brushing his, and follow his gaze outside.

Against a darkening sky, a stream of white light shimmers across the horizon. It curves with the land, reaching up into the stars, spreading as far as the eye can see.

I draw a deep breath. "Is that..."

"The Wall of Light," says Kaden reverently.

I am dazzled by its glow. Overwhelmed by its sheer size. I do not think, in all my life, that I have ever seen something so beautiful.

Kaden chuckles at my response. "I remember the first time I saw it. It was a night, much like this. I was but a little boy. My guardian, a man who was neither my friend nor my family, led me to the gates of the Cliff. It was the first time I had ever stepped foot outside my tiny village. The first time I had gazed upon a mountain, or the snow, or a castle. An old man waited outside to greet me. His name was Master Orcael, I learned, and he was there to test me. To see if I was truly a Twin Spirit. I do not know the exact test he performed, but I passed, and he beckoned me closer. My guardian was well happy to be rid of me, and left without another word, as Orcael asked me to leave my possessions behind. I clutched the scarf around my neck. It was my mother's, I explained, the last piece I had of her, and I would not give it up. The Master said I had no choice, but I did not budge, and after half a night out in the cold, finally he sighed and said I may keep the bloody scarf. He took my hand then, and guided me inside the Cliff. He became my closest mentor after that. I learned more from him than I did from anyone else."

It feels good, hearing one of Kaden's stories again, feeling this artificial wall between us fade away.

"I never knew my father," I say softly. He may already know this, but I say it anyway. "He died before I was born. My mother was my only guide, my only rock in this world, but sometimes I wonder how different my life would have been if my father was still alive. If my mother never married Pat. But then I realize that if that were the case, Kyle and Caleb and Kara would never have been born, and I feel foolish and selfish for even thinking it. For how can I wish them away just to make my own life easier?"

Kaden scoots closer, slowly taking my hand in his. "Sometimes, one needs to be foolish and selfish." He pauses, eyes gazing into my mine. "I was wrong earlier. The kiss was not a mistake. I see now that I said what I said out of fear. I have had many friends at the Cliff, held many people close, and I have seen all but one fade away. It is... hard... for me to let someone in, but... I want to let you in, Sky. I want to share with you the things I have kept locked away. And I want you to do the same. I want to see you smile, and I want to be the reason for that smile. I hope we can have that someday."

I think of all the things I have left to do. My training. My search for Pike. But in all this, I feel the need for more, the need for connection and joy and calm. This journey has made me realize that I cannot live for vengeance alone. That is no life. I squeeze his hand, holding his eyes with mine. "I hope so too," I say. "One day."

I lean in, my lips searching for his.

The carriage rattles beneath us, pulling our bodies apart.

I slump down, thinking the moment passed.

But then Kaden reaches for me and pulls my face to his. Our lips meet, and we hold our kiss longer than before, deepening it, letting the passion build between us and flow through us. When he leans away, I feel the absence, the cold left on my mouth after his warmth retreats. He smiles, and gestures to the window. "We're here," he says. "We're at the Cliff."

I stare outside, at the mountain that rises over the horizon, one side of the stone cut away to form a cliff, another trailing down like a tail. "It looks like a dragon," I say. "Is that how it got its name?"

"Yes and no," Kaden says. "Legend has it that it *is* a dragon. One of the Elder Dragons whose bones became stone as he died. They say the land is sacred, touched by dragonfire."

As we ride closer, I see a shape take form at the top of the mountain. A castle that spans the entire cliffside, carved from the very earth. Nine thick, round towers rise from its vast walls, and only one winding path leads to the massive steel gate. Catapults and small battlements line the walls. Plain windows shine in the moonlight. While the Palace of Storms showed off its opulence, Dragoncliff is a rougher creature. More rugged in its purpose, yet no less impressive. In some ways, it is even more menacing, for it has no time for luxuries and games. It is a fortress built for war. A place built for death.

The carriage halts before the gates, and Kaden opens the door and helps me out. The driver nods her head to us and tugs on the reins, pulling the horses around. "I'll get your horses tucked in at the

Cliff's stables, then I'd best be getting back before the sun sets all the way. Kaden, you'll be coming down for a tankard of mead soon?"

"You know I will, Jules," he says with a wave.

She winks as she leaves, and Kaden ushers me across the drawbridge and into the main courtyard of the castle. There are benches scattered throughout, and evergreen pines and thick shrubbery surround the stone paths winding through the fortress. I see a few people in the distance practicing with swords on a field of snow. They don't seem to notice us as Kaden guides me past them and to the many buildings that line the courtyard. "You'll get a proper tour when training begins. For now, I'll give you the basics. If you follow that path," he says, pointing to a cobbled walkway that leads to the right, "you'll find a large arena used for combat and weapons training. You'll be spending a lot of time in there."

I nod and keep pace with him.

"To the left is the dormitory wing, where all Ashlords have their private rooms, as well as a shared common area. You are not permitted inside, unless invited by an Ashlord, of course," he says.

Snow crunches under my feet and I breathe in the chill of the early evening air as I notice a group of men and women running laps in the distance, half naked, their breath fogging. A man cloaked in furs yells orders at them, as well as a slew of curses. "Early training," explains Kaden, as he continues. "Further down is the northern wing. The forge is there. The armory, as well as the Infirmary, which you'll likely need a fair amount in your first year."

He takes us to the northern wing and into a large room lit by torches and lined with every kind of weapon imaginable: swords, clubs, spears, bows. In the center, a tall, muscular woman performs a handstand with only one hand, her crimson hair falling to the cold black floor. Her feet are bare, her leggings covered in black leather, her chest wrapped in a dark binder. Her eyes are closed, face calm, and in her free palm she holds a coiled whip.

Three men surround her. They are all armed with swords and shields and clad in chainmail. And yet for some reason, they are the ones who look nervous.

"Attack!" yells the woman.

The men lunge forward. But before they can even reach her, she snaps her whip through the air in a circle, tripping them all, sending them crashing into the floor. Before they can stand, she pushes off the ground with one arm, leaping and spinning through the air. As she lands, her whip curls around one of the men's blades, and she yanks it away, catching the blade for herself. As the men jump to their feet, she is upon them, blade flashing through the air. She lunges at the man closest to her, and feigns slashing his throat. "You're dead, Brodsky."

The second man tries to strike her from behind.

She spins, dropping as she does, and kicks him at the knees. He falls, and she swings the blade at his throat. "Dead."

Then she leaps at the third man, knocking his blade away with one swift movement and landing on his shoulder, legs around his head. She twists her body, bringing them both to the ground, her sword pointed at his heart. "Dead."

She jumps off him, landing on her feet, as the three men stand, groaning and panting. "Dead. Dead. Dead," she says, shaking her head disapprovingly and grabbing a glass of water from a nearby table. She sips on it slowly, her breath calm. Then she turns suddenly, cracking her whip against the floor, bringing the three men back to attention. "What were your mistakes?"

Kaden laughs and walks over to her. "Their first mistake was fighting you at all."

The woman grins at Kaden, and they hug affectionately, then her smile fades. "I'm sorry I couldn't accompany you. Did all go well?"

"As well as could be expected," he says wearily. "I'll tell you about it later. But right now I must introduce you to our newest recruit." He turns to me, ushering me forward. "Sky, this is Phoenix, my partner. Phoenix, this is Sky Knightly."

Her eyes fall on me, and I can see she's sizing me up, and I realize I want this woman to like me, or at least respect me, because I want the skills she possesses. I do not yet know the gender norms of Nirandel, but it never hurts to have another woman at your back. Especially one like her.

"A pleasure to meet you," I say, raising my hand.

She ignores it, wrinkling her nose at my words. "You're an Earthling," she says, picking up my accent. "You'll be lost amongst those who were raised here. But... ", she cocks her head, as if trying to dig deeper into me, "train hard, and you may just survive."

I swallow at those mildly encouraging words. "Are you... are you the best here?" I ask, remembering her impressive display moments earlier.

She laughs. "One of them. Kaden here isn't bad himself."

I gesture at the three men still waiting at attention. "What about them? Where do they rank?"

She side-eyes them, clearly still disappointed in their performance. "In a fight against most, they are skilled, strong and competent. But they are not the best, and likely never will be at this rate."

I can't tell if she means those last words, or if she's just saying them to piss the men off and get them to work harder. But I suspect it's the former.

"What do you think?" Phoenix asks, wrapping her arm around me and leading me to the men. "Do you think they have what it takes to rise in the ranks?"

I know she's testing me, but I'm not sure what answer she wants. I consider her question and recall their technique and skill. "No, I don't," I say finally.

"Why is that?" she asks.

"As you said, they are strong and skilled. They are soldiers who could follow orders and maybe even lead a small group under a more skilled commander. But they lack creativity. They can't visualize possibilities in their opponent and therefore can't foresee the unexpected. Without that talent, which is hard—if not impossible—to learn, they will always be stuck at this level, no matter how much they practice." I force myself to maintain eye contact with her, despite the intensity of her stare.

"And how do you know these things? Are you a warrior?" she asks skeptically.

"No," I say. "I know very little about wars and armies and combat techniques. I don't know how to fight people, but I know how to fight fires, and my training and experience has taught me a lot about how people think and how they view the world. Some firefighters can predict the fire's course, because they learn to become the fire. It requires creativity. It requires a way of thinking that isn't always linear. Those who approached the job like these men approach fighting couldn't do that. They could apply the necessary techniques to put out a fire, but they couldn't take charge and beat a strong blaze that lacked predictability."

I wait for her response, and after a very long moment she smiles and places a hand on my shoulder. "I like this one, Kaden," she says. "I think she just might have a place here." She releases me and looks to her friend. "I've got to get back to training, but bring her around again sometime."

As we leave the room, I let out a breath I didn't realize I was holding. "Is she always that intense?"

He shrugs. "Mostly, yes. But you get used to it. After a few years." He grins playfully, then takes my hand. "It's time I showed you your quarters."

He guides me back outside into the biting wind, but the closeness of his body and the feel of his hand in mine lends some warmth to the frigid walk. We pass a round stone building, white and plain, and set at some distance from the others. It is different from the rest of the fortress, and it takes me a moment to realize why. It has no windows.

"What is that place?" I ask.

Kaden follows my gaze, then frowns, his hand tightening around mine. "The Asylum. When a Twin Spirit pushes themselves too far before they are ready, their Spirit can become Corrupted. It takes over their will, turns their eyes red, and makes them little more than the Fenrial we fought in the woods. When that happens, the Corrupted Twin Spirit is sent to the Asylum, where they are cared for and kept safe while a... cure... is developed for the condition." His words sound bitter. "When I first began my training, I lost many friends to Corruption. You will probably face the same."

I don't ask him anything more, hesitant to bring up more of his pain, as we pass a stone statue of a woman clad in armor, a veil upon her face. But Kaden notices my gaze and speaks anyway. "That is Illian, the first Ashlord. They say she slayed over a thousand dragons and gave her life to protect the Wall of Light."

I nudge him with my elbow. "I've heard you're making quiet the legend for yourself as well, Darkflame."

"I am nothing like Illian," he says quickly.

I seem to have offended him, though I don't understand why. I'm about to ask him about it, when he gestures at a simple, three story stone building in front of us. "Here are the Training Quarters. It is where you and the rest of the Ashlings will stay." He guides me inside and up a set of stairs, then stops in front of a door. "This is where we must part ways," he says, facing me, his hand still clutching mine. "We will not see each other again for a while. I will be busy with my duties, you with your training." He looks like he wants to say more, but doesn't.

I step forward, placing my free hand on his chest. "Thank you. For teaching me. For guiding me here."

"It was my duty," he says plainly. Then adds more cheerfully. "But as Albert Einstein once said, 'Love is a better teacher than duty'."

He leans in and his lips gently graze mine before he steps back, letting my hand fall. "I hope to see you again, Sky Knightly. Perhaps then, we will be freer persons, ready to give each other so much more." Then he turns around and walks into the darkness, red scarf dancing behind him though there is no wind.

20

ASHLINGS

My lips still burn with the heat of Kaden's kiss as I walk into a large stone room filled with beds lining the north and south walls. Eight in total, each with a trunk at the foot, a small bookshelf by the head, and furs for blankets. There are seven others already present, so it would seem I'm the last to arrive.

No one speaks. In fact most don't even look up from what they're doing. A man and woman sitting on a bed in the corner together sneer at me as I walk by.

I say hi to the quiet room, but everyone ignores me, so I shuffle in and pick a bed that looks unused, towards the back of the room. A neatly folded pile of gray clothing is stacked on the pillow—presumably meant as a change of clothes and something to sleep in. In the bed next to me sits a young girl, no more than twelve or thirteen, with straight black hair, pale skin and dark eyes. She's petite, quiet, and sits in silence sharpening a knife.

I look around, trying to get my bearings, already missing my time with Kaden on the road, though my backside is relieved to be done with that carriage.

The room is large and drafty. There's a large window but curtains are drawn over it. The only lighting comes from two fireplaces, one on each side of the room, and a handful of candles that sit on the bookshelves by the beds. The stone walls are covered with dark tapestries, presumably to keep the draft to a minimum. Underfoot is a large rug that covers the span of the room, but still the cold chill of stone in winter seeps through the attempts at warmth. I sit on the bed and it's as hard and uncomfortable as it looks.

Across from me a young man with narrow eyes and long, slim fingers sits in bed reading a huge tome of a book with a cracked brown leather cover. Next to him an Ashling sits cross-legged eating an apple. They have black straight hair cut at an asymmetrical angle and sharp features that belie their gender. A giant beast of a man with a pale bald head covered in tribal tattoos sits across from them, staring quietly into space, and an older man, maybe 40-something with skin the color of twilight, sits to the other side and browses through the books in his bookcase. The last two look the most comfortable here. He is the blond, tan, ultimate pretty boy, while she looks like an untamed lion with her wild red hair and green eyes. They scoffed at me with the same looks when I first walked in, as if they were better than me and everyone else here. They are sitting in the same bed, whispering to each other.

I turn to the quiet girl next to me. "Do you mind if I take this bed?"

She shrugs without looking up. "Don't care."

The sound of stone against steel fills the space between us as she continues to sharpen what already looks like an incredibly lethal blade. "I'm Sky," I say. "Sky Knightly."

"Raven," she says, maintaining eye contact with her knife.

"Hi, Raven." I calm my voice, as if talking to a feral animal that might dart away or attack at any moment. "You seem so much... younger than everyone else here," I say, hoping to draw her in to conversation.

She finally looks up with eyes nearly as black as her hair. "You don't choose when you become a Broken One," she says. "And I didn't want to be part of the Ashmites."

"Ashmites?"

She nods. "They're still technically Ashlings, but everyone calls the little kids Ashmites. The Spirits take all ages. You can't very well place adults with three year olds for training, can you? They have their own section of the castle, away from everyone else. But you'll likely see them from time to time."

"Why did you want to be with the adults?" I'm trying to imagine what it must be like for those young children, taken from their families, their lives, thrust into this life of training. How horrid. And then my mind turns to Kara, and I fight away a grief that is still so raw and fresh it nearly chokes me. I shake my head, as if by doing so I can shake out the memories. I will never survive this life if I think of her every minute.

The girl before me pauses before answering, returning her gaze to the knife. "I find little children annoying. They talk too much." She looks around, narrowing her eyes at the two huddled together whispering. "But I'm finding adults can be worse."

The blond pretty boy looks up, though she hadn't spoken loudly. "Do you have a problem with us, Ashmite?"

"I have a problem with everyone," she says, without any variation in her tone or expression. "Goodnight, now." She blows out her candle and crawls under the furs on her bed, closing her eyes.

The redhead yawns. "We should all get some rest now. We'll need it for training tomorrow."

Both her and pretty boy have a similar accent. An intersection of western European and something else I can't quite place, though hers sounds more rehearsed than his. They definitely sound upper class.

"You know," says the one with an apple, "statistically speaking only forty percent of us will graduate. So, the weaker ones shouldn't bother trying, really." Their alto voice sounds bored, and has a noticeably different inflection from the redhead and blond. Less staccato. More fluid.

"Who are the weaker ones?" I ask.

They don't answer for a while, all their focus on the apple. Then finally... "You. The little one, and the bookworm. You three might as well give up."

The bookworm snaps his tome shut. "This juvenile dialogue bores me," he says with a very formal dialect, each word clipped and proper. "I need to find somewhere quiet."

"Are you making fun of us?" pretty boy asks, his face hardening from the perceived threat to his ego.

"No, just stating the obvious. And you, with the apple, you're wrong. The forty perfect graduation rate applies to the whole regiment, not a single squad. All any of us has to do is perform above average, and we can all take the Ash. Simple as that. Now, if you don't mind, I am done with this form of communication."

"This form of... What did he just say?" Pretty boy asks the girl next to him.

The older man speaks, and I'm surprised to hear he has a very French accent. "He said this bickering is pointless, and it's time we all had some sleep. I, for one, agree. *Oui?*"

The French man situates himself in bed, but as he moves to lie down, he catches my eyes and gestures for me to sit. So I do, facing him.

"I am Enzo. We are from the same world, *Oui?*"

I thought perhaps that was true, but wasn't sure. I smile at the confirmation. "*Oui,*" I say, wishing I'd paid more attention in high school French.

"The big man there, he is Bix. He is from the Frozen Mountains, high in the north. They have very different customs, from what I understand. The boy with the book, he is Zev. He is from the Sunstar Isles of the east. The one with an apple is Naoki. As far as I can tell, they're from the west. That's all I've gleaned thus far."

"They?" I ask, curiously.

Enzo shrugs. "Their gender is unknown, they are, how you say? Like water?"

"Gender fluid?" I ask.

"Yes, in our world, that is what I think. Here everyone calls Naoki 'they' instead of he or she."

"One of our volunteer firefighters is the same," I say.

Enzo nods, and then continues. "The blond is Landon. He's from a wealthy family in Al'Kalesh, down south. His family is somehow connected to the Emperor, or so they say. And the woman, she's Mabel. She says she's from a high born house, but something doesn't ring true in her story," he says.

I'm impressed by his assessment and appreciate his kindness in telling me everyone's name. I tell him as much.

"I was always good at reading people," he says without arrogance. "Some say my family exploited this in me, but who is to say what is exploitation and what is necessity for survival, *Oui*?" He yawns and lies down. "Sleep well, Sky Knightly. We'll talk again soon."

I pull off my heavy cloak and put it and the extra clothes in my trunk and then crawl under the thick furs. The pillow is made of feathers, and some of them poke at my face as I try to sleep, but that's not what keeps me awake, despite massive fatigue.

Mabel is still talking with Landon on his bed, and though they feign whispering, it's more like stage whispering. I know they want us all to hear them, and their giggles and guffaws begin to rattle my already frayed nerves.

"Can you please be quiet?" I ask as politely as I can.

They ignore me, of course. I'm about to walk over there and use my 'mom voice' on them, but Bix gets there first. Without saying a word, he picks them up, one arm around each of their torsos, and places them gently on either side of him. Then he flops down on the bed between them and closes his eyes.

I nearly choke trying to hold in a startled laugh, but I watch to see what they do next. Bix takes up the entirety of the bed, so Landon and Mabel aren't so much laying on the bed as clinging to Bix as he bear hugs them both. I wonder how long they'll last.

It doesn't take long before Mabel sighs and scoots off to sleep on her own bed.

Landon holds out longer, but eventually gives up once the big man starts snoring. He grabs a spare fur and sleeps on the floor.

This is going to be a long night, I think, as I try to get comfortable once more.

SOMETHING STARTLES ME AWAKE, and it takes me a beat to remember where I am and what's happened to me. For a blessed moment I thought I was home and that one of the kids had gotten into something. Then reality crashes in on me, and I suck in my breath to keep a sob from escaping.

I look around, trying to assess what woke me. It's still dark out, and yet there is a man yelling at us from the door. A man with a shockingly large white wolf standing next to him. "Rise and shine, Ashlings. Your first day of training begins now."

Mabel raises her head a moment. "But it's still dark out."

"Perhaps you'd prefer to spend this time cleaning the privy?" The man says. "I believe I have a toothpick you can use to scrape away the shit."

Mabel bolts up. "No sir, I would prefer to begin training," she says, suddenly awake.

"That's what I thought. Let's go, Ashlings."

Zev throws a cloak over his shoulders. "If you don't mind me asking sir, who are you?"

"You can call me Master Vane. And this," he says, pointing to his giant wolf, "is Master Wolf. And today, my little Ashlings, you will learn what real pain feels like."

Master Vane is a tall man with dirty blond hair that falls to his shoulders. He appears rather ageless, but if I had to I'd place him in his 30s. He's tan, muscular and carries himself like a man always ready for battle. He wears furs and leather and looks comfortable in this cold climate as we follow him through the halls and into the snowy courtyard.

Ice crunches under our feet and I shiver and breathe out white mist. There are patches of grass here and there, struggling to survive the winter. A wall of gray stone surrounds the courtyard, topped with pyres of blue fire.

Umi appears on my shoulder, chirping into my ear and shivering. I scratch his chin to calm him.

We form a line and Master Vane paces in front of us like a drill sergeant, the wolf at his side staring at us with eyes too smart to belong to a normal beast.

"This will be your new world," he says. "Within these walls, you will find pain, suffering, tragedy. Within these walls, you will find you are captives. Slaves. Less than human. Within these walls, you will grow to understand what the dragons must feel like, trapped as they are. Hunted. Tortured. Abused. And once you feel as they do, once you have put yourselves in their skins, then, and only then, will you have even a chance at learning to fight with the fervor they do. With the fierce beauty and majestic power they inspire." He stares at each of us in turn. When he passes me, he stops, locking his startling blue eyes with mine, as if he can see into my soul. "Within these walls, you will find your limits. And... if you are lucky, you will find yourselves."

A few squad members frown at his words, but something of what he says sinks into my soul, waiting to be studied more closely.

"For your first lesson," he says, "you will be learning transmutation." He walks over to eight columns of wood, each at least nine feet tall and two feet wide. They're planted into the ground several feet from each other. Vane orders each of us to pick a column and stand behind it, facing him.

He stands in front of a ninth column set apart from ours. His is twice as thick and made of stone, rather than wood. "The ability to change a part of your body into that of your Spirit's is critical to your core training and Spirit wielding. Your goal for today: Transmute one of your hands into a weapon, and cut the pillar before you in two. Just so." He jumps forward, swinging his right hand through the air. Midway it transforms, skin turning into white fur, nails into claws, and he slashes through the stone, rending it in two, then lands on the ground on the other side of it as his arm reverts back to normal. The stone crashes down behind him, stirring snow and dirt into the air. His wolf celebrates his accomplishment with a brief but impressive howl that is nearly deafening.

"We will spend three days on this training," Vane says, not even out of breath from the exertion. "The first to break a pillar in two shall be awarded one talisman." He holds up one of the stones with glyphs that Kaden used to fight the Corrupted Spirit on the mountain. "The first Ashling to earn five talisman will be named squad leader for the duration of your training."

Landon smirks at that, and it's clear he has leadership in his sights. No one else seems to care much either way. I'm too nervous about passing to even worry about being the best at the moment. I feel like I did when I first started training to be a volunteer firefighter. Everything was so foreign and new. I worried I wouldn't be strong enough to carry the equipment, or wouldn't be able to move fast enough in the gear. It was hard at first. But I grew stronger and more capable each day. I steel myself now to not give up. To stay focused. I got this, I remind myself.

Vane is still pacing, his wolf at his side. "Anyone who doesn't break their pillar in half with the use of transmutation by the end of the three days will be sent to the Charred. From then on, your eternal duty will be to serve all the needs of this fortress. Any questions?"

There's a deep and worried silence, and some look shocked by his announcement. Mabel raises her voice first. "So being a Charred One means doing menial labor? Like cleaning the rooms?"

Vane moves to stand in front of her. "Like cleaning shit, Ashling. Who do you think keeps your privy from smelling to high heaven with waste?"

Her face pales under his glare, and perhaps from the consideration of what sounds like slavery here.

"Now, everyone begin."

Wait, what? That's all the instruction we're given? Just... do it? A sheen of perspiration forms on my forehead as I look around to see if anyone else is freaking out, or if they all know what to do. Maybe I can get a clue from them. My fellow squad members are mostly looking at their hands, their faces full of fierce concentration. Enzo swipes at the air before him, maybe preparing?

I think back to my fight with Pike, when I tried to stop him. I did this, didn't I? My hand turned into a silver claw. But how did I do it?

Something crashes to my side and everyone turns to look.

Raven, the smallest and youngest of us all, stands there, her hand a giant black sickle, the pillar before her torn in half. Landon stares at her, open jawed. Everyone does, in fact. Everyone but Vane, who approaches her with an appreciative smile on his face. "And the first talisman goes to Raven." He tosses her the small stone and she examines it briefly then slips it into a pouch at her waist.

"Raven, you're free to retire to the common room while your peers continue their work."

She nods, glances at me briefly, and then walks away.

The others, Landon and Mabel in particular, glare at her as she leaves.

I sigh and turn back to my wooden pillar. I don't have time for rivalries. I need to learn as much as I can as fast as I can.

I swipe at the air, like I saw Enzo doing, while I visualize my arm turning into a claw. Nothing happens. I keep trying. Again and again.

An hour passes, and Bix breaks his pillar using what looks like sharpened shells made of steel. He guffaws loudly, pounding his chest, then walks out smiling.

Moments later, Mabel breaks hers. Her hand quickly transmutes from something scaly looking back to unblemished flesh, and she jumps and cheers as she's dismissed.

When night falls, there are still five of us who have yet to break the pillar, and Vane sends us back to the barracks to sleep.

My arm is aching, my shoulders are on fire. I want to soak in a hot bath, but I'm too tired and sore. I give a fleeting thought to spending some time in the library to see if I can research some instruction on how to transmute, but I can't keep my eyes open and nearly knock myself out walking into a stone wall.

The next morning, before sunrise, we are woken again. After a breakfast of porridge in the dining hall, those of us still struggling return to our pillars. Raven, Bix and Mabel are excused for the day to read, take baths, or explore the castle and library.

To say I'm jealous would be an understatement.

To say I'm tired would be a joke.

But I don't let that stop me. I've fought blazing fires in the high heat of summer for twelve hours straight, day after day, when wild fires spread in California. Breaking only to maintain my gear, restock the engine and sleep for a few hours. I can do this. This is nothing.

And so I give it my everything as Vane walks around inspecting us.

"Feel the Spirit within you," he says. "Imagine that you are both one. Of one mind. Of one body. Then focus on your intent. And strike!"

I nod and I focus on imagining myself as a silver dragon. *Break the pillar. Break the pillar!*

I strike, my fist hits the wood, and the skin on my knuckles crack open, spilling blood. I hold my hand to my chest as tears of pain sting my eyes.

Landon is next to finish. His hand turns into a golden claw and he slices the pillar in two. He looks quite smug as he leaves the rest of us behind.

After him is Zev. He looks almost surprised when he finally succeeds. Then relieved. As he passes me I whisper to him, desperation hitting me hard. "How did you do it?"

"I'm sorry," he says, frowning. "But information is a valuable commodity here. One I'm not willing to share."

The sun sets on our second day, leaving me, Enzo and Naoki still unable to transmute.

Vane is about to call us to head to dinner and bed, but as he opens his mouth to speak, Enzo cuts through his pillar with a massive elephant foot.

"Job well done," Vane says. He turns to look at me and Naoki. "Looks like you are the last two remaining."

I glance at Naoki to see how they're handling the stress, but they're looking down at their feet. If I don't succeed tomorrow, I'll have to join the Charred Ones, and all of this, everything, all the sacrifices I've made—leaving my brothers behind, leaving my work, my best friend... all of it will have been for naught. I'll never master my powers. Never avenge Kara. Never return home as I promised Kyle.

I squeeze my fists. I can't fail. I won't.

"Maybe I'll bring everyone back tomorrow to share some tips with the two of you," Zane says with some sympathy in his eyes.

Good luck with that, I think. I already know they won't. They'll just gloat as they watch Naoki and me fail over and over again.

Dinner is a tasteless affair that I don't register in my brain, too distracted am I by what's to come. That night, I toss and turn in my hard little bed, unable to sleep. I go over the moment I transmuted in front of Pike over and over again. How could I do it so easily then, and not at all now? What was different?

"Hey," someone whispers to me.

I turn over and see Raven kneeling by the side of my bed.

"Come with me," she says as she stands and walks away. Everyone else is asleep, and I'm pretty sure leaving our sleeping quarters is breaking some rules, but...

She turns. "That is, if you want to pass tomorrow. If not, don't come. I don't really care either way."

Her words are all the motivation I need to make up my mind. I follow her just as she disappears through the door.

We walk through the dark hallways as she uses a candle to light our way amidst the shadows. I glance over my shoulder regularly, fearing one of the masters catching us.

We travel down a staircase, and as I watch the candlelight flicker around her, I shiver. There's something spooky about this girl. In the darkness she reminds me of a pale ghost haunting the halls.

We are outside now, walking through a small graveyard. She stops by one of the gravestones, and behind it is a wall carved with a giant tree. People, carved in relief, are gathered around the tree, worshipping it. Raven runs her small hand down the center of the tree, stopping near the base, and then she pushes. Stone grinds against stone, a loud echo in the quiet of the night, and I almost jump.

The gravestone slides out of its place, revealing stairs leading somewhere underground.

"What is this?" I ask.

"A secret passage," she says, her voice calm and emotionless. "I found it yesterday while exploring the grounds. I thought it could be a good place for training in the middle of the night."

Right.

She walks down the stairs, into a pitch black hole. I hesitate for a moment, wondering if this is a smart idea. She's a young girl, but she's clearly skilled in the use of Spirit. But she seems to want to help me, and why would she want to hurt me? It's not like I'm any threat to her.

In the end, I follow her, because at this point I'm willing to risk my safety if it means even a small chance of learning something to help me pass tomorrow. I feel the weight of this test pressing down on me like an anvil on my chest. Failure is not an option.

It's a long walk down the winding stairs of questionable safety. I imagine trying to fight a fire in a structure like this and shudder. At least it's made of stone. We finally reach a large circular chamber that I can only see in castoffs of shadows. Raven walks around the chamber lighting other candles with her own until a soft orange glow fills the space. There are at least a dozen doors leading out of the chamber in all directions.

"What is this place?" I ask in a whisper. It feels almost sacrilegious to speak too loudly here.

"Probably an old part of the castle no longer in use," she says, not bothering to whisper. Her voices echoes off the chamber walls, sounding louder than it should. "Though, it also might be a dungeon for torturing people. It's about a fifty-fifty chance either way, I think."

I wait for the punch line, but she's dead serious. I shudder and look around for any torture devices or jail cells.

As if reading my mind she shrugs. "The torture would happen further in, likely down one of those halls."

I walk to the nearest opening and peer through. "It's caved in," I say, laying a hand on the rubble before me.

"A few of them are," she says, "but not all of them."

I walk to another, this one open and I walk down the hall. Raven follows me. I hear something. "Water," I say. "I hear water dripping." I creep forward, and step into the water before I see it, my boots soaking through. Great.

There's a gap in the wall before me, from which water gushes into a giant pool blocking the hall. It must be draining somewhere though, because this is the only place that seems flooded.

"So, I know this is exciting and all, but do you want to train or not?" Raven says with a frown.

I turn back to face her, thoughts of the flooded hall and where it may lead leaving my mind in an instant as reality crashes back down on my shoulders. "Yes. I'll do whatever it takes to become an Ashlord," I say as we walk back to the original chamber.

"Good. Why?" She turns to face me, reading my eyes as we stand in the center of the chamber.

Her question is so fast, so brazen, and so... personal, it catches me off guard. I think of what generic response I could give that wouldn't reveal too much. But I can see in her eyes that she's studying me, looking for the truth. "My... my daughter was taken from me," I say, surprising myself with the truth. My body fills with a blend of grief and rage as I speak, my fists clenching. "And learning to control my power and becoming an Ashlord... it's the only hope I have of catching the man who took her and bringing him to justice."

"I see," she says, still showing no emotion. "Then think of your daughter as you attempt to transmute. When you strike at the pillar, imagine not the column before you, but whoever it is who took your child. Understand?"

I nod. "Yes, I understand."

She moves aside, and with a wave of her hand dark shadows swirl from the floor, forming a column. Something hangs on it. A black mask with black feathers. It reminds me of a scarecrow. How did she make this? What kind of magic is she using? I didn't even see her use a talisman.

"How do you know so much?" I ask.

"It's easy for me," she says. "Always has been." She doesn't offer more, and I don't pry. I don't want to make her angry just as she's trying to help me.

"Ready?" she asks.

Not really, I think. But I nod. "Ready." I hold out my arm, and in my mind I don't see the scarecrow, I see Pike. His face hollow, his skin tight, gems protruding from muscle and flesh. And I lunge, ready to tear his throat out.

My hand flies through the pillar of smoke, and I look down, crestfallen. It's still just my bruised hand. I failed. Again.

"Good," Raven says.

I look up in surprise.

"You transmuted for a moment."

"What?"

I look down at my hand.

"See the silver?" She points, showing a streak of silver dust where my hand used to be. "You left a trail. Now, try again."

I let my fingers trail through the faint dust that's already fading. I did it? The thought elates me, even if it was just for a moment. It means I can do it again.

And I do. Over and over I practice. I train through the night, and before the sun rises, Raven and I sneak back into the sleeping quarters. "Everyone here seems to be treating this like a competition," I whisper once we're back in bed. "Like they need to keep every advantage they can to themselves. But you don't. Why?"

"You mean why did I help you?"

"Yes."

She stares at the ceiling, quiet for a moment. "I suppose, because if I were a mother, and I had my kid taken away, I'd want help getting them back."

"So you wouldn't have helped me if I had a less noble reason?"

Her voice is cold. "If you'd had a less noble reason, you'd never have learned."

When the sun comes up, I reach the field first. Naoki is late, joining after Vane arrives with the rest of our squad. I'm ready, and as soon as he's watching, I swing my arm at the column, and in it, I see Pike holding my baby, taking her away. Leaving my family broken and bloody. All the anger in me pulses and my skin changes to silver scales around my arm. My nails transmute to claws. I slice through the pillar.

And it doesn't collapse.

"She failed," Mable whispers.

"No," Raven says, pointing. "Look."

I kick the pillar, knocking the top half off, and I see Master Vane smile. I'd cut it through so clean you could barely see the slice. But it was there, long and deep. I did it. I passed the first test.

Relief fills me as I leave Naoki and Vane on the field, while I head to the baths for a much needed soak.

I did it. But this was only the first.

21

CHARRED

Naoki does not pass the test.

After my bath and a walk to think, I returned to the courtyard to see how they were doing. It was close to sunset, and I'd hoped to see it empty, but Zane stood out there with his wolf, while Naoki struggled to transmute. Over and over.

To no avail.

The rest of our squad mates sat and watched in stunned silence.

No one scoffed or mocked.

I think they were all too shocked.

I know I was.

Tears streamed down their face as the sun finally faded and Vane frowned. "It is time. I am sorry."

His words sounded sincere, and his face looked haggard as he walked Naoki into the fortress.

We all head to our beds now, and we wait. Naoki does not return. A girl comes in later and takes the bedding and any personal affects from their space and leaves. Just like that, Naoki is gone.

"They're Charred now," Landon says. We've barely begun training and already Naoki's out. Just because they became a Broken One, just because they couldn't figure out transmutation, they'll now have to spend the rest of their life as a slave. Where's the justice in that?

Everyone is dejected as the candles burn low and light from the fire dances on the walls. Zev, who hasn't touched his books all night, speaks first, breaking the heavy silence. "I read the first trial has minimal instruction on purpose. To weed out those with so little natural talent that it would take them decades to gain even basic control over their powers. They're too dangerous to be allowed to wonder free. So they're made Charred, their Spirits snuffed out, and they serve those of the Ash until they die."

"What do you mean their Spirit is snuffed out?" I ask. I think about my bracelet and how it controlled my power for a time. Is it like that?

Zev shrugs. "They undergo some kind of procedure and lose the ability to summon their Spirit. I've tried to learn more, but the details are a tightly guarded secret of the Ashpriests."

"Ashpriests?" I've heard of Ashknights and Ashlords, but this is new.

"There are four sects for those of the Ash," Zev says. "The Ashlings, who learn. The Ashknights, who protect. The Ashlords, who command. And the Ashpriests, who remember. The priests are a group dedicated to the knowledge of Spirits as well as managing the fortress and the Charred."

"And then there is the fifth sect," Landon says.

Zev scoffs. "A myth told by superstitious nursemaids to keep children in line."

"It's no myth, I tell you," he says, leaning forward on his bed, his voice low. "There is a fifth sect. The Ashwraiths, they call them. Who conspire. A secret group comprised of the most talented Broken Ones, working in the night to manipulate the land. Turning noble houses against one another. Assassinating those who oppose the Cliff."

Mabel tsks at him. "Dragoncliff avoids interfering in matters of politics," she says, tossing a lock of red hair to the side. "Everyone knows this. For centuries they've remained neutral throughout wars and feuds."

Landon chuckles. "Or so they want you to believe."

Bix nods, surprising everyone with his deep, booming voice in the quiet of their room. "My people, too, speak of the Ashwraiths. But they are not agents of the Cliff, no. They are deserters. Ashlords who left the Cliff and betrayed their sacred vows, and Charred who escaped. They hide in the Waning Woods, where their Spirits have become corrupted, their powers greater. It is they who cause children to go missing in the forest. It is they who summon Corrupted Spirits to attack villages."

I shudder at his words, but Landon laughs again. "Listen to yourself. *Those* are the nursemaid tales meant to scare children."

Bix nods solemnly. "It does scare the children. And it should scare you as well."

Zev leans in. "All these tales are ridiculous. If any of the myths are even slightly true, it's that Ashwraiths live within the Wall, deserters who hide within the mountains. It's the one place they actually have a chance to avoid being caught by Ashlords, as long as they manage to avoid the dragons as well. Though it's unlikely they can survive in such an environment for long, it's not impossible, I suppose." Zev smiles gruesomely. "Still, those dragons are starving."

Landon rolls his yes. "Really? Twin Spirits living beyond the Wall is more realistic than a powerful organization using assassins to influence and control?"

Zev rubs his chin. "Assassins are not completely out of the question. However, if Dragoncliff had decided to enter politics, then why does the Emperor rule and not our Headmaster? Think about it. The only people stronger than Twin Spirits were High Dragons, and they were all killed off during the Rising. Why would Dragoncliff let the Emperor have power, instead of taking it for itself, if power was the goal?"

Landon shrugs. "Who says power is the goal?"

Mabel shakes her head. "Listen to yourselves, trying to analyze folk stories. Ashwraiths don't exit. If they did, we'd have accounts of them, just as we do dragons and various Spirits."

Zev nods. "I agree. There would be some official record of their existence, even if not here, then at the palace."

"I wonder... " Landon says, frowning, "what Naoki would have thought about this."

We all look at their starkly empty bed, and our somber moods return. It could have been any one of us who made Charred. It was almost me. I was so focused on trying to get myself past the first trial, I didn't think much about Naoki's struggles. It didn't occur to me to ask Raven to let them join our training. I could have saved them. Maybe they would still be here with us if I had. I glance at Raven, who isn't looking at anyone. Instead, she's sharpening her blade again.

Eventually we blow out our candles and tuck ourselves into bed, but I can't sleep, despite my physical and mental fatigue. After hours of tossing and turning, I give up and crawl out of bed to use the privy and relieve a full bladder.

I enter a stone room full of crude stone toilet seats that contain reusable clay pots. I do my business, trying not to breathe too deeply, and as I'm about to leave, someone dressed in gray robes enters. They bend over one of the toilets and begin scooping brown sludge into a bucket.

I catch the side of their face in candlelight, and see dark purple rings under familiar eyes.

"Naoki?"

"Do not look at me," they whisper in a pained voice without making eye contact.

"But I—"

"Is there something you require, Mistress?" they ask, staring at their feet. Their voice is dead, cold, a recitation of some line they're forced to speak.

"No. I just wanted to talk. To see how you are."

"You must not talk with Charred, Mistress. It is beneath you. Now, if you will excuse me—"

A woman steps into the privy wearing dark gray robes. She's thick-boned and has her raven hair pulled into a severe bun. She has a rope tied around her waist. "Do you not recall what I told you, Charred One?" She says in a harsh voice to Naoki. "You do not speak to those above you."

I'm appalled as Naoki drops to their knees and puts their forehead on the filthy floor. "I am sorry, Watcher. She addressed me first. I thought it rude not to respond."

"It was rude to even look upon her. To even stand in her presence." The Watcher walks forward, untying the rope around her waist as she does. She holds it above Naoki. "Your transgression must be removed through pain. Remove your robes."

I gasp. "What are you doing?"

"Do not question me, Ashling," she says. "This Charred is new, and she must be taught our ways. Go now, or stay if you like. But do not interfere again." She turns away from me to Naoki, who's back is bare as they bend their head to the floor. The Watcher raises her rope and strikes down.

I catch the rope with my hand, my skin transmuting to avoid injury.

The Watcher's eyes go wide. "How dare you—"

"Are you not a Charred One as well?" I challenge her. She must be, else why would she be in this role.

She glares at me, without speaking. "Then am I not *your* superior, yet you dare speak to me. Chastise me. Command me."

I pull on the rope and the Watcher loses balance and falls face first next to the bucket of shit and piss.

"Come, Naoki," I say, handing them robes to cover themselves.

The Watcher stands, and I expect a fight, but she does not move. Her voice is calm. Collected. "I know you seek to help them, Ashling. But what you do will only make their life harder. They are Charred now. Their existence is dedicated to taking care of this fortress and nothing more. The faster they accept this, the better for everyone. Do not try to give them hope when there is none to be had."

She walks past me then and commands Naoki to follow her.

Naoki slips on their robe and walks past me. I try to grab their hand, but they brush me away. "This is the way things must be, Sky. I have accepted it. So please, accept it as well, for my sake."

When they leaves I am left alone in the cold darkness, wondering what kind of torture they endured that could break a person's spirit in one day.

They ask me to accept this, but how can I ever accept injustice?

22

BLOOD AND TEARS

I see Naoki only once in the next few days. Their paleness has deepened into an unhealthy sallowness that serves to highlight their sharpened cheekbones and the dark half-moons under their eyes. Naoki and I don't speak, and they don't make eye contact with me, but as they walk away I notice dark red lashes across the backs of their calves. I shudder as I consider what kind of torture Naoki has endured already.

I want to talk to someone about it, but who? Raven is remote and not good at empathy. Mabel and Landon seem to actively hate anyone not them. Zev disdains everyone and prefers books to people. Bix and Enzo seem okay, but are earnestly trying to learn everything they can, and so there is little time to make friends.

I'm lonely, and I miss Blake. I miss our talks late into the night, where we would tell each other everything over ice cream and cheap beer. I miss my fire family, and the easy camaraderie that was forged in battle and boredom. And I miss the kids so much my chest aches when I think of them. I see them each night in my dreams, and it's a bittersweet kind of crushing of my heart. There's a moment—a flash of a moment really—each morning, when I'm just waking up, and consciousness isn't fully upon me yet. When I forget where I am and what's happened. When I expect sticky hands to touch my face and wake me. Or Kara's impatient cry to jolt me back to my reality. And then my eyes flutter open and I remember, and I have to suck in a sob as it all crashes down on me anew.

Each morning, I lose them all again.

And each time, it hurts just as much.

Time should heal this. Or make it more bearable. That's what they say, isn't it? I don't know whether that's a relief or just a different kind of loss. The raw pain is a penance, a reminder of why I'm here. To lose that is to lose part of myself.

But night is the hardest. During the day I am kept too busy by lessons, training, physically grueling workouts, reading, horseback riding, sword fighting, and Spirit work to think beyond the moment. It's a blessing, to be kept on the brink of such exhaustion. I'd never sleep otherwise.

Over the next few days, the lessons intensify. We spend time in the forest gathering herbs and learning their uses. We learn how to track, and practice finding prints, covering our own, noticing when a branch or stick or twig or leaf is even the slightest bit displaced. We are challenged to use our Spirit to heighten our own senses, which aides many of us in the tracking.

"We may only be tracking animals now, but these skills will serve you when tracking dragons," Master Vane says.

We learn how to make camp and how to find and prepare food in the wild. This knowledge seems new to most, even Raven. Only Bix seems to have a greater mastery of outdoor survival, though he still listens as attentively as the rest of us.

We are hungry and sore at the end of each day, and Bix picks up two points. One for tracking a deer faster than the rest of us, and the other for setting up the best camp.

Despite the challenge of it all, or maybe because of it, I finally feel like I'm getting the hang of this life at the Cliff. I've spent time camping with my family when I was a kid. And I learned a lot of survival skills with the fire department. It feels good having some skill at what we're doing.

That fragile dash of confidence is destroyed when we begin combat training.

It's not quite dawn yet as we line up in the training arena. Master Vane—who seems to never need sleep or sustenance and I'm convinced is more machine than man—demonstrates hand-to-hand combat skills for us to mimic.

He makes it look so easy I almost laugh.

Until I try it myself and realize it's not at all easy.

After a few repetitions, he pairs us off and commands us to spar. The Ashling with the best technique will receive a point by the end of the day.

I'm paired with Landon, and I'm not holding my breath at getting that point.

Raven's with Mabel. Zev is with Bix and Enzo waits to have a turn later with one of us since Naoki is now gone.

"Don't worry," says Landon, with a crooked smile. "I'll go easy at first."

Yeah, right.

He throws a right hook, but I duck under and rush him with my body, knocking him to the ground and pinning him. Not a move Vane taught us, but hey, whatever works.

He flails about, unable to escape from my hold. "Come on, what kind of move was that?"

I grin down at him, my hair falling to the side of his face. "The kind of move you learn to take down bullies in the fifth grade," I say, applying more pressure on his neck with my elbow. "Do you give up?"

He squirms some more, his face turning red from the exertion and embarrassment, and when he realizes he's not getting out of this, he taps my arm twice. The signal to end the fight.

Master Vane walks by and smirks at Landon. "Suppose your tutors didn't teach you this, huh Ashling? Did they only believe in the delicate arts?"

Landon frowns, then stands while massaging his throat, his eyes fierce. He raises his fists in fighting form. "Again."

We spar. And we spar again. And again. I take most of the wins, though he gets me a few times. We take breaks to catch our breath and get water, and I use that time to watch the other pairs. Raven fairs well, moving faster than I've ever seen her. She may be small, but she's strong, fast and agile, as she dances around Mabel, tripping her up and twisting her joints. Mabel gets in a few punches, hitting Raven in the side with considerable force, but it doesn't slow the young girl down. It's as if she doesn't even feel it.

Since Enzo has been waiting on the sidelines, Vane eventually sends him to take Raven's place. I guess he figures Raven doesn't need more practice. Enzo and Mabel prove an even match, constantly tiring themselves out with neither of them taking many wins.

But I spend most of my time watching Zev and Bix.

The big man rushes his small opponent, but Zev dashes out of the way in an instant, then grabs Bix by the wrist, twisting in some strange manner I've never seen until the giant collapses. With screams of pain, he taps out and Zev stands victorious, the gloat filling his face. "Care to try again?" he asks smugly.

Bix wipes his eyes, and I wonder if he's covering up tears. "You too fast, little demon man," Bix says. "Too good. Where you learn fighting like that?"

"My father taught a class of Hetow back home. Every day I was forced to join him by the beach and train. I'd much rather have been reading, but now, I'm grateful my parents made me practice."

"Your father must be a great warrior," Bix says, his booming voice full of admiration. "I would like to meet him one day."

Zev smiles at that and offers his hand to help the giant man up. A symbolic gesture, given that Zev would not be able to lift Bix, but it is not lost on Bix, whose mood improves.

We've all sustained our share of bruises when Vane stops us halfway through the day and tells us to line up. "Now it is time you learn to infuse your actions with the strength of your Spirits. You must punch harder. Run faster. Jump higher."

He points to two beams about sixteen feet high, positioned side by side in the northwest corner of the arena. Another beam crosses between them around four feet from the top, making a really tall, stylized 'H'. "You will line up and take turns trying to jump over the beam. The first to succeed gets a talisman."

I'm first in line, which is... awesome. Because who doesn't want to be the first to fall flat on their face?

But, I give it my all.

I run as hard as I can.

I jump as high as I can.

And I fail completely. Though I don't fall flat on my face, so that's a plus. "That thing must be twelve feet high," I say, in what is definitely not a whiny voice I would have scolded the kids for.

Landon jumps about four feet, then groans. "How is this even possible?"

One after another, we each fail.

Raven is last, and we watch, expecting her to be as unimpressive as the rest of us.

She doesn't even run. She just walks up to the bar. And honestly, I don't blame her. After seeing everyone else try and fail, why bother doing something you know isn't possible?

But...

She jumps in one fluid, effortless movement that defies gravity. Literally. Because she keeps gliding. Fifteen feet into the air, over the beam, and then lands softly on the other side.

There is a stunned silence and then I clap and whoop, hollering and cheering for her.

But I realize no one else claps. Or cheers. Or even smiles. Most of them glare at her, as if she's done something wrong.

Bix is the only one not sending her dagger eyes. He just looks perplexed and disappointed in himself.

Landon sneers. "Good at everything without even trying. Some of us actually have to work for our abilities. She doesn't even share how she does it. Screw her."

My instincts kick in and I ram into him then, pinning him down and holding my elbow against his throat. "Is that how you talk to a kid? Huh? Does that make you feel better about yourself? Is your ego really so fragile and delicate?" I raise a fist and aim it at his precious face.

Someone grabs my robes and pulls, and I fly across the arena and land hard in the dirt, scraping my arms and legs and jolting my insides.

Master Vane stands over me. He was the one who threw me like I was a rag doll. He looks between me and Landon, a scowl on his face. "Both of you, thirty laps. Now," he barks.

I do as he says, not looking at Landon even once as I run. I can hear Landon behind me. He makes good time, but I've trained in fire-fighter gear that weighs a ton. This is nothing.

I can hear Vane awarding points as I make the laps. Raven gets one for jumping, Zev for sparring.

I finish before Landon and head to the waterfalls to rinse off in private. As I stand underneath the pouring waters, I let my frustration out in tears that disappear into the lake. I'm sick of living with these selfish people who only look out for themselves. I'm sick of the constant training when what I really want to do is find Pike.

I continue my venting until all the bitterness and anger I've been carrying pours out of me.

It is in this emptiness that I find stillness. That I find some reflection of peace.

My temper has cooled and I've locked down my emotions by the time I return to the barracks.

The general mood when I arrive is cheerfulness. Even Landon and Mabel seem happier than normal.

"Where's Raven?" I ask, realizing she's the only one missing.

"She has gone to bathroom," Enzo says, using the same word I would use.

She comes back in as we're talking, and goes to lay in her bed without looking at any of us. As soon as she lies down, I hear something pop, and red stickiness explodes all over everything.

Raven sits up, her body covered in red goo. She looks at her hands, her eyes wide with horror.

Landon and Mabel burst out laughing.

I have a fair amount of the red crap all over me too, and it takes a moment for my brain to process what it is. "Is this... blood?" I ask, sniffing at my hands.

No one answers.

Raven doesn't say anything, just jumps from the bed and runs out the room.

The laughter grows louder. Bix is the only one not joining in.

I turn and stand in the center of the room, my hands balled into fists as I try to control my temper. It takes an act of will to keep me from beating the bloody hell out of them. Instead, I stare down each of them. "How dare you!" I say, holding their gaze, forcing them to hear me. To see me. To see what they've done. I do not yell. Quite the opposite. My voice is dangerously quiet. "How dare you do that to her."

Landon doesn't back down. "She needed to be taught a lesson," he says. "Taught some humility."

"Humility? You think she doesn't have humility just because she's better than you? You're the one who likes to talk about how good you are. How good your life used to be. We're just all nuisances to you, aren't we? You have better things do to than be here, don't you? You're a fool. You're the one who needs to learn humility. And kindness."

Landon walks closer to me, getting in my face. "You had best shut your mouth," he says with a sneer, his hands balling into fists.

"The girl got what she deserved," Mabel says, tossing her long red hair to the side.

I glance at both of them, wondering how to handle this. If it comes to a fight, Mabel is better than Landon.

Mabel sees my hesitation and pounces on it, standing side by side with Landon. "But I'm starting to think maybe you need a lesson too. How about it?"

Her and Landon advance, then freeze.

Bix walks up beside me. He points at the two of them and cracks his knuckles.

Landon rolls his eyes. "Fine. Guess your lesson will just have to wait."

He and Mabel turn, but Bix walks up behind them, grabs them both by the collars, and lifts them up until they are dangling from his arms like angry little dolls. They try to fight him, but his arms are so long they can't even reach him.

"I with Sky. You leave others alone, understand?" he says.

They fight a bit more, and Mabel bites Bix's arm, but he doesn't flinch.

Finally they give up.

"Yes, we understand."

He drops them and returns to his bed. "Good."

I meet Bix's eyes and nod my thanks, then I address the whole room. "Has it not occurred to any of you to wonder how Raven got this good at everything at such a young age?"

I can see by their confused expressions it has not. Idiots.

"She's just a kid. And yet she can beat all of us at just about anything." I walk closer to Landon and Mabel. "What kind of life do you think she would have had to make her into such a weapon?" I stand there silently, forcing each of them to consider my question. To really think about what that poor girl has endured.

When Landon and Mabel drop their heads in something I hope is shame, I turn and grab a blanket and change of clothes and then leave them in silence to think about what they've done.

It occurs to me then that my role might not be super solider. My role here might just be mom. I'm not the oldest, or the best. But I know how to make a family. Maybe that's what my squad needs from me more than anything.

But right now, Raven needs me the most.

I CHECK for her first in the baths, but they are empty. So I think of where she would go to be alone, and I remember the passage under the stone grave.

I find her in the round chamber, clean, wet, and wrapped in a towel. She sits on the floor in a corner, her knees pulled to her chest, her face pressed into arms as sobs shake her body.

Saying nothing, I sit beside her. We stay like that for some time, not saying anything. I just want her to know she has my support. Nothing more. Her sobs echo in the chamber, filling our space with her grief, until, eventually, they slowly subside and she finally looks up and stares at the ceiling. "Why do they hate me?"

"Because they hate themselves," I say. "They hate their own weakness. And you remind them of just how much they have left to learn."

She turns to face me, then flinches, pulling her arms to her chest. "What's wrong?" I ask.

She says nothing, but moves her arms away, revealing a giant purple bruise under her shoulder.

"Did this happen during sparring?" I ask.

She nods.

"How did you continue training after that?" I ask, remembering how she kept beating Mabel even after taking hit after hit. How she gracefully jumped into the sky, earning another talisman. How she never showed any pain or discomfort.

"I'm used to it," she says.

Her words are so straightforward. As if it should be obvious. Like this is all she's ever known, so what else would she do. It's her acceptance of this pain that breaks my heart the most. She knows nothing else, and so this has become her normal.

"We should get you to the Infirmary," I say. "They need to check for broken ribs."

She doesn't respond, so I smile at her. "Come on. I can go with you."

After a moment, she nods. I offer her the blanket, wrapping it around her as I help her stand, and that's when I see the scars lining her back. Layers of them, each older than the next. What did they do to her, I wonder.

As we slowly make our way out of the tunnels, I try to lighten the mood a little. "I always see you walking in your measured way. I can't believe how fast you were during the sparring."

The side of her lips curls. "Maybe it's all the energy I conserve."

I'm not sure, but I think Raven may have just made a joke. I take the risk and chuckle, and then slowly, hesitantly, she starts to laugh as well. Like a door opening after a long winter, and we laugh some more, forgetting even why, letting the giddiness steal us away from a moment.

Then something crashes into stone, the sound reverberating through the many halls.

And we both freeze as we realize...

We are not alone.

23

ORCAEL

We jump up, then rush to the side, hiding behind one of the rocks near the caved-in passages. "The lantern," whispers Raven.

I nod and snuff out the flame, putting the lantern down by my side. We stay low as light spreads over the ceiling, and footsteps echo in the distance, growing louder, closer.

"What about this passage?" asks a low, familiar voice. It's Kaden. I know for certain.

"The Masters know of this one," replies a second voice. Feminine. Phoenix.

I consider leaving my hiding spot and revealing myself to Kaden. But we're not supposed to be here, and though I trust Kaden completely, I do not yet know what to think of Phoenix, so I stay hidden.

"Just because the Masters know of the catacombs, doesn't mean they monitor them," says Kaden. "We could use the passage if we needed to get in quick."

"I hope... I hope it doesn't come to that," says Phoenix, her voice sad.

"I know. Me too." Kaden's reply drifts off.

The footsteps fade. The light wains. They must be heading down another passage.

Phoenix says something in response, but they are too far for me to make out the words. I wonder what they were talking about. What they meant. Once the light on the ceiling is gone, and the silence has returned, I poke my head up, scanning the chamber. I see nothing, so I gesture to Raven. "They're gone. Come."

I hold out my hand to her.

She takes it and stands. I'm surprised she embraced my help, but glad she did. "We should head back," I whisper.

She nods, and we walk through darkness, feeling our way, since I can't relight the lantern.

I think we've found our way back to the staircase, but then I realize they are stairs heading down and not up. It's the wrong way, but as I turn to leave, I hear something in the darkness.

A cry.

"Someone's down there," I say.

"Or some*thing*," says Raven. "We should leave it."

I know she's probably right. But that cry sounded wounded, pleading, and my protective instincts kick in. "Stay here if you'd like," I say, descending the stairs carefully, trying not to fall and break my neck.

A light flickers in the distance. I jump back, worried someone is passing through the tunnels again, but then I realize the light isn't moving. It must be coming from a stationary source.

I creep forward, easier, now that I can see my steps, and arrive in a small passageway lit by a torch on the wall. Something stirs in the corner, in the shadows. I hear the cry again.

I move forward, trying to make out the shape. A large black cat lies in the corner of the room, splayed out on its side, eyes open, still.

The cat is dead.

Something wiggles around its belly. I reach into the darkness and feel a little bit of fur. I take it in my hands, holding it up. A tiny kitten, fur gray and wild, stares up at me. It makes a sound, the cry I heard before. The poor thing was trying to nurse from its dead mother.

"You should leave it," says Raven, who stands behind me, though I didn't hear her approach. "It's the runt. It stayed because it was too weak to leave."

I hold the kitten up, examining its thin body, its giant blue eyes. They remind me of another pair of eyes. Another time. "I won't abandon those who can't defend themselves," I say, clutching the kitten against my chest and standing as I turn. "Just because something is weak, doesn't mean it's worthless."

Raven shrugs. "Bring it if you want."

I hold the kitten up for her to see and say with utter sincerity, "This one will be a part of the squad."

It takes a while to find our way back up the stairs and toward the hidden door. When we reach the Ashling living quarters, we freeze. Master Vane stands in the doorway, arms crossed. He looks us up and down disapprovingly, then scoffs. "I thought it'd be the other two."

I EXPECT to be made Charred. Instead, Master Vane gives us chores. "A month in the kitchens for you," he says to Raven, then points at me. "A month in the library for you."

I raise an eyebrow, skeptically. "Is the punishment... reading?"

Raven giggles, then clasps a hand over her mouth.

Master Vane's eyes go wide, and I swear smoke comes out from his nostrils. "Two months for that comment. And yes... the punishment is reading. Reading every title and author and number you come across as you handle the reorganizing of the library. The cataloging system has been out of date for years, and Master Orcael has been asking for an assistant just as long. I think you will do perfectly. When you're not reorganizing the stacks, I expect you to be cleaning the floors, dusting the shelves, and doing anything else Master Orcael may require? Do you understand, Ashling?"

"Yes, Master," I say, standing straight.

"What... is... that?" he asks, pointing at my arms.

I smile sheepishly. "It's... um... a kitten, Master."

"A kitten?" he chews on the word, as if its new to him. "A kitten? Did you venture out into the night to get a pet, Ashling?"

"No, Master. It was just there, and it needed help, and—"

"I don't want to know," he says, shaking his head. "The more details I know of what you did down there, the more likely I'll have to make you Charred. Let's just say you got lost, and I found you in the hallway. You were never in the catacombs. You will never be in the catacombs again. Understood, Ashlings?"

"Yes, Master," we both say in unison.

I raise the kitten in my hands. "So does that mean we can—"

"As long as I don't see the beast, I don't care. Keep it away from Wolf. And keep it away from me." He turns around then, disappearing down the hallway.

Raven and I exchange a glance and a shrug.

We bring the kitten up to our quarters. Though it is the middle of the night, no one is asleep. It seems they have been thinking.

Bix raises a large finger, pointing at the furry bundle in my arms. "It cannot be. Is that a..."

"It is."

"Can I hold it?"

"You can."

The big man's eyes turn glassy as he takes the little kitten into his arms. It grabs onto his finger, nibbling on the nail. Bix giggles. "Oh, he is a fierce one. A mighty hunter he will make one day. Does he have a name yet?"

I notice the others have huddled around, even Mabel and Landon, entranced by the little kitten.

I look around to each of them. "I don't know yet. Anyone have a suggestion?"

Raven is the first to speak. She walks forward, past me, taking one of the kitten's paws into her own hand. Her face is softer than before. Her voice is shaky, lacking the confidence she usually possesses. "What about Ashpaw?" she asks. "Because he's one of us."

Everyone nods in agreement, even Mabel and Landon.

"That is a fine name," thunders Bix, lifting up the kitten. "Ashpaw. You are one of us now."

We spend the rest of the night taking turns cuddling the little gray feline, and when everyone is asleep, and I too am about to fall into slumber, I notice Raven sitting in the corner, whispering secret words to the kitten in her arms.

THE NEXT DAY we train in sparring again. Then attempt to jump the H. All of us do better. All of us still fail. Even Raven.

When she walks up to the pole, she makes a small leap, barely reaching the top, then shrugs.

"What is wrong with you, Ashling?" asks Master Vane.

"I don't know, Master," she says innocently.

As we head back to our quarters, I nudge her. "Why didn't you make the jump? You know you could have."

She just shrugs again.

While the others take the night off, we begin our chores. I find the library from memory and walk through the giant gilded doors, closing them behind me. Shelves filled to the brim with books rise up to the ceiling, which must be at least four stories tall. Ladders on wheels stand on tracks, for use in reaching the higher manuscripts. Spacious tables fill the center of the room, some empty, some covered in stacks of books. The library is vacant at this late hour. The only light comes from a few glowing orbs placed on the tables. Talismans, I realize, glowing a pale blue. There are no candles here, no torches or fireplaces. No fire.

"Hello?" I call out, walking forward. "My name is Sky Knightly. I—"

"Be a dear and pass me that book on the table, won't you?" comes an old, gruff voice.

I grab the book next to me, then walk forward, through the stacks of shelves until I come upon a man on a ladder. Blue robes fall from his shoulders. A long gray beard grows from his chin, reaching down to his belt. A monocle sits on one of his dark beady eyes. His face is full of lines, showing a lifetime of history. More than a lifetime.

He holds out his arm, not looking at me, and, realizing what he wants, I hand him the book. He studies the spine carefully. "Ah, that's the one. Thank you, my dear." He slides the book into an open spot on the shelf, then descends the ladder and holds out his hand. "I am Master Orcael. But you may call me simply Orcael."

I shake his hand. "Nice to meet you, Orcael. I'm Sky. Sky Knightly."

"Would you care to join me for tea, Sky?"

I shrug. "That sounds nice, but I'm pretty sure I'm supposed to help you reorganize the library, or Master Vane will throw a fit."

Orcael waves a hand dismissively. "Oh, don't you worry about him. You are here to assist me, and I need assistance with tea."

I chuckle and follow him to a table where a pot is positioned over a glowing blue talisman. I grab two nearby cups and pour us each a drink. Orcael breathes in the steam from his tea deeply, and sighs with satisfaction. "Now that is a good cup of tea. I will show you how to make one, in time. The process is very specific. A lost art, really."

I smile and sip the hot liquid. It warms my mouth and fills me with a fresh minty taste.

"Now," says Orcael, tapping a pen decorated with dragonstone against the table. "to business. What do you know of The Valarata?"

"Um... nothing," I say sheepishly.

He frowns, bushy gray eyebrows pushing together like a puppy. "Oh, that will not do. That will not do at all." He pauses, composing himself, then begins in a more singsong voice. "The Valarata is an ancient poem. It chronicles the battle between Val and Nir before the Wall of Light was created. It is, to date, the most complete account on the matter. I, however, intend to write something even more thorough." His eyes beam with excitement. "The only way, of course, is to compile information from a variety of sources. There have been many different accounts, many different extrapolations from historians. I intend to combine them into one volume. But, I am getting ahead of myself. First, we must go back to the Valarata. It is special for many reasons. One in particular interests me. It is the oldest, and, in truth, only legitimate record of the Mask of Nir."

I've never head of the mask, and it peeks my interest. Orcael must notice my curiosity, because he smiles and continues. "You see, it is said that Nir did not defeat Val the first time. Nor the second. Nor even the third. Again and again he lost, but each time he had a secret weapon. His mask, which allowed him to travel back in time, to repeat his war with Val over and over, until he decided to trick his brother and create the Wall of Light. When Nir died, the Valarata says his mask was buried with his corpse in the Dragon Graveyard. A place only found in stories." He pauses, voice growing serious. "The poem says one more thing. It says the mask was smooth and faceless, and if found, it could be used again. One final time."

Something tugs at my mind. A memory I do not have.

"You... you wish to find this mask?" I ask.

He nods, rubbing his hands together with glee. "Most say it is a myth. But if not... imagine the implications? A way to travel through time, even if it is only once. The possibilities are endless." Then he shrugs. "And if the mask is but a tale, I will still write the most comprehensive account of Nir ever told. You shall help me. You will scour this library and move all books even remotely connected to the Valarata into one section, as per the new cataloging system. This should appease Master Vane and help me with my mission all at once."

I smile, taking another sip of the tea. "This seems important to you. Personal, I mean."

He glances down, eyes suddenly heavy. "Like most, I grew up hearing tales of Nir, and yet, I know so little about him. I want to know more. I want to know the truth. It is something I have wanted since I was little, I suppose."

I set my tea down, scanning the stacks. "Where do I begin?"

THE NEXT DAY we are given a new challenge in the training yard. "Today," says Master Vane as he paces before us, snow crunching under his boots. "We will focus on Beckoning. Whoever summons the largest manifestation of their Spirit by the end of the day, gets the talisman." He glances at Raven and Landon. They are both tied with four talisman, and this exercise will finally decide our Squad leader if one of them prevails.

"Begin," he roars. As usual, he doesn't provide any instruction, to suss out the naturally gifted from those who are not.

For the first time, I get to see everyone's Spirit. Well, almost everyone's. Bix summons one so small, none but Master Vane get a glimpse. Zev beckons a small beetle about the size of his hand. He looks displeased with his accomplishment, but it's the best he can do. Mabel conjures a pale blue fish that glides around her arm. It stretches from her wrist to her elbow, bigger than Zev's Spirit, but not by much. Enzo is the next to find success. He summons an elephant, about half his height, and beams proudly. I beckon Umi, and find that I cannot make him as large as when I faced off against the Fenrial or Pike, but I come close. He stands as tall as me, wings shielding me from the sun. Raven nods approvingly in my direction. Landon smirks smugly, and outdoes us all. A golden light flashes before him, solidifying into a tiger twice as tall as Umi. Black stripes streak across his golden-red fur, and he shimmers like a flickering flame.

Master Vane nods, impressed, then turns to Raven.

She is the last to go. Sheepishly, she holds up her hands, raw from a night of scrubbing dishes, and reveals a small black bird. A raven.

Vane sighs, a disappointed look on his face, and gestures to Landon. "Well, it appears..."

As he talks, I run up to Raven and whisper at her. "I know what you're doing."

She looks shocked, caught in something embarrassing. "I..."

"My little brother Kyle did the same thing in sixth grade. He was the best in the class in math. So good the other kids started teasing him. Nerd, they called him. Loser. And day by day, Kyle's math grade began to fall. Not because he was struggling with the subject matter. But because he was tired of being bullied. He let those little bastards get their way. Let them make him smaller, dumber. But I wouldn't have it. I told him he had every right to be the best at math in his class. I told him he had every right to be all he was." I pause. "Then I sat in for the next few classes, and I made sure Kyle answered all the questions I knew he could, and I made sure the other kids left him alone. And day by day, Kyle's math grade went up."

I grab Raven's hand and stare fiercely into her eyes. "You have every right to be all you are, Raven. Don't let those little bastards get their way. Don't let them make you small."

I let her go then, my breath heavy from the intensity of the moment.

Raven stares at her hand, at the bird symbol on her wrist. Then she looks up, eyes small but ferocious. She throws up her arms.

And in the sky a shadow forms, so large it blocks out the sun.

Landon gasps, gazing at the giant bird hovering above us. The others look on in awe. At the sharp claws that glint in the light. At the dark wings that beat like a heart.

Master Vane crosses his arms, grinning. He glances at me knowingly, then walks up to Raven and raises her arm in the air. "Listen closely, Ashlings. This is your leader!"

Everyone but Landon cheers.

MASTER VANE EXCUSES us early and says we may have the next three days to rest in honor of our leader. Raven and I are included in this, and excused from our punishment during this time. I hit the baths first, to wash away the muck and sweat, and by the time I return to our quarters, everyone is settled in and chatting, while Ashpaw runs around playing with a ball of yarn that wasn't there before.

"My sister is getting married tomorrow," says Mabel, as she brushes her thick red hair. "You're all welcome to come."

Landon, who still seems annoyed at losing, scoffs. "Your sister just happens to be getting married during the three days we have free?"

Mabel smacks his shoulder with the brush. "We have kept in touch with letters. I heard Ashlings got time off after getting a Squad leader. I thought the next few days might be free, and now I can confirm it. The wedding will happen, and I will get to see my sister as a bride, thank you very much."

She puts down her brush and walks over to me and Raven by the door. Her tone is softer now. "You two may come as well, if you'd like."

I glance at Raven, leaving it up to her.

"Fine," she says, shrugging. "Sounds interesting."

'Thank you," says Mabel, nodding quickly. "It will be an honor to have you there." Then she returns to her bed and starts braiding her hair. I wonder if that was an apology of sorts. It's not enough, but it is a start.

I head to my bed, excited to get a proper night's rest, when I see it. I point at the gray sack on my sheets. "What's that?" I ask.

Enzo glances at the bag. "It was here before, when we arrived."

"We thought it was yours," says Zev wearily.

I take a step forward and open the top of the sack with my hand. What lays inside makes my blood run cold. I turn away, vomiting onto the floor.

"What in all the worlds?" barks Landon, jumping to his feet.

I try to stop the retching. To stop the tears pouring down my face.

But I cannot control my sorrow, my rage, my fear. The emotions overwhelm me, making me their plaything.

When I have emptied my stomach, I collapse at the side of my bed, crying into the sheets. Someone touches me on the shoulder. It is Raven, her small hand a comforting feeling.

"What's wrong?" asks Mable, voice concerned.

I cannot speak. Because to say it will make it real, and it cannot be real. It cannot.

Landon steps forward and unfurls the bag, letting the contents spill out. "Oh," he says simply.

Zev sees the package and bends over, vomiting as I did. Mabel clutches her mouth, gasping, and Enzo shakes his head in disbelief, retreating back to his bed. Bix drops his gaze, eyes dark.

Sprawled over the bed is a pile of bones. They are delicate, brittle things, and little more than a handful. They are a child's bones. And with them lies a blue blanket. The blanket I used to wrap Kara in. The blanket she was swaddled in the night she was taken.

24

MEMORIES OF GRAY

I cry well into the night. At some point, I pass out from exhaustion. The next morning, I wake in the midday—because for once we have no training—and I take the little sack out into the courtyard and bury the bones under a pale white tree.

The rest of my squad follows me and watches as I dig a small hole in the snow with my bare hands, as I lay down the little bones and cover them with earth, as I clutch the blanket tightly to my heart.

As the tears fall down my cheeks.

My squad mates do not ask me questions, and for that I am grateful. Bix brings over a sword—I am not sure from where—and lies it near the grave. "So they may have protection in the world beyond," he says, by way of explanation. Mabel leans toward me and whispers the prayers of her people. Zev recites a passage from one of his books. *And so I return to the earth, my goodly home.* They do not know who I am burying, or why I truly grieve, but they have seen the bones of a child, and they share in my sadness.

I stay there for hours, my body numb to the cold. Skip warned me this would happen, but I did not believe it at first, and later I had forgotten— made myself forget, I think. But the truth has come to crush me once again, to reopen wounds that were just beginning to heal.

The others leave one by one. And for a fleeting moment I think of Kaden. I wish he was here. He alone would understand my pain.

Raven is the last to stay. She shows no signs of being affected by the cold, though I know she must be freezing. "These are the bones of your daughter, aren't they?"

I look up at her in surprise, but then remember I told her the truth of why I am here when she helped me pass the first test. I nod, the cracks in my heart deepening.

"She loved you," Raven says. "And if she had the chance to grow older and to know you better, I think she would have loved you even more." She takes my hand then, gently, and leads me back inside the fortress. I am grateful, for otherwise I may have never returned.

Mabel doesn't bring up the wedding again until the next day. "There will be drinks. People to dance with," she says with a beaten down sort of cheerfulness.

"I'll go," I say quickly, because I need to go, need to keep myself preoccupied and away from the dark thoughts that forever take up residence in my mind. The rest agree to go as well, and we pack that night. Zev asks me about the sack of bones and I confess a small part of the truth. Beneath that tree lies the remains of a loved one, and I don't know how their remains came to be here. As I lay in bed, the sorrow and heartache strong within me, Ashpaw crawls under the blankets next to me and snuggles against my chin. As he purrs, the sadness feels a little lighter, the guilt a little smaller, until finally I fall asleep.

WE LEAVE the next morning before the sun has risen, riding through the darkness carrying torches. Mabel and Landon lead the group, their heads bent together as they talk quietly, casting glances at Raven and me when they think we aren't looking, their expressions hidden in shadows.

Zev and Bix take the middle, and somehow Zev has managed to figure out how to ride while reading under torchlight. His horse seems to know what to do without much guidance from the distracted bookworm. Bix, on the other hand, is all present. His horse is huge, the size of a small house to accommodate his giant body, and he looks ready to gallop into battle rather than attend a country wedding.

We must seem an odd sight to any passerby, a mismatched band, all wearing our gray weathered training robes, fur cloaks draped over our shoulders to keep us warm. Wolf fur for most of us. Boxen fur for Bix, due to his size.

We left the snow and truest cold on the Cliff, but there's still a nip in the air this early in the morning. Our breath still turns to mist with each exhale.

I'm used to mornings such as these. Too early for rest of the world. Not just from Ash training, but from back home too. Fire shifts that last three or four days, with calls at all hours. Some of my favorite memories are being with my crew in the middle of the night, coming back to the station from a call where we helped someone. The streets empty, the sky full of stars. There's a place by the train tracks where you can see what Blake called the nightly Zombie apocalypse. Every night around midnight all the homeless would shuffle down the old train tracks like a mob of zombies. It was eerie, but also kind of beautiful in its way. I never knew where they were going, how coordinated it was, or if it was just their time to own the small California town without worry or harassment. We let them be, and they did their thing.

The world is a different beast at night. In some strange way, the fading of the sun and the light of moon and stars reveals more secrets than it hides, showing the shadow side of the world we live in. I've always preferred the night.

The sun has its perks, however, and as it rises, it brings warmth and brighter moods. The road we travel has begun to widen and become more populated with other travelers. One man, guiding a donkey and dressed in rags, spits at my horse as he passes by, fury in his eyes.

"What was that about?" I ask, as the man disappears behind us.

"Those of Ash are not well liked," Raven says. She rides to my right, her spine straight, her posture and form perfect. She looks as if she was born on a horse. She also looks pissed.

"The service we provide—that of slaying dragons past the Wall— is not one readily felt by most common folk," Raven says. "They blame us for their high taxes, disparage us for the goods they must send off to the Cliff."

I sigh. "That doesn't sound all that different from my job back home. People are only grateful for firefighters when they need us, but no one ever wants to *need* someone like us. And the funding is never there."

She raises an eyebrow at me. "And what crime did you commit to be placed in such a position?"

"Crime?" I shake my head, smiling. "No. I chose the work."

Her jaw drops. Eyes go wide. "You chose this *voluntarily*?"

"I did. I wanted a job where I could help people. And... " I pause, not sure how this will sound. "I've always been drawn to fires. There's something in the flames that calls to me."

She nods as if this is the most normal thing in the world to say, and then her mask returns, hiding her emotions. Once again I wonder... What must her life have been like to make her this hard so young? What happened to make her a Broken One?

I resolve to ask her, because though she can be hard to talk to, she's the closest thing I have to a friend here, and I think she needs me as much as I need her. "Raven, what—"

"There was, there was, a maiden most fair," Bix breaks out into song, his voice booming over my own. "And I did, I did, show her most care." No one else seems to know the words, but this doesn't stop the big man from fluctuating off key at the top of his lungs in a jagged rhythm that makes me smile despite myself. Soon enough, we're all clapping along, roaring out a word here and there. And my talk with Raven is forgotten.

Midday, and after more songs than I can keep track of, we arrive in town, but the excitement in our group is not diminished by the long and dusty ride. My body has toughened up since this training began. I thought I was in decent shape as a firefighter. After all, we have to wear fifty-pound gear while battling infernos on a regular basis. But this is a whole other level. Hours and hours, day after day, training all day, studying all night, rinse and repeat. It's nice to have a break.

The village is small, so small I can see where it begins and ends from where I sit. The houses are almost all one story, never more than two, their roofs covered in hay, or rarely, tile. The streets are nothing more than mud. The people side-eye us with suspicious glances as they go about their day, trading goods, sewing fishing nets, tending pigs. When one of the women notices Mabel, her face softens. "It can't be... Mabel? Is it really you?"

Mabel hops off her horse and wraps the old woman in a hug. "You didn't think I'd miss my own sister's wedding now, did you, Aunt Mary?"

Aunt Mary smiles at her niece, then looks around, cheeks red, as if caught in some scandal. "Not everyone here be glad to see you again, you hear?" she says quietly. "Best keep an eye out. Folk can be rough to your... your—"

"My kind," says Mabel, sighing, eyes heavy. "Don't worry Aunt Mary. If there's one advantage to being my kind, it's that I'll be safe."

Aunt Mary nods, though she looks no more at ease. She glances curiously over Mabel's shoulder at the rest of us. "Are these your friends?"

"My squad," corrects Mabel. For some reason, she seems sad to say it. Slowly, she turns to us, gesturing at her aunt, and makes the introductions. We each dismount and walk over to say hello. Most of us stick to a polite handshake. Bix grabs the woman in a huge hug and lifts her off the ground. I swear, she's about to break in half, but she just laughs, patting Bix on the shoulder, and he puts her down, beaming.

"Where you be staying?" asks Aunt Mary.

"The Mudpie," says Mabel.

The Mudpie, it turns out, is the filthiest inn in town and looks like something you might find on the bottom of your shoe. It's tiny, rundown, and I can smell the rot and piss well before we arrive.

Mabel guides us around the inn to a barn where a boy no older than ten takes charge of our horses and promises to brush them down and feed and water them. I'm reluctant to hand over Moon to him, but he wins her over quickly with a clump of sugar from his pocket and then smiles a toothless grin at me. "She sure is a pretty one," he says with a rough accent.

I introduce them and then follow my squad through broken wooden doors. The smell hits me even harder, and I can't figure out if it's human waste or what passes for food. Either way, I think I'll be fasting while I'm here.

Mabel finds the innkeeper, a large woman with a hunched back and thin gray hair. She's called Old Granich by her customers, and Raven walks up to negotiate our rooms. As squad leader, she has the money and is in charge, which draws a few curious looks at such a young girl leading a group of Ashlings.

We divide into two rooms, with the men in one and women in another, at the insistence of the Old Granich, never mind that we all share sleeping quarters at the Cliff. As we walk up rickety steps, I lean to Mabel and whisper. "Is there nowhere else we can stay? This place... "

"All the other inns are full for the wedding and apparently have refused to host 'our kind'," she says with no small amount of disgust. "As it is we had to pay higher prices for this gem of a place. Despite her high morals, Old Granich is the only one in town who can be bought."

This response to our *kind* is not one I felt while traveling with Kaden. Perhaps it is because he is the Darkflame, the hero of Al'Kalesh, while we are untested Ash who do nothing but train and drain resources.

Our room is tiny, with three sketchy looking mats on a dirt-packed floor and a dusty washbasin and pitcher on a lone table. The water in the basin has clearly been used by others, and has bits of I don't know what floating in it.

Mabel sniffs her nose in disgust, gritting her jaw. "If they only knew what we have to endure for their ungrateful hides. I used to be considered family here, and now, it's like I'm some dirty northerner come to steal their food, or worse." She glances apologetically at Bix in the hallway. "No offense."

He just shrugs, as if to say he understands.

Raven closes the door, and we all change our clothing in silence. I'd been looking forward to a bath, but realize quickly that I've no chance of becoming clean in this place, so I use my cloak to slough off as much dirt and dust as I can before putting on my nice clothes.

After training began, we were given an allowance to buy some personal supplies and clothing at the Dragoncliff market for wearing to events like this. I bought a simple dress made in cerulean blue with white beads around the neckline. It compliments my eyes and my figure and is a welcome change from the Ashling robes I haven't taken off since training began, except to bathe of course.

We join the men downstairs, and I note the differences in each of their clothing preferences. Landon is, not surprisingly, dressed like a nobleman, in velvet and satin and gold. Bix, I'm guessing, is wearing something his people consider appropriate for a wedding, but to my untrained eye still looks like something you'd wear to raid a village: steel bracers, leather pants, nothing to cover his chest, and his Boxen fur to cover his head and back. Enzo, despite being less dressed up than Landon, is perhaps the most dashing of the group, and I catch Mabel glancing at him, probably agreeing. His red vest and white cloak look made for him, like a second skin, complimenting rather than distracting from his handsome face and striking complexion. Zev, the smallest of the men, appears very formal in his black robes, as if he's left one type of school for another. As we study the men, they too study us.

Mabel is dressed plainly, in a green gown tied at the back with yellow lace. I had expected her to be more like Landon, more regal and lavish, after seeing them conspire, but I realize I was wrong about her. She is no noble's daughter, but a peasant girl who grew up in this mucky town, probably struggling to survive even worse than I struggled in Ukiah.

And Raven, well, she chose to keep her robes on. Come to think of it, I never saw her buy other clothes.

We march out of the inn in a line and head down the street, to the center of the village where the wedding will take place. The entire town comes alive in anticipation for the celebration, hanging colorful banners on ropes between buildings, setting up games and large tents. Ribbons adorn nearly every post, chair and table, woven together with purple flowers, casting a sweet scent that almost covers up the smell of horse dung and body sweat. And while most of the adults prepare, the children play in the mud laughing and giggling, and a woman with long golden hair sits on a stool positioned on a wooden stage, playing a lyre and singing in a language I don't understand, her voice bright and haunting and beautiful. While people greet each other with warm handshakes, hugs and laughter, our squad is given a wide berth. Even without our robes, it's clear we are outsiders.

Our squad doesn't stay together for long. Landon and Mabel leave with each other, likely to find her sister and soon-to-be brother-in-law. Bix joins a group of men and one woman who are competing with bows and arrows. The prize looks to be the kiss of a beautiful woman.

Raven stays with me, and we follow the sound of squeaking until we find a group of kids chasing pigs in the mud. We watch for a moment at a safe distance from the flying dirt.

Zev walks up behind us, a book tucked under his arm. "Whoever catches a pig first gets to keep it. That will feed a family for a month. Each sends their fastest child to compete. It's a great honor."

Before long, bells ring, and everyone gathers in the center to see the couple wed. The music changes to something slower, more ... ethereal, and the bride and groom walk down a path of flowers. Long purple robes embroidered with golden leaves fall from their shoulders, and wreaths of garland rest on their heads. They look happy, more than happy even, as if all their dreams are coming true.

It is a happiness I will never possess.

Not since I lost Kara. Not since I left Caleb and Kyle and Blake.

I could have had it though, in another life. If Pat had never made that deal. I could have raised Kara and my siblings, and maybe I could have met a man. Someone gentle and kind. Someone like Kaden, perhaps, but simpler. A doctor, or a teacher. And together we could have been happy. Together, we could have this wedding, or one much like it, surrounded by our families and loved ones.

But it will not be.

It cannot be.

My loved ones are gone. And even marriage is forbidden for my kind—too keep us focused on our sacred duty, they say.

The ceremony, conducted by the eldest woman and man from each family, is brief. The young couple vows to protect, love and guide each other, in this life and the next. Then a red ribbon is pulled from the bride's hair and wrapped around their wrists, and the crowd cheers.

Friends and family stand in line to greet the couple, and I see Mabel walk up and hug her sister, who she calls Avelyn. They share the same red hair and freckled skin, but Mabel's sister is older, face happier, but also wearier. They exchange a few words I cannot hear, and then the music changes, and the dancing beings.

The newlyweds do not dance first, as they would in my culture. Instead, it is the elders, the ones who performed the ceremony, that begin to the cheers and merriment of all. Others join in soon, and somewhere a bar opens, and I see people sharing cups of mead and glasses of something sparkly. Mabel stays close to her sister while dancing with Aunt Mary. Landon dances off to the side with a pretty young blonde, while Bix enters a wrestling match in the mud. The other villagers look at him with distaste, then admiration as he wins round after round, as Raven and I watch from afar, Zev standing with us. I think he likes being able to expound on his knowledge of culture and history to someone who knows so little of this world. I don't mind, and in fact appreciate his tidbits of information, as I feel woefully out of sorts here.

Enzo is nowhere to be seen.

At first, I think he has found somewhere private, then I realize he is at the bar, head down, hand curled around a mug of ale. His face is somber, his eyes glossy. I join him at his table, leaving Raven and Zev to watch the festivities. While other tables are full, ours, of course, is not. I order a drink for myself, and sip the thick ale slowly. "Why so gloomy?" I ask, after a moment, my tone light.

"Weddings are hard," he says with his thick French accent. I can see him searching for the right words. "They bring to mind memories, gray ones. They are like... " he pauses, searching. "Like sweet and bitter at once. I can't decide if I want to remember or forget. *Tu comprende?*"

"Yes." I take another sip of ale, trying to drown out my own memories. "If you forget, you kill a piece of yourself, but if you remember, you die all over again."

He nods. "*Exactemont.*" He goes quiet for a while, then speaks softly. "I was married once. Before." He pauses. "It is harder than I thought, being here, at a wedding. Remembering my own. Remembering her. We were married a year when we had our first child. A girl. The sweetest thing." He looks up then, and smiles through tears. "She was getting her first tooth in when it happened. We were driving her around late at night to help her sleep. She liked the lull of the engine. But we had to stop for gas. It wasn't a good part of Paris, but I didn't notice until it was too late. A man came at me with a knife. Wanted to rob me. I would have given him everything. I cared not for those things, but then he saw my wife. She was beautiful. Young. And then he wanted her."

Before I came to this world, I would have cried at his story. Now, I do not cry, but I do feel the sadness bubbling within me, threatening to spill out. I take a deep breath and reach for his free hand and hold it as he continues.

"I fought him, and the knife slid into my... " he cocks his head. "How you say? Belly?" He pats his stomach with his drink.

"Yes, belly. Stomach. Abdomen." I give him the English words, my voice cracking.

He continues. "The pain, it lit something up in me. And then... " He closes his eyes again, and pulls his hand away. He takes another drink and a sob breaks inside him. "There was fire. It blew up the tanks. It blew up my little family."

I gasp, imagining what would have happened if I hadn't gone with Kaden, if I lost control, if I killed Kyle and Caleb. I do not think I could live with such grief, but somehow Enzo does.

"I alone survived," he says, finally. "The authorities, they say it was accident. I was not punished for my murders. But when they came for me, when they told me what I had become, I knew I had no choice but to leave. I could not be around people. The day the Ashknights came for me I was... how you say?" He feigns slitting his own throat.

"Suicidal." I say softly.

He nods. "I couldn't live with what I had done. But the Ashknights, they gave me another way. I can fight for others. I can try to... atone."

I say nothing, because there is nothing that will make this easier, nothing that will stop the pain in his heart. Instead, I put my arm around his shoulders and let him cry as I sit with him. Sometimes, there are no words left. Sometimes, the best you can do for someone is stay with their sorrow.

After a time, he stands, his tears dry, his face a little less sad. "I wish to sleep now. You have been a kind friend, Sky Knightly. Go, enjoy the rest of your—"

He freezes, eyes looking past me.

A woman screams from behind.

I turn, trying to figure out what is wrong. It is not difficult.

Three massive black stallions charge through the center of the village, carrying *things* with spikes and tails and tattoos and no eyes.

Shadows.

And I know the one in the front.

Sylus.

25

SPIRITS

The music stops. The villagers freeze. "Well, well. We have stumbled upon a wedding," says Sylus, his forked tongue tasting the air. "And here I thought this town had nothing to offer but some bedding and ale. What luck!"

Avelyn, Mabel's sister, steps forward. "We don't want any trouble here," she says. "You're welcome to the best rooms at the best inns. But please leave us to celebrate with family."

Sylus laughs, and it is filled with a cold malice. "Are we, servants of the Emperor, may he never burn, not entitled to enjoy the festivities as well? To partake in the local customs of the people we defend?"

Avelyn lowers her eyes. "Of course. Please enjoy."

The three Shadows chuckle and dismount. The one with large horns stalks over to the archery range and forces a kiss from the woman offering one to the victor. He does not compete, and he does not stop at a kiss as he gropes her breasts while the nearby villagers watch helplessly. The third Shadow, the smallest, jumps into the pigpen and, with his unnatural speed, catches the largest pig in an instant. He lifts it up over his head, then slices open its belly with his claws and laughs as the guts spill out at his feet. Sylus grabs Avelyn by the waist and spins her around. "My turn for a dance, love," he hisses.

Aunt Mary frowns, but doesn't object. No one will, if they had anything to lose.

But I have nothing left to lose. Not anymore.

I step forward, about to intervene, when Landon jumps in front of Sylus and transmutes his hand into a golden claw. "Step away from her now," he says, voice quiet and tense.

Sylus does not let go, and his accomplices come to his side. "Think you can fight three Shadows on your own, boy?" asks Sylus.

"You don't recognize my voice, do you?" asks Landon, grinning.

Sylus tilts his head, then finally let's go of Avelyn, turning his body to face the Ashling. "Ah, I do know you. Landon, once of the House of Lioncrest. How does it feel to not only lose your family name but also your betrothed? I look forward to the day I get to bed such a sweet young thing. Do you think she likes it rough? I certainly hope so, for her sake."

Landon glares at Sylus, and I can see his tiger Spirit pulsing within him, fighting to be free, to destroy the enemy they face, but Landon maintains control, vein throbbing on his neck.

It is quiet, everything silent except for the breeze that thrashes around Landon's golden cape and his dirty blond hair as all eyes are fixed on the Ashling and the Shadow. As all are still.

All except me.

I walk forward until I stand beside Landon, and I transmute my hand into a silver dragon claw. Despite our problems, I need Landon to know he is not alone in this. That I am on his side.

The Shadow smiles, noticing me for the first time.

But then Mabel joins us, hand turning into a gray dagger, and his smile fades a little. Then Bix walks up behind us, body transforming, turning into a hard emerald shell of armor, and Zev and Raven both join us, using Spirit to transmute parts of their bodies into weapons. Even Enzo—the sorrow swept from his face and now replaced with anger—joins us, his hand now a tusk.

And the Shadow smiles no longer.

"You know," says Landon. "I heard a most interesting rumor back at court, and if it were true... well... I wonder... " he says, pausing to ponder. "What would happen if the Emperor, may he never burn, discovered you've been collecting extra taxes using his name and keeping them for yourself? It would be interesting to find out, don't you think?"

Sylus clenches his jaw, flexing his hand over and over. He looks ready to pounce, but then his head moves, and he seems to notice the rest of us again, and his body goes slack. "Come, my brothers," he yells to his comrades. "This party has grown stale, and we have better places to be."

Without further words, they mount their giant black horses, and ride out of the village. When they are fully gone we drop our transmutations, and only then do the villagers seem to sigh collectively and move once again. They rush up to us, and for a moment I fear they will attack us for spoiling their party, but instead they clasp our shoulders and shake our hands. Avelyn hugs me, then Landon, then the rest of us. They ply us with mead and food, with candied apples and buttered breads and freshly roasted meats, with the honey pies and sweet cakes they had hidden in their kitchens. Before, we were outcasts, but now we are heroes.

Bix eats his body weight and drinks twice that and dances with the largest woman I've ever seen, and we help the butcher properly store the pig's meat that must be used before it goes bad.

I sip at my drink and wander about, lost in my own thoughts. This world is so unlike my own. Different in every way you can imagine. But at the core, we all want love, happiness, connection, and moments of unfiltered joy. We all want to live in a just world of fairness and truth.

Well, most of us do.

And then there are people like Sylus. Like Pike. Who see other people not as equals, but as things to be used for their own pleasure and needs. When will it change? *Can* it change? I do not know, and I don't think I will ever find out.

When I realize my cup is empty I find the open bar and see

Landon sitting there, nursing his own mug. My first instinct is to go somewhere else, but then I remember how Landon stood up for Avelyn, and I remember my goal of trying to bring this squad together, so I take a seat next to him and ask for a refill.

He doesn't say anything, so I break the silence. "I don't get you," I say, sipping the ale. "One moment you're complaining about being an Ashling and treating the rest of us as if we're beneath you, the next you're standing up to a Shadow for some people you hardly know. It doesn't make sense."

"I..." he sighs. "I don't think you're beneath me. It's just..." He sighs again. "It's complicated."

"What isn't?"

He nods, but doesn't reply.

And I decide to share something personal with him first, in hopes that he will open himself to me. "The bones I buried," I say quietly. "They were my daughter's."

He blinks. "I'm sorry."

I pat his arm gently. "If you really want to help, how about you distract me and tell me this complicated thing. We have time... for once."

He chews on his bottom lip, then nods, and begins in earnest. "I never liked being a Lord's son," he says, speech slightly slurred from drink. "There were perks, of course. Private lessons from the best tutors, servants tending to my ever need, the best food, wine and clothing. A private stable full of horses, and a beautiful manor to call home. But as I got older, I began to see through the facade of splendor." He glances up at me to see if I'm still listening.

I am, and he continues.

"I saw how the servants were beaten if they ever made mistakes. I saw how their only real choice was to work for my house or starve to death. I saw the mistresses my father took—some willing, some too fearful to say no, and I saw how it affected my mother. How she began to drink more and more. How she became crueler to all those around her, even her children. It corrupted her, broke her. And in her anger, she would beat the servant boy whenever her own children had done wrong. She would make her children watch as the boy's back ran bloody at the flick of a whip."

I shiver at his tale, and notice how he distances himself from it even now, in his language and the way he tells the story.

"I began to hate my life. Even the privilege felt like a prison. And I could never change anything. My mother and father were immortal, after all. Unless one of them was murdered, I would never rule our house. The only thing I had... was her. My Meredith."

When he says her name, his voice breaks, and he pauses, taking a deep breath before continuing. "I knew I would be married off to whoever was most beneficial for my family's alliances. I had resigned myself to a loveless marriage. But the fate's blessed me, or so I thought. The girl my family chose was my soul mate in every way. She was beautiful, of course, but I cared little about that. She had a kind heart, and that was where her true beauty lived. And she was clever and shared my vision for what the future could be, if we ever started our own house. Then we could end the cycle of beatings, abuse, and cruelty that ruled my life."

I picture it, the happiness he must have felt being betrothed to someone he actually loved who loved him back, and then I remember the snide comment Sylus made about bedding someone, and I grit my teeth.

Landon continues. "Then, the fire happened. My mother, in a drunken rage, had set flames to my father's quarters while he and a lover were inside. She wanted them to burn, not caring for anyone else caught in the building. When I returned to the manor from a day of hunting with friends, I saw it ablaze. It lit up the sky like something unnatural, and turned a cold day hot.

"I rushed in, saving all I could find. My servant, Arbal, who taught me cards and wisdom and who I considered one of my mentors. The stable boy, Pettin, who always took extra care of my horses. The handmaiden, Mira, who treated my mother and father with such kindness, despite the treatment they gave her. I got them all out in time. Our guards had already saved mother and father first, of course, and it seemed all had been rescued." He pauses, taking another drink, his hand shaking now.

"But then I heard the scream. Someone was still in the manor. I rushed in again, but before I could reach whoever was still trapped, the roof collapsed on me, and all went dark. I awoke later. The guards had pulled me from the fire, but left the young boy still trapped to die. They didn't even try to save him. All that mattered was the Lord's son was safe." Landon looks at me with swollen red eyes. "He died because of me. Because my name was 'better' than his."

He's silent for a moment, and the bartender refills both of our drinks before he continues. "It took weeks for me to recover. But even that was too quick for all my injuries. It was a miracle. That's when I learned I'd become a Broken One. The Ashlords came for me, and I had two choices. Disinherit my family name, give up my right to marry, and join the Cliff, or die by their hands." He laughs, but it's empty of mirth. "It seemed no choice at all. And so I'm here. My hope of making a difference stolen from me, and the love of my life betrothed to someone else. I shouldn't be so surprised, really. This world has a way of crushing anything good."

We are both quiet for some time. I always assumed Landon hated the Cliff because it lacked the comforts he was accustomed to, but of course, it wasn't so simple. Too often we judge people by our own standards and preconceptions and miss the truth of the thing entirely.

I take another drink. And another.

And then a quiet voice speaks from behind us. Raven. "Is that when you found your Spirit, Landon," she asks? "In the fire?" She's been standing behind us, it seems, listening the whole time.

I worry Landon will be mad, but instead he nods, lips curling in a half smile.

"What do you call him?" she asks.

And then the smile becomes full, his face relaxing for the first time in our conversation, and a golden shimmer appears on his shoulder. It solidifies into a cat... a small golden tiger with black stripes. "I call him Rako, after the boy who died," says Landon, stroking the feline under the chin. The purr is so loud, it draws the attention of others, and then Bix, Zev, Enzo, and Mabel join us at the table, looking at Rako eagerly. Raven sits down as well, and the little tiger then jumps onto the table and walks around, brushing past me as he explores everyone's drinks.

Raven holds out her hand, and on it appears a little black bird. A raven, like her, and I wonder if it's a coincidence, or if she had a different name before getting her Spirit.

"She is Muninn," Raven says. "Like the old stories."

Rako hisses at the bird, but Muninn seems unimpressed and climbs Raven's arm to perch on her shoulder and preen her feathers, as if she hasn't a care in the world.

Landon nods. "Thank you for sharing her. And... " He looks down, but then forces his eyes back up to meet Raven's. "I'm sorry. For what I did. It was cruel and unnecessary."

Raven's face is expressionless, and everyone at the table seems to hold their breath as we wait for her response. Eventually, she blinks and a small smile appears on her usually solemn face. "It's forgiven."

Mabel speaks up then, her face contrite. "I apologize as well. I let my temper get the better of me, just as my pa always warned me about. I should never have done that."

"Thank you," Raven says. "Apology accepted."

A look of relief flickers over Mabel's face, and then she smiles more brightly and holds up her arm. A blue fish appears above it, as if made of water, swirling around her hand. "This is Mako. He's a fierce little beast."

My eyes widen. "Is he floating in real water?"

She holds her arm out to me. "Feel it."

I tentatively reach my hand across the table and touch the fish. He's solid, with the scales you'd expect on any fish, and the water he dances in is wet and cool. He flips his tail and dives around Mabel's arm, defying gravity, and then the bird notices the fish, and the tiger stares at them both and licks his lips. Fortunately, they seem to be keeping their distance from each other.

All eyes turn to Zev next, who sits beside Mabel.

He sighs and rolls his eyes, closing the book he was reading while we talked. "I suppose I'll go next. This is Zip." He holds his hand open and a large gray beetle materializes on his palm. It has little pincers on its head and intricate designs etched onto its exoskeleton. It reminds me of the Scabrial Kaden once spoke of, and I ask Zev if that is the term for his Spirit, and he says it is, for once impressed by my knowledge.

Enzo is next, and he winks at us before lifting his goblet out of the way and clearing the space before him. I wonder why, until his Spirit appears with a loud thump that shakes the table and spills all of our drinks.

"By fire, a little warning next time?" Zev says as his beetle sloshes about in spilled ale next to the small elephant on the table. Well, small is a relative term. It takes up a good bit of the table, but for its species it is absolutely mini. It's gray, and completely adorable, and when it raises its tiny trunk and lets out a loud trumpet, causing many to turn and stare at our squad, Enzo beams and scratches his Spirit on the head. "This is Penelope. She's a dear."

"Just keep her away from Zip," Zev says grumpily.

Zip, on the other hand, seems just as charmed by Penelope as the rest of us, and buzzes over to her, landing on her back. The elephant doesn't seem to mind, and walks over to the spilled ale, taking some up in its trunk, then spraying it around the table. Zev shrieks and I can't help but laugh.

My laughing dies out fast though, when all eyes turn to me, and I realize they're expecting me to show *my* Spirit. I beckon Umi and he appears on my shoulder, his silver scales shining in the moonlight. He is inexplicably sleepy and yawns loudly, before hopping down and mingling with the other Spirits. "His name is Umi," I say, as he nibbles on Landon's finger playfully.

Next, all eyes turn to Bix. He shrugs and says, "Maybe later."

"Do you wish for guidance to summon your Spirit?" Raven asks practically.

"No," the big guy admits, his face turning slightly red. "It is just... my people do not believe as others. While all of you came here after tragedy, after being forced out of your homes, I came here of my own will."

There's a shocked silence as everyone stares. Mabel's mouth drops open. "What do you mean?" she asks.

"We follow the old ways," he says. "Amongst my people it is an honor to become Twin Spirit. We are not Broken Ones. We are made whole by our Spirit. It is those without Spirit who are incomplete. At the age of twelve, under a new moon, boys and girls who have been chosen for their bravery are sent into the Dark Forest with no supplies and only the animal skins they wear on their backs. They are told to return under the light of the full moon, not before. Those who return with Twin Spirits have honored the ancestors. Those who have not try again the next year, and the next, until they too pass our ancestor's test. And then there are those who never return." He pauses, a flash of grief crossing his face before his stoic expression returns. "It took me longer than anyone else in my tribe to become a Twin Spirit. Too long, the village elders said, and my Spirit... it is not an honorable one because of my weakness."

Landon scoffs. "Your Spirit is a part of you. I see nothing dishonorable about that."

"I agree," Mabel says. "You have nothing to be ashamed of."

"They're right," I say, amazed that I'm agreeing with Mabel and Landon for once, and Enzo, Zev and Raven all nod their heads as well.

Bix's face turns redder than ever, and he cups his hands together as if holding a small egg between his palms. "All right, then." He moves one hand away and reveals a tiny little turtle smaller than his fingers. "Meet Gaf the Mighty." Bix looks at the tiny creature adoringly, then pulls something out of his pocket and holds it up to the turtle. "He really likes it if you feed him chestnuts," the big man explains.

"He's so cute!" I say.

"He's adorable," says Mable, as we all gather closer to admire Gaf.

Bix looks at us all sheepishly. I've never seen him so insecure. "You think he is... fine?"

"I think he's wonderful," I say honestly. The others nod as well.

And finally, Bix smiles. "Gaf the Mighty likes you, Sky of the Knightly clan. He says you may pet him."

I rub my index finger under the turtle's chin, and he nudges against me and makes a little chirping sound.

The others beg for a chance to pet Gaf too, and it isn't long before Bix has to pour himself another drink. And another.

Eventually the bar closes and the party ends, and we make our way through the quiet streets to our rooms. And as we walk, I smile. Because for the first time, I think I may actually be able to find some happiness in this strange new world.

26

WALL OF LIGHT

Our break is short-lived. We head back to the Cliff the next day, after a restful sleep in a very comfortable inn, where we each enjoy private rooms, private baths and beds that feel majestic.

It's a bitter pill to swallow, returning to training again, but there's a lightness to our group that didn't exist before. The journey home is full of talking, laughing, sharing stories and training tips. Our squad is finally becoming what I'd imagined when I first arrived.

Family. Of a sort.

We have some free time when we return, and I use it to study more of the books I've borrowed from the library. Somewhere, someone must have written something that gives me a clue as to Pike's whereabouts. Somewhere there must be information that can help me end his reign of tyranny over people's lives. My research lasts late into the night.

That proves a mistake, as I am jolted awake pre-dawn by the bellowing voice of Master Vane.

"Move it," he orders, as my squad-mates wake reluctantly, dressing slowly. It's easier for me. My time in the fire department got me used to waking for midnight calls, dressing and moving fast, so I'm ready first, though Raven is a close second and shows no signs of the sleepiness the others exhibit.

Once again I wonder what kind of life this teen girl has had that this is her norm.

"What's going on?" Landon asks.

"I just received word from the Wall," Vane says. "We have a special training opportunity today, but only if you move fast, Ashlings. Dragons wait for no one."

My heart skips a beat at the word dragons. We're surrounded by their lore, here on the Cliff, and people talk as if they are as real as dogs or cats, but I have yet to see one beyond my own Spirit and Kaden's. And even that was shocking. Dragons! I live in a world where dragons exist. It's electrifying.

He marches out the door, his wolf at his heel, and we follow him down to the stables. "Think we're going to the Wall then?" Enzo asks. His French accent is always thicker when he's tired or drinking, I've noticed.

"Seems so."

He frowns. "But we've hardly any training. Isn't that dangerous?"

Before I can respond, Vane bellows another order to hurry our asses, speeding past on his giant brown horse, his white wolf howling into the dark morning at his side.

I nuzzle Moon, running a hand over the black star on her head, the only mark on her sleek white body, and then mount her and guide her toward the trail.

This isn't a leisurely ride, and my thighs ache as we grow closer to the Wall. A shimmering blue light fills the sky, like shining, iridescent colored glass against the darkness. Before us there is a stone arch that forms a partial circle creating a break in the Wall. Like a gateway. Glyphs that look like High Dracus line the edge, and at the top is carved a crude drawing of a dragon eye. From the center hangs a large blue-purple gem shaped like the iris of an eye that shoots beams of blue and purple light.

And in front of the Wall stands a row of people chained to each other by the waist. About two dozen women and men have gathered, and they block our way. But they are not dressed as warriors. More like priests, in long robes of black with purple tippets that hang down like scarves, similar to the stoles of Catholic priests on my world.

"Why are they blocking us?" I ask no one in particular, but I'm not surprised when Zev answers.

"They're Wall Worshipers. They believe the Wall of Light wasn't erected to keep dragons contained, but to protect them."

"Protect them from what?" I'm trying to imagine what's more dangerous than a thunder of dragons.

His lips curl into a sardonic grin. "From us."

I raise an eyebrow at that.

"It's absurd of course. Dragons are inexplicably strong and fast. Without the Wall on our side, they'd destroy humanity in mere weeks. It's highly improbable that whoever built the Wall did so to protect *them* from *us.*"

"What do you mean, whoever?" I ask. "I thought Nir created the wall."

"That's the most popular story, of course," Zev says. "But I don't believe it. Elder Dragons are just a myth invented to appease simple minds." He shakes his head and locks of dark hair fall into his eyes that he brushes away distractedly.

"So if he didn't create it, who did?"

He shrugs, and I see others listening to him as well. It seems I'm not the only one curious about the history of this place.

"No one knows for certain," he says. "The Wall Worshippers believe the story of Nir and the Elder Dragons. Personally, I think the High Dragons banded together to erect the wall. They had great power and many soldiers under their control. Of course, they spent most of their time fighting each other for control of the lands, but I imagine back in ancient times, when the Elder Dragons ruled all the lands, the High Dragons could have banded together to overthrow their gods. With their combined power they could have created the wall. Unfortunately, whatever that power was, it's lost now. There are no High Dragons left after the Rising."

"Turn back," says a man with a purple pointed hat and a beard threaded with silver. He stands in the center of the blockade and the group defers to him. "Turn back before you desecrate the sacred light once more."

Landon scoffs. "Let us through, priest. Without Ashknights defending the wall, you and all your kind would be dead. All of us would. Killed by your precious gods."

The man frowns, but does not back down. "You know not of what you speak, but the gods forgive you. The truth comes to us all in due time."

Landon looks around nervously, wondering what he should do. It's the thought on everyone's mind.

Vane jumps down from his horse and walks toward the priests, his wolf, as always, at his heel.

They look frightened of Vane, but they don't abandon their positions. "Turn back, defiler, lest the wrath of the gods curse you and turn you to ash where you stand. We are prepared to die for our gods. Are you truly prepared to harm those who do not bare arms against you? Would you sacrifice the lives of unarmed men and women for our beliefs?"

Vane walks up to the old man and grabs him by his chains. "Move."

"No!" he screams.

The others begin chanting in an ancient language, their voices carrying far and wide. Somewhere beyond the wall I hear an inhuman screech. Was that a dragon? Umi crouches around my neck at the sound.

"I will stand strong," the priest says. "I will—"

Vane pulls on the chains, yanking the entire group to the side as if they were dolls strung together. A few collapse to the ground, but none seem seriously injured, and the Wall is no longer blocked from our passage.

"Just how strong is he?" I whisper.

"Some say he has the strength of ten men," Mabel says, her eyes glued to the muscular man, her lips parted slightly. "Others say a hundred."

Zev scoffs. "Unlikely."

Mabel doesn't seem to hear Zev, or the disdain in his voice. "They say Master Vane's not from this world, but came here once to train and now returns on occasion to teach. Mark my words, this is only a taste of what a Twin Spirit can accomplish." There's a glow to her eyes as she speaks, and I wonder if she's dreaming of power, or just dreaming of Master Vane's muscles. Probably both.

To the side of the Wall, the head priest struggles to stand with the support of two of his followers and then leads his people back to their protest position, but Vane steps on a link of the chain, holding him and the entire group back. "Ashlings, forward," he says, gesturing to the circle of stone.

Once we ride up to the gate, Vane catches up on horseback and motions to a man and woman positioned by the archway next to a giant stone wheel. They nod simultaneously and clasp handles on the wheel, then turn. The stone moves the chain that holds the purple crystal, and it begins to rise, pulling it so high that it disappears within the ring of stone and the light it casts out disappears with it. This has created an opening under the archway, allowing people to pass. As we ride through, I move my horse to the side, where Vane waits, watching us pass. "Can we touch the light?" I ask.

He nods. "Go ahead, Ashling."

I reach out my hand towards the glowing iridescent blue wall, and when my skin connects with it, it pushes back, like a wave of wind charged with static. My fingers feel weak and my head fuzzy as the energy of the Wall pulses through me.

Landon, who stopped to watch, grabs my arms and pulls it away. "You okay?"

I nod, feeling better now that I'm no longer touching it.

Vane glances at me. "The Wall of Light blocks Spirits as well as flesh from passing. That is why there are no Spirits, Pure or Corrupted, within these walls, save the ones we bring within us." He rides on and we follow.

Zev and Landon ride on either side of me and Zev shares more of his book knowledge. "Dragons who absorb Spirits grow in strength and Spirit. That is why the Wall keeps them weaker."

"It seems to make Twin Spirits like us weaker as well," I say. "At least while we're touching the light."

He nods.

Vane leads us deeper into the Ashlands. "When you become Ashknights, it will be your duty to defend this wall. Your entire training will be dedicated to preparing you for this task. Today you will watch and observe only. Mind the women and men you see today. They are what you are trying to become. Ask them any questions you may have, but do not waste their time with nonsense or distract them during critical moments."

There will be critical moments? The full weight of where we are hits me at once. We're in dragon territory now.

My palms sweat as we pass a stone tower with a pyre of wood at the top.

"That's one of the watchtowers," Vane says. "It is guarded at all times and lit if dragons are spotted near the wall, warning those at the gates."

The pyre of wood is burning an orange and red blaze high into the sky.

Dragons are near.

We ride on, traveling a dirt path that seems to be made from horses stomping over it time and time again.

We still have no sun by the time we reach our destination, and I wonder how early—or rather late—we left. We must not have gotten more than an hour or two of sleep. I see Zev yawn and Mabel's eyelids flutter from exhaustion.

But all signs of sleep deprevation vanish quickly when Vane moves us forward to see what we've been brought here for. We have arrived at one of the outposts, and two large wagons sit, tethered to several massive Boxen.

One wagon carries supplies, and the other carries a ballista.

Three Ashknights sit on the wagons in dark cloaks with spears at their sides.

Vane leads us to a huge pit dug into the earth. We dismount our horses and lean in to see what is trapped there.

My breath catches in my throat and I can't stop staring at the creature below. It's the size of a small house and is screeching so loud it's almost deafening. It has reptilian wings and is clawing at the sides of the caves. Its body glows with scales that look like gemstones. More specifically, like dragonstone.

"This is a Hatchling," Vane says. "Or what you might know as a baby dragon."

27

HATCHLING

I stare, wide-eyed, and I can see I'm not the only one of my squad mates who is in awe. But it's Enzo and I who are most stunned by this. With everything that has happened... losing my baby, dying, getting a dragon Spirit, even seeing Kaden transform, I realize I still haven't fully processed that all this is real. That this is a world with dragons. I grew up on a world that doesn't have dragons. That doesn't believe they exist. Dragons were myth. Fairytales. Fantasies. But here, right here in front of my own eyes, is a dragon. A real, living, breathing dragon. Not a Spirit. Not a shape-shifting human. A full on fire-breathing dragon.

And if this giant beast is a baby, I don't know that I want to meet its mother.

"It's huge," Mabel says. "How'd you catch it?"

"And can't it fly out?" I ask.

"Dragons can't fly until they reach full maturity," Vane says. "The young ones are easier to hunt and harvest. We dig a large, deep pit, like this one, then build a patch over it out of thin wood that we cover with leaves. Then we toss some raw meat in the center of it and wait. When the hatchling goes for the meat, the wood can't support its weight, and it breaks. The hatchling falls into the pit, trapped. Then, we kill it."

I can see the dragon trample over bits of wood and leaves beneath its claws as it frantically tires to find a way out of the hole. I feel bad for it, and wonder how I will do this job, killing dragons. It feels... wrong.

Sad.

Like hunting puppies.

Giant man-killing puppies with claws and teeth the size of children. But still.

"Ready Cilia?" Vane calls.

One of the Ashknights, a woman with short, golden hair, nods. "Ready." She maneuvers the ballista and aims it down at the hatchling. Her comrades talk as she gets the dragon in her sights.

"Bet you twenty coppers she hits it the first time," a dark haired man says.

The tawny man next to him laughs. "Bet you thirty she doesn't."

"Thirty. So be it." They shake and Cilia rolls her eyes. "Don't you two have anything better to do?" she asks.

"You mean other than watch you do all the hard work? Nah. Think we're good here," the dark haired man says with good humor.

She chuckles, then returns her focus to the hatchling, taking aim. She releases the bolt and it flies into the pit, striking the hatchling near the tail. The baby dragon hisses in fury and turns its head toward us, shrieking.

I shiver at the sound. It's haunting, like a child possessed and screaming into the wind.

The tawny one laughs. "Missed. Pay up."

The other sighs and pulls out some coins from a pouch at his belt.

Celia takes aim again. This time, the bolt embeds itself in the hatchling's head, piercing its skull. I suck in my breath, holding it as I watch the life drain out of the poor beast. Its body jerks, its cry dies out in one final flare of agony, and then it collapses. It twitches a few times, then goes still.

"Good shot," says the Ashknight who lost the original bet. "Hope you weren't holding back the first time."

She shrugs, a small grin playing on her lips.

"Wait, you weren't holding back? Were you?"

The other man laughs with a loud guffaw and slaps the loser on the back. "Life lessons, my friend. Shouldn't have pissed her off last week in drills."

Celia doesn't reply to their banter, but instead tosses him a rope from one of the wagons. "Come. Let's pull it up before the day gets away from us."

Vane turns to us, and I remember to breathe again. "Watch carefully. This will be your job someday."

The Ashknights jump into the pit and tie ropes around the hatchling's body, then they jump out, using their Spirit power fluidly, as an extension of themselves. The ropes are tied to the two carts, and the Ashknights guide them forward, using the strength of the Boxen's pulling them to drag the hatchling out of the pit.

We get a closer look at the baby dragon now. It's dark blue, not black—as it had looked in the pit. And its body seems made of crystal, reflecting fractals of light in all directions as the sun hits it. Like my necklace.

The hatchling is beautiful. Majestic. And now, dead.

The Ashknights get to work like hunters skinning and gutting its kill. They remove the horns and spikes first, filling canvas bags with their loot.

"They collect the dragonstone," Vane says. "Which will be ground into powder and used to make powerful concoctions. The most famous one, of course, extends life. Bottles of it will be sold to the noble houses throughout Nirandel, and in exchange, Dragoncliff will receive the funds it needs for weapons, training and maintenance of the fort."

"So this is just a business transaction?" I ask, a bit appalled by this. Hunting for profit. Killing for greed.

Vane looks at me, but I can't read his expression. "These hunts serve many functions. They keep our Ashknights fight ready. They keep our organization funded so that we can continue to protect the worlds from Corrupted Spirits, and so that we can continue to train future Ashknights and Ashlords."

"If dragonstone is so valuable, why not breed the dragons in captivity to harvest them?"

"Some have tried," he says. "But dragons need room to grow. Put a small hatchling in a cage and it will never outgrow it. Thus, it will never reach maturity and you will never be able to breed more. Unfortunately, there is no material strong enough to hold a fully-grown dragon. The Wall of Light is as close to a cage as we can get. It's dangerous within the Wall, and you can't take a living dragon out."

"Why not?" Enzo asks.

"A man tried it once," Vane says. "Felius the Fool they call him now. Took three dragons out for experimentation. Soon enough, they absorbed a Spirit that came close enough to them. They grew stronger in size and magic, and they broke free, destroying an entire village. It took six Ashlords to put them down, and one died in that fight."

Landon's hand curls into a fist. "But this... " He looks at the hatchling, who has had more of its parts removed as we talked. "This is slaughter. I thought I was leaving a corrupt world behind, where the strong fed off the weak, but I see this is the same. Always the same."

I glance at the blond by my side, my sympathies siding with him. This is hard to take in. Hard to stomach the thought that my life will be one of a dragon killer.

Vane moves closer to Landon, standing inches from his face. "You think this is dishonorable? Killing hatchlings? Would you rather leave them be until they are fully grown? Until they are the size of mountains? Until they come for the Wall and shatter the gates and destroy all you hold dear?"

Landon's face pales, and my heart thumps louder in my chest. Vane steps back to look at all of us. "Believe me. You will face a grown dragon soon enough. And on that day, you will wish you could have killed it as a hatchling."

He paces in front of us. "There are drakes who fly within these walls, behemoths who tower over hills, and ancient ones larger than any creature you can imagine. We must do what we can to curb their numbers. If not, another Sundering will come. Sooner than you think."

I crane my neck to whisper to Zev. "What's a Sundering?"

"A time when dragons attacked the Wall, attempting to breach it. The legends say there have been three Sunderings throughout history, and that another will come again. Some prophets say this will be soon, but they are ravings of madmen and are not taken seriously. But this is why Ashknights must defend the Wall. If the dragons ever broke free, they would consume all the Spirits and all the flesh in the world, and then move on to the next, and the next, until nothing is left."

My eyes widen. "Dragons can move between worlds?" I ask, my voice hushed as the Ashknights finish their task.

Zev nods. "When a dragon absorbs a Spirit, it gains powers no one fully understands. One of those powers is to travel between worlds. It's happened before. A dragon breaks through a gate, absorbs a Spirit, then ends up on Gai." He turns to look at me. "That's your world. That's where your stories of dragons come from. Ashlords quickly depart and put the beast down before it grows even more powerful. It is one reason Ashknights guard the Wall while Ashlords travel the worlds. A dragon who has escaped and fed off a Spirit is the greatest threat humanity has ever seen."

I pause, soaking in that information. It's a lot to take in. I think of all the tales of valiant knights defeating dragons. Of all the lore and history that my world has about these creatures, even while believing it is fantasy. But this makes sense. Why else would so many cultures have stories like these? Shared images and symbols and myths about great winged beasts? Where else do fantasy and myth come from if not hidden truths buried by time and trickery?

"Why not have your strongest Ashlords manning the Wall?" I ask. "If the threat is that great."

"It used to be so, once," he says. "But the Sundering is more myth than history now, and the lords of the realms care more about

Corrupted Spirits than dragons they never see. That threat isn't real to them, whereas family and friends getting taken by a Spirit... that is. To them, our true role is to control the Spirits. To them, the Wall is just an excuse to keep the gemstone trade to ourselves. If some had their way, the Ashlords would no longer even guard the Wall of Light—"

"Stop whispering and pay attention," Vane says, pointing to the Ashknights. "One day, this will be your duty, and you're going to wish you had learned all you can now."

"Yes, Master," Zev and I say in unison, as we turn our eyes to the bags of dragonstone being loaded into the cart. I look back at the dragon, and shudder to see what remains. It is a pile of meat. Nothing more. Even the bones have been harvested. "Is there no use for what is left?" I ask, my eyes glued to the macabre sight.

Vane follows my eyes, and his face is hard. Expressionless. As always. "The other dragons will feed on the remains. Dragon meat is considered tainted by many humans, unlucky or sacrilegious to eat by others."

"Sacrilegious? So they honor the old ways in this, but are fine harvesting the rest of body and ingesting it for power?" I ask, my bias clearly showing.

"Humans are not consistent creatures," Vane says softly. "They cover their own sins with pretty lies and justifications. To attempt to find reason in that is a wasteful use of time."

"You speak as if you are not human," I say, studying the enigmatic master more closely.

He raises an eyebrow at me, but we are interrupted as Celia shouts from one of the wagons. "Everyone mount up. Let's get out of here."

Vane walks away, leading his wolf toward his horse, and I mount mine and follow as we ride for the gate, this time more slowly with the wagons carrying the weight of the harvested dragon's body.

"We travel by the ridge," Celia says, turning the cart to the right.

Vane frowns. "Not many places to maneuver there, should the need arise."

"But it provides cover from the skies," she says. "Gods willing, we'll pass through these lands unnoticed."

"Gods willing," Vane says, but he does not seem convinced of this plan, and I get a pit in my stomach. The kind of pit I would get when a fire was about to go sideways.

I learned to listen to this pit, but I have no power, influence or authority here. So I keep my wits about me, stay focused, and do as I'm told.

I stay close to Vane while the rest trail behind us.

"These lands remind me of my realm," Vane says, surprising me. "It is a cold region, but wild and free, with tall trees and wide mountains. Good for hunting."

"So it's true you're not from this world?" I ask, pulling my horse closer to his so we can speak more freely.

"I am not. As you are not," he says, looking at me. "My wife, she is from your world. It was tough for her, at first, coming to a strange land. Giving up the modern conveniences Gai offers. She had to learn much the same way as you, to master a new power, to negotiate the politics, social norms and moralities of a place so foreign." He pauses, still looking closely at me. I try not to squirm under his scrutiny. "She'd like you. And you'd like her. You both have a great deal of compassion. Just do not let that get you killed."

I'm surprised he's shared so much with me, and his comment about his wife makes me smile. "Why are you here then? You seem to miss her."

"Her and our daughter," he says with a faraway look. His wolf seems to hear us and gives a soft bark at the talk of them. "But coming here wasn't a choice. Not really."

I think of my own choice that wasn't really a choice. If I had refused, so many bad things could have—would have—happened.

"Tell me about your home and your family," I say, wondering if I'm pushing this conversation too hard, but curious about this man who has been teaching us.

He tells me of lands in the North, the brutal cold, the harsh beauty. How on long hunts with his wolf he would stay warm by a fire in caves at night. "My wife... she is not free to be here. She has other responsibilities in our world. But when we are together, she is my everything. She pulls me out of myself, and we dance outside at night under the goddess moons and stars."

He speaks of his wife with such tenderness that I almost don't recognize the man who barks orders at us all day every day until we can barely walk. "That sounds... incredible. How—"

"Quiet." His face is hard once more. Commander. Master. The man in love with a woman back home is gone, as he raises his hand and closes his eyes. Listening.

His wolf is just as still beside him, nose in the air, as if trying to catch an elusive scent.

I look around and see nothing, but I close my eyes and focus my senses. And then I hear it. A collective flapping in the wind, like a dozen beating hearts.

And my own heart skips a beat. Because I know what this sound is.

The dragons are coming.

RED DRAGON

"**T**ake defensive positions!" screams Cilia. "Protect the Ashlings."

"We can help," Landon calls out, drawing his sword.

I draw mine as well, and see others doing the same, but I feel ill-prepared to fight a dragon. My mouth goes dry and my skin feels too hot.

"Just keep your heads down and don't die," Cilia says. "That's the best you can do for us right now."

A dragon flies above us, engulfing the sky in its massive silhouette. "Is that full grown?" I whisper, huddled with the others of my squad.

Zev shakes his head, wide-eyed. "Not big enough. It's a drake. Basically a teenager."

I gasp. It's huge. It looks as if it could swallow me whole. And it's *not* full-grown. Holy hell. No wonder they kill them when they're hatchlings.

The drake is gleaming in the sun with blue dragonstone scales as it swoops down and grabs one of the Boxen pulling the wagons. The great beast screeches in pain, foam forming at its nostrils as it struggles against the claws of the dragon, fighting to regain its freedom.

Blood drips from it as deep gashes pierce its flesh, carving into its soft brown fur. It's horrible to watch, but we are powerless to do anything but stand and pray to whatever gods any of us may believe in. I hear Bix mumbling something that sounds like a prayer under his breath. The rest of us stare in shock and fear and awe.

Cilia rushes to the ballista on the other wagon and swerves it around to face the drake, but before she can fire a shot, the young dragon flies just above her and drops the dying Boxen onto the ballista.

Cilia dives off the wagon, using her Spirit to avoid injury, as the poor animal collides with the weapon, and the entire wagon crashes beneath the weight of the beast, shattering into useless pieces of wood and metal.

Another screech fills the air, and two more drakes appear in the sky above us.

"Everyone!" Vane yells. "Grab the dragonstone and ride for the wall. I'll hold them off."

He jumps then, and a piece of the cliff juts out under his feet. It slides upwards, following his movements toward the drakes. Then he leaps and, using his great sword, slashes one across the neck, severing its head. As he falls, another stone juts out under him, catching him.

"How's he doing that?" I ask, as I grab a bag of the dragonstone and tie it to my horse.

"Must be his Spirit," Zev says. "It appears rumors of his skill have not been overstated. Interesting."

I grab another bag and a blue horn slips out. I pick it up and am about to put it in my bag when a drake swoops down in front of us, ramming into the horses, sending them flying and just barely missing us.

"What are they doing?" Zev asks. "It's almost as if they're trying to cut off our escape. But they're supposed to be mindless."

"Even animals know how to hunt," I whisper, watching as the drakes seem to coordinate another attack on us.

"Keep moving," Cilia says. "Head to the wall on foot."

Another drake heads our way, and we look toward the direction of

the Wall, but Vane... we can't just leave him to fight two more drakes.

What if more show up?

One of the Ashknights, the dark haired one who lost the bet, grabs me by the shoulders and pulls. "Come. Did you not hear her?"

We move then, all of us in messy formation, carrying what we can, but mostly trying to get away as quickly as possible. Cilia jumps into the air, sword forward, a white Spirit spiraling around her. It's a silver swan that seems to glow.

She pushes the blade forward, into the drake's mouth, the steel tearing through its head, but then the jaws collapse around her body, breaking it in two, killing her instantly.

I freeze, paralyzed by the brutality of it. The drake drops her body, both of them now dead.

The Ashknight hides a face full of pain. "Come. Move it, Ashlings."

"But Cilia," I say. "We need to get her body."

"It's too late. She's dead," he says.

"What do you mean? Won't she regenerate?"

The Ashknight pulls me away from the carnage. "There's no regenerating after a dragon kills you. There's no sanctuary. She's gone, and if you don't move, she will have died in vain."

I move then, and my fear escalates as his words sink in. I'm used to feeling mortal. To feeling like this fire could be the last fire I fight. But my battle with Pike changed something in me. Gave me a small feeling of invincibility.

That feeling died with Cilia.

We can be killed, and quite easily it appears.

This is madness.

The remaining drake lands near his fallen brother, near Cilia's body still trapped in the dead drake's mouth. The drake leans over the bodies and... something changes in it. Its spikes and horns shimmer blue and he seems to get bigger.

"He's absorbing her Spirit," Zev says. "He's going to grow more powerful. He—"

The drake dashes then, faster than it moved before.

I feel it move past me, and the dark haired Ashknight jumps between me and the drake to protect me.

It all happens so fast.

He pushes me to the ground, and as I struggle to stand, to help in whatever feeble way I can, the drake sinks long, sharp teeth into his torso and shakes him like a cat playing with a toy.

His friend curses, and the Ashknight screams, blood spraying from his mouth.

The remaining Ashknight jumps toward the drake, attacking with speed and agility, sword aimed at its mouth. He's trying the same move Cilia pulled.

Giving his life to slay a drake.

But this one is faster now. Stronger. Deadlier even than before.

It dashes around him, then swipes at him with claws, ripping through his chest and throat, killing him instantly.

He's dead.

All the Ashknights are dead.

The drake turns to face us now, its eyes and body glowing as it absorbs two new spirits. It grows visibly bigger, stronger.

We back away, our swords held in wavering hands. Only Raven looks calm. Ready.

Even Bix, our fierce warrior, quakes a bit at the sight.

"Stay together," I whisper to them. "Keep our backs together. Swords up. Spirit at the ready. There's seven of us and one of him. We can do this." My words are meant to bolster morale, but they fall flat as we are all too terrified to heed them.

We know we're about to be dragon food.

Just as the drake is set to lunge at us, Vane catches up, moving on a stone slab like a surfer on waves. "Run," he yells. "Run!" He jumps at the dragon, and before I turn to run, I see them clash in the sky.

We flee down the road, running at full speed, using our Spirits to make us faster.

"Seems like Vane might just hold it off," Landon says, as the drake and Master Vane fade into the distance.

It would be easy to imagine we were just in training right now, doing our daily run, pushing ourselves to prepare for a future of dragon fighting and Spirit hunting.

Almost.

Until a new drake arrives. This one is smaller than the others, but still bigger than the hatchling. It hid under the cover of the forest and dashes out to attack us once Vane is too far away to intervene. As if it knows we are the weak link.

It lunges for Landon first, it's claws grabbing his leg, as if trying to pull him back into the forest with it.

Landon screams in pain and attempts to attack it with his sword, but his aim is off. Raven attacks, cutting the dragon with the black sickle her hand transmutes into, instantly severing its head.

The drake falls to the ground, dead, and Landon collapses as the claws loosen around his leg.

Umi chatters in my ear, shaking in fear as I kneel by Landon to offer first aid. His leg is mangled, and though he will regenerate, it won't be fast enough. I tear off cloth from my cloak and grab a stick to form a makeshift splint. I use the stick to stabilize his leg, then wrap the cloth tightly around the wounds. "This will stem the bleeding and keep your leg stable, but infection is a risk until it heals," I tell him.

He nods, his face contorted in pain. "Thank you."

His eyes flick to Raven, who stands watching. "And you. You saved my life."

She shrugs, and Bix tries to help him up, but Landon pushes him away. "No, I'll only slow you down. Get out of here. All of you."

Bix ignores Landon's protests and lifts him easily into his arms, carrying him like a child. "We get out together, or not at all."

"He's right," I say. "We have to stick together."

No one responds. Bix and I exchange a glance. The others seem frozen. Terrorized by the events of today. They need a leader, I realize. Someone to focus them. I look to Raven, our Squad Leader, but she's looking to me, waiting for me to make a decision. Her body is covered in dragon blood, and she looks pale. Scared. I remind myself that though she may be the most deadly fighter of us all, she's still only a kid, however hardened her life has made her.

This falls to me. I need to get us all out of here. I suck in my breath and close my eyes, imagining my training in the fire department. The times we stuck by each other during horrible wild fires that spread through our forests. The long days and nights of never ending fire fighting, where everything smelled of smoke that was impossible to wash off, and the days we all bled together and it seemed as if the entire state of California would burn to the ground if we didn't do our jobs.

I can do this.

I open my eyes and meet each of theirs. I steel myself with resolve and purpose. "We need to head through the woods," I say. "There's more cover that way." I turn to Bix. "How long can you carry him?" I worry for the big man's stamina.

Bix smiles. "I carry bear bigger than this man many miles after hunt, to praise of my people. He is nothing."

Landon would likely take offense at that, if he didn't look ready to pass out. I hand him a flask of water. "Drink."

He obliges, and I feel his head. It's warm but not too hot. Still, he's badly injured. We need to hurry.

"Follow me," I tell the group.

I expect one of them to object. To say I don't have a right to lead them. But none do.

This day is fading. And we are all exhausted as the sun begins to set and the forest is cloaked in darkness. The moons aren't strong enough to penetrate the tall canopy of trees above us beyond a stray beam of pale light here and there.

Based on how long we've been walking, we should be close to the Wall. I say as much, and this gives everyone a burst of confidence. Our pace increases, and we see something in the distance.

"It must be the Wall," Mabel says.

She sounds relieved, as we all are.

I run ahead to scout the area and nearly hit a wall of black stone, face first. My hands brace the impact, palms scraping against jagged bits of stone. "It's not the Wall," I say, as they approach.

Bix looks up at the structure before us. "It's a cliff."

"There must be a way around," Enzo says.

"No time for that," Raven says as she leaps onto the side of the cliff, digging her transmuted hands into stone. "Come. We must climb."

"Wait. We have to secure Landon to Bix so his hands are free." We tear more of our cloaks and make something resembling a baby wrap parents on my world use to carry their infants. We strap Landon to Bix's back, making sure the fabric will hold. Landon is silent during this, whether from pain or frustration at being incapacitated I do not know.

When Bix is ready, we face the cliff. No one but Raven looks keen on making this climb. Our Spirit powers are still rather rough for most of us, but we have been trained for this. More or less. And we need to keep moving. This might be our only way forward. From the vantage point of the cliff we should be able to see which direction the Wall of Light is in.

I jump after Raven, my hands transmuting into silver claws that clutch the stone with ease. One hand slips as the stone breaks, but I regain my balance and climb.

Bix lands at my side, the rock crumbling beneath his weight as he scales the cliff with more ease than I would have thought, given his size and burden.

Enzo and Mabel follow, and we climb as fast as we can.

Until we see them.

Something in the sky. "What is that?" Enzo asks, his voice shaking, his accent so thick I can barely understand him.

I turn to look and see what he's pointing at. A dragon in the distance, making loops in the sky, but not coming toward us. It's red, and it's huge. The size of a mountain. That's no drake. That's a full-grown dragon.

Zev reaches the top of the cliff and pulls himself up to standing, Raven beside him. "I've never heard of that kind," he says, and I don't know whether he means the color or the size or something else.

"Why doesn't it attack?" Mabel asks as she climbs faster.

"It's waiting for something," I say quietly.

The dragon lands above us, on the peak of the mountain connected to our cliff. It roars, shaking the ground with its thunderous voice. A moment later we hear the beating of wings approaching. In mass.

"It's calling for reinforcements," I say. "Climb. Faster!"

One dragon breaks free of the thunder and swoops down, catching Enzo's arm with a giant claw, pulling him off the cliff.

Enzo screams as crimson lines open up in his flesh.

"No!" I yell, and without thinking, acting entirely on instinct, I jump, transmuting as I do, and hit the dragon in the head. It's like hitting a boulder with a feather, but it distracts the beast long enough for me to grab Enzo. We fall, his arm ripping from the dragon's claw, his blood spraying into the sky.

I use Spirit to pull us up, and it's as if I'm flying as I throw Enzo's body onto the cliff's ledge, while I land beside him.

Another drake comes at us, and Raven attacks this one, holding it off.

And then another comes.

There's no time to think. To plan. To strategize.

Bix throws his spear and it hits the drake in the shoulder. The thunder of dragons disappears into the clouds, only to return in a new formation.

"They're cooperating. Like they have a battle plan," I say. "But how?"

I use the distraction to make a fast tourniquet for Enzo's arm, and he stands, shaky but ready to fight, holding his sword in his good hand.

"Get in a semi-circle," I shout. "Backs to the cliff. Protect Enzo and Landon." We place them within our circle. They are both armed, but we know they can't fight effectively yet. Raven, Bix, Mabel, Zev and I take positions to surround our injured friends. The dragons are in flight again, heading straight for us.

There's another roar, this one huge, closer, and it shakes the ground beneath us. Pieces of the cliff break off in chunks from the vibrations. It's the red dragon, closer than ever, flying overhead. It opens its mouth and spews fire.

The ball of flame shoots down at us and I leap to the side to avoid instant incineration. The ball explodes when it hits the ground, and Bix falls to the side, his skin burning. He yells in pain and fear. Zev is trying to drag Landon away from the flames.

Raven helps Enzo.

I throw my cloak over Bix to help put out of the fire. "Roll on the ground," I tell him. "Then pour cold water on the burns as quickly as possible."

There are three drakes coming for us. Now that we are divided, our ranks broken, our people injured.

They know. They know we are at our weakest.

That we are vulnerable as prey.

They've picked us off, one by one. Taken our leaders, then each other, until we could easily be killed.

I don't know what to do. I reach for my sword that fell from my hand during the explosion, and I see the hatchling's dragonstone horn that must have fallen out of the bag on my hip.

I hold it in my hand and stare at it, my mind tumbling in on itself. Is this what we have all died for? Some bits of dragonstone to make people live longer? To make them more powerful? Was this worth the loss of so much life? Cilia and the other Ashknights? The injuries and possible death of my squad?

I choke on a sob, scared not just for me, but for all of us.

This isn't over yet.

I won't let this be my last stand.

Not here.

Not now.

Not today.

I grip the dragonstone in my hand and stand, facing the dragons as they descend on us. My Spirit wells in me, and the stone begins to glow in my hand, turning hot as it does. Then it shatters, and a burst of power punches into me with such force I lose breath. I see strands of my hair blowing in the wind and it has turned silver and glows. I look down at my hands and see they are glowing too.

And then light explodes out of me, like a star going supernova. My body lifts from the ground and into the air, and I realize I'm riding a dragon. My Spirit.

This is the first time Umi's manifested this size, and all at once we are connected, him and I.

His body takes form under mine, becoming solid. He roars and white lightning bursts from his mouth.

It incinerates two of the drakes, killing them instantly. The third dives out of the way, trying to fly around me, but my dragon lifts a claw and smacks it out of the air, as if it were a gnat.

The drake hits the cliff, its body breaking, and it falls to the ground.

I feel at one with Umi. His arm is my arm. His power, my power.

More drakes arrive on the horizon. At least a dozen.

I will burn them out of the sky.

I don't even feel human anymore. Just... power. All I feel is power.

The drakes form a V in the sky and come at me, ready to strike.

But a roar echoes through the mountains, shaking the ground once again. The red dragon has been watching from the peak, and as it bellows into the night, the drakes stop and turn midair, staying in perfect formation as they disappear into the night sky.

Was the red dragon controlling them? It certainly seemed to.

The red dragon stares at me for a moment, then turns and flies away, it's huge body getting smaller and smaller until it's no longer visible.

In an instant, the power I felt fades, and my limbs weaken. I fall off my dragon, which vanishes back into Spirit.

I'm losing consciousness as I fall through the sky.

Then something catches me, and different hands carry me, laying me gently on the earth. Above me, through fractured vision, I see my friends, and then the world turns blurry and fades out.

29

AN EMBER IN THE ASH

My eyes peel open slowly. My head pounds and my heart beats frantically as adrenaline surges through me. Where am I? What's happened?

I lift my head to look around, to get my bearings. I'm covered in someone's cloak, my head on someone's lap. There's a fire burning. A cave. I'm in a cave with my squad.

Raven's face leans over me. "Don't move too quickly. You're still weak."

I nod as she helps me sit up. Every bone in my body, every muscle holding them together aches like nothing I've ever felt. I feel completely drained and utterly exhausted.

Landon and Mabel share a cloak on the other side of the fire. Both are sleeping. Bix is leaning against the wall of the cave, his eyes closed and Enzo snores loudly next to him, his head lulling onto the big man's shoulder. Zev is awake and watching me with a strange expression on his face.

"What happened?" I ask.

My voice seems to wake the others, and slowly they all sit up, stretch, yawn, and scoot closer to the fire.

"M'lady has awoken," Landon says, and I can't tell if he's mocking me or serious.

"Do you remember what you did?" Raven asks softly, her eyes flicking away from mine.

Fragments of it come racing back. The dragonstone shattering in my hand. The surge of power. Fighting off the drakes. I nod. "A bit, but I don't understand."

Zev cocks his head, still staring at me. "Your kind was thought to be dead. Killed in the Rising. And yet, here you are, the last of the High Dragons. You should be queen of these lands."

I suck in my breath and stare at them all. "Are you serious?" I flash to our classes on the history of this world. On High Dragons, and the power they wielded. The ability to use dragonstone to channel great power. Only a High Dragon born with the blood of dragons could do that. Only the royalty, but as they said, the last of them died during the Rising.

"You killed those drakes like it was nothing," Mabel says.

"So what does this mean?" I ask, trying to wrap my head around this. Eyes turn to Landon, who seems most knowledgeable of the nobility in this world.

"I don't know," he says. "By right you should be ruler. By blood, at least. But the High Dragons were deliberately killed off, their reign thwarted and stolen by Emperor Titus, first of his name, and ruler of all of Nirandel. He's banished the worship of dragons and publicly kills any Wall Worshiper he finds. The only permissible religion is the worship of him. If he knew you were alive, he'd assassinate you in your sleep and harvest your blood."

I shiver at that. At all of it.

Enzo finally speaks. "What do you know of your early life? Of how you got to Gai?"

I tell them of my mother, how she was from another country—or so I thought. Of how she didn't speak about her past. About Pat and the kids.

And then I tell them how I came to be here. About Pike and Kara and the horrible things that happened. "The bones you saw... those were the bones of Kara, the little girl I raised since birth. Pike killed her."

"Ashwraiths," Bix whispers. "It is true. All of it is true."

"You must have been taken from this world during the Rising and sent to Gai for safety. Your mother saved your life." Zev says.

"But wasn't the Rising thousands of years ago?" I ask, confused by all of this.

"Time is an illusion," Zev says, echoing the words from my dream. "Since time moves differently between worlds, you could have been taken to Gai and raised there, where only twenty-something years passed, while here thousands of years passed. And now you're back."

"So... time here moves faster than time on Gai?" Enzo asks. This is a new concept for us both.

"It can," Zev says. "Honestly, have none of you read The Time Maker's Dilemma, by Russgrand Norlic?"

We all stare at him blankly, and he rolls his eyes and sighs. "Ok, here's the short lesson. On each of the Nine Worlds, time is internally consistent. But when crossing over from one world to another, you aren't just making a vertical jump, you are piercing the fabric of time itself. Anywhere from a minute to a thousand years could pass while only a second has passed for you. Or a lifetime passes for you when it's only been a few weeks elsewhere. There is no method to it, much to the dismay of those who study this. One theory is that every time someone travels between worlds, it changes the flow of time in all worlds, thus it is impossible to map or track reliably."

"So... this is real? I'm a High Dragon?" It feels... surreal. Unbeliev-able. My mother seemed pretty human, so that means my father must be High Dragon. Is that why she never spoke of him? Of her life before? Who is my father, then? What happened to him?

"None of us can ever tell anyone," Landon says, his face hard, his eyes intent. "Sky saved our lives. The least we can do is not get her killed."

"Agreed," Mabel says, surprising me. They each in turn nod their heads, vowing to keep my secret.

I look at them and wonder what happens next. Not just the immediate next of where do we go and how do we survive, but beyond that. I don't feel any different. I'm still the same old Sky. But they are looking at me with new eyes, seeing things in me I don't fully understand. Enzo is the only one who looks at me the same. He and I, we are from the same world. Or at least, raised on the same world. I realize with a start that I must have been born on Nirandel. This, then, is my home. How strange. But Enzo and I, we weren't weened on stories of High Dragons. We do have royalty though, and I can see Enzo's face shift as he realizes that's what I am.

I shift the conversation to something else, needing time to contemplate all this. "What of the injuries. Landon, Enzo, how are you?"

"We've both healed fully," Landon says. "The regeneration is complete."

"And everyone else?"

They all nod and murmur that any injuries sustained have healed.

"How long until daybreak?" I ask.

"About three hours," Raven says.

"Then we stay here until sunrise," I say, and I realize how natural it feels to assume the role of leader.

They agree, and in exhaustion I sink against the wall of the cave and accept a drink from Raven.

"Any news of Vane?" I ask.

"None," Landon says.

I sigh. What I'm about to say will likely not sit well with this group, but it has to be said. "I know we were heading to the Wall when all this happened, but I expected Vane to catch up with us. If he hasn't... we have to go back for him."

"Are you nuts?" Zev asks. "We're on the wrong side of the Wall, and sitting ducks for hungry dragons. You saw how they attacked. You saw the red dragon. It was controlling them, organizing them, I'd bet my books on it."

Landon nods. "I've never heard of anything like this before. It shouldn't be possible."

"But then it left," I say, remembering the look the red dragon gave me before flying off.

"Maybe because it knew you were High Dragon?" Mabel asks.

"Or maybe because Sky summoned the biggest Spirit ever seen," Bix says proudly. "Your dragon, it is huge. Very honorable Spirit."

I pat the big man's hand and smile.

"Nothing has changed," Mabel says. "Vane told us to leave. We leave. We are barely trained to fight hatchlings, let alone a thunder of drakes led by what we saw last night."

"And so we leave him behind to die?" I ask, looking into each of their eyes. "He has a wife and daughter back home, did you know that? When he speaks of her his eyes light up and his face softens. He loves her deeply. She waits for him. They both do. Would you steal him from his family?"

They don't say anything, and I can see their determination wavering. "I was a firefighter before coming here. I risked my life nearly every day to save strangers from burning buildings, or stop forest fires from spreading. We never went in alone, and we never left someone behind. Vane risked his life to give us a head start. We can't leave him behind."

I pause, trying to asses their mood, their emotions, before I lay down my final argument. "And besides, Mabel is wrong. Something has changed. We now have a weapon we didn't before."

I see the moment their eyes register understanding, and I smile, showing more confidence than I feel. "How many still have the bags of dragonstone we were told to collect and carry back to the Cliff?"

They each rummage into their cloaks and pull out what they have. "I can use them," I say, collecting what I can carry in my own pouch, and giving back what I can't. "I can protect us, and Vane too."

"He's likely already dead, and we will be too if we don't go for help," Enzo says.

"Something tells me that man is harder to kill than a dragon," I say, and someone chuckles in response.

"Shouldn't we at least send someone back, to fetch help and alert the Cliff to what's happened?" Mabel asks.

"I shall go!" Bix says. "I am best tracker and can find the Wall and bring help."

It's not a bad plan but... "I'm the only thing we know can kill the dragons. If we separate, we're more vulnerable." I look at Bix. "Plus, you *are* the best tracker, which is why I need you to help us find Vane."

He nods in agreement, pleased that he is that important.

"And... wouldn't the Cliff know something's wrong?" I ask. "We were supposed to be back by now. Some of our horses bolted, and maybe they made it back. Either way, surely they would be sending help soon?"

I'm not sure about that last part, as I have no idea how things are handled in situations such as these, but it's what I would do in their shoes.

I look to Raven. "What do you think? You're the leader."

She shrugs, looking around at everyone, then back at me. "I'll follow you."

Landon nods. "I'll follow you too, Sky."

Bix, Mabel and Enzo all lend their verbal support, and then all eyes turn to Zev.

He rolls his eyes and sighs. "Fine. It's a death march, but if we're going to die, we might as well do it together."

I hope he's wrong about that, but I'm glad we are all in agreement. Still, we have a few hours. So we each put into a pile what little food and water we have left and we divide it amongst everyone. It's not enough, and my stomach feels hollow—empty—even after filling it with what I can. But it will do to keep us moving and give us some energy.

"Does anyone know what's edible in these woods?" I ask, as I chew the last bit of dried meat and wash it down with a sip of water. None of us can afford to use all our water until we find another source.

"I've memorized all the books of herbology in my mother's library," Zev volunteers. "I assume the Ashlands would have similar vegetation as outside the Wall."

"You've memorized them?" I ask, stunned.

Zev nods. "It's not hard. I just look at it and it flashes in my mind, staying there permanently."

"On Gai we call that eidetic memory. Though if it's real at all it's quite rare," I say.

"I've gotten pretty good at scrounging," Mabel says. "No books to study, but living on the streets gave me a good instinct for what's edible and what's not."

We all look at her wide-eyed. "You lived on the streets? I thought you were of noble birth," Landon says.

"I had a family name, early on, but my father squandered our wealth gambling and whoring," she says softly, pulling her knees to her chest and staring at the fire as she speaks. "Eventually we had nothing. He died, and my mother... well, she took her own life from shame, and I think, a fear of living without. My sister and I were just children, and we ended up on the streets, struggling to stay alive. Eventually we joined the Band of Thieves, and they protected us and taught us how to survive. But the Band of Cut Throats was a constant threat, encroaching on our territory and employing much more vicious and deadly techniques to rule. It was during a fight with them that I was badly injured and left for dead in the alleys. My sister, she'd already left. I'd... I'd traded some favors to get her a job as a maid in a noble house, to keep her safe. Anyways, that night, I became a Twin Spirit, and then the Ashlords found me."

The cave falls silent as the tragedy of her story sinks into us.

Landon positions himself closer to her and puts an arm around her shoulder. "You were brave. And smart. The Ashlords are lucky to have you."

There are tears in her eyes when she looks up at him and smiles. "I thought if you knew you'd hate me."

He laughs sardonically. "I have no right to judge anyone after the atrocities my family has committed."

I remember back to the night of the wedding, what Landon said of his family. And of the woman he left behind to join the Ashlords.

So much pain here. Enzo with his dead family. Landon with his lost fiancée and dreams of righting wrong. Mabel with her street life, and who knows what else. Bix seems to have had it the easiest, but even he suffered shame and sadness for not living up to what his tribe expected of him.

My eyes turn to Zev, who remains an enigma. He and Raven are the only two who haven't shared their stories, other than Naoki, who was with us only a few days and never had a chance. I often wonder how they're doing, and sometimes see them in the halls scurrying to their next job, and I feel a sadness wash through me that there's nothing I can do to make their life better.

Zev catches my eye and presses his lips together. "All right. I guess it's my turn to get all maudlin for our little squad bonding moment." His voice is sarcastic, but there's something in his face that makes me think he's grateful to have someone to share this burden with.

"I was from a noble family," he says. "From the Dragonbreath Islands of the east. My family clan was one of the largest and most powerful of the islands, and valued hunting in the great waters and trading stories over fire pits at night. I never fit in, but I was the oldest son and there were many expectations for me to fulfill, in particular, who my bride would be. I was set to marry a woman from another family of equal name and rank, one I had grown up around. But she wasn't the one I wanted. She wasn't the one I loved." He stares into the fire, his voice wavering. "It was her brother, Danir. He and I... we were lovers. We... we had a fool's plan to run away together. To find a small village far from our islands and make a life planting food and drinking mead until we grew old together. I would collect books and read, and he would draw and play music, and we would lead a simple life where no one would bother us."

He looks up, waiting to see if we say anything. Perhaps waiting for judgment, but I scoot closer to him and place a hand on his arm, showing him that I care. And that I don't judge him.

He nods and continues. "We were found out, of course. It was his sister. She caught us in a... compromising position one day in the barn, and she ran to tell her parents. They were furious, as were mine, and they arranged to teach us both a lesson. That night I was dragged from bed, a hood shoved over my head, and taken to the dungeons, where I was hung from chains and beaten for days. I was given only enough water to not die, and no food. I was cut and whipped and tortured, until it finally happened."

"They did this to you on purpose?" I ask, shocked.

He nods. "It's not uncommon. Many noble houses deliberately turn a disappointing heir into a Broken One. Sometimes they become a Twin Spirit, and serve the Ashlords. Sometimes they become a Corrupted One and are killed. Either way, they are no longer a problem."

"That's... that's horrific," I say, appalled.

He nods. "That's how I ended up here."

Tears fill my eyes. "What happened to Danir?"

He drops his head, and his voice cracks. "He became a Corrupted One. Even in this, the gods wouldn't let us be together."

So he's dead, and Zev is here.

Bix pulls out a flask, but it's not the one that's been holding his water. "In the Frozen Mountains we never go to a fight without the fire of the gods." He takes a swig and passes it around. Mabel is next, and she nearly gags. "By the gods what is that?" she asks, wiping her lips and crinkling her face.

"It is fire of the gods," Bix says, as if it obvious.

Zev hands me the flask and I take a drink and feel it burning down my throat and into my stomach. I worry it will burn a hole right through my body and come pouring out of me, along with all my organs. "Holy hell, that's fire all right, but whether from gods or devils I'm not sure," I say, passing it on.

Everyone laughs at that. And we talk of brighter things for the next few hours, until the first rays of light spill into the cave.

"It's time," I say, standing. My strength has mostly returned, and everyone looks well enough, though we are all clearly nervous about this plan that could get us all killed.

Bix takes the lead, and we begin our journey retracing our steps. "We need some kind of cover to avoid getting picked off one by one if the drakes come back," I say.

Raven points to the large green leaves that grow from a plant on our path. They are huge, and I smile. "Perfect."

We each grab one of the leaves, and straps of leather from our cloak. I show them my plan by placing the leaf on my head and tying it in place. It holds its form and creates a kind of floppy hat that covers my body if viewed from above.

Zev and Landon frown, and the handsome blond sighs. "This is not an attractive look."

But they both do as instructed, and we walk in tight formation, so that from above we look like green foliage.

Moving green foliage. But still. It's better than nothing, and we don't know how intelligent the dragons are, or if they are really controlled by the red dragon, or where that dragon is. So many questions. So much uncertainty. But we have to move forward as best we can.

We walk for hours, mostly in silence. We are fearful of attracting any attention to ourselves. Occasionally we hear the distant sound of dragon calls or wings flapping. Once I see the silhouette of a dragon through the dense trees, but none attack. Not yet at least.

Bix continues to leads us, slowly but steadily. We return to where the fighting began, the bodies of the Ashknights gone, presumably eaten by dragons or other predators that might live in these forests.

The horses that died are picked clean to the bone. The dragons feasted on our carnage.

Occasionally we stop so Mabel or Zev can find edible roots and berries for us to partially satiate our hunger on.

And we keep following the trail Vane and his wolf left. It leads away from the Wall. There is blood. Torn plant and tree. Disturbed earth and stone.

We are weary. We are sore. But still we move. No one complains. No one suggests we turn back. And for that, I am grateful. For that, my respect for my squad grows.

It's late afternoon and we are resting under a tree, nibbling on a bitter root that turns my stomach, but that Bix assures me will "put fire in my belly and hair on my chest"—though I'm not sure I want either of those things—when we hear a growl.

We stand, flanking each other, swords out, Spirits on call, when a giant white wolf approaches us.

He's blood-stained and limping, and I nearly weep from happiness. "Master Wolf, where's Master Vane?" I ask, approaching the beautiful creature with my palm out. The wolf sniffs my hand, then licks it and whines.

"He's a wolf. He doesn't understand you," Zev says with disdain.

I ignore him and wait.

The wolf barks once, then turns and walks away from us.

I follow him and the rest follow me.

The wolf leads us through a maze of trees to a makeshift fortress formed from the earth through the use of Spirit.

Inside is Master Vane.

I crawl in and he opens his eyes and scowls. "I thought I told you Ashlings to get back to the Cliff."

"We don't leave our people behind," I say. I wait for him to scold me more, but he sits up and flinches. "How badly are you hurt?"

I give him water and what remains of my bitter root. He ignores the root but accepts the water. To his side I see a dead rabbit, bloodless but with meat still on its bones. The wolf must have been hunting.

"I'm fine. Let's get out of here." He crawls out of the fortress with me and stands to face our group. "How you seven survived you'll have to share when we get back to the Cliff. In the meantime, follow me, and stay quiet and alert."

He looks at the leaf hats we're wearing and shakes his head. "Clever. Ridiculous, but clever. Someone get me a leaf."

WE TRAVEL IN SILENCE, following his lead and avoiding any areas that would get us in more trouble.

When we finally catch sight of the Wall, I nearly sag in relief.

Those last few steps are fraught with fear. We are so close, I can almost taste freedom. But we aren't there yet.

Screeching fills the sky in the distance. Flaps of wings sound too close for comfort.

We sprint the last leg of the journey, and once outside the Wall, we all fall to the ground, exhausted and relieved.

And then the cavalry finally arrives.

Ashknights with horses, wagons and food, sent to find us when only a few riderless horses returned to the Cliff.

The ride home is jolting, but still we all somehow manage to sleep on and off after having our fill of food and drink.

We are relieved of our duties and training the next day and given potions that are promised to increase our stamina and strength and restore our balance. We soak in hot baths, eat carb-laden foods and lounge in bed reading and talking.

I enjoy a long walk through the gardens in the afternoon, with Ashpaw joining me, as I contemplate what I've learned about myself on this journey. What it means. Was my father really a High Dragon? What does it mean that I have dragon blood flowing through my veins?

I think back to the journal I found in the hidden compartment in my closet, back in Ukiah. To the strange writing I saw in there. The dragon on the cover. The symbol on my arm and the fact that my mom somehow knew enough magic to form a bracelet that would block the leaking of my Spirit, to keep the Ashlords from finding me. Or perhaps, to keep the Emperor's Shadows from finding me.

I'm startled out of my thoughts when Kaden jogs toward me, his face one of relief as he pulls me into a hug. I let myself sink into him, into the hardness of his body and the gentleness of his embrace. Into his scent and into the feel of him. Ashpaw weaves in and out of our legs purring and rubbing himself against us.

Kaden brushes a lock of hair out of my face. "I was tracking a Corrupted Spirit when rumor spread that a dragon attack left Ashknights dead. I came back as quickly as I could. Were you injured?" His eyes travel the length of my body, looking for wounds.

My stomach flip-flops at seeing him. It feels a lifetime since I first came here and had to say goodbye to him to embrace my training. I rest a palm on his cheek, soaking up the hard set of his chin and the piercing gaze of his eyes. "I'm fine. Others didn't fare as well. It was brutal." I pause, then step closer to him, reaching for his hands. "I've missed you."

"I haven't stopped thinking of you," he says. "Much to the chastisement of Phoenix, who swears I'm too distracted."

Distractions in this line of work can get us killed. And I don't want to be the reason he dies. But I can't turn away from him, and so we steal a few hours, hiding out in the garden, sharing thoughts and a few forbidden kisses, before we're forced to say goodbye yet again.

When I return to my room, my squad is there, and they look as if they've been talking about me.

They are all staring, and I stand awkwardly, Ashpaw at my heels. "What's going on?"

Landon steps forward first. "We've been talking. About... who you are and what you went through. About what you told us about your daughter and Pike."

I nod, waiting for him to continue.

"You saved our lives," Mabel says. "And you saved Vane's life. We wouldn't have gone back for him if not for you. You put others first, always sacrificing yourself in the process."

"We owe you a blood debt," Landon says. He pulls out his sword, and then they all pull out swords and kneel before me, heads bowed.

Landon speaks for all of them. "You are the true ruler of this kingdom. We vow to follow where you lead. To protect your identity. Our swords are yours. And when this training is over and we are free to travel between worlds, we vow to aid you in finding Pike and avenging your family. We will be your knights. Now and always."

And then their voices join as they chant, "Long live the queen of dragons."

"Long live the queen."

30

ASHKNIGHTS

THREE YEARS LATER

I'M NOT who I once was. I'm somehow more. And less. Changed and the same. I exist in a contradiction. The me who lived in Ukiah, who watched The Bachelor with Blake while drinking cheap wine, who dreamed of fighting fires and saving lives, who suffered the abuse of an addict step-father, who raised three kids who weren't mine, but who I loved as if they were... this girl is still in me somewhere. When I dream at night it's of her. Of them. Of that life.

But those dreams are growing further apart.

The faces in them are dimming.

The events becoming less focused. More feeling than details.

I'm not her anymore. Not really.

But I wouldn't be this version of myself if she hadn't existed.

I've been at Dragoncliff for three years now.

I've trained until my body aches and bleeds and studied until my mind grows numb. I've bonded with my squad in ways I never imagined possible, as we live, breathe, eat, sleep, bathe and bleed together.

We started as eight.

Now we are seven.

And soon, we will take our final test together. Soon, we will be Ashknights...

Because if we fail, we all end up Charred.

I still see Naoki from time to time, but I barely recognize them anymore. They're not the person they used to be when our little squad was first formed. The last time I saw them, I noticed they had a distinct limp. Whatever is done to the Charred, it's no life at all.

I have seen Kaden, from time to time, these last few years, but our moments together have grown further and further apart, and our relationship more distant. There is no space in our lives for those things we dreamed of as we traveled to the Cliff, no space for something *more*.

Yet today, the day my life irrevocably changes yet again, he surprises me downstairs with breakfast. His face is harder since I last saw him, his eyes wearier, as he hands me a bowl of porridge. I try to eat, but my stomach is too full of butterflies.

"You're ready for the test," he says, his blue eyes pulling me in the way they do. "I have seen you train in the courtyard."

My glance drops back down to my food, because I do not *feel* ready.

He takes my hand in his. "I'll be waiting for you when it's over."

I struggle not to let my mind follow a darker path, but there is too much between us, too much history to ignore the pain that lingers in my heart like a thorn wedged inside my chest. "Have you found anything? Have you any news?"

His eyes drop. I don't have to clarify who I'm talking about. He knows. He always knows. "There have been no signs of Pike," he says somberly. "I'm sorry."

I am sad, but not surprised. This has been his answer for three years now, after all.

I clear my throat. "This is another step. Another step toward Pike. Passing the test today."

He nods solemnly. I know he still mourns the loss of his best friend. Still suffers the burn of vengeance in his desire to find the Outcast and bring her to justice for what she's done.

This too, we share.

And I wonder, will we ever have something between us that isn't rooted in pain?

We part ways, and I wander to the training field where I know I'll find my squad stretching and warming up. We don't know what the challenge will be today, but we know we must succeed at all costs.

Bix is sparring with Raven, their swords clashing loudly in the quiet morning. She is fast. He is strong. They strengthen each other's weakness by training together.

Enzo and Mabel have grown much closer over the years than I would have imagined, and I see them sometimes sneaking away to be alone together. They engage in hand-to-hand combat, combining different martial arts styles from this world and Gai. Their bodies move gracefully, flowing together as one, like a dance they no longer have to think about. I can see what has become between them and hope they find what little happiness they can in this world.

My mind flits back to Kaden and I wonder... but it's only ever a wondering. I have too much else to focus on. Too much else to master in my life.

Love takes a piece of our soul, of our heart, and holds it hostage. I don't have any pieces left to give right now.

Landon and Zev are unlikely friends, but friends they have become. Like brothers, they are now, and though any one of us would take a drake's claw for the other, these two are now tied even more tightly. It's not romantic. At least, I don't think. Landon has never gotten over the girl he left behind to join the Ashlords, and Zev still mourns the death of his lover. But they share a platonic kind of love that is stronger than passion, having found comfort and solace in each other that has both softened and strengthened them. No longer are they both so barbed with anger, that brittle kind of strength that turns to dust. Now they have a strength that comes from the soul, that is tempered by empathy and understanding. By wisdom. It has been rewarding to see them grow closer. Today, they practice Transmuting and fighting with their Spirits as they ready themselves for the trial.

We've all grown so much in our time together.

We never speak of the allegiance they swore to me. Of who I really am, and what my role in this world could be—should be—if you go by their beliefs. But it has formed a new kind of foundation underneath our friendship.

And it has set me outside the squad in a way.

Raven relinquished the position of Squad Leader to me with the support of the group.

Their fates now rest on my shoulders, and it is a heavier burden than I sometimes know what to do with.

But I won't let them down.

They pause their sparring when I arrive, each giving a small nod of the head—the only kind of concession I could be talked into, since Bix and Landon felt obligated to do full bows befitting the High Dragon status at first. But I don't want them to see me as something *other*, as something beyond them.

"It has come to this," I say, smiling. "We have been through much, and today we will prove we are true Ashknights." I make eye contact with each of them. "I'm proud to call you each my squad mates. And even prouder to call you my friends."

Master Vane and his white wolf come forward then. The man hasn't aged or changed in all the years we've known him. Not a single new line mars his face, but I see the weight of time's passage in his eyes. He misses his wife. His daughter. His home.

This will be our last day with him. After this, he returns to his world and his life. For better or worse, our training as Ashlings will be complete.

"Ashlings, are you ready?" he asks.

"Yes, Master," we say in unison.

He smiles. "Good, because it begins whether you are ready or not. Today, we cross the Wall yet again, and you will show what you have mastered during your time here."

We mount our horses and set forth. The journey is mostly a quiet one, each of us lost in thoughts, or overcome with nervous energy. Occasionally Bix makes a joke, then laughs at it so loudly and with such abandon that we can't help but join in. Even if his jokes aren't funny, or we don't understand them, his boundless joy always cheers us.

We have no idea what to expect from this trial. Everything about the process of becoming an Ashknight is a tightly guarded secret, but given we are going beyond the Wall, I'm guessing it includes dragons.

My hands dampen at the thought, and I close my eyes and let the smells of fresh flowers fill my nostrils as I enjoy the sun on my face and the gentle breeze in the air. My horse has become an extension of me, with all the training we've done together, and I don't have to guide her much as we follow the well-trodden path from Dragoncliff to the Wall.

My breath hitches as we pass through the gates and into the Ashlands. I look up, instinctively, but see no silhouettes of flying creatures marring the bright sky. I strain my senses but hear nothing that would give me worry.

Still, I stay on guard. We all do.

None of us have forgotten the bloodshed, the lives lost, the terror of our first time within the Wall.

Vane takes us a different way this time, north through dense countryside until we arrive at wide arena. It looks ancient, with crumbling stone walls, but it seems to still be functional. And in the center...

In the center is a dragon.

Scales dark and shiny. Wing membranes red.

This is no hatchling or drake.

This is full grown.

Perhaps even larger than the red dragon.

And it looks pissed.

Heavy chains have pinned each of its legs and wings to the earth. It writhes and screams in anger and pain, trying to break free. Nine Ashknights stand at the ready, weapons drawn, waiting. The ground beneath us shakes and our horses neigh and pull against their reins. I steady Moon but keep my eyes focused on the dragon.

Vane dismounts and paces in front of us, his wolf as always at his heels. "Meet your trial," he says, gesturing to the dragon. "Its bonds will be undone, and you will have no outside aid. Your task is to kill the dragon and carve out its heart. If you do this, you will become Ashknights."

"What if it flies away?" Zev asks, voice trembling.

"It won't. It's angry. And hungry."

Just... great. "What happens if we cannot defeat the dragon?" I ask. "If we reach a standstill?"

"I can assure you," says Master Vane grimly. "By the end of today, either your squad or the dragon will be dead." He lifts a finger. "However, your leader may *call* for reinforcements. But in doing so, your entire squad forfeits the challenge, and you will all be made Charred."

They all look to me, and I swallow my fear and worry, because I may have to decide between our lives and being Charred.

"Dismount, ready yourselves, and prepare to begin," Vane shouts.

We settle our horses beside a nearby stream and come together before entering the arena.

"How do you want me to handle reinforcements?" I ask.

"Don't call for them," Landon says firmly.

Zev nods. "We win this, or we die. I will not be Charred."

I look to the others. Bix nods. "Agreed. To die by dragon is honorable. To become Charred is not."

Raven shrugs. Even after all these years I still feel like I know her the best and least of all. "I agree," she says.

Mabel and Enzo look at each other, and he reaches for her hand, squeezing it. They don't let go just yet, and I know they are thinking about what this means for each other as well as themselves. Enzo speaks first. "It is as you say, Charred is not a life to live."

Mabel nods, turning her body closer to Enzo. "Don't call in the reinforcements."

"Okay, if everyone's sure," I look each of them in the eyes. "Then we need to give it our all. No holding back. I'm not ready to die yet."

"There will be no death for us today, Sky of the Knightly clan," Bix says, pulling his fist over his heart in salute.

The others do the same, and I am humbled and scared, but also determined not to fail them or myself.

We walk back to the arena together. "We're ready to begin," I tell Vane.

He looks at us a moment, assessing. Then nods. "I believe you are."

LANDON GRABS his lance off his steed. A long white weapon engraved with two glyphs: Density, to make the weapon unbreakable, and Weight, to make the weapon lighter. He is the only one of us to prefer an Imbued weapon over a Transmute one.

In the last three years, we have studied the arts of Beckoning, Transmuting, and Imbuing. Each of us can now summon our Spirits at our size or larger. Each of us Transmute various parts of our body. And each of us knows how to Imbue, inscribing coins with glyphs to create talismans, and inscribing weapons to empower them. Orcael, instead of Vane, led our Imbuing lessons and taught us how to make the necessary ink required for the process by crushing dragonstone and mixing it with liquid. Zev, with his keen memory, proved to be most talented at Imbuing and made many of the talismans we will use today.

All seven of our squad step into the arena, and as we do, Vane signals the nearby Ashknights, and they unchain the dragon, then retreat backwards. As soon as the giant serpent sees us, it fires flame in our direction.

We disperse, avoiding the flames and surrounding the dragon. I need to end this fight quickly, before any of my friends are injured or worse, so I reach into my cloak and pull out a disintegrate talisman and fling it at the beast's chest. The dragon repositions, and my coin misses the mark, hitting a claw instead. The giant nail begins to boil and wither away until it is completely gone. The dragon hisses, then strikes out at Bix with its uninjured claw. The large Twin Spirit isn't fast enough to evade the attack, and instead Transmutes Spirit armor, turning the skin below his neck into a hard emerald shell. He throws up his arms, clad in tortoise like shields, and blocks the dragon's assault. The force of the blow pushes him back, but he stands unharmed, grinning in a storm of dust.

Raven Transmutes a pair of black wings that sprout from her back and flies into the sky, flanking the dragon and striking it from behind with her black Transmuted sickle. Landon strikes at the serpent's feet with his lance, hitting a thigh and causing the beast to recoil, while Mabel tosses a talisman into the air. The coin hits a wing, and a giant gust of wind explodes from the glyph, pushing the dragon off balance and causing it to collapse. She used a wind talisman, I realize, to bring the dragon down.

I take advantage of the moment and toss another disintegrate glyph at the beast's head, but it jumps into the sky, avoiding the coin, and spins, lashing out with its tail. The movement is so quick, it catches all of us off guard, and the tail slams into everyone but Enzo, tossing us into the arena wall. We hit hard against the stone and collapse into the dust. Before we can recover, the dragon rears its head and shoots a cone of flame at us. While before we were fast enough to evade, now we are on our knees, injured, slow. The fire will hit us. It will burn us away. Perhaps reinforcements can save us, but I will not call them. I will not betray the wishes of my friends. I reach for a barrier talisman in a final attempt to survive, but I am not fast enough. The flame is upon us.

And then Enzo lands in front of us, arms raised. He Beckons his Spirit before him, a large elephant, and it meets the fire head on. The flame will burn his Spirit. It will melt away its flesh and bones and incinerate us. But somehow... Somehow the Enzo's Spirit holds.

He yells as his entire body tenses, jaw clenched, veins pulsing, and he resists the fire. How is he doing this? It shouldn't be possible?

I snap out of my thoughts and signal for the rest of the squad to circle the dragon. I Transmute silver wings and dash around the fire, and before the beast knows we have moved, before it can see us over its own flame, I flick a disintegrate talisman at the back of its neck. My aim is true, and the coin burns through the dragon's scales, sinks into its flesh and turns its blood into acid. The mighty beast wails and wreathes in pain as it stops breathing fire and collapses backwards. Its eyes melt out of its socket. Its scales and flesh start to peel away. The dragon takes on final breath, and then its body falls still. And I realize, we have won.

THERE's a heady mix of elation, relief and joy in the air as we all look upon the magnificent corpse of the dragon. But our trial isn't technically over until we harvest the heart.

I climb the dragon's belly, using what remains of the scales to pull myself up, and when I stand atop it, I raise my silver claw, and I slash down, opening up its chest in one clean strike.

It doesn't take long to extricate the heart. But there is something strange about the muscle. It no longer looks living, but hard, as if it solidified in death. As if it became dragonstone. The largest I have ever seen. It pulses faintly in my hand, glowing a soft red.

Wearing my silver Spirit armor, I slide down the dragon's body and hold the heart up to Vane.

My squad joins me, taking positions by my side. We are exhausted. Injured. Bleeding.

But we did it.

Vane nods and examines our prize. "A dragon's heart never truly dies," he says. "Even when the dragon does. It is what makes the heart so powerful. So coveted."

He hands me a leather bag. "Carry it in this, and take great care. You will need it for your final ceremony tonight."

"Our final ceremony?" I ask, my mind numb. Tired. Trying to catch up to the reality of my life.

He nods. "Tonight six of you will be initiated into the Order of Ashknights."

I let out a breath, a smile creeping to my face, until I do the math and pause. "No... there are seven of us."

I turn then, and, for the first time since the battle ended, truly look at each of my friends. Their eyes do the same, until we all land on Enzo.

I feel the blood drain from my face, as Mabel cries out, then covers her mouth, trembling.

Enzo looks up, confused. "What is the matter?" He looks to Mabel, reaching for her hand, but she pulls away.

"Enzo..." I say softly, my throat thick with emotion. "Your eyes. They're red. You've become Corrupted."

31

DRAGON HEART

Enzo collapses to his knees, shaking. "I... " he runs a hand over his bald head, his skin covered in sweat. "I..."

Mabel kneels in front of him and takes his face into her hands. Her eyes fill with tears. "You saved us. You're the reason we aren't all dead right now."

He looks up, red eyes menacingly replacing his own dark brown. "I pushed too hard, didn't I? I doomed myself." He caresses her face with a shaking hand. "I doomed us."

She's sobbing now. "You didn't," she says, voice cracking. "You saved us. This isn't the end. Someday, they will find a cure." She looks up at Vane, her blue eyes pleading. "Won't they? There's hope, isn't there?"

Vane frowns, but he nods. "My wife would say there is always hope. While you yet breathe, you have hope. She's not been wrong yet."

Mabel gives a small smile to our fierce teacher, and then turns back to Enzo. "See? Even Vane says so. There's hope. I won't give up on you."

Ashknights come forward, one on each side, and I realize they are there to take him away.

Mabel realizes it too, and chokes back a sob, then leans in to kiss him deeply.

They whisper something to each other, and then Enzo is led away.

We stand and watch, none of us knowing quite what to say or do. We were told early on what happens to Corrupted Ones. There is a special place for them at the Cliff, where they are treated and cared for in a safe place, where they can't misuse their power to harm anyone. He will be safe.

That's the lie I tell myself.

The same lie I used to tell myself about Charred Ones.

That burning out their Spirit was for their own safety. For everyone's safety. That it gave them a way to live in peace.

But I've seen how Naoki has been treated.

And I don't trust Dragoncliff to care for anyone who is no longer useful to their purposes.

Still, I don't give voice to my concerns. Who would it help? Instead, I put my arm around Mabel and stand with her, holding silent space while she grieves.

Vane gives us as much time as he can, but we are still in dangerous lands and must get back to the Wall.

I carry the dragon heart with me, and the remaining Ashknights harvest the rest of the dragon while Vane, the wolf, and our squad—minus Enzo—head back in silence.

This should have been a time for celebrating.

But now we are drowning in a complex juxtaposition of mourning and relief.

Relief that we didn't die.

Mourning because we lost one of our own. And that cuts at something much deeper.

Mabel feels Enzo's loss the most, and when we return to our quarters, she goes straight to his bed and lies down, holding his spare robes close to her.

The rest of us leave, to give her privacy to mourn in peace.

"What do you think will happen tonight?" Zev asks, once the six of us—seven if you count our cat—are in the courtyard.

Ashpaw follows at our feet, winding in and out between us, purring. He seems happy we're back safely. I pick up the little guy, and he nuzzles his head against my hand. "I have no clue." I turn to Landon and Bix. "Surely you've heard something about the ceremony? Rumors? Hints? Whispers?"

"In my tribe, it is never spoken of," Bix says. "Even brothers who come back to see family once they are Ashlords, they wag no tongues about this thing."

Landon nods. "It truly is a heavily guarded secret."

My hand falls to the pouch at my waist which now carries the dragon heart. Though bulky and awkward to carry, I didn't want to leave it unattended. "I wonder what they need the heart for?"

No one has an answer, so we walk in silence. Snow crunches under our feet as we make our way around the castle. We don't have a clear destination, but the fresh air does us good.

We see other squads training, but we aren't close enough to interact with them. Though many live and train in this castle, we have always been kept so busy within our own squad that we are left with little time for anything else, including outside relationships. There's always, of course, the occasional rumor of two people from different squads falling in love and sneaking off to be together, though how they find the time I'll never know.

My mind flashes to Kaden, and I wonder where he is and what he's doing right now. I thought he'd find me once we returned, but I haven't seen him around at all today.

As the sun sets, we turn and make our way back to our quarters. I set Ashpaw on my bed, and he finds a comfortable spot to curl into for a nap. Mabel is still sitting on Enzo's bed, but her eyes are dry, and she looks ready enough for whatever tonight holds.

Vane comes in sometime later, his wolf at his side. "Ashlings, it is time. Tonight you will be made Ashknights. Wear your dress robes and follow me."

Our dress robes are black with silver accents. We've only worn them a few times since we've been at the Cliff. I dig mine out of the bottom of my trunk and put it on over my black leggings and binder. The others do the same, and then Vane hands us each a candle, lighting them as he does.

"Now, follow me quietly."

The moons are high in the sky, and all three are full, a rare site that only occurs once a year in this world. I imagine how we must look from a bird's eye view. A line of people dressed in black, small splashes of flame striking against the darkness. Moonlight bathing us in a pale hue. Otherworldly. Sacred. Ethereal.

Vane takes us around the castle and through a passage I never noticed before. We walk down, into the tunnels, and then down further, through long dark hallways. I wonder if the candles are cere-monial or practical. Maybe both.

We are led into a cavernous room caved out of stone into the form of a circle. The walls hold torches spaced evenly apart. But it is the center that gives us pause.

A great fire burns in an open stone pit large enough to cook an entire Boxen, and ancient glyphs are carved into the floor around the flame.

Master Orcael stands at the far end of the room, and in the shadows I see two Ashlords on either side, each holding some kind of pulley attached to the wall. A flicker of firelight flashes long enough for me to recognize one of them.

Kaden.

Warmth spreads in my chest as I realize he will be here for my ceremony.

Following a nod from Vane, we form ourselves around the fire. When we are in position, Master Orcael speaks.

"You have been called here by the Ancient Ones to take your vows in the presence of the Eternal Fire, first forged by Nir himself, with the flames and breath he used to create humanity. And since that day, tended to by those of Ash, lest we lose the blessings the Ancient One bestowed upon us." His voice is deep, and it reverberates throughout the stone chamber, creating haunting echoes.

"And now, you will take a piece of Nir's fire with you." He looks to me. "Ashling Sky, do you have the dragon heart?"

I nod and pull it out of the pouch. Master Ocrael smiles and nods to Kaden and Phoenix who are still standing by the wall. They each pull on a lever and stone grinds against stone above our heads.

I look up and see the ceiling moving apart, revealing a moon door.

"We stand before the Eternal Fire and below the Dragon Moons on this sacred of days. We bequeath the Ancient Ones to grant our pleas and pass their power onto us." His gray eyes turn to mine. "Sky, throw the heart into the flame."

The moment is heavy, weighted with history and layered with future expectations.

Sweat drips down my face, stinging my eyes, and pools between my breasts and under my arms. I hold my hand as close to the flames as I can without burning myself, then toss the heart in.

The flames crackle and hiss, then turn white, burning larger and hotter, blazing toward the sky, shooting past the moon door into the night.

We all stand transfixed by the vision of the fire, and I wonder, has it really been kept alive all these centuries? Is this really the flame breathed by an Ancient One?

As the fire continues to burn, Master Orcael leads us in a chant we studied in preparation for this day. It is as old as the flames, we are told, in a language no longer spoken or understood, but it invokes the magic of the Ancient Ones.

My mouth rounds to form the unfamiliar sounds, but soon the poetry of the words, the heat of the flames, the sacredness of this space takes over any other thought, and I find myself lost to the intonations and deeper meaning, swaying in place as my body is consumed by the magic of the moment. It feels eternal, but eventually the flames die down to their original size, and a gush of wind steals the breath from each of us.

The chanting stops.

And burning in the fire before each of us... is a fragment of the heart.

"Remove your cloaks," Master Orcael says.

We follow his command, removing our cloaks until we are all standing shirtless.

"Reach into the flames and pick up your piece of the dragon heart," he instructs.

Eyes turn to each other, as we each wonder what will happen when we follow these instructions.

I can tell my squad is nervous, so I step forward first, and thrust my hand into the flames.

I expect to be burned. I've been burned before, and it's unlike any other kind of injury. First, you feel a sharp pain. Then it's almost numb as nerve cells are killed. Then the burn dives deeper into you, finding new ways to torture you.

I wince, but nothing happens. The flames lick around my arm harmlessly, and I pull out my piece of dragon heart.

It's hot in my hand, almost searing in its heat, but still it does not burn.

The others see what I've done and follow suit, until we are all holding our pieces of the heart.

"Say your vows," he says.

We studied these as well, and so we are ready. Our voices come as one as we recite the words we've committed to memory.

"Before the Eternal Fire and the flame of the Ancient One, I commit myself, body, mind and soul, to the Order of Ash. To protect, to serve, to sacrifice for the Nine Worlds. To guard the Wall of Light and protect the children of Nir from any threat, within or without. I swear this to Nir and Gai, to Ava and Inf, to Heln and Spri, to Var and Min and Undi. In this and all things, may dragon blood make me strong. In this and all things, may dragon eyes guide my path. In this and all things, may dragon wings take me far. In this and all things, may dragon heart give me life. In this and all things, may dragon spirit give me courage. In this and all things, may dragon scales make me strong. In this and all things, may dragon bones reform me. In this and all things, may dragon mind make me wise. And in this and all things, may dragon fire light my way." The words feel more than words, they feel like magic made real as they crawl over my skin and embed themselves inside me.

"Now, place the heart over your own, and press it into your body."

I look up in surprise. In confusion. But I know I cannot speak or ask questions. I cannot break the sacredness of the moment.

I have to trust.

I have to believe.

And so I take another leap of faith, and hold the heart against my chest. I can feel my own pulse pounding in my ear as I push the stone against my flesh.

It burns my chest in ways it doesn't my hand, and I nearly drop it.

Someone across from me calls out in pain, but I stay focused.

I press harder, pushing it into my flesh, like pushing a stone into bread dough.

And to my astonishment, it sinks in.

Pain flashes fiercely in my body, and I bite my tongue until it bleeds to hold in my scream. My whole body feels on fire. Not from the outside, but from within. As if a burning inferno was lit inside my chest and is spreading to all my other organs.

I drop to my knees on the stone floor, my skin splitting open from the impact, but I hardly notice or care.

The fire consumes me. Eats away at my tissue. At my soul. At my mind.

Everything spins. Bile rises in my throat, but it feels like the flames of a dragon rather than vomit as I spew it out on the ground before me. Tears burn my eyes and turn to steam on my cheeks. Sweat pours out of me, but dries instantly on my body. The room around me topples onto itself, and all goes dark.

EVERYWHERE AROUND ME IS FIRE. Flames growing brighter and

stronger. A voice silences the blaze, but orange glow still permeates my vision.

"You are of the Chosen. You are a child of Ash. Rise, Ashknights, and take your place amongst your kin."

I blink and see Master Orcael standing before us. It was his voice I heard. I stand on shaky legs and look around. My squad mates are all here, and a softly glowing ember burns in each of their chests. I look down at mine, and see the same red glow from the dragon heart peeking out through my flesh, as if a part of me. It pulses to my own heartbeat, and I realize what has happened.

It is done. I am an Ashknight.

With a dragon heart beating in my chest.

32

GOODBYES

That night there is no talking as we make our way back to our room. We imagined ourselves celebrating, once upon a time, when we were a year or two into our training and envisioning what it would be like to get to this point. We imagined all of us would be here, aside from Naoki. But they had left us so early on, that while losing them was a tragedy, it didn't reshape the core of our group the way losing Enzo has. He won the day for us, and lost everything in turn.

We all sleep deeply, heavily. Our bodies still adjusting to the new hearts beating inside each of us. The faint glow of red casting ominous shadows on the stone walls. I'm told the glow will fade in time, that it will only be visible when using Spirit. But for now, its pulse is strong and bright.

My insides feel different when I wake. I no longer feel the pain of last night, but I feel something. Something new worming into my body, a kind of shadow creeping into my veins, changing me. I look around to see if anyone else is affected, but I can't tell. We all look spent. Sad. Exhilarated. A contradictory mix of emotions that none of us can quite reconcile.

Master Vane greets us as he has done every day for years, with a booming voice and his wolf by his side, before the sun rises.

"Good morning, Ashlings." His eyes twinkle and he smiles. "Or should I say, Ashknights."

We all stand at attention, eyes focused on him. We have no idea what happens next. No one prepared us for this part.

"I am proud of each and every one of you," he says in a quieter voice. "This road has been hard. Long. Perilous. But here you are. Stronger, tougher, more skilled in your use of Spirit. You might think you are done, that you have completed your training." He paces, making eye contact with us. "Your training is just beginning."

There are a few sighs as we consider what he means. How hard we've worked. How far we've pushed ourselves over the years.

"But alas, this will be goodbye for us. My time here is complete, for now, and I will be returning to my world." There's a bittersweet edge to his words. He will miss this. Us. We will miss him. But he gets to be back with his wife, his daughter. His family.

"I couldn't leave without saying goodbye. And without apologizing."

My eyebrow raises in surprise.

"I am responsible for Naoki and Enzo. I should have trained them better. Pushed them harder so they wouldn't break. It's a burden I could not share with you, as your master. But I'm no longer your master. Now, I am just Vane. Now, we are equals."

He grasps each of our arms and nods, until he reaches me. Then he smiles. "I will be telling my wife about you. Someday you two should meet. In the meantime... " he leans in, whispering so only I can hear. "Trust no one with your true identity. Do not assume that your secret is safe. Do not trust the Ashlords. There are a great many political machinations at work right now, and you are at the center of most of them. Watch yourself, and know this." He pulls back to look me in the eyes. "You have a friend in me."

My mouth drops. "How long have you known?" I ask.

He just smiles. "I knew before you did." He turns and walks away, then stops before he reaches the door. "Be well, Ashknights. Guard each other. Guard yourselves. It is only then that you can guard the Nine Worlds."

The room seems emptier once Vane is gone, and I suck in a deep breath and turn to my squad. "Anyone know what happens next?"

"You get a better living arrangement," a familiar voice says from behind me.

I turn to see Kaden and Phoenix standing there, both smiling.

His look lingers on me longer than the rest, before he speaks again. "Ashknights, this room is now needed for the incoming Ashlings. You will be enjoying much nicer accommodations. Pack your things and meet us at the barn. It's time for a field trip."

They leave as suddenly as they came, and the six of us stand there, mouths agape. Everything is moving too fast. But this is the way of it. We lived the same routine day in and day out for years, and now it's all shifting under our feet. What we thought was concrete was really just sand.

Quicksand.

"Are we leaving the Cliff?" Mabel asks, some tentative hope in her voice.

It's not that this hasn't been a good place to us. We have access to everything we need. But the walls start closing in on you after a while, being so isolated and removed from the world.

Landon shrugs, his eyes finding Zev. "Your books say anything about this?"

"Not specifically," he says, while filling his bag mostly with said books. "Though of course Ashknights and Ashlords have a variety of living arrangements depending on what or who they are assigned to. I had thought we would get what most new Ashknights get... stuck at the Wall in their shitty squatter huts."

I shudder, and hope very much that we do not end up in one of those huts by the Wall.

It doesn't take us long to pack our meager belongings, though Ashpaw is less excited about this adventure. I carry him in a makeshift pouch I wear at my chest. He claws and hisses at first, but eventually settles down as we head to the barn. Kaden and Phoenix wait for us with their horses. I mount Moon and we all travel down the long cliff.

I have a million questions I want to ask, but the narrow, rocky road that leads from the Cliff to the village is precarious and requires us travel in single file. There's no chance to ride up to Kaden's side and talk to him.

Instead, I ride behind him, and watch the ease with which he handles himself on horseback. How his strong back and arms are relaxed but in perfect form. How his thighs grip the horse so that he's never completely resting on the saddle. A rush of warmth passes through me as my mind flashes to our first kiss, interrupted by Skip. How new this world seemed back then. How crazy and scary and overwhelming it all was.

Now it's home. Now, I have to struggle to remember what I left behind. It's only been a few years, but some days it feels like a thousand lifetimes. Everything here is completely different. No world wide web connects us to everything and everyone. Here the world is smaller, shrunken onto itself based on where you can get on foot or horseback. Carriage if you're lucky. I've seen the same handful of faces every day since I arrived. I've eaten the same foods for each meal. Repeated the same routines.

But then, no matter how big the world is, or how well connected the people on Gai fancy themselves with their cell phones and internet... at the end of the day aren't we all creatures of habit? Seeing the same faces, doing the same things, thinking the same bloody thoughts, day in and day out until we die. My life may not really be as different as I thought.

We reach the end of the winding road and I loosen the reins a bit on my horse so she can nip at the high growing grass that we pass.

Kaden takes us through the nearby village, to the end, where we find ourselves passing through the richer neighborhoods, where homes are bigger and built further apart, where the children are dressed in nicer clothing and the families have staff that work for them in their homes.

We stop at the end of a dirt lane.

Kaden looks up and beams. "Here's your new home."

Zev frowns. "This is your idea of a *better* living arrangement?"

I'm glad he said it, because I'm sure it's what we are all thinking.

It's big, the manor that looms before us. It's definitely big.

It's also a complete mess. Shutters falling off windows. A porch that looks like it will cave in with a strong wind. Peeling paint and rotting wood. Weeds overgrown in the expansive yard and extended property.

We all tie our horses to poles, since a quick glance at the stables shows that the hey is rotting with mold and bugs and would likely kill any horse we housed in there.

Kaden ignores Zev's barbed comment and leads us to the porch, but before he can open the door, it opens on its own.

No, not on its own. A man stands at the entrance, dressed in fine clothes that present a sharp contrast to the shambles of the manor. He wears long black robes that look made of satin, and a heavy golden key hangs around his neck. He's got a white beard that lands at his sternum in a sharp point, and eyebrows that form points above his eyes, giving him a menacing look. But when he smiles, laugh lines crinkle around his eyes, softening his face. "You have arrived. Lovely."

The man steps out of the door. "You must forgive the state of things. This beauty has been too long neglected." He looks at Kaden and Phoenix with no small amount of reproach on his weathered face. "But now that we have a proper squad here, all that is about to change."

Kaden chuckles. "This is Drenwald Appleseed, the Keeper of Dragoneyes Manor."

Drenwald bows his head. "It is an honor to be of service here once more."

From behind him a young man appears, no more than fourteen years old. "This is my apprentice, Devon Appleseed. Someday he will take over as Keeper and wear the Keys of his calling. Our family has served as Keepers to the Order of Ash since the time of the elder dragons." He bows deeply, and little Appleseed, as I can't help but think of him in my head, mimics his elder.

Kaden turns to us. "This will be your home now. And you are now our squad," he says, referring to himself and Phoenix.

Landon raises an eyebrow. "I heard you don't take squads under your command anymore."

Kaden acknowledges his words with a slight head nod. "All things change." His eyes flicker to mine briefly, before he makes eye contact with each of us. "You six have proven yourselves exceptional. You will not be wasted at the Wall. You will be trained in advanced skills typically reserved for Ashlords. Henceforth we are the Dragoneyes Squad."

A thrill of excitement runs up my spine as I consider what this means. Not only will I be closer to Kaden, but I will learn more. Have more freedom. Train harder. I might actually have a chance of finding Pike and avenging Kara.

As if reading my mind, Kaden looks at me again, his eyes carrying all of our shared secrets and regrets. "Come, we will show you around before work begins."

The tour is brief, but eye-opening. The entryway is huge, with vaulted ceilings and an old candelabra with remnants of dripping wax clinging to it. Next, is the Great Hall, which is furnished with chairs and couches covered in canvas on one side and four large rectangular tables positioned to form a square, with a huge fire pit in the center. You could comfortably seat the entire village at these tables. A large fireplace with a year's worth of ash piled in it is the focal point of the sitting area. The kitchen is designed with large banquets in mind, with oversized pots and pans, ovens for baking and generous fireplaces for smoking and roasting food.

Connected to the kitchen are the buttery with barrels of ale and wine, and the pantry, which should be filled with food, but houses only a lump of something that has since grown fuzz, and rotten straw. I assume the storeroom is just as empty. The wash room has two large baths for hot and cold water, the Keeper says. "It is a custom for some to alternate between the two for enhanced blood flow and youth." The baths could fit our entire squad and then some, but they have been drained of water and are collecting dust and mold.

And then there is the garderobe, which contains the most disgusting toilets I've ever seen. We can't even enter the room without gagging. I don't envy whoever gets that clean up job, though judging by the look on little Appleseed's young face, he's the likely victim. Poor kid.

The library is massive, but dusty, with many books disintegrating from lack of care. "Careful of the books, they have paper mites that also enjoy human flesh."

Zev pulls his hand back from the bookshelf so fast the book falls to the ground, sending up a mushroom cloud of dust.

Landon chuckles and Zev shrugs casually, but I notice he keeps checking his hand for flesh eating mites.

"And finally," Kaden says, waving his arm dramatically toward another hall, "we have the solar. Where everyone gets their own, private sleeping quarters."

This perks us all up. We've been sleeping as a group for years, but there isn't a single one of us that doesn't crave privacy. I thought living with Pat, Blake and the kids was chaos, but at least I had my own room.

We make our way into this wing of the house with a lot more enthusiasm, and even though everything is in need of cleaning and repair, we each claim a room. I take the time to let Ashpaw out of the pouch on my chest. He's been getting restless since we arrived.

My room, like the others, is large, with a fireplace, what looks to be a queen sized bed, a desk, dresser, side drawers and a two person wooden table. Ashpaw jumps from my arms and begins sniffing around, exploring all the secrets only a cat can find. I gingerly test the bed and when no bugs crawl out, I sit. It's more comfortable than I expected. I sniff the mattress and am pleasantly surprised at how fresh it smells.

"The Keeper had the beds cleaned, re-stuffed and stitched first thing," a boy's voice says. I look up and see little Appleseed.

"I'm Devon," he says.

"I'm Sky. Nice to meet you."

He doesn't smile, but his serious expression softens as Ashpaw comes out from hiding to rub against his legs.

"I'm impressed," I say. "He doesn't normally like anyone but me and my squad. But you... he likes."

"I 'aint... " he pauses, correcting himself as his face squishes together in frustration. "I have never lived with a cat before. Where did you get him?"

"You know how it is. Two souls meant to be always find each other eventually."

He squints as though he does not in fact know how it is. I change the subject, sussing out something he said. "You live here then? Full time?"

I assumed they came and went like normal employees. But of course, not here, in this world. That's not how things are.

He nods. "We lived somewhere else before, but the Keeper, he was waiting for this one to need him again. It's where he was born, you see. Where I should have been born."

"Ah. Well, welcome home to you both then. And please, thank him for making the bedding suitable. I have a feeling we will all need a good rest after today."

Devon chuckles unexpectedly, then nods and dashes out, but not before saying quickly. "I'll bring you linens right away."

He's gone before I can reply. I think for another moment about the boy, this place, this new chapter in my life. Then I slide off the bed, open the curtains to a window in the room, and then give Ashpaw a pat on the head and a stern warning to use the outside for his bathroom needs.

I return to the Great Hall and wait as the rest of the squad returns from exploring their new quarters.

Phoenix turns to face the six of us. "You need to get this manor into proper living condition. There are also the outside areas that need tending to. The stables, the training arena, the gardens, the forge. Kaden and I have some errands to run while Keeper Drenwald gives you each your new assignments."

They both turn to leave as Drenwald nods and takes over. He assesses each of us, asking for our names, which we give, and within a moment seems to feel confident in assigning us our tasks.

"Zev, you will repair and restock the library." Zev's eyes brighten and I suppress a smile. Maybe the old man has some psychic abilities after all.

"Bix, head to the forge and do what you can. It needs to be fully functioning." Bix nods and seems proud of such an honorable task.

Mabel is assigned the garden, and I'm surprised she smiles at that, looking relieved. I didn't know she knows how to garden.

Landon is given the training arena and Raven the kitchen.

I'm praying I'm not assigned the toilets, but the Keeper says I'm responsible for the stables, and that he and Devon will handle the rest.

The poor boy turns even more pale than he is already, with the tips of his ears turning red.

We exchange glances at each other, and I know we're all thinking the same thing. How do we fix up this place? It will involve a lot of manual labor and many trips to the village for supplies.

It's daunting. I stand before the stalls and see how much bad hay has to be removed and burned, and the scrubbing, painting, wood repair... all of it. But I smile.

This is hard work, but it's straightforward. It's therapeutic. Straining my muscles, sweating, watching as the space changes in front of my eyes.

I pick up a rake and begin. Ashpaw joins me from time to time to meow something very important. Mostly I ignore him and keep working.

By the end of the day, I'm sweaty, dirty, sore and exhausted. I'm also the happiest I've been in a long time.

The three moons are out, though two are already waning and my stomach rumbles from hunger, but first I must bathe. I skip the baths inside the manor, figuring they likely haven't even been filled yet, and head out to a lake I remember seeing on the property.

I bring a change of clothes and a towel, and do a cursory inspection to make sure I'm alone. Then I strip off all my clothes and walk into the water.

The shock of cold hits me first, causing goosebumps to appear all over my body. But then my body sinks into the dark depths, the moons reflecting off the surface, the air cool and clean, the sound of water trickling and crickets serenading the night with their unique song. I suck in my breath and submerge my head.

I use a washcloth to rub the dirt and grime from my body and wash my hair, then dive back in and swim, letting the long strokes carry me further into the lake.

I don't know how long I stay in, laying on my back staring at the moons and stars, my breath even and regulated, my heart calm, even with its new and different beat. Instead of *lub dub, lub dub,* my heart now beats to *lub lub dub, lub lub dub.* I don't understand the change, or how or why it is even possible, but I can hear and feel the difference. And now, I lay naked in the lake, listening to my own heart, feeling the newness of it. *Lub lub dub. Lub lub dub.*

A splash of water pulls me out of my reverie, and I lurch to my side, throwing myself off balance. My face is submerged under water, and I pull out, right myself and spit out water I inhaled.

Then, a face appears before me, bobbing on the top of the water like an apple, the moon casting him in silhouette. "I thought I was alone," Kaden says.

"So did I," I reply.

As he swims closer, his face catches the moonlight. He looks ethereal in the water, in the night, with the moons, and for a moment I feel as if we are in a dream, dancing on water and moonbeams.

"You did a good job on the stables," he says, which makes me want to laugh, because what kind of line is that right now, right here. But he is Kaden. And I am me. And this is all we know how to say to each other. All we know how to speak.

But I want things to change. And so... I change it.

I drift my body closer to him, filling in the gap between us, and under the moons, with lake water dripping over our faces, I kiss Kaden Varis.

And this time, neither of us pulls away, and no one interrupts us.

33

DRAGONEYES MANOR

It takes us a fortnight to get the manor in reasonable living condition. But by the night of the Mother Moon—where one moon is full and the other two are crescent—we are ready to celebrate our achievements with a small feast and copious amounts of locally brewed mead and a sweet wine that comes from further north.

"My family owns the vineyard that this wine is from," Landon tells us, holding up his goblet.

Mabel raises her eyebrow. "It's delicious. And pretty popular in these parts. Is that where their money comes from?"

Mabel is always interested in where the money is, but I don't blame her. Even at my poorest in Ukiah, I still had a roof over my head and food. She's gone through some hellish experiences living on the streets, and I'm sure I haven't heard all her stories. The ones I've heard are fodder for nightmares on their own.

The Great Hall feels less drafty, with a fire blazing, fresh tapestries hung on the walls, rugs on the stone floor, and candles and sconces lit throughout. There's a warm glow that settles on us as we occupy one of the tables. It's covered in large platters of food. Meats spiced and cooked with fat drippings, fresh vegetables from a local farm, salad, fruit, fruit pies, chocolate tortes, nuts and berries, spicy soups and fresh baked bread dripping with hand churned butter. My mouth waters. We were fed at the Cliff, of course, but nothing like this.

The eight of us sip our drinks, and sink our teeth into various delectables as the Keeper and little Appleseed flit in and out removing things and bringing new things. I sit next to Kaden, our knees touching. Each touch between us sends an electrical current up my spine, and I love it. The last few weeks have been magical. Between seeing the manor turned from a dump into a truly beautiful home, to stealing kisses with Kaden in between work shifts and training, I've enjoyed every minute of our time here so far. Part of me wishes we could stay this way forever, but beyond this little bubble are other terrors we must eventually face.

Just not tonight.

I look around the table at my friends. At Landon and Zev talking quietly about something, heads close. Bix is telling Mabel a story with a lot of guffawing and banging his goblet down, splashing mead over Mabel's hand at one point. She doesn't seem to mind though. He's a good distraction from what must be an awful sadness about Enzo.

Raven sits quietly, as always, eating small bites of her food. Phoenix is talking to her, trying to draw her out, but Raven only answers in brief nods or mono-syllabic responses. Still, she's here. Amongst friends. Amongst family.

I smile at Kaden and his face transforms from hard and determined to a radiant kind of joy when he smiles back. I love that face.

"It's been a long time since this manor held so much laughter," Phoenix says, a melancholy in her voice.

Kaden's smile fades, and his eyes take on a far-away look. "Alec was with us then."

"You lived here before?" I ask.

Phoenix nods. "Before so many of our squad members died, this was our home." She tells stories of what it was like back then. What Alec was like. How close they all were. And I learn more about

Phoenix herself. About her deep loyalty to those she loves. I can see she would do anything for Kaden.

We stay up late. Drinking. Talking. Singing. Telling stories. I learn about more legends and old tales that children on this world grew up hearing. Dragon stories, mostly. I store it all to memory, and think about the library Zev did a remarkable job restocking and repairing. I don't know how he managed it, but he's acquired a collection of books that would make Master Orcael green with envy. I'm excited to peruse the selection and see what more I can learn about the world I was born to.

Kaden squeezes my knee under the table then stands. "Tomorrow we have an early morning. Your official Ashknight training begins. Don't stay up too late."

He gives me a knowing look and takes his leave. I wait as long as I can, engaging in conversation with Bix and Mabel and laughing at a weird joke Bix tells.

When enough time passes, I stand, excusing myself.

Everyone but Phoenix nods then returns to their conversations.

But Phoenix follows me with her eyes as I leave the Great Hall and head to the Solar. But where I should turn right to my quarters, I turn left. To Kaden's.

It's not that we're trying to keep it a secret. I'm sure everyone knows something is going on between us. It's a tight group and we're always together. Mostly we want to explore this on our own. Privately. Discreetly. Before 'coming out' with anything big. It's all still so new for us, despite how long we've known each other. And technically, what we have is all we're allowed, in the Order of Ash. Dalliances. Physical comfort. Nothing more.

At first I was worried it would ruffle feathers with Phoenix, but Kaden assured me it isn't like that between them and never has been. Friends only, he said. Like brother and sister.

Still, brothers and sisters can be proprietary too, and I see how she looks at me when I'm with Kaden. Something about our relationship doesn't sit well with her, and I don't know what, if not jealousy.

As I reach his door, I push away those thoughts and focus on only one thing, enjoying another night with the man I'm falling in love with.

The man I've maybe always been in love with.

I push the door open and Kaden is standing with his back to me, shirtless. I suck in my breath and close the door behind me as he turns and smiles, then pulls me into his arms.

THE NEXT MORNING comes too early. Kaden and I are entwined in each other's limbs when he wakes me with a kiss on my forehead. "It's time," he says.

I yawn and untangle myself from him. It's still dark outside, and I sigh. "Can't we at least wait until sunrise?"

He chuckles. "Half the day would be wasted then."

I groan and roll my eyes. "How do you get up at this time every morning without an alarm?"

"Discipline and training," he says.

After another kiss, this one longer, deeper... I leave his room to get ready for the day.

Breakfast is waiting for us downstairs, and bleary eyed and slightly hungover we all suck down tea and nibble on biscuits and eggs before heading to the training arena.

Kaden and Phoenix stand before us. The sun is only barely beginning to illuminate the arena.

"Today you're going to learn about Sanctuary," Kaden says. "Specifically, the importance of it, and how to enter each other's Sanctuary."

My mind flashes to my fight with Pike. To dying. To Kaden meeting me in my Sanctuary. Cold sweat breaks out on my skin. I haven't thought of that day in some time.

His eyes hold mine in understanding as he continues. "As you know, it is very hard to kill an Ashknight or Ashlord." He taps his chest, where his dragon heart lives. "We are immortal now. We will not die a natural death, but we can be killed. A dragon can kill us instantly. It is believed they have the power to kill us both in our physical form and in Sanctuary at the same time. We don't know how or why. But that's not the only way we can die. If the person you're fighting knows how to enter Sanctuary, they can enter yours and kill you there if they've weakened or killed your body. So you must learn how to do this, and how to defend yourself within it."

He paces in front of us. "You will each be assigned a partner and you will practice with them. You will take turns entering each other's Sanctuary and sparring. Since your bodies are healthy and you are not dead, you will not be overly harmed in Sanctuary, but be careful. This isn't the time to let all your powers loose. You are more vulnerable in Sanctuary than anywhere else."

He breaks up the teams, assigning Landon and Zev together, Bix and Mabel. I expect to get Raven, but Phoenix takes her, leaving me with Kaden. I smile in relief.

"I figured you wouldn't want someone else in there, after what happened before," he says by way of explanation.

I nod. "Thank you."

I'm shaking as we begin. We sit cross legged in front of each other, and he gives instructions to the whole group as he faces me. "Close your eyes and let your body relax. Connect physically with your partner to help with this initial phase. Eventually you will not need to be touching."

His hands take mine. They are warm and dry, and mine are cold and damp. He squeezes them in comfort.

"Slide deeper into your Spirit, and if you stay calm and observe, you will see a light in the center of your being. This is how you access Sanctuary. Everyone's light will be different, but you will all have one."

I see mine. It's a light blue and glowing. I reach for it mentally, and step into it. Kaden's voice is faint, as if he's talking from very far away. I hear him telling us to go into our Sanctuary and explore, then come back out.

My Sanctuary has changed, as if seasons have passed. It is fall, with golden and red leaves falling from trees. It smells of pumpkin spice and corn mazes. My eyes wander through the space, then I find that light again and come out, my hands still clutched by Kaden's. His eyes are already open when I open mine.

"You okay?" he asks.

I nod.

"Next," he says to everyone, "you will take turns finding each other's Sanctuary and joining your partner in theirs. No fighting just yet. Explore. Talk. And then leave."

Kaden already knows how to enter mine, so he encourages me to enter his. This time I have to focus on his energy. It's harder, but not as hard as I expected. He is glowing a soft orange light, and as I reach for it, I slip in.

"You did it quickly," he says. He's sitting on the top of a cliff over-looking a lake and mountains. There are birds flying above and a deer drinking from the lake below.

"I guess my Spirit knows you well," I say, sitting beside him. I lean my head against his shoulder and he kisses the top of my head as I say, "It's beautiful here."

"Not always," he says. "Our Sanctuary is our inner mirror. In times of great anger or turmoil, Sanctuary changes."

I shudder as I try to imagine what that would look like. "Wouldn't dying have made mine ugly then?"

"It could have. But at the core, you are a peaceful person. Even in the worst of it, your heart is pure and good." He lifts my face to look at me. "It's part of what I love about you."

"It is?" My heart is beating too fast, and butterflies swarm my stomach.

"It is. I love you, Sky. I shouldn't, but I do."

I melt against him. "I love you too, Kaden."

He doesn't explain why he feels he shouldn't love me, and I don't ask. Things are complicated. But I don't care. I'll take it. I thought I could protect my heart by keeping it closed off to love, but Kaden snuck in, and now I realize that we only cripple ourselves when we close ourselves to love. To family. To community. We humans are not islands. We need each other.

I reluctantly return to my own body, but what was said stays in my heart, and I'm smiling when we open our eyes.

We are about to do this again, switching partners, when a black messenger raven flies over us and toward the manor.

Kaden sees it and frowns.

It doesn't take long before little Appleseed runs out and hands Kaden a small slip of paper. Kaden reads it, his brow furrowing.

"A local village is under attack and needs our help. They say that a Corrupted Spirit is killing the children and animals. We must leave now. Everyone, ready your horses and plan to be gone a few days."

34

CORRUPTED ONE

Kaden gives us more details on the way. It turns out we are heading to the same village we went to for Mabel's sister's wedding.

"You okay?" I ask Mabel as we ride side by side. The weather has warmed in recent months, inviting an early summer into the usually cold lands. I shrug off my cloak as sweat pools under my arms.

She shrugs. "I haven't heard from her in some time. I just hope she's well, and not one of the victims."

"The message made it sound like mostly children were targets," I say, though this is hardly a comfort.

"I... I've done a lot of things I'm not proud of in my life. To survive. To get out of the slums." Mabel glances at me, and I nod to show I'm listening and not judging. "But I'm not ashamed of anything I did that helped my little sister start an honest life for herself. I did my best to protect her from the life I had to live."

"I understand," I say, thinking back to my life. "I suffered a lot to protect my kids. And still, I lost my little girl. It seems no matter what we do, or how much we sacrifice, we can't control the fates of those we love."

As pep talks go, this one fails miserably, but there is a shared camaraderie in the pain we've both suffered trying to take care of the people we love most.

We arrive late in the day, with the sun low and heavy in the sky. Our horses are hot and thirsty and so are we. We stay at the nicest inn this time, the one we ended up in after standing up to the Shadows. The inn keeper's son takes over care of our horses while we make our way in. A plump woman stands behind a well-worn counter. Her weathered hands polish a spot with a dirty rag, but it's clearly a nervous gesture, not an effective one. She is a homely woman in most respects, except for her eyes. They are hazel with hints of green, and in them I see the young woman she must have been once upon a time, with her own hopes and dreams and desires. I wonder what her younger self would think of her current life. She looks up when we approach and greets us somberly.

"Wish we'd be seeing ya on brighter occasion," she says in the thick accent that's common in these parts. "A pleasure having ya here for the wedding before. Sure did make that occasion a better 'un." She stretches the word 'occasion' like she's just learned it.

She narrows her eyes at Kaden and Phoenix when she spots them. "Don't recognize these two though. And missing another one, aren't ya?"

"You've a good memory," I say, taking the lead, since she remembers me. "This is Kaden and Phoenix, Ashlords who are part of our squad now that we're Ashknights. We're missing Enzo, who didn't make it through training."

A deeper sorrow fills us all as we reflect on our last time here, drinking and talking and getting to know each other. It was our first real breakthrough as a squad. As friends.

The woman, Alba, I remember now, nods. "It does be the way of things, the changing and the coming and the going of folks. Well, your rooms be ready with fresh linen and water. I'll expect you want to freshen and wet your lips before talking to the town council? Everyone's a flutter about the happenings lately. Monstrous beasts stealin' our youngin'. Men sent out to hunt them and never coming home. Whole village is in uproar about it. Had a meeting we did.

That's when I suggested calling you. You'd done us so much good before, figured you could help again."

I nod. "Thank you for the accommodations, and yes, if we could take a moment to freshen up from our travels, then we'd very much like to talk to everyone who knows anything about what happened. The sooner we can figure out what's going on, the safer you all will be."

This inn is far superior to the one we started with on our last trip here so long ago, and I'm pleased to see the rooms are still relatively well-cared for. A minimum amount of bugs and dust and spider webs. Water that is mostly fresh. It will do.

I splash water over my face and change my tunic into something not covered in road dust, before joining my squad downstairs.

Kaden and Phoenix are sitting, heads bent low together, talking in whispers. Everyone else is already drinking and eating. I sit across from Kaden and take a deep drink of the watered-down mead to wash the dust out of my throat. "So, what next?"

Kaden clears his throat, but Phoenix answers first. "We speak with the town council, then interview everyone, as you said. Then we track and see what we're dealing with."

I nod and Kaden winks at me as we finish our meal, then head to the Commons, where the council has already been called, or so we've been told.

The village council consists of three middle-aged white men in ornately carved chairs. Before them are rows of hay stacks placed for everyone else to sit.

The men wear black robes with golden clasps and each hold staffs that look custom made. Everything about their presentation is a pretentious nod to what little power they wield in this tiny village. The eight of us walk in, but rather than sitting on the stacks, we stand before the council looking rather impressive, if I do say so myself. Our power is not for show. It is real, and it effective.

There's something about these men that rub me the wrong way without them even saying anything. Particularly the man in the middle, who looks to be in charge. His eyes are small and beady, his salt and pepper hair is plastered to his head with some kind of animal fat, and he has a lecherous way about him that makes my skin crawl. He keeps glancing at Raven and licking his lips. I shift my eyes to her to make sure she's okay, but her face is expressionless.

The man to his right looks like he's done his best to emulate the middle man, down to the same part in his hair. It's only the man on the left that smiles at us when we arrive, and seems grateful that we are here. He has warm brown eyes and gray hair that flops around his face. He reminds me of a kindly grandfather.

"I am Head Council Charles Lambarington Rothcrust," the bloated man in the middle says. His accent is manufactured. That of someone trying to sound above their rank. "And these are my seconds; Jerrit Rubling Dreaklest to my left and Frankelton Mortlur Karspurple to my right." Jerrit visibly cringes when Charles uses his whole name. Conversely, Frankelton puffs up like one of those poisonous fish.

"We've called you here today to give you the opportunity to perform your sworn duty to this realm by ridding us of the devil that is hunting and killing our children. It is, if I may say, a disappointment that we needed to call you at all. That your people haven't managed in all these years of existence, with all the financial charity you receive from the kingdom, to rid us completely of the need for these tragic events."

Kaden and I exchange exasperated glances, and he clears his throat, cutting off Charles before he can continue. "Gentlemen, time is of the essence. Are any of you personally connected with any of the victims? Or a witness to anything that happened?"

Charles pouts his lips at being interrupted. "We have, of course, spoken at length to each and every—"

"That's all well and good," I say, not bothering to hide my frustration. "But we need the names and locations of those who lost loved ones or witnessed what happened so that we can interview them directly."

Charles glares at me, then returns his eyes to Kaden. "I believe the men were speaking. If you could please control that girl."

Are you kidding me?

Kaden smirks at Charles. "If you had any idea how powerful 'that girl' is, you'd be eating your tongue before speaking to her, or about her, that way." Kaden looks to me to continue.

I turn back to Charles. "If you're unable to help us, we will take our leave and begin asking around. This is a waste of our time, and will likely lead to more innocent people getting hurt."

Charles eyes bulge out his wide face, but before he can sputter some defense, Jerrit stands. "Of course. Forgive us for interfering." He comes around the table and hands a piece of paper to me. "Here are the names of the victims, their immediate family members, dates and times they were last scene, and other individuals with possible knowledge of what happened. I'd start with Penny Stratus. Her daughter was the first taken, and she claims to have seen a monster in the shape of a dog the night it happened."

I accept the paper and glance over it, then nod. "Thank you. We'll be in touch."

The eight of us turn and walk out without another word. I can hear the council members begin to argue as Charles chastises Jerrit for 'usurping' him. I have to choke back a laugh at that. These men have really set themselves up as little kings.

Once outside, Kaden and I study the paper. It includes a roughly drawn map of the village, with X marks to indicate the homes of the victims.

"Let's divide and conquer," I suggest. "We each take one of these names, get as much information as we can, then meet back at the inn to discuss the next step?"

Kaden nods. "Smart plan." He rattles off names and pairs people up. He and I take Penny Stratus.

She lives in what I'd generously refer to as a shack in a run down corner of the small village. When we arrive, she's bent over a cast iron pot hanging above a fire just outside her home. She sees us, then looks back down at her pot. "Makin' stew, I am. For Caroline. She be comin' home any time now. That's what they said."

I glance inside the pot, but it looks mostly like water with a rabbit foot floating in it. The woman herself looks probably twenty years older than I imagine she is, with hair turned white and skin leathered with lines. She has two front teeth missing and chapped lips she nervously licks every few seconds. The smell emanating from her makes it clear she hasn't bathed or changed clothes in some time.

"Who told you she'd be coming home?" I ask.

"The Councilmen. They be in charge here and said she'd come home."

Kaden and I sit in the dirt next to her by the fire as she continues stirring the rabbit foot. "Can you tell us what happened?" Kaden asks.

"The devil done took my baby," the woman says, sniffling through emotion. "She was a tiny tike. Only nine years on this wretched earth. I heard an animal outside late that night. Didn't sound like no normal beast neither. Sounded sick. Twisted. I grabbed a stick to beat it away, and saw red eyes glowing in the dark. Then it walked closer and I screamed. It weren't alive, but it were. Its skin crawled on its body, showing all its bits and insides like they was coming out of its belly. Its teeth dripped with red. I ran back inside to get my baby, to take her somewhere safe, but when I returned she weren't there. I looked everywhere, but never found her. The devil took her. Swear it on the dragon eye. She were the first, but weren't the last. More's gone since then too. Other little girls, just like her."

We ask the woman to show us where she saw the beast, and she walks us around back, toward a clearing that feeds into a forest. After, she allows us to look in her home. In one corner there's a broken table with two chairs and a few shelves for what should be food and supplies but mostly holds dust. On the other side of the room is a small chest with a broken lock hanging off it, and a bed of hay covered by a thin blanket. It's a heartbreaking scene. But it leaves us no clue about what happened to her daughter.

"Was there any blood?" I ask. "In your home or outside?"

She nods and opens the trunk, then hands us a small blanket. "Is hers. She was sleeping with it that night, and I found it on the bed, like this."

The blanket has a few tears and some dried blood. "Do you mind if we take this?" I ask.

"Give it back though, will you? It's all I have now. She were supposed to have a good life. They promised. If she served, she would be rewarded. She's a smart girl, not dumb like me. She could've been something."

Her last words give me pause. "Who is 'they'? Who was she serving?"

"The councilmen," the woman says, as if it should be obvious.

"She served them?" Kaden asks. "In what way?"

The woman struggles with her words, her eyes glazing over. "In the ways. The ways of service. It be tradition. They want them young, to teach them, then they can rise up and get good work. In proper home's. Make a good marriage. Get a chance at something. She won't be like me. Won't do what I've had to do to keep food in our bellies." She stirs the pot again and lapses into silence.

We try asking a few more questions, but she just hums under her breath as if she can't hear us.

We leave the woman to her own grief and examine the wooded area around her shack. "What do you make of this?" I ask. "If I didn't know better, I'd say she's on drugs. Is that a thing here?" For as long as I have lived on this world, there is still so much I don't know. I've been very sheltered at the Cliff.

"There are ways," he says as we continue investigating for any signs of struggle, blood, trails. "Herbs and plants that can be used to alter the mental state. Alcohol is common. It's also possible she's just very broken. She hasn't had an easy life."

"No, she hasn't." I don't readily spot anything that can help us and I sigh in frustration. "Landon and Bix both have Spirits with unusually good senses of smell. Maybe we should ask them to sniff around, see if they can catch a blood trail?"

Kaden nods. "And they can compare the scent to other abduction scenes."

"I wonder if anyone else got any clues to help us," I say as we head back to the inn.

Kaden and I are first to arrive, and we order lunch and drinks for everyone as we wait. Eventually the rest begin trickling in, and none look particularly happy.

Once we are all there, Kaden asks for reports. Bix and Mabel go first, with Mabel taking the lead. "I talked to my sister." Her eyes flick to me and she smiles. "She's safe. And expecting her first child! She's heard all the rumors, but didn't know anything first hand. Then we talked to the father of the second victim. His wife died a few years ago, and he's been raising his little girl alone. They're poor, and he's broken. Can hardly see or think straight anymore."

I glance at Kaden, who raises his eyebrow. This sounds like our woman. "Did he say anything about the night she was taken?"

Mabel shrugs. "Not a lot. He heard a noise, thought he saw glowing eyes. Went to look but nothing was there, then came back and his daughter was gone."

"Nothing else?" I ask, desperate for some clue.

She takes a long swig of ale before answering. "He did mention something about how things were improving for them. That she'd been selected to serve."

My heart beats more rapidly. "To serve? The councilmen?"

"Yes," she says. "Why? Did yours say the same?"

Kaden and I nod.

"As did ours," Phoenix says. "Raven and I interviewed a mom who also was poor, alone, and out of sorts. Her daughter was serving the councilmen."

I look to Zev and Landon, and Landon nods. "Same story with us. Poor mom, looking crazy, rambling about how her daughter Lucy would have a good future."

"So, four little girls around the same age go missing, and all of them come from poor single-parent homes, and all of them are connected to the council? Maybe we need to talk to the council members alone," I say. I think of the leader, Charles, and how he looked at Raven, my skin crawls. Raven has grown during her years in the Order of Ash, but she still looks very young. Too young for a man of his age to be ogling.

I cringe when I consider where this is going.

"My sister said the council didn't want to call us in," Mabel says. "That the villagers basically forced their hand."

"Interesting."

"What about the sightings?" Zev says. "More than just the parents claim to have seen things. Red eyes glowing in the woods. A dog that looks undead and as if its body is pushing out of its skin."

"Who else saw this?" I ask.

He shrugs. "Ask anyone at the market and they will likely have some story. How much is true eye witness account and how much is imagination fueled by fear and fascination of the macabre, who knows?"

That's the tricky bit. Who do we trust?

I pull out the blanket with blood and put it on the table in front of me. "Landon, Bix, we need you to take this and use your Spirit senses to track this blood." I give them directions to where Caroline was abducted, and instruct them to cross match the scent with the other crime scenes. "I'm going to have a chat with a particular councilman. The rest of you, talk to everyone in the village. See if you can pin down who was where when. Find out more about this program for the girls. See if anyone knows anything about it. Have other girls gone through this 'service' and actually come out with a good life? Better prospects?"

Alba comes to collect our plates and tsks at what I say. "Them be up to no good, you ask me."

"The councilmen?"

She nods. "They have stories. Girls who served, then went on to marry higher up in other villages, or got good jobs working in noble houses in the capital. Nonsense. We ain't never seen those girls again. My son Billy, he took a shining to a little girl once. They played. Were friends. Would catch tadpoles at the lake. She went into service. They said she had a better life somewhere now, but Billy and me, we looked for her. Talked to her mum. Never found out nothing. Mum said she didn't hear from her but knew she was happy. Now mum is living it up in a nice house with fancy clothes and more food than one person needs."

Kaden and I exchange glances. Someone is making girls disappear from this village, but it doesn't sound like a Spirit.

It sounds like a man.

35

POWER CORRUPTS

We track Charles down at his house. It's not hard to find, as it's the most garish and ostentatious house in the village. He's had custom work done to create moldings and statues of nymphs and dragons and all manner of detail that individually could be really beautiful but collectively are an overpowering display of gaudiness.

When his Keeper invites us in, I'm not surprised to find that it's even worse. Gold everywhere. How does this man afford such things? How can anyone earn this much money in such a small village?

He makes us wait in the library for quite some time. It's a power play, and it's frustrating as hell. I run a finger over the leather books that line his bookshelves. "These haven't been read," I say to Kaden.

He nods. "I noticed."

"This man has the depth of a teaspoon," I say.

Kaden winks at me. "That's probably an insult to teaspoons."

Someone behind us clears his throat and we turn to see Charles standing there in what I imagine to be the most refined clothing he owns. Top coat, hat, cape, all shiny and adorned with gold. His hair is pushed into something like a pompadour, with more animal fat to keep it in place. I can smell it from here and it turns my stomach.

"I expected you would be out hunting a Corrupted Spirit, not harassing the head councilman," he says, his lips pushing out strings of saliva as he talks.

"This is part of our investigation," I say. "You failed to mention all the girls who have gone missing were part of some kind of service to your council."

His eyes widen, and then he waves at us dismissively. "That? Oh that's nothing. Just something we started to help the more impoverished families. They can't afford to care for their children, and those children have no future. So we train them, allowing them to serve in our homes and to learn proper ways of speaking and acting. They learn skills such as cooking, cleaning, managing a home, and then when they are older, we help place them, either with good families or in good marriages, depending on their aptitude."

"Aptitude being another word for who turned out better looking to sell off in marriage." It's a statement, not a question.

He narrows his eyes at me. "Better than those poor girls growing up and selling their bodies to men to buy food. They would have no future without us."

"Then where are the girls you have placed? Why do their parents not hear from them, if their lives are so good now?" Kaden asks.

"Do you think they want to be reminded of this hovel, once they get out?" Charles asks. "Do you think they have fond memories of parents who beat them, or neglect them, or are willing to sell them to pay for their vices? Those girls choose not to come back. We don't force that on them."

If I didn't find this man so vile, and this whole thing so questionable, I might believe him. His words make a certain kind of sense, if viewed through a lens I don't possess.

But all my instincts tell me something much bigger is going on. This isn't as altruistic as it looks. Men like this don't do anything out of kindness. There's always something in it for them.

"How do you afford to live this way?" I ask. "If this village is such a hovel, as you said."

"Not all of us were born here. I was sent here by the Emperor himself—may he never burn—to serve him in creating order from chaos. I am doing my divine duty to His Majesty by being here. My family has long been part of the royal line, going back generations. In fact," he puffs out his chest as he continues, "it would only take five-hundred and sixty-two people to die, for me to become Emperor myself!"

I don't know what to say to this, so I keep my mouth shut. The delusion in this one is strong.

I'm about to ask more, when the Keeper comes in. "I'm sorry to disturb, but our guests have an urgent message."

Kaden and I walk quickly to the front door, and find Landon and Bix waiting. "There's something you need to see," Landon says. "Immediately."

We nod and make our excuses, promising to return soon. I hate leaving Charles before we've finished questioning him, but we must.

Bix leads us to the clearing where Caroline disappeared. "We've been tracking the scent," Bix says. "There is same smell each place. Three smells. The girls. Something Corrupted. And this."

He holds up a silver button, and I take it, turning it over in my hand. It's a simple thing, without any embellishments on it. "You said you smelled something Corrupted?" I ask.

They both nod.

"Are you positive?" Kaden asks.

"Very." Landon wrinkles his nose in disgust. "It's a distinctive smell, like rotting flesh mixed with magic. The villagers saw something. They weren't imagining it. What they saw, I don't know. But there is a Corrupted Spirit attacking this town. There's one more thing you need to see."

We follow them deeper into the woods and Landon points at something by a tree. Kaden and I creep closer, and I recoil instinctively. "What is that?"

It's crawling with bugs and looks like a rotting intestine.

Kaden furrows his brow. "It's a piece of decomposing dog that was taken over by a Corrupted Spirit."

"How can you get all that from... this?" I point with my toe, still standing a few feet back. I don't need special Spirit senses to smell how awful this is.

"Experience," Kaden says, without elaborating.

We head back to the clearing and I recount what we know. "The girls all serve the council. They all went missing within a week of each other. There's definitely a Corrupted Spirit involved. And then there's this button." I look down at it. Something is niggling the back of my mind, but I can't place it.

"Can either of you tell who it belongs to?" I ask.

"Not yet," Landon says. "We'd have to canvas the whole village and smell each person to place the scent."

"Do it." I offer the button, but Bix shakes his head. "We have the scent. Don't need button."

They take their leave, and Kaden and I consider our next step. "We need to search the woods for the Spirit," I say.

He nods. "But not alone. Let me find Phoenix, create a plan. See what Landon and Bix uncover."

"Sounds good. I'm going to find out if there are any other girls part of the service club the council's got going. She could be the next victim and will need guarding."

He reaches for my hand and pulls me into his chest. "Be careful. There's something more going on, I can feel it."

"As someone recently pointed out, this girl is pretty powerful. I'll be fine."

He's smiling as he kisses me, and I kiss him back, my arms wrapping around him to pull him closer.

When we pull away, it is with reluctance. I want more. But that will have to wait.

I decide to head to the inn first. Alba seems to know just about everything happening in town. Maybe she'll know if there are any other girls involved.

On my way there I see Jerrit coming out of a bakery, arms laden with fresh loaves wrapped in cloth. He sees me and smiles, heading toward me. I stop to wait for him.

"How is the investigation coming along?" he asks, offering me a chunk of bread. It's still warm and I accept it and bite into it while he talks. "This whole business has really been a fright for the people of this village. We are a small community, so what happens to one affects all."

I swallow my bread and glance at him. "We have some leads we are exploring."

There is flour on my hands from the bread and I wipe them on my legs as I walk with Jerrit. "Charles told us about the girls working in service to the council," I say, watching his expression from the corner of my eye. I wouldn't have noticed anything unusual. He remains passive. His body relaxed. But he has one tell. A twitch of his fingers tightening around the bread he's holding.

"Yes, it's something we started to— "

"To help the less fortunate. He explained. That's really generous of you all." I try to keep my voice light, sincere. But the pieces are falling into place. I double check to make sure, but yes, I'm right.

He's wearing his guilt as surely as if he held a bloody knife.

"It was you, wasn't it?" I say.

He looks over to me, a shocked expression on his face. "I don't know what you mean. Surely you've found evidence of a Corrupted Spirit."

Evidence he made sure we'd find. "Oh we did, and we'll find the Spirit and handle it, but that's not what endangered those girls."

We've been walking through the village, and I realize we have made it all the way to the edge of the woods.

I should be more careful, but I'm an Ashknight. He's human. What could he possibly to do me? I'm not a little girl.

He sits on a rock and places his bread bundle by his hip, then folds his hands on his lap. "You're a clever one. How did you know?"

I pull the silver button out of my pouch. "This is yours. I suspected it before seeing you in this cloak, but you've confirmed it."

He looks down at his cloak with silver buttons. One is missing. He fingers it. "I wondered where it went to."

"It came off the night you took Caroline."

"How did you know it was mine before?"

"It's silver. No one in this village can afford silver. Except the council. But the others, they wear gold. You like to imagine yourself a man of the people. You like to offset their ostentation with your own insincere humility."

He nods, a small smile forming on his lips. "Perceptive. If only you were younger... "

I sneer at him. "Do you use the girls yourselves, or are you just selling them to the highest bidding pervert you can find?"

"They aren't my taste, though I had to do some level of... skill testing."

I cringe and try to resist killing him on the spot. I need to hear the rest. To know the whole story in case there are others involved.

"They are lucrative business," he says. "Unfortunately, Charles and Frankelton were becoming suspicious. They genuinely believed all the money we brought in came from grateful families looking for a good maid. As if those couldn't be found on every street corner. They didn't realize we were grooming these girls for something far more specific."

"What happened to the four girls who have gone missing?" I ask, while quietly seething with rage..

"They have been sold," he says. "Fortunately, having a Corrupted Spirit loose near the village helped cover this up. Though, with all the suspicion, I will have to alert the Emperor that this location is no longer viable. He will surely find me another town or village better suited to the disappearing of wayward waifs."

"The Emperor knows?"

Jerrit laughs. "Knows? He commissioned me himself to start this little business—may he never burn. He needed to appease certain powerful nobles with unique tastes."

He stands, and a cold sweat breaks out all over my body. Suddenly, I don't feel well. My stomach roils and my head spins.

"But you're asking the wrong questions, Ash Girl. You should be asking yourself why I'm telling you all this. Doesn't it seem odd, that I would confess everything to you right here and now? Without worry? Are you starting to feel sick? Off balance?"

I stumble and grab onto a tree to regain my balance. I reach within for my Spirit, but I can't access it. I'm too weak. I fall to my knees in the dirt, scraping my knee on a root.

"I can't let you go now, but the Spirit I captured will need some company. I need her a little longer to keep terrorizing this town. Long enough for me to leave without a trace."

The bread. He poisoned the bread. Then I see the red eyes, glowing in the woods. An inhuman growl fills the air around us, and I topple to the side, darkness crowding in on me.

When I wake, I am cold, shivering, and I turn onto my side and vomit up everything in my stomach. It stinks of digested food and bad ale, and the smell of it makes me vomit again, until I have nothing left but bile.

I push myself up then, my head spinning as I try to figure out where I am.

The light from a fire flickers over stone walls. Red eyes glow at me from the other side of the fire. My body aches, and my ankle is ripped open as if by sharp teeth. I have scrapes that go up my legs, torso and arms, as if I was dragged over rock and dirt. Did the corrupted dog bite into my ankle and pull me into this cave?

"I am surprised the man let you live," a girl's voice says softly.

I can't see her at first, but then the light of the fire flickers against the wall, and I see. She is a girl, maybe twelve years old, and she is trapped by vines that keep her pinned to the stone. Her chin drops to her chest and her eyes are bloodshot. Red. Corrupted.

"Who are you?"

"I am... I don't know anymore who I am. Or who I was. I know only what I'm meant to be. I am the sacrifice. The one meant to keep the Nine Worlds safe."

Her words are riddles to me, said in a soft, child-like voice with an accent I can't place. "You're the Corrupted Spirit that's been hurting people in the village?"

She holds her head up, her dark hair falling away from her face as she does. "I am, but I have not."

The dog walks up to her and begins nuzzling her. "He is my eyes and ears. I see and I collect, but still the man keeps me here."

"Jerrit put you in here? Why?"

"This was my wish. My one favor granted. I wanted to be free, just for a time, before I was to be sacrificed. Pike said it would be so. But once I was free, I did not want to go back. Then, when the man found me, I couldn't go back."

My heart skips a beat and my mouth goes dry. I walk to the girl, standing close to her face. "Pike? You know Pike?"

She nods, her eyes opening and closing slowly. "I worked for him. I know all about him." Her eyes focus on mine and she grins. "I can tell you everything you want to know, if you help me."

I step back, not sure what to say or do. "What do you mean you were meant to be a sacrifice? For whom? Is this part of what the council is doing to the girls?"

She laughs, but it's the laugh of someone losing their mind. "This has nothing to do with them. *I* have nothing to do with them. Don't you see? The man was just using me to cover up his misdeeds, as all men are wont to do. It's in their nature—men—to abuse and use and demand and cover up and do it all again and again and again. They grab the power and abuse the power and create dark spots every-where, over everyone's eyes, and in their mouths and on their faces and in their noses. Dark spots everywhere. Full of blood. Full of decay. Full of dead things pretending to be living."

I try to parse out the truth from the rant, but it's hard to know what's real and what's not. "Tell me, please. What do you know of Pike? Of what's happening to the girls here? Tell me!" My voice carries and echoes in the small chamber of the cave.

The undead dog growls at me and I step back, fear surging within me as I remember what I'm facing.

"You said you wanted help," I say, trying to change the mood. "What kind of help?"

She giggles. "A helping hand. A helping spade. A help a help a help. We all need help. I need the help of dragons. Only the dragons can help any of us anymore."

She pauses, then sucks in air and looks at me, her eyes clear for just a moment. "You. You. YOU!"

I stumble back as she screams, as she struggles against her confinement. Her fingernails break off as she fights to free herself from the vines, leaving chips of nail and bloody lines over the foliage.

"I don't know what that means," I say, though inside I'm terrified she knows what I really am. Can she tell I'm of dragon blood?

"I need the skin of a dragon, and I need to leave. Far away. Far along. Away and along and goodbye to this dreary place."

"The skin of a dragon? You mean a dragonstone?"

She nods, her face lighting up.

I struggle with what to do next, because I have a dragonstone. I keep one on me at all times, just in case. But I don't want to give it to her. She's Corrupted and insane and could kill the whole village if she escapes.

"And you need to leave? Like, leave this world?"

She nods again.

"So you need a travel talisman," I say.

"A talisman, a tail, a traveling tail of tales," she sings, off key. "But not just that, I need a guide. Yes, a guide for a god. For the sacrifice of dragons. For the good girl who took the place of the other."

My head begins to pound and I lean against the cave's wall and try to think, pinching my nose as I do. "Ok, so a dragonstone, a travel talisman, and we'd have to get to a fountain or body of water under the proper star alignment. I haven't learned to use travel talisman yet. We'd need someone's help."

"Oh fooey, fooey, gooey on you. You can do it. It's in your blood, silly dragon."

"Won't you please just tell me what you know about Pike? I'll do my best to help you if you tell me." She knows something. Something about Kara. About what happened to my baby. And I need to know.

"Get away from it," a voice from the mouth of the cave calls.

I turn around in shock, surprised to see Raven there. "How did you find me?" I ask.

"I tracked your scent," she says. "I smelled something off and knew you were in trouble. There was a stone blocking the entrance to this cave, so I used my Spirit to move it."

She turns to the Corrupted Spirit, and begins to transmute.

"Raven, no! She has answers I need."

But Raven isn't listening. She attacks the girl, and the girl begins to transform, breaking free of her bonds as easily as flicking away ribbon on a present. Her body lengthens and grows in bulk. Her hair falls out in chunks, with her scalp attached. Human skin festers and boils until unnatural bones and chunks of flesh are exposed.

There is no more talking.

The girl, if she'd ever been there to begin with, is gone.

In her place is a mindless monster, and Raven is fighting it alone.

I muster my strength and search inward for my Spirit. I grab onto the thread of light I see. The drugs in my system are wearing off. Transmuting my hand, I lash out at the beast. It roars but attacks. We run to the mouth of the cave and pour out of it. The sunlight stings my eyes.

"We can't let it escape," Raven says.

I nod and we guard the opening, waiting for it to lunge at us.

When it gets closer, I throw down a talisman to create an explosion that forces it back.

I reach for another talisman to create a shield, but the creature is faster than me, and it runs out, knocking into Raven and sending her crashing into a large rock. Her head splits with a hard crack and blood pours out. Her eyes flutter, but do not open.

The beast lunges toward her unconscious body with a knife-like hand jutting out, ready to impale her.

I throw myself between them, blocking with my own dragon claw.

The force send me back, and I'm still dizzy and injured from Jerrit. When my head hits the ground, I feel pain shooting into my brain and blood in my mouth.

I force myself to my knees, and am still transmuted and fighting the monster, when her dog makes a move for Raven.

He's too close. I have to take my eyes off the monster to swipe at the dog. My dragon arm pushes through his neck and he falls to the ground, but as I roll to my back the monster is about to land on me.

I know this will be it.

If this girl is trained in Sanctuary, I could die for real this time.

Just as its about to strike a blow that I might not be able to stop, a figure falls from the sky and lands on the beast's back, stabbing it through the heart with a sword. They throw a purification talisman onto the beast, and the form slowly returns to that of the girl, who is dying.

I spit blood from my mouth and look up to see who saved us.

It's a woman in white with red accents. Her face is covered by a mask, but her hair is red and spirals down her back.

"You're the Outcast," I say, my breath still coming in gasps. I crawl over to Raven to check on her.

"She's alive. She'll have a headache, but she'll live."

"Why did you save us?" I ask.

She walks toward us, and kneels before me. "I want to talk. I have something important to tell you."

My mouth opens, then closes.

"I know you who are," she says. "What you are. I was there that day. When you showed your power. That you are of the dragon blood. And I need to know something."

My blood runs cold. "Who are you?"

"She's the monster who killed my best friend," Kaden says.

I turn my head and he's standing there, sword drawn, ready to kill. "We need to capture her. Now."

He attacks, and the Outcast dodges easily. "You don't understand," she says. "I'm not your enemy."

Kaden isn't listening, or doesn't care, or doesn't believe her. He keeps attacking, and I expect to see her die quickly. But she proves to be a match for Kaden, which seems to surprise him even more than me.

And then, as Kaden lunges, about to make contact. She just disappears.

It's as if she teleported.

There one second, gone the next.

Just as I have done in the past.

36

THE RED DRAGON

"**W**here did she go?" Kaden looks around, wide-eyed and full of adrenaline.

I can finally stand, and I run to him on wobbly legs, throwing my arms around him. His eyes focus on me, and he frowns. "Are you injured?"

I laugh, because everything on my body hurts so much that I don't even know what's serious and what's not.

He looks more closely at my whole body and sighs. "You need a healer. We need to get out of here, get the squad and return to Dragoncliff to report what's happened."

"I agree, but first, there's something you need to know. Jerrit did this. Did everything. He trapped a Corrupted Spirit and poisoned me. He... " I'm about to tell him everything that happened to those poor girls, but he brushes the hair off my face and the words die on my lips.

"I know. After we separated I found out some things that didn't make sense. Long story short, we got a reluctant confession out of Jerrit. The remaining council members are trying to track down what happened to the girls, and Jerrit is being hanged at sunrise."

"That's fast," I whisper, bile filling my throat.

"It has to be. If what he said is true and this is sanctioned by the Emperor, the village can't afford to wait." He kisses me softly. "We've done our part. Now, we must leave. You're hurt. Raven is unconscious, and I just let a murderer escape."

I limp along with him until we reach Raven. He lifts her gently and carries her as if she weighs nothing. "The village isn't far. Can you make it?"

I nod. My ankle hurts, everything hurts, but I'm already starting to heal.

Kaden speaks again, but doesn't turn to face me. "Sky, I need to tell you something."

There's something in his voice that makes me fear what he's about to say. "Okay..."

"I know you're High Dragon." He stops and turns to face me. Raven is between us, separating us. "I knew there was a chance the Outcast would show up. We think she's after you."

"Me? Why?"

"Because you have power. You are the most powerful person in this world right now, even if you don't know how to fully access that power. That makes you a danger to some, a weapon to others. It's why we have to get back to the Cliff. Immediately. You're not safe here."

We begin walking again and I ask, "How long have you known? And what did you mean by 'we'?"

Before he can answer, there is a great roar in the sky.

We both look up, and there, coming toward us, are dragons.

Many. Many. Dragons. The largest thunder I have ever seen.

"How?" I stutter.

"The Wall, it must be fading. A Sundering maybe? Or... look!" He points.

I see the red dragon from before. Surrounded by drakes and smaller dragons. But this time, the red dragon is closer. Close enough to see the rider on it.

"That's her. She's controlling them. The Outcast is behind this!" Kaden is livid.

And scared.

We both are.

We are in no condition to fight that many dragons. Raven is still out cold. I'm injured. Our squad is still back at the village. We are no match for what awaits us.

"Take Raven back to the village. You have to run," I tell him.

I pull out the dragonstone I keep hidden in my pouch and hold it in my fist. I look to see if Kaden listened, but of course he didn't. He set Raven under a tree and is running back to me. Stupid man.

I close my eyes and focus on my power, and I channel the largest dragon I ever have. Umi roars from me full of fire and rage, and heads straight for the dragons that are descending on us.

My feelings of victory are short lived as the red dragon fights with Umi. They battle and I feel it in my bones. Every lash. Every cut. Every wound.

I focus harder, trying to send more power to help him fight. But he's losing. The other drakes and dragons are coming to aid the red dragon, surrounding Umi until he can't escape or fight them all.

I feel the moment he's killed and dissipates into the air, and I sink to the ground, my power draining from me like water from a broken cup. I feel empty, and I know I will not be able to channel again anytime soon.

Kaden reaches me, his eyes wide.

Tears leak from my eyes. "I told you to run. You just killed yourself and Raven."

He kneels before me. "Do you trust me?"

"Of course. But that doesn't change our fate."

"I can save us, but you have to trust me. I promise I will explain everything later. And... I'm sorry." He kisses me softly. "Please don't forget I love you."

I sit in stunned silence, wondering what he's sorry for. Trying to make sense of his words, as he closes his eyes.

He's clearly reaching for Spirit. He'll go out fighting, of course he will. I will watch him die, and then I will die. I can only hope they will spare Raven. Maybe she will regain consciousness and get to the village.

Power washes over Kaden, and he begins to glow as he summons his Spirit.

A huge black and red dragon that looks demonic and very powerful. The dragon he transmuted into when he rescued me from Skip's inn.

Kaden opens his eyes, and I hear a gasp behind me.

Raven is there, staring at us both, blood dripping down her face.

Kaden swears, and it takes me a moment to make sense of everything.

His eyes.

They are red.

Kaden is Corrupted.

He turns away from us and mounts his dragon, then takes to the sky to fight.

Raven sinks to the ground beside me and I put an arm around her. She lets me. We watch, silently. Waiting.

I'm numb inside. Or think I am. But I'm also scared. Can you be numb and scared?

I can't lose Kaden.

Not to this fight.

Not to the Corruption.

But it didn't seem sudden. He knew.

He knows he's corrupted, and he never told me.

But how? How is this, is any of this, even possible? Corrupted ones can't control it. They go mad. They are deadly. He is none of those things.

The dragons fight above us, and one of their drakes falls from the sky, dead. Another follows. Kaden fights like a beast possessed. I've never seen anything like it.

Except.

Except I have.

In the Corrupted.

When another dragon falls dead from the sky, the Outcast pulls out of the fight, and the red dragon leads what's left away, unwilling to lose any more of her thunder to Kaden's ferocity.

He lands before us, his dragon dissipating as he runs to me, his eyes still glowing red. "Sky, I can explain."

"They saw you!" Phoenix is here now, but I didn't hear her arrive. She looks pissed.

"No, wait!" Kaden holds out his hand, but before he can reach us, I feel something hard hit my head, and I fall to the ground, passing out before my head hits the rock.

37

ALON LONDAL

I have been betrayed.

For years, I trained to be an Ashknight because of Kaden's guidance, and now he has trapped me in a cell. Were his promises to help me defeat Pike all hollow? Were our stolen kisses all lies? Did he have something else planned all along?

And what of his eyes...

Red eyes mean a Corrupted Spirit, and yet Phoenix wasn't even surprised. She knew he was Corrupted. She knew and she wanted it kept secret. She would rather us captured than talk. Maybe she would rather us dead.

But we still breathe. And we will be free.

Heavy shackles cover my wrists, steel rings engraved with nullify glyphs. They remind me of my wrist brace, but even stronger in their effect. I can't feel my Spirit at all, and all my attempts at transmuting and beckoning leave me nothing but tired.

Raven has barely spoken since we woke a few hours ago. She sits next to me, her small pale body feeble compared to the massive chains that link us to the stone walls. Her skin is purple around the wrist, bruised from the tight confines of metal. There is an emptiness in her eyes. More so than usual. She has always been distant, but now...

Now she is defeated.

My lips are cracked, my throat dry. We've not had water since we woke, and I do not know how long we were here while unconscious. There are no windows in our cell. Only torches of blue flame on the opposite side of the bars, castling long shadows. I do not know if it is night or day. If we are above ground or below. I know nothing but the cold hard floor, the ache in my bones, and the growing hunger within.

A droplet of water falls from the ceiling before me, adding to a slowly growing puddle. Perhaps it is raining. Perhaps we are beneath snow. Drip. Drop. The water falls. Drip. Drop. The sound buries itself in my mind, and a headache grows. I cannot sleep. I cannot relax. How long will this go on for?

Will we be prisoners for days, weeks, years? Or will they kill us?

They can try.

As soon as someone enters my cell, I will be upon them, fighting tooth and nail. I will free myself to honor my promise to Kara, or I will die trying.

A rattle. A groan of wood.

Someone just opened a door.

Footsteps.

A man emerges from the shadows.

Kaden.

He stands before the bars, his face tired, his eyes... normal.

The red is gone.

But how?

There is no cure for Corruption. Not yet. That is what they seek to discover in the Asylum.

"I'm sorry," says Kaden softly. "If it were up to me, you would never have been put in these cells—"

"Then free us," I say.

He frowns. "I can't. It is not for me to decide, you see."

I stand, walking forward, chains rattling behind me. "Then who decides?"

He sighs, saying nothing.

Raven looks up at him. "You were Corrupted. Now you're not. How?"

He leans forward, clasping the bars with his hand. "There is much you don't understand. The Masters have been lying to you. About Corruption. About the Asylum."

I take another step forward. If I can grab Kaden's hand, maybe I can pull him against the bars, wrap my arm around his throat, take him prisoner and negotiate a release.

"Tell us the truth then," says Raven.

One more step. I almost have him.

Kaden pulls his hands away, grabbing a set of keys from his belt. "I can't tell you. But I will show you."

He unlocks the cell, then steps within. He is in reach now. I can grab him, but I don't. Why don't I? This could be another trick. Another lie.

But there is truth in Kaden's eyes. He wants to show us something. He wants us to understand.

With a key, he unlocks the chains, and they fall to the ground with a thud. I raise up my arms. "Now the shackles," I say.

He shakes his head. "That I cannot do. Not until you swear to do no harm within these walls."

"I swear." It is a lie. I choose freedom over truth.

"It is not to me you must swear, but to another." He puts the keys back on his belt. I consider grabbing them. Together, Raven and I could overpower him and—

"I know you're thinking of escape," says Kaden, glancing at us both. "Perhaps you could take the keys, though I have access to Spirit and you do not. Perhaps, you could remove your shackles and defeat me, though I am an Ashlord and you but knights. But I swear to you, there is another here you cannot defeat. And if you run, she will kill you." He pauses, clenching his fist, his eyes intense. "Do not run. I beg you."

I see the sorrow in him, and it softens me. Somehow, he is on our side in this. I do not know how. But I hear it in the way he speaks. It wasn't he who knocked us out. It was Phoenix, and he seemed against it. There is more in play here than I know. Much more.

Kaden grabs a torch from the wall and motions for us to follow, and so we do, leaving the cell behind. He guides us past other cells, most empty but for two. One holds an old man, another a younger woman, both shackled like us. "Who are they?" I ask, their faces unfamiliar.

"Criminals," says Kaden. "The woman awaits trial. The man carries out his sentence."

"Are we in the King's dungeons?" I ask.

"No." He does not elaborate, leading us up a set of spiral stairs. The stone walls are old and cracked. Ancient symbols are etched into the ceiling.

Raven glances at me. "Remind you of anywhere?" she whispers.

I nod. The catacombs beneath Dragoncliff. Is that where we are? It is not long until we reach a doorway and emerge into a giant cavern, so tall and wide I can barely believe we are underground. Crystal stalagmites glitter like stars in the ceiling. Blue flames flicker in the distance, lighting doors and windows carved into stone walls, and roads weaving between blocks of dark rock. A vast pool of water casts reflections in the center of the cavern, large enough to be a lake. Waterfalls pour from stone, thundering in the distance. Giant trees, with tops like mushroom, reach high above, glowing a pale blue in the darkness. This place would seem an underground sanctuary, if not for the people.

They are everywhere, bustling about, filling stalls around the roads, washing clothes in the lake, chatting on rooftops, bathing beneath the waterfalls. Most wear gray robes. A few, like Kaden, wear black.

"This is a city," I say.

Kaden nods, raising his torch higher. "Welcome to Alon Londal. Home of the Ashwraiths."

"THEY'RE REAL," whispers Raven, her eyes locked on the city. "The Ashwraiths... All this time... I thought I knew... I thought I knew... " She talks more to herself than us. I have rarely seen her surprised.

My mind mulls over everything I've recently learned. I remember Kaden's eyes. The Corruption. And a thought forms. "Are Ashwraiths Corrupted Twin Spirits?" I ask.

Kaden nods. "Yes, and no. Corruption is not what you have been led to believe. It is not a disease to be cured. It is not a curse. It is but the next step for the bond between Spirit and man. An evolution."

I raise an eyebrow. "But when one's Spirit becomes corrupted, doesn't the Spirit take over their mind? Make them dangerous?"

Kaden guides us forward, talking as we walk. "At first, yes, it makes one dangerous. But is a Broken One not dangerous? Is an untrained Twin Spirit not dangerous? Those who become Corrupted shouldn't be locked away. They should be trained."

Two men pass us on the way. They look at Raven and me with suspicion, but to Kaden they bow their heads.

"Are all these people Ashwraiths?" I ask.

"Yes."

"But there must be hundreds."

"And you're wondering how they all ended up here," says Kaden. His voice takes on false sincerity. "All Corrupted Ones are sent to the Asylum. Those who flee are hunted down. Within the Asylum, Corrupted Ones receive treatment and shelter while a cure is developed for their condition." His voice returns to normal. "That is what all Ashlings are told. What we all come to believe."

"You mean... they lied?" I ask.

"Oh, they lied. Let me show you how much." He guides us into a tunnel, and we walk up until we reach a dead end, a brick wall before us. A man and woman stand on either side of the wall, wielding spears; the first weapons I've seen in Alon Londal. When they recognize Kaden, they bow their heads.

"Lord Kaden," says the man. "How may we be of service?"

Raven and I exchange a look. Bowing and calling people lords is something for the nobility, not Twin Spirits. Yet these people seem to do more than bow for Kaden. There is respect in their voices. Reverence in their eyes. Who is Kaden to these people?

The Ashlord smiles. "Anyone new come through the doors?" he asks.

"A woman," says the man. "An Ashknight who pushed herself beyond the Wall."

"Who tends to her?" asks Kaden. "Meric?"

"Iona, my lord," replies the man.

"Ah. Iona has a tender heart," says Kaden. "She will do well. Now, my company and I must pass."

The man and woman glance at the shackles on our wrists and frown. They don't appear to agree with what Kaden is doing, but they offer no argument. "Yes, my lord," replies the woman. She pulls a black lever on the cave wall, and the bricks before us slide out of the way.

We follow Kaden forward and enter a new chamber. Where everything in Alon Londal was black stone, here it is white. White walls, white ceilings. There is nothing else. It is an empty chamber, the size of a barracks. High above, I see something in the wall. A door of black steel. There is something familiar about the door. About the size of the chamber and the white walls.

And then I understand.

"This... This is the Asylum," I say.

Raven gasps. "But there's nothing here."

Kaden walks forward, gesturing at the empty space. "The Asylum was never a place to treat Corrupted Ones. Simply a place to lock them away."

I bend down, rubbing my fingers against the floor, wiping away a layer of dust. "But if there's no treatment, why not simply kill anyone who becomes Corrupted?" I ask. "Why the lie?"

"The Corrupted were killed," says Kaden," back in the ancient days. Back before Illian."

"The first Ashlord," I say, remembering Illian's statue at Dragon

Cliff. "The one who ended the first Sundering, sealing a breach in the wall, and becoming Corrupted in the process. They say, with her last act of lucidity, she took her own life."

"Another lie," says Kaden. "Let me tell you the tale of Illian. Let me tell you the truth that was kept from you."

"ILLIAN, like all who become Corrupted, could not control herself at first. Her followers had a choice. Kill her like they did all Corrupted before, or try to find a cure. They could not bring themselves to murder their great leader and friend, so they trapped her instead. In this place. It was not long before all Corrupted were placed here as well. No one wanted to kill their friends. This was an easier choice. A simpler choice. Lock your friends away until a cure was found. It made sense. It eased the conscience. But as the years went by, no cure was found. As centuries passed, all hope for the Corrupted began to fade. This place, this prison, was no longer the beacon of hope it once was. And so the Masters, in an attempt to boost morale, devised a story. They had converted the prison into an Asylum, where the Corrupted were treated with care and where a cure was being developed. But they sent no doctors and nurses into the Asylum. And the cure... the cure had long been abandoned.

"The lies appeased the people, however, and in time, the story of Illian changed as well. There was no honor to joining the Asylum. Illian took her own life instead, they said. I wonder if it was to try and encourage others to do the same.

"The Masters abandoned those who were corrupted. They left them locked away for centuries. And then something happened no one expected. Illian, the oldest of us, began to regain control. It took many years with no guidance, but somehow, she succeeded. She regained balance with her Spirit, and became lucid once more. The other prisoners did not harm her. Nor each other. Their connection, the fact that they were all ascended, kept them safe. And Illian began to seek a way out. She could not breach the door, for it was sealed with many glyphs and barriers. But she could dig.

"For years Illian dug through the walls and earth. She sought to find the lands outside, to see the sun and moon once more, but instead she reached something else. A forgotten part of the catacombs beneath Dragoncliff. A place so large it could hold all those within the Asylum and more.

"Illian thought to leave then. To make her way through the catacombs until she reached the Cliff and then freedom. But she would have to leave the other Corrupted behind. Men and women she had spent centuries with. Men and women she had grown to care for even though they had never shared words. None had died, for the Corrupted were immortal, whether they had earned dragon hearts or not. And so she stayed with them and began began to teach them control.

"It took many years, for Illian barely understood what she herself had learned. But in time, her first pupil, Yosa, became lucid as well. He and Illian had achieved a level of ability with Spirit never seen before. They could do things the Masters had never envisioned. And they began to train the rest. They did not call them Corrupted, for they realized the inherent lie in that word. When one pushed themselves too hard, when their Spirit took over and their eyes turned red, they had simply reached the next part of their journey. A journey none ever thought could be completed. But Illian and Yosa proved them wrong. They and their pupils became something new, something more even than Twin Spirits, and so they no longer called themselves Corrupted, but Ascended.

"In time, there were hundreds of them. They thought to leave the catacombs then. To return to the Cliff and show the Masters the errors of their ways. But what if they were not believed? What if they were seen as a threat? For how does one prove that they are themselves and not a Spirit merely playing at human? If the Masters refused them, a great war would begin. And the Ascended, still relatively small in number, would die.

"So they decided to bide their time. To build a city in the very caverns below the Cliff, and to live as best they could until the moment was right. Until they could return to the surface once more, and none would dare challenge them.

"Perhaps you're wondering why the Masters never caught on? Why they never realized the Asylum had grown empty? There are two doors you see. An Ascended is taken past the first when they are forced inside the Asylum. The second door is then opened remotely, and a further contraption, a moving wall, pushes the Ascended inside the pit where we now stand. There are no windows. No way to look within. For the Masters feared what they would see. And even more, they feared their prisoners' escape.

"As the years passed, more and more Ascended were tossed inside the Asylum. They were taken into the city now called Alon Londal, and they were taught control. In time, they named themselves Ashwraiths, a title from legends, but one they wore proudly. A reminder that they were real, though others had forgotten.

"Their numbers grew. They were almost ready return to the surface. But first, they needed to weaken the empire that ruled the land. They needed to send someone out into the world, someone who could manipulate events in their favor. But their faces were known. Illian's most of all.

But soon they had someone known by no one. The first of his kind.

For Illian and Yosa had a child.

And that child was me."

38

ILLIAN

"But if this is true..." says Raven, "Then..."

Before she can finish her sentence, a man steps through the tunnel behind us. His robes are gray. His skin dark. His smile is wide and he looks happier than I've ever seen him.

"It's good to see you again," says Enzo with a thick French accent.

Raven runs into his arms, hugging him fiercely. She hides her eyes against his chest, but I can hear the soft whimper of sobs. "I missed you so much," she says.

Enzo caresses her hair. "And I missed you, little one. But I'm taken care of well here. I learn many things."

I wrap an arm around them both. "I'm glad you're safe."

"Me too," he says. "I thought my life was over. Worse than Charred. For the first few days, I lived in a dream, my body not my own. But then I hear a voice. Distant. Then closer. It guides me. I follow. A little the first day. Then more. I find the voice, in my mind, in my Sanctuary. It is a person. Iona, she calls herself. Tells me not all is lost. That I am not really Corrupted. That I simply need more training. So I learn from her. And one day, I find balance once more. And then I am in my body. And then I am meeting people and eating food and having a room all for myself. And now I am seeing you again."

Raven pulls away, her eyes red, but her face happy. "How did you find us?"

"Lord Kaden sent a message. Told me I could meet you here." He bows his head to the Ashlord, and I see the same reverence in his eyes for Kaden as I saw in the guards.

Enzo looks down at our shackled wrists and frowns. "What is the meaning of these?" he asks.

Kaden stands by my side. "They are yet to take the oath to our liege and lord."

"I see." Enzo locks eyes with me. "All will be well soon, I promise. The lord is understanding. No harm will come to you if you swear to peace."

Kaden clears his throat. "I wish you could have more time to talk, but I'm afraid we must move on. Perhaps, Enzo, you can accompany us to the throne room."

"Yes, my lord."

Enzo, Raven, and I follow Kaden back down the tunnel of stone, and into the heart of Alon Londal. A few Ashwraiths glance our way, but most go about their business, exchanging coin for goods I don't recognize: glowing pale blue mushrooms, crude utensils made of black steel, sapphire fishing nets that stretch to three times their size.

"It seems your people have made a world of their own here," I say.

Kaden smiles. "We had to make do with what the underground provides. The vegetation is different here. The animals as well." He bends down and picks a rock up from the ground. No. Not a rock. A dozen little legs expand from its shell, and it runs around Kaden's palm. "Rockbugs, we call them. These are small and harmless, but their cousins..." He shudders. "Their cousins the Rockdwellers are another matter. Five times the size of a person. Their pincers capable of snapping a man in two. They're tasty meat though." He scoops the Rockbug from its stone shell and plops it into his mouth.

My stomach turns at the sight.

Kaden grins, picking up another bug. "You should try one—"

"No. No, thank you," I say, pulling back.

Enzo holds out his arm. "I'd like one, please." He chews down on the Rockbug, grimacing. "Every time I think maybe it'll taste better now. And every time I am wrong."

Raven chuckles.

A thought comes to mind. "Do the Masters drop food down into the Asylum?" I ask.

Kaden shakes his head. "The Ascended do not need food to survive. Our Spirit is so strong it sustains the body. We do grow hungry though, and we still enjoy taste. So food is a delicacy of sorts. Sometimes, we bring some juicy meat from the surface."

"We?" I raise an eyebrow. "Are there more like you? More Ashwraiths from birth?"

"There are," he says. "I was the first but not the last."

"Is Phoenix..."

"No. What you know of Phoenix is true. I met her when I first joined the Cliff. We trained together. Bled together. One night, when we were still children, she followed me into the catacombs. I was careful, but she was sneakier, and she trailed me all the way to Alon Londal. By the time I noticed her, she had already seen the truth of things. I told her all there was to know, and she swore to keep my secret."

I lower my head. "You could have told me, you know."

"I know," he says. "But it is not only my life on the line, but the life of thousands. The fewer people know, the safer we all are. And... I didn't want secrets between you and your squad. You needed to trust each other explicitly, and this would have gotten in the way."

My squad... "What happened to them after the dragons attacked?" I ask.

Enzo frowns. "This too, I wish to know."

Raven crosses her arms, eyeing Kaden suspiciously.

He sighs. "Phoenix ordered them to return to Dragoneyes Manor. We both agreed to tell them you were injured in battle and recovering safely at the Cliff." He pauses. "They ask about you often. Bix is physically ill with worry."

I imagine the poor giant bent over a toilet, spewing out his guts. Oh, Bix. How I miss him. How I miss all of them.

"How long have we been here?" I ask, feeling confident I will get true answers now that Kaden has shared his story.

"Only a day," he says. "And please, don't be too hard on Phoenix. She shouldn't have knocked you out, but she panicked. You must understand, she thought my life was on the line. She has protected my secret since we were children."

Raven's face softens a bit. "She will do anything for those she cares about. I saw it in her eyes. It... it reminded me of you, Sky."

I pause, suddenly overcome with tenderness. "I... I suppose I would have done the same for my squad as Phoenix did for you." I grin. "Though I would have tried talking first."

"We're here," says Kaden, as we reach a giant metal gate three times my height, images of people and Spirits carved into the steel. It takes four men to pull the gate open, the steel groaning throughout the caverns.

Enzo lowers his voice. "Once inside, you must show the outmost respect. Do not speak unless spoken to. And do not make threats, please. Your freedom depends on this."

I nod. "So who are we meeting?"

Kaden gestures forward into the darkness. "Our liege and lord. The first of our kind. My mother. Lord Illian."

WE ENTER a hall of black and silver stone. Guards clad in dark armor line each side, their faces hidden behind mouthless masks. Kaden leads us forward, and at the end of the room, we reach her. Illian. She is a mirror of her statue, clad in silver armor, a gray veil upon her face, sitting on a stone throne.

"Kneel," whispers Enzo.

Raven and I exchange a look.

We stand firm.

And then Illian speaks, her voice gentle and soft. "I have seen you in my dreams... standing amongst a field of ash." Her words echo across the space and she sounds as close as if she was standing beside me. Her eyes are hidden behind the veil, and I do not know if she speaks to me or Raven or both. She raises a gloved hand, her fingers long and thin, and gestures at our shackles. "Those are unnecessary."

I expect Kaden to unlock our restraints.

Instead Illian flicks her wrist.

And the shackles fall unbound at our feet.

How? How does she have this power?

Are these the things a trained Corrupted can accomplish?

"Thank you," I say, rubbing at the cracked skin on my wrist. "We will do no harm to you or your people. I swear it." And I do mean it, unless someone gives me—

"Unless someone gives you cause to do otherwise," finishes Illian.

Did she just... Did she just read my thoughts?

The Lord of Ashwraiths turns her head to the side, and I see a hint of a smile beneath the veil, lips stained black on a pale face. "Thoughts and words are but ripples in an ocean to me. I see and hear so much more. The past. The present. The future. They draw closer and closer, folding in on each other." She clenches and unclenches her hand. "I believe one day I will lose my sanity once again. The Spirit can comprehend so much more than the mind, after all. But do not fear... Perhaps our kind are not meant to live forever. Perhaps we must choose to Ascend to something even higher. Leave the body behind. Once and for all."

She turns her face back to us, smile fading. "You have questions."

I nod, trembling, caught off guard by her abilities. "When can we go—"

"You may leave whenever you wish. But you will not. You will stay and hear what I have to say. You will find it most interesting. You will wish to ask why Kaden did not bring you to me sooner, but know that you were not ready before." Illian smiles a chilling smile. "I will tell you what I have seen. But to understand the future, you must first understand the past. You know the secret of the Asylum. Now learn the secret of the Ashpriests. The secret of the Wall of Light. One man stands at the center of it all. The one you seek. The one who calls himself Pike. I will tell you how his story began. Only you can tell me how it will end."

———

"YOU KNOW that Nir created the Wall of Light to keep the dragons at bay," she says, falling into a rhythmic vocal pattern that draws me into her story. "What you do not know is that every millennium the Wall fades, the light wanes, and a Sundering begins. You see, the Wall is not eternal, not without help at least. Someone must keep it alight.

"Two were tasked with the duty. Ordained by Nir himself. Me, and the one you know as Pike.

"We were friends, once. I, the first Twin Spirit, and Pike, the first child of Nir. Not the first human, no. You see, Pike...

"Pike is a son of Nir. A dragon.

"That is why none can match him in battle. Why he has powers Twin Spirits cannot comprehend. The skin he wears is not his own. But an Illusion. He has had many faces. Many names. Pike was but one of the first. One I knew.

"When Nir created the Wall of Light, he tasked us with its protection. Together, we oversaw the creation of Dragoncliff and the training of the first Ashlings. By the elder dragon, I was named the first Ashlord, and Pike the first Ashpriest. I was tasked the command of Ashknights in defense of the Wall. Pike was tasked to remember and uphold of the Code of Ash. You may have heard of it... but there is a part you have not heard. The key to keeping the Wall alight.

"It requires sacrifice.

"A Twin Spirit must give themselves to the light. Their body and soul burned until nothing but ash remains.

"They must be placed on the Pyre of Light. The pyre only found in the Dream that Cannot be Dreamt.

"The sacrifice must be strong, trained in the highest arts of our order. At first, the strongest Ashlords and Ashknights were enough. Each millennium or so, one would willingly sacrifice themselves to the light. But as each cycle of the Wall passed, Pike and I became aware of something. The Sunderings grew closer together, the need for sacrifice more common, and the strength of the Spirit required stronger. In time, only those who were trained from birth were strong enough for the light. But they were few. Too few. So Pike began to seek them out with the strongest devotion.

"And when once the sacrifices were willing, they began to have no say in the matter.

"At first, I approved. For what else was there to do but keep the Wall alight? Yet, as the centuries wore on, I grew tired of the death, of the endless battle between man and dragon. I sought to break the cycle.

"I delved into the ancient caves left behind by the elder dragons. I studied their magics, seeking to understand the spell that created the Wall of Light in the first place. It took many years, but finally I learned the truth. Nir had never completed the spell. His injuries at the hand of Val's children prevented him from doing so. The Wall of Light wasn't meant to simply contain the dragons, but to burn them out. To kill them once and for all.

"And it could still be done. If the sacrifice was strong enough, the Wall of Light would burn brighter than ever, so bright that all dragons within would burn to ash, and our eternal struggle would finally end.

"Pike and I both agreed, there was only one strong enough for such a sacrifice.

"The child of Nir, the first Ashpriest, Pike himself.

"He took the duty. When the time came, he would give himself to the light, putting an end to the need for more death.

A day later, I received word. Some of my Ashknights were attacked beyond the wall. Pike and I rushed out to help them. As I passed beyond the gates, they sealed behind me. And too late I realized... There was no attack. No dragons. Only Pike standing on the other side of the Wall. "I'm sorry, my friend," he said. "But I cannot give my life. There would be no one to lead otherwise."

"He walked away. Left me to die.

"And the dragons came.

"Hundreds of them.

"I fought with all my strength.

"I would make it back somehow. I would tell others the truth. That Pike could end the battles, the sacrifices, but he would rather give the lives of others than his own. He had lived too long to think otherwise. And if he could not give himself willingly, then I would make him. One final sacrifice to end it all.

"I fought with all my strength.

"And the Corruption took hold.

"Amidst a thousand corpses I fell into insanity.

"My Ashknights found me then. But I could not tell them the truth. I could not speak. To me, they were but a dream I could only watch. I watched them debate my life. My future. In the end, they locked me away, and Pike's betrayal went unpunished.

"The cycle continued.

"The Wall would fade.

"A Sundering would come.

"Dragons would fly over Nirandel.

"Hundreds would die.

"A sacrifice would be made.

"The Wall relit.

"And so it would be as it always was." She sits forward, her eyes glued to me.

"I have seen you in a vision, standing in the Dream that Cannot be Dreamt, the choice before you. Let the Wall fade and the dragons reign. Sacrifice the Twin Spirit trained from birth and let the cycle continue. Or place Pike upon the pyre and end the cycle once and for all."

She pauses. "The ritual to rekindle the Wall of Light can only be done during a Sundering, and only when the three moons are high in the sky at the mid point of night. You have until then to find your daughter."

I freeze. My blood runs cold. "Kara... Kara is dead."

"No," says Illian. "She lives. She is the next sacrifice. That is her purpose. You know, somewhere deep within, this to be true."

"I..." my voice cracks. "I buried her bones."

"There are many ways to get bones. They were not the bones of your daughter. She has been trained as the next sacrifice."

My heart speeds up. My palms sweat. My head spins. Kara may yet live. I may yet save her.

Illian continues. "But first, you must find the dragon who fights his own kind. The first Ashpriest, my old friend, Pike, son of Nir. You must find him, for the Dream that Cannot be Dreamt is his Sanctuary."

39

THE SUNDERING

My mind overflows with what Lord Illian has told me. Kara is alive. It's not too late. I can still save her.

But Pike... he could be anyone. What if he's a friend? Someone I trust? Is that possible?

Whoever he is, he has great power, and he can change faces. Perhaps Pike isn't his only identity. Perhaps he has a more inconspicuous one that he uses to go about everyday life. "Can you see Pike's identities with your abilities?" I ask.

The woman—Kaden's mother, I keep reminding myself—tilts her head, considering. "It is possible I have seen one of his faces, but how could I be sure? He hides his transformations well," Illian says.

How do you track an enemy who can look like anyone at any time? "There must be some way to detect his true self," I say. I won't allow frustration or the impossibleness of this situation to deter me. Granted, it was hard enough to track this man when he was just one man with a single, identifiable face. But this?

My mind flashes to when I first met him. When I tried to describe what he looked like to Dean and Blake. Could this explain why they didn't understand me?

"The first Ashpriest always relished his abilities, and enjoyed using them to gain the awe and admiration of the public. Seek out those who do things you cannot explain," she says.

Her words trigger an idea that's been slowly growing in my mind. "I need to get to the library at the Cliff. If Pike has lived for centuries, then at least one of his identities is likely in the histories."

"But how will you ferret him out?" Kaden asks.

"I'll search for miracles. Wonders. Something will stand out."

Kaden sighs. "I've tried a similar approach before. There are too many tales. Too few ways to separate fact from fiction."

"It's a start, at least." I say, thoughts spinning in my mind. "When is the next Sundering expected?" I ask.

Kaden's eyes turn dark. "You've seen the dragons beyond the Wall. You know what it means."

"So it's begun," I say, finally facing the truth. I'd hoped... for what? More time. That this wouldn't happen just yet. But alas, we must deal with the reality we are given, for true suffering comes from fighting reality.

Kaden nods. "All Ashlords and knights have been summoned to the Wall. They will defend any gates that tear open."

"Our squadron?" I should be with them. My squad. My friends.

"They are on their way to the South Gate last I heard," says Kaden.

I'm torn. I need to lead my squad and defend the South Gate, but I also need to find Pike. Fast. Before he sacrifices Kara. But how much time do I even have? A week. A day? An hour?

Except... if he doesn't make the next sacrifice, then the Wall will fall. The dragons will raid all the worlds. Humanity will be devoured.

"Your mind is racing, spinning into dozens of webs," Lord Illian says. "You worry about your choice, and yet even with free will, we cannot escape fate. It is your fate to find Pike. It is what must be to save the Nine Worlds."

I hope this is the right choice, but Illian's words give me confidence. "Take me to the library."

Illian nods, a small smile playing on her lips. "Escort our guests, my son. Then I expect your return. We have preparations of our own to make. The time has come."

He gives a small bow to his mother, then leads Raven and I out, with Enzo joining us.

We are halfway through the passageway before I dare ask, "What did she mean by preparations?"

Kaden frowns and his face hardens. "While the Sundering is at hand, Nirandel will be in chaos. It is the opportunity the Ashwraiths have been waiting for."

"Opportunity for what?" I fear I will not like his answer, and I reach for his hand and squeeze it.

"We will make the transition as peaceful as possible. We will target the Emperor and his Shadows. Once they are eliminated, we will demand surrender from the army and the common people. If all goes well, everyone will lay down their arms. Those who wish to stay under our rule, may. Those who wish to leave will have a chance to travel north, to start a new community there."

It is as I feared. "And what if people don't lay down their arms?"

"Then much blood will be spilled," he says somberly.

"How can you do this? Potentially kill hundreds, maybe thousands of people, at a time when the people need defending the most?"

"What would you have us do?"

"If your people helped fight the dragons, helped prevent the Sundering, we could save so many more. Then, you could talk with the Emperor. Show him how you can control your powers. How you helped save this world, and all the worlds. Create peace. Maybe you can get land to call your own." Even as I say the words I know how pathetic they are. I've seen the long arm of the Emperor, how he abuses those he's meant to care for. He will not stand for any challenge to his rulership.

Kaden glances at me as we walk, his face still hard, but his hand in mine is warm and comforting. "The Emperor annihilated every single High Dragon when they burned his wife. Our kind has murdered children, destroyed entire villages. We had no control of course, without training, but do you think Emperor Titus will care? Do you think anyone will?" He pauses. "No. We tried peace once, long ago, back when the High Dragons reigned. We sent a party to treat with them, to tell them the truth of our ways. The High Dragons agreed to meet, but it was only a trap. They captured our diplomats and sent them to torture. They wanted to know the location of our base, our weakness. As far as I know, everyone one of ours died rather than betray their people. Their bodies were dissected, I heard, studied after their Spirits were killed in their Sanctuaries."

I'm silent as we continue to walk down the darkened halls, lit only by sporadic torches on the walls.

Kaden shifts his eyes to me, his hand tightening on mine a fraction. "I do not expect you to agree with what we're doing," he says, "but I hope you can at least understand. My people have been mistreated for millenniums, living underground like insects, scrapping for food and tools. While Titus and his ilk live in leisure on the backs of others. We will make far better rulers than him. In our world, everyone will have a place to call their own."

As we pass from the halls, we enter the large chamber where it seems most of this underground world is centered. There are stalls for crafting, small homes for families to live together, and I pay more attention to the details as we walk by this time. I notice swords of obsidian being sharpened. Metal being forged in blue flame.

I glance at Enzo. "How do you feel about all this?"

"Titus, Sylus... their kind must be removed from power. And," he pauses and looks around the darkened space. "It will be nice to look upon the sun once more."

If that's true for Enzo, who has not been here long, I can only imagine how so many others feel. They are pale, deprived of sunlight, of fresh air, fresh food, space. They have been left here to die, and yet they carved for themselves something more. They were left in their madness, and yet they clawed their way out of it and learned how to control their powers.

While I don't relish war, and this timing is unfortunate, I also understand. There is a wrong that needs righted. Justice is needed for these people. And when I remember what I've learned about the Emperor. The kinds of things he's done. The kind of leader he is, I know this has to be.

It seems the blood of the innocent is always payment for change.

Kaden and Enzo lead us up a tunnel until we reach a dead end. Kaden pulls a lever on the wall and the stone slides away revealing sunlight and grass and trees. I inhale sharply, and the fresh scent of flowers and sun fill me.

We step out and I see that behind us is the mountain of Dragoncliff, which makes sense given that Alon Londal exists below in the catacombs.

Kaden reaches up to brush his thumb along my cheek as he holds my eyes with his. "Enzo and I must return. I wish I could help you search for Pike, help you save Kara—"

I put my hand over the one he has against my cheek. "But you have to do this. I understand. And I would do the same if I were you."

Relief fills his face and he leans in to kiss me.

We let the kiss linger, ignoring Enzo and Raven and the urgent needs that propel us forward. For this one moment, we allow time to stand still.

A tear leaks out of my eye when he pulls away. "We may never see each other again," I whisper, afraid to speak this out loud lest it comes true.

He wipes the tear from my eye. "That won't happen. Look at all we've lived through. We will find each other again. After. Our story isn't over yet, Miss Knightly."

Kaden turns away and leads Enzo back into the catacombs, and I rub my eyes and take a step toward Dragoncliff.

The Sundering is upon us.

Everything is about to change.

It's time to return and finish this.

DRAGONCLIFF IS BESIEGED by a flurry of activity when we arrive.

Ashknights are loading ballistas on the wall. Anyone who can fight, from Ashlings to Ashlords, are sharpening blades and preparing their weapons. The Charred are visible in larger numbers. Usually they go about their business unseen, but now they are everywhere, helping in tasks that they are not normally called to do.

We see one Ashling cowering behind a shrub, quivering as he sharpens his sword. He's just a kid and clearly not ready to go to war, but today, everyone must fight if needed.

Raven and I find our squad setting up a ballista on the south side as Phoenix calls out commands. When they see us, they drop everything and run, giving hugs and asking questions over each other. "Are you two well? We heard you were recovering?"

I smile at them. "We're better now. I'd heard you were on your way to the Wall?"

"Change of plans," says Phoenix. "News came. The dragons broke through the South Gate. The Wall faded in that area and they've taken over. They'll have to pass this way to reach any inhabitable areas, so we'll make our stand here."

"Time to put all that training to use," says Landon.

Phoenix grabs me by the arm and pulls me away from the others. She whispers in my ear. "I'm sorry for what I did... I..."

"It's alright. I would have done the same for Kaden."

She probes my soul with her eyes. "You know then... everything?"

I nod. "Raven and I both do. And we won't tell anyone. Not until the war begins."

Her eyes flick to the dark-haired girl who has her back to us as she looks out toward the Wall. Phoenix nods. "Very well then, you might as well help prepare."

I turn to everyone. "There's something else I must do. There is someone I must find."

"The man who took your daughter," says Mabel.

"Yes, but there's more to it than any of us knew." I tell them just enough so they understand. So they know that I wouldn't abandon them right now if it weren't urgent. If it didn't mean the fates of the worlds, not just my daughter. I don't betray Lord Illian or her people. That is their secret to reveal when the time is right.

"So... " Zev says. "If we find Pike and throw him in the Wall, problem solved?"

"Basically, yes," I say, grinning at his way with words.

"Then we go with you," says Bix. "We swore."

Phoenix balks at this. "You are under my command and right now, we are all needed here, defending the Cliff and the rest of this world. We can't spare anyone right now. I'm sorry."

Landon steps forward. "With respect, Sky is our leader, today and always. We follow her command." They each step forward, flanking Landon, lending their support. "If you want our help in finding Pike, we are yours. If you want us here, we will fight."

My heart feels bruised by such loyalty, when I know I am likely acting on a fool's hope. What are the chances I can find Pike when everyone else has failed? But still, I must try. To save Kara. And to put a stop to the sacrifices permanently and save countless others.

"Thank you," I tell them, but you are needed here. All of Nirandel needs you to defend them from the Sundering. And I need you to keep this castle in one piece or all my work will be for naught."

They exchange looks, then as one they kneel with swords held point down. "We will do as you command," Landon says.

"Be safe. Be strong. Fight well. You all are more than my squad, you're my family, and I will see you all again when this is over." I make eye contact with each of them and then turn to Phoenix, who's face is unreadable. Her command, which given her rank is hers by right, was just ignored, and she could see that as a great insult. "Please take care of my squad. Lead them well."

I make sure my squad hears my words, so they know I am leaving Phoenix in charge. Phoenix looks relieved, though still annoyed by the exchange. She resumes issuing orders as I turn to leave, and I hope this isn't the last time I see my friends alive.

But it's hard to walk away, and I falter, looking back toward them. Can I really leave them to fight without me? But I know I must stop Pike. I can't fail Kara again. She will die tonight when the moons are at their highest if I don't do this. And it will keep happening. Again and again. No, Pike has to be stopped.

"Go," says Bix, who sees me hesitate. "We be here waiting for you when you get back."

"Yes. Those dragons will wish they stayed behind the Wall where they belong," jokes Landon.

"We'll beat them," says Mabel. "Working together."

Zev shrugs. "By my calculations, I do think the odds are in our favor. Go. Kill Pike and save the Nine Worlds."

Raven smiles at me, and nods.

With all their blessings, I head for the library. I will find Pike and save Kara before it's too late.

40

UNLIKELY ALLIES

When I reach the library, it is empty except for Master Orcael. "What are you doing here?" he asks. "Everyone has been sent to the walls."

"Special order from Phoenix," I lie. "She needs me to research something that could help in battle."

He adjusts his monocle. "Perhaps I may be of some assistance."

Yes. He could be very helpful. No one knows this library like Master Orcael, and a theory has been forming in my mind, one I'm hoping these books can help prove. I considered what would someone with that much power do? Would they be content living in shadows on another world, stealing kids and training them? Or would they want something more?

Pike has powers beyond anyone. He is likely the strongest person on Nirandel.

So... why not start my research with the strongest person on Nirandel?

Emperor Titus himself.

"I need histories on the emperor," I say. "Biographies, stories, battle accounts, everything."

"As you wish," he says, and in moments he brings me a pile of books. He leaves and returns with more books. Then more. The piles grow beside me as I begin to skim through them.

The Emperor's Shadows have powers that they keep secret. Powers no one else knows about. Abilities that allow them to kill Twin Spirits. This alone could point to the Emperor being Pike. But perhaps he just recruited Pike as one of his Shadows.

But why would someone so powerful be content working under someone else?

Still, I need more definitive proof before I try to confront the Emperor of all Nirandel.

I continue speed reading, and quickly devour passages that describe the Emperor's great feasts. How he outmaneuvered the High Dragons in battle, despite having fewer numbers. That alone is worth pausing for. The High Dragons and the power of the dragons, and greater forces, and yet Titus beat them and then brought the middle class into power after the High Dragons were all dead.

It's a powerful argument for him being Pike, but not entirely conclusive.

And if I'm right, how will I get an audience with the Emperor? Maybe Illian can help, if they are going after the Emperor during the Sundering?

Still, a case could be made Pike is just one of his Shadows. Or none of them. Maybe he prefers to stay out of the way. On another world. Controlling from a distance. How can I possibly understand a mind like his?

I'm so lost in thought, bent over the books that smell of paper and leather and ancient mothballs, that when Master Orcael approaches, I nearly jump out of my seat.

"Perhaps if I knew specifics I could be of more help?" he says.

I close my eyes and pinch the bridge of my nose, then stretch my neck and arms. "I'm looking for someone," I say, trying to explain my situation without giving too much away. "I learned they're using a false name. Their true identity is secret, but I suspect it may be in one of these books."

"I see," the old master says, stroking his beard. "This is going to take a lot of time. I best make some tea."

He returns with tea for us both, as I keep looking. I sip at the tea and strain my eyes reading through the histories, deciphering headache inducing fonts. Hours pass. The sun begins to set. I feel cloistered within the thick walls of the library. Like I'm in another world. Another life. I try not to think of my friends. Of all the people who could die today. I have to figure out this riddle.

The letters begin swimming before my eyes, no longer making sense. My muscles feel weak and tired. I need to stretch. To think. To get a new perspective and breathe fresh air. I swallow the rest of my tea and head to the balcony where Master Orcael stands, smoking a pipe and looking toward the horizon.

"The Wall of Light shines less brightly than before. There's hardly any of its luminescence left," Master Orcael says as he stares into the distance. "Soon it will be gone completely."

I want to tell him it will be all right. That the wall will be fixed, but I don't know what will happen, and I try not to make promises I can't keep. Instead I say what I believe. "We'll survive." I pat his arm. "Sunderings have come and gone and yet Dragoncliff remains."

"Yes," he says as he chews on his pipe, smoke filling the air. "We remain."

I'm about to return to my books when something dark appears over the setting sun. A silhouette in the sky. Then another. And another. Dozens of them. Beating wings against the horizon fill the sky with fire and promises of death.

"They are coming," the master says. "It won't be long now until the walls are besieged."

I run back to the books, a panic filling me. I'm out of time. But there's something I'm missing, something playing on the edge of my mind. I reach for the thought but it flits away, like trying to catch a cloud. Frustrated, I slam my fist into a thick leather tome, tears of anger burning my eyes. If I fail at this, if I don't figure this out, it's all over. Kara's dies and Pike will get away with it. We will continue to war with dragons, sacrificing our lives to defend the worlds. The cycle never ends.

I close my eyes and draw on memories of what my mother taught me when I was young. About slowing my breathing, focusing.

I hear her voice in my head and let myself sink deeper into my mind. My breathing calms. My heart rate slows.

I need to start at the beginning, I realize. The very beginning.

My eyes pop open, and in a frenzy I move books around, looking for the earliest account of the emperor. Before his wife was burned. Before he became a warrior. Before he became a ruler.

Because I've been looking at this all wrong.

I find what I need in a small black book. It's not a historical account like the rest, more like a story. I flip to the first page and begin reading.

"Titus lived a life of solitude, in a manor bestowed to him by relatives long gone. The place had long been in disarray, for he had no guests, and no one to entertain. The nearby villagers ignored him and told tales of Titus and his manor. Some called him an Ashwraith. Others a Corrupted Spirit. Over the years, the tales grew until all the villagers feared Titus

All but one.

A young woman.

Seeking to become an alchemist.

She heard the manor had a library, and so, against the wishes of her family and friends, she traveled there.

At first, Titus turned her away. He wanted to be left alone.

But the young woman persisted. She offered to tidy up the manor in exchange for access to the library.

Titus said no once more.

And so she waited three days and three nights outside his door.

Finally... on the fourth day, the door opened, and Titus allowed her inside.

She marveled at the library, at all the knowledge hidden there.

She took a room at the manor and began her studies, as well as her efforts at restoration.

Days turned into weeks.

Weeks turned into years.

And eventually, the young woman and Titus fell in love.

For the first time in a long time, Titus had opened himself up to another, and together they lived happily.

Then one day the woman left to collect herbs for her alchemy. As she plucked leaves, the High Dragon Elarius and his cohort rode by on their way to the village. Elarius, upon seeing the woman, was mesmerized by her beauty. He ordered her to join him on his journey. He would take her as a concubine, he said.

The woman explained she already had a husband. She would be returning home. But Elarius did not allow it. He ordered his men to capture the woman and imprison her. Until she decided to be his concubine, she would not have freedom.

For three days and three nights she wept in a cell.

On the fourth night, Elarius came to see her.

This was her final chance, he said. She must become his, or suffer the consequences.

The woman said she belonged to no man. And then she spat in Elarius's face.

He dragged her from the cell, and burned her at the stake for all the village to see.

When Titus heard of what befell his wife, he cried out with rage.

He rode to the village and rallied those who had been friend or family to his wife.

Together, they overthrew Elarius, lord of the land, and burned his body until nothing but ash remained.

In the years to come, Titus would become a great warrior, a conqueror and ruler. But he would never stop being the man who fell in love with a young woman dreaming of becoming an alchemist.

She had stolen his heart.

And taught him how to love.

You will not read of her in the histories, except for her simple role as catalyst in the great uprising.

But she was so much more than that.

She was a person, and her name was Eliana.

I FREEZE. Memories chilling me to the bone. Memories of my mother on her death bed.

"Eliana. I am scared, my friend. I am scared."

Eliana...

My mother knew her... the Eliana from the story.

And it clicks. Everything in my mind reshuffles, and I finally understand the truth. Not just about Pike, but about myself.

Eliana and Titus had a child.

A daughter.

A High Dragon.

Half human, half dragon.

Me.

My mum kept me safe, but she was not my true mother.

My mother was Eliana, and my father was Titus.

And if she was human.

And he was a dragon.

Then Titus, the first of his name, Emperor of Nirandel, is Pike...

And I am his daughter.

THE KNOWLEDGE SLAMS into my gut like a fist. Everything I thought I knew about myself, my life, it was all a lie. Why hadn't my mother—who wasn't my mother—told me the truth? Why had she let me grow up believing the lie?

I ball my hands into fists and feel my nails pierce the flesh on my palms. I don't have time for a personal crisis right now. My first priority has to be stopping Pike. The rest can come later.

I need to reach Kaden. He or his mother can help me get to the Emperor—to Pike. There's still time.

I stand quickly, my hand hitting my tea cup off the table, and it shatters to the floor.

My knees buckle beneath me.

I grab my chair to stop from falling.

What's happening to me?

My body is sluggish. Disobedient to my mind. I cannot move at will.

Tap. Tap. Tap.

The tapping of a cane.

Master Orcael walks in from the balcony, a cane in his hand that was not there before.

Tap. Tap. Tap.

A cane with tri-colored wood. Tipped with what I now know to be a dragonstone.

"No... " my voice sounds strained. Too quiet. More like air escaping through my lips. I need to stand, but my body grows weaker.

"I am so very sorry, my dear," says Master Orcael, "but I cannot allow you to leave. A Sundering is upon us, and I have a duty to fulfill. A duty, I suspect, you intend to interrupt."

He moves closer to me and smiles. "A shame you had to find out this way," he says, his voice changing as he speaks, becoming rough. "I did so enjoy our nightly talks."

As I watch helplessly, he begins to transform. His skin reshapes itself, his beard shortens. His gray robes darken until they are black. He pulls a hat from his coat and places it on his head, and in that moment, he becomes the image from my memories. From my nightmares. The enemy I hunt.

Pike.

He's been right here the whole time, and I never knew. We had tea together. Talked. Laughed. Commiserated. I thought him a friend.

Bile rises in my throat, burning the back of my tongue.

The monster before me grins. "You were clever to study the emperor so closely. Not the first, of course. There have been others before you who discovered Titus and I were one in the same, but they are gone now. Like you, they forgot to consider one important factor."

He motions all around. "My home. Did they really believe I would abandon it? That I would not spend my days here any longer?" He taps his cane. "The palace is lovely to be sure, but it will never replace the Cliff. The books. The view."

I can't just sit here paralyzed while he prattles on. I need to fight. I try to transmute my hand, but nothing happens. My legs buckle more. I am losing control of my body. "What did you do to me?"

"What I did to the others," he says. "Moonshade, a very powerful herb, capable of causing temporary paralysis. Easy to blend in to tea." He pauses, his eyes distant, somber. "My wife taught me of Moonshade, you know. We'd pick it together in the gardens. But that was long ago. I was a different man then."

I want to dismiss him as a madman—and he is, to be sure—but the sadness in his eyes is genuine. If I can't fight him, maybe I can persuade him. "I know about you and Illian. I know about you and Eliana. The world betrayed you, I understand. Illian wanted you to give up your life. Wanted you to die, though she was your friend. Eliana was taken from you. Killed for being who she was. All those you held dear are lost to you. But—"

"But what?" He sneers at me, his face losing that placid facade he usually maintains. "Should I return my sacrifice to their home and let the world burn instead?" He shakes his head. "Everything I have done, everything I do, is necessary. Without me, dragons would consume Nirandel and all the Nine Worlds. Without me, the corrupt High Dragons would still rule. Don't you see? I make this world bearable. I, alone."

"It is our friends who make this world bearable," I say, remembering Bix, Landon, Mabel, Zev, Enzo and Raven, and the night we swore we would never leave each other. "It is those we love who make this world bearable."

"Those who I love are gone," says Pike. "The world took them away. It will do the same to you in time. It always does."

I feel my energy spent. I am about to collapse, my body unable to move while my mind still works. I need a burst of strength. I need... a dragonstone. If I had one I could...

I remember Orcael's—Pike's pen—the decorative stone at the top.

I see it on the table.

"Now," says Pike, "it is time we go somewhere more comfortable. Somewhere you cannot interfere."

He steps forward.

With my remaining strength, I reach for the pen, and clasp onto the dragonstone.

And I shatter it.

The dragonstone explodes, along with the pen, and energy surges through my body. I stand tall, facing Pike.

His eyes go wide. "How is this possible?"

He seems stunned. No one else would have been able to break through the effects of the Moonshade. Not without dragon blood and a dragonstone.

This is my chance.

This energy will only last a moment. I can already feel the effects of the drug resurfacing.

I have to make the right choice.

Fight?

Run?

What do I do?

I can't afford to think. I must just act.

So I do.

I blink and appear at the balcony, using my powers.

And then.

I jump.

I fall.

I try to transmute my wings, but the power is already fading. I have no strength. The paralysis returns.

My eyes close.

When I hit the ground, my body will break. I will regenerate in Sanctuary. But Pike will find me.

Still, there is hope. Maybe one of my friends will find me first.

I think of my squad. Of Kara. Of my boys back home. Of all the things I have to live for.

I think of the life I've had. The good and bad. The misery and the joy. It is the bitter that makes the sweet palatable. I've come to see this. To see that we would not want a life that had no challenge. That did not push us and test us and polish us. We are meant to be more than what we pretend to be.

Blake told me that once. I believed him then.

I believe him now.

I have not given up hope. Even now.

A lightness fills me, and I surrender to what is.

And then, arms wrap around me. A warm embrace. Someone holding me close.

We glide through the air.

I'm no longer falling.

Someone came.

Someone saved me.

Kaden?

I peel my eyes open.

And then I see her.

Holding me.

Saving me.

Her masked face above me.

The Outcast.

I FALL INTO DREAMS.

Into a field of grass.

A silver tree.

And two stone graves.

My Sanctuary.

I sit amongst the flowers, their smells playing with my nose, and then I sense it.

A presence not my own.

Pike steps out before me, his black cloak drifting in the wind. His eyes scrutinize me. "You are High Dragon," he says, perplexed. "But I killed them all. All of them except..." There is panic in his eyes, and fear. "No... you cannot be..."

"I am," I say softly. "My mother was Eliana and my father, the man called Titus, the man called Orcael, the man called Pike."

"No... you were stillborn. You were dead. I saw it. I felt it. All my hopes. All my dreams for you. They died that day. We could never conceive again. I was going to raise you to rule the worlds. But you died, as did my dreams that day." He smashes his fist against the tree and leaves fall.

"I was dead," I say, the pieces falling into place, "but somehow, I already had my Spirit. My body regenerated. My mother hid me from you, gave me to her friend, the woman who raised me." I cock my head to look at him, as I think back to what it must have been like for my birth mother. "Perhaps Eliana saw you for what you truly were. What you truly are."

Pike shakes his head. "I saw you. You were dead." He pauses, looking at the flowers. "Do not look for me in the coming hours. Do not interfere. Once the Sundering is finished and the sacrifice given, I will find you. Perhaps... perhaps we can start again."

He fades away, disappearing.

And then I wake.

41

NA'RAZIM

My eyes peel open, the world a blur coming slowly into focus.

A familiar face leans over me. Their black short hair curling around their cheeks.

Naoki.

"Good to have you back," Naoki says.

They hold a mug of something warm at my lips and support my head as I sip at it. The bitterness of the brew zings at my mouth and I cough.

Naoki smiles apologetically. "Dragon's Breath. It grows on the mountains during winter. Horrible tasting, even with honey added, but is known for helping rebuild a person's constitution. It's particularly useful when someone's been poisoned."

With Naoki's help I prop myself up enough to look around. I'm in a simple room carved from rock, almost like a cave. I lay on a mat on the floor with a wool blanket tucked around me.

My memories come back slowly, sledging through my mind.

The Cliff.

The Sundering.

Pike.

The Outcast.

I sit up straight, my heart pounding faster in my chest as the urgency of the situation returns. "Where are we?" I try to stand, but fall back down, my body still weak from the poison.

Naoki catches me, making sure I don't bang my head as I lay back down. "You must be careful," they say. "You were passed out for hours. You are still recovering."

Only hours. Good. I haven't missed a day. There's still time. "I need to get back." Back to my friends. Back to Pike. I need to stop him. To stop the Sundering.

"Soon," says Naoki. "But first you must rest."

"Where is the Outcast?" I ask, scanning the room. She saved me—twice now—but still I don't trust her. Not after she killed Kaden's friend.

"She is close," Naoki says. "She will be glad you are awake."

"Where are we?" I repeat again. If Naoki is working with the Outcast, I don't trust them fully either. I need to figure out what's going on, and then find Pike.

"Please, Sky, you must relax. I know this is disorienting, but the more you see, the more you will understand." Naoki eyes plead silently with me.

I remember the day I saw the Watcher whip Naoki, how broken and alone they looked. The day I saw the what it means to be Charred. The memory softens my response.

"Where are we?" I ask again.

"Na'Razim," Naoki says.

My gasp is audible, and something like excitement and fear bubble up inside me. "But I thought that was just a story."

"It is real," says Naoki. "A place where people live beyond the Wall. The place I grew up."

Grew up? "So are you... are you a Worshipper of the Wall?"

"Yes, but my father is the priest. I just believe in the teachings."

"But... if you lived beyond the Wall... how did you become an Ashling? How did anyone find you?"

Naoki straightens their back, their tone proud. "I came to the Cliff myself. I volunteered."

"Volunteered?"

"To become a Twin Spirit. I spent three nights in the Ashlands alone. The experience broke me, and I gained a Spirit. Then I snuck past the Wall and arrived at the Cliff. I joined the Ashlings. And then I failed the first test to become Charred."

"You mean... you failed on purpose? Why would you do such a thing?" I can't keep the incredulity from my voice. I've seen what Naoki endured. To do so by choice seems... mad.

"The path of an Ashling did not concern me. As Charred, I had instant access to many parts of the fortress you have probably yet to see. I heard and saw things that the Ashlords kept secret. No one notices the Charred cleaning their chamber pot or refiling their water, even as they discuss battle plans and strategy."

"You're a spy? Why? For who?"

"For this city," Naoki says. "I deliver information to help prevent the killing of hatchlings. I hear things in the fortress, which gates are manned, what patrols are heading out."

"But how do you leave the Cliff? The Charred are never supposed to leave."

Naoki nods. "It is true. We are not. They fear we will remove our braces." She rolls up her gray sleeve, revealing a brace around her wrist, covering her Spirit Mark, much like the armband I used to wear.

It makes sense now. "So the Ashpriests don't actually burn out your Spirit. They just contain it. That is why they can't simply let you leave."

"Yes. If we were to take off our bracer, we would be as dangerous as any untrained Twin Spirit. So they watch us closely, very closely. But I know how to make a drink that makes one very sleepy, and I give it to my Watcher every night. And I know a passage in the fortress, through the catacombs, that leads out past the Wall." Naoki pauses. "It is small. Too small for dragons. But perfect for me."

I try to process all this information. A disturbing thought comes to mind. If Naoki spies for the Outcast... "Are you the reason we were attacked beyond the Wall three years ago? The reason we almost died?"

Naoki bows their head. "Yes. I had heard of the hatchling catch and the path that might be taken." Naoki looks up, tears in their eyes. "I am sorry. I did not know it was your squad that would go." Their face tenses, as a resolve replaces the grief. "But even had I known, I would not have done differently. But then things changed. The Red Queen, she told us everything. She told us what you are."

"The Red Queen?" I ask.

"The one you call the Outcast... she was there... atop the red dragon," says Naoki.

Pieces begin to click together. It makes sense she would have been atop the red dragon then. She would have seen me shatter the dragonstone. She would have realized who I was. A High Dragon.

"She said you would want to help us," Naoki says, a new light in their eyes.

"Help you do what?" I ask.

"Help bring peace between dragon and mankind," Naoki says, as if it's obvious.

Because I am half dragon, they think I will fight for the them. But... "The dragons are beasts," I say. "Monsters who would kill all men and Spirits."

Naoki shakes their head. "This is not true. We can live together. You saw the Red Queen atop her dragon. There can be peace between us. That is the great lie told by the Emperor and the Masters. That the dragons are a threat to be locked beyond this Wall. But they are not. At least... not all of them. Many are angry at the way they have been treated. Many want to kill man. But there are still those who want peace. Those who live in and protect this city," Naoki says. "I will show you." They gesture outside through the open door.

I nod, and she helps me up more slowly this time. I feel blood traveling to my legs, waking them up with pinpricks of pain. Everything aches, and my muscles still feels sluggish, but I take one tentative step, and then another, as Naoki offers their arm for support.

And then we step outside into a world I could not have imagined.

A giant city built within a huge crater stretches far below and above me. The sky is clear and blue, and is filled with dragons flying.

More dragons than I've ever seen in one place.

They are black and white and shades of blue. Some breathe fire, others ice.

I look down again, and I can barely see the bottom of the crater, but there, in the center, lies a massive dragon. Larger by far than anything I've seen.

"That is Mother," Naoki says with reverence. "Adragasa. She protects us from the dragons who would wish us dead."

Hatchlings who would normally seem massive, but look small from so high up, snap at each other and hiss fire as they slither around Adragasa. "Are they playing?"

"Yes. They are learning how to be great hunters," says Naoki. "I can bring you closer if you'd like."

It's tempting, but the images of dragon jaws clamping shut on Clli still haunt me. The crunch of bone. The spray of blood. The screams. "No, thanks." I'm not quite ready to be close to them if I don't have to be.

An older man, hunchbacked, with a cane of gnarled wood walks up through the stone paths that wind through the walls of the crater like veins, connecting the carved out living spaces. "A wondrous site, is it not? Two species, both capable of extreme destruction and creation, co-existing in one place."

Naoki smiles and gestures at the man. "Sky, this is Makoto, my father, and High Priest of the Wall of Light."

"Are you the leader here?" I ask.

"More a guide than leader," he says, smiling. His face shows the map of his years lived, but his eyes are bright and sharp. "I teach the truth of things. What others do with the truth is up to them. I see Naoki has begun to show you our city. What do you think of it?"

I look around at the wonder of it all and bite my lip. "I... I don't understand. I've seen dragons act like mindless beasts. I've seen them attack my friends, kill my comrades without a thought. And yet the dragons here seem uninterested in people. Why don't they attack us?"

He nods, a sympathetic look on his face. "Dragons, like all things, are innocent at birth. They want to hunt, they want to eat, yes, but like us they put limitations upon themselves. Just as some cultures may eat chicken but not dog, some dragons may eat Boxen but not people. It is not for the food that dragon attacks man."

"Then why? Their Spirits?"

He shakes his head. "When one of you Ashknights sees a dragon, what do you do first?"

"Consider retreat. If retreat is not possible, take the offensive."

"And when a dragon sees one of you Ashknights, what does it do first?"

I see where he is going. "You mean dragons only fight us because they have to."

"When a hatchling is slaughtered, should the pack not fight back? When a drake is cut down, should its brothers and sisters do nothing? When a wall is erected, keeping an entire species trapped and separated from their main source of substance, should they not seek to break free?"

"So dragons don't hunt us for food... but vengeance?" I can hardly believe this.

"Vengeance, liberty, desperation... the dragons have many reasons as varied and natural as our own. What do you call it, when two major forces come in conflict?"

"A war," I say, pieces clicking together.

He nods sagely, as if he can sense my understanding. "War is a complicated thing. It washes away innocence. Reduces some to their basest instincts. It forms heroes and legends. It drives progress. And yet how many suffer in the end? Is one side always right and one always wrong? Is there ever truly a victor?"

"And you have these answers?"

He chuckles. "Sadly no. I have but the questions. It is for each of us alone to find the answers."

I clench my fist. "Dragons attack my friends while we speak. They slaughter my comrades and burn villages to ash. If you want me to believe that dragons and people can live in peace, then stop the Sundering."

"I am afraid I cannot," says Makoto. "While Adragasa believes peace is attainable, many of her fellow dragons do not. They have been treated as beasts far too long. It is hatred and vengeance that drives them now, and they will not stop until all their oppressors are gone."

"Oppressors? The dragons almost destroyed the Nine Worlds," I say. "That is why Nir trapped them within the Wall in the first place."

"Perhaps," Makoto says, nodding his head, "but how many of those dragons are still alive today? How many new generations have suffered for the sins of others?"

I... I never considered that.

Makoto turns toward the path. "Come. It is time you spoke to the Red Queen."

"So she rules you?" I ask.

"Her title is an honorific, but some would prefer it to be more," says Makoto.

"The Red Queen has a way with dragons," says Naoki. "They listen to her more than most, respect her even. She has helped secure peace with a great deal of dragon clans. And she is a great warrior. She has helped keep us safe for many years."

There is awe in her eyes. I see she is enthralled by this Red Queen, and probably wants to emulate her.

"She is a murderer," I say, wiping away the gleam in her eye. "She killed an Ashlord."

Makoto and Naoki exchange a glance. They do not seem shocked or disturbed by my words.

Makoto sighs. "Though I share the truth of things, this truth I will leave for the Red Queen to share."

Naoki shrugs and smiles. "You'll understand when you meet. Much is yet to be revealed."

I want to ask Naoki what they mean, but we reach the end of a hall, where a thick red curtain acts as a door to another room.

Makoto moves it aside, revealing an arena with walls made of the stone crater, sand for a floor, and an open ceiling.

In the center, crouched outside a gray tent, is the Outcast. She is clad in white armor with red accents, her white featureless mask covering her face, her red hair drifting in the wind as she sinks her knife into the body of a large Boxen stretched before her. She appears to be gutting it.

I step forward. It's time the Outcast and I have a long talk.

42

THE RED QUEEN

I expect Naoki and the old priest to join me, but they let the curtain fall in front of them, leaving me alone with the Outcast.

My Spirit glows within me, warm and bright, and I grasp a thread of it, ready to transmute if necessary. I have no idea what to expect from this woman. She is my enemy, but she has saved my life. She is a murderer, but she is trying to bring peace, if the old man is to be believed.

I step forward until I am a few feet from her. She continues to carve at the Boxen.

"No need to hold onto Spirit. I'm not going to hurt you." She looks up, her hands dripping blood. "And I'm not the enemy Kaden believes me to be. There are things he does not know." Her accent sounds slightly different then the locals, but close enough that she's clearly been here awhile.

"Things? What things?" I ask.

"Things that are his to hear. When the time is right."

She talks so vaguely. I don't have time for this. "I need to get back to the Cliff."

"You are free to go," says the Outcast, pointing back at the curtained doorway with the tip of her bloody knife. "It's a three days ride from here to Dragoncliff."

"Three days... then how did we get here so quickly?" I pause. "Does it have something to do with how you vanish into thin air?"

She finally pauses and looks back up at me. "Yes."

I wonder if it's like my blinking ability. And if they are similar, then how? And why? What does the Outcast want with me?

The Outcast refocuses her gaze on the carcass between us and pulls out the guts. I reel from the smell, fighting down nausea, but she doesn't flinch. She starts to cut off small pieces of meat and collect them in a pile on a white rag. She talks as she works. "I do not want the Sundering, I just want for people to stop hunting the dragons. They keep them from Spirit, but then they hunt them too, for dragonstone. They can stop, and they can give us access to Spirit if they so chose, but they don't, because they've made a monopoly of corpses. Better to live outside the Wall, but dragons can make do within if they are left in peace."

She stands, picking up the rag. "Come. I want to show you something."

I walk around the splayed Boxen and follow the Outcast to the tent. The flap is pulled away and reveals a dark den covered in cracked shells, broken eggs and...

"Baby dragons?" I ask, awe in my voice.

There are seven of them, and small enough to fit in the palm of my hand. They are nuzzled together in the center of their nest, and they chirp at each other and wiggle about. Their scales are nearly translucent, as if the color is still growing in them, and they seem to glow from some fire within. Their core, where their magic is made.

The Outcast takes a piece of meat from the pile and holds it up to the closest baby. It approaches tentatively, its tiny tail whooshing around, its tiny paper-like wings flapping futilely. When its closer, it pauses, as if waiting for something bad to happen. Then it sniffs, and a tiny puff of fire bursts out of its mouth. The Outcast tosses the piece of meat toward the dragon, and it catches it from the air and eats it.

"They've just learned that," the strange woman next to me says, her voice carrying all the pride of a mother.

One doesn't have to give birth to be a mother, I remind myself.

"They're so small," I say. "I thought hatchlings were huge?"

"They grow quickly," says the Outcast. "These are newborns. They will only stay this little a couple of days. Very few people have ever seen dragons this young." She hands me a piece of meat.

I'm surprised she would trust me, but I take the meat. "Why show me this? What if I killed them? It's my duty to hunt dragons."

"I'd kill you before you could touch them," says the Outcast plainly.

I asses the situation. She and I are about the same height and weight. So depending on how much training she's had, that could tilt the scale. By the set of her shoulders and the strength in her posture, it's clear she means it. She will let no harm come to her babies.

But harm sometimes comes, whether we mean for it to or not.

I hold out the meat for the smallest dragon who watched the first feeding with a kind of longing I can relate to. The little one is hesitant at first, sniffing the air and my hand. Then, as if something finally convinces the baby dragon that I'm safe, it puffs itself up and blows a tiny burst of flames. I toss the meat into it and the dragon catches it with its teeth and finds a hiding spot alone to eat without the nagging of its siblings.

I feel my heart shifting. Melting. Softening. There are secrets to this city. Marvels I couldn't have imagined. There is life here. Love. Beauty. Magic. Wonder.

But it also represents everything that is threatening the people I love. My friends are in danger. Pike's next victim is in danger. I must help them.

"What do you want with me?" I ask. "Why rescue me? Why bring me here?"

"You're a High Dragon. You have power that is long since gone. Power that can heal nations. Join with us. What life is there for you out there? If the Masters find out what you are, you're dead. If the Emperor finds out what you are, you're dead." She stares me down, her arms crossed over her chest, as if she knows what I'm going to say next.

"I intend to kill the Emperor," I say.

The Outcast pauses at this. She seems to be waiting for me to continue.

"I met him years ago, but he was using a different name then," I explain. "One you may have heard. Pike. He stole my daughter. Killed her. Like he's killing another tonight."

"And you intend to stop this sacrifice?"

"I do. I won't let him kill another innocent."

"Even if that means the Sundering will continue?"

"Yes." I don't tell her the other option. Where I kill Pike and destroy all dragons. The choice had seemed so clear before, when this conflict was black and white. Monster against human. Being here has destroyed that certainty. It has carved doubts into my heart, and now I... I don't know what to do. How can I possibly make a decision like this that will affect the fates of the Nine Worlds and everyone I've ever loved?

But, of course, I say none of that out loud. Instead, I let her believe that I'll do anything to stop Pike. Which, of course, I will. Even if that means deceiving the Outcast.

"I like this plan," she says, nodding. "I too, have an issue with Pike. Perhaps we can work together." She flips the knife over in her hands. "But first we must play a game."

"I don't have time for games. I need to get back—"

"It's a very simple game. Each of us tells a story. A story of how we came to be who we are. If I believe your story, I'll help you. If I don't, then you're free to leave alone. See? Simple. To make things easier, I'll start. Perhaps then you'll understand what truly happened to Kaden's friend. Perhaps then you'll understand who I am." She takes off her mask, revealing a pale, elfin face with dark brown eyes. Revealing a face almost exactly like my own.

"My name is Sky Knightly, and this is my story."

43

ADRAGASA

My name is Sky Knightly. Like you, I lost Kara to Pike. Like you, I traveled to Dragoncliff and trained to become an Ashlord. Like you, I found Pike during the Sundering.

And then...

I failed.

I could not defeat him.

Though I used all my power, though I became Corrupted in the battle, my dragon and hair turning red, I could not win.

And so Pike sacrificed Kara to the Pyre of Souls. But it was not enough. The Wall was so weak that even her death could not restore the light, and the dragons swept over the Nine Worlds. I saw my friends burn. My loved ones die. But I endured.

The dragons did not kill me. I think they felt some sort of kinship with my High Dragon blood, and so they left me to wonder a world of ash. Pike too, remained, though I did not see him again for a many moons. It took ages for me to regain full control of my Spirit, to learn the abilities Kaden had spoken of before he died. And when I finally awoke, I set out to fix my failure.

For millennium, I searched for the Dragon Graveyard, and one night, in a distant world now forgotten, I found the resting place of the Elder Dragons. There, amongst a corpse the size of Nirandel, I uncovered the Mask of Nir. I placed it upon my face, and then, as foretold, I could see the ocean of time. I could see the ripples of specific events, the waves of lifetimes repeating again and again. I dove into the water, into a time before I lost Kara.

I set out to change events. First, I went to a ruin where Kaden had told me he and Alec fought a Scabrial once. I killed Alec then, as you probably know. He was not who you think. Not who Kaden thinks. He was in Pike's service after making dealings with the Emperor. During the Sundering, he would have betrayed you, as he had betrayed me, leading to Kaden's death. I could not allow it, and so I removed Alec from the timeline.

I considered telling Kaden who I was, what I was doing, but he had yet to meet you, or me, if you will, and so there was no reason for him to trust me, no reason for him to care.

I decided to keep my identity hidden, my changes to the timelines as deliberate as possible. I burned certain ships that carried weapons for the Emperor. I assassinated some of his strongest Shadows and supporters.

But the next part of my plan, the most crucial part, did not go as planned. Despite a millennium of training, I still could not defeat Pike in battle. As we clashed on the Frozen Mountains, he struck a near mortal blow, and I barely escaped, blinking away into the Ashlands. I had mastered the ability, allowing myself to travel far distances in an instant, though it made me weary.

It took months to recover. Pike's blow nearly destroyed both my body and my Sanctuary. I could not stop him from taking Kara as I had planned, as I lay recovering in a cave under the care of Naoki and her father. So I developed a new strategy.

If I could not stop Pike, perhaps I could stop the Sundering. Or at least *change* it. Perhaps, by the time the Wall of Light faded, I could convince the dragons not to destroy the Nine Worlds, but to seek peace. Perhaps I could convince them to make a life for themselves out of more than just death.

And so, I began to travel amongst the dragon clans, speaking of a better future, of a time of peace and prosperity. Some clans listened. Some I made listen through power and force. Eventually, they began to embrace my idea, because I wasn't on the side of humans. Because I showed them, through my actions of destroying patrols, of slaying those of Ash who invaded the Ashlands past the Wall, I showed them I was on the side of dragon.

You may think me cruel, for killing those I had trained with at the Cliff. But you must understand, at the start, I only tried to scare them off, to stop their attacks on hatchlings. But the Ashknights always fought. They killed dragons because I had hesitated. So I stopped hesitating. I would always send a warning. A roar, or the beating of wings. But after, it was war. The Ashknights could flee or they could die.

It is why I attacked your group past the Wall. I did not know you would be there, because our timelines, our destinies had begun to diverge at that point. If I had known, I may have acted differently, I'm not sure. But once I saw you beckon Umi and slay the dragons I had come to know, the dragons who had become my family, I pulled back. I decided to watch over you from that point on, realizing that you were perhaps in more danger than I had been. It is why I was there when you battled the Ashwraith in the cave. Why I was there to catch you when you fell from the library balcony.

And it is why you are here, as the Sundering has begun, and the Cliff is under siege.

It was the compromise I had to make.

The dragons would not destroy the Nine Worlds. They would put centuries of hatred aside and spare billions of people, but the Cliff they could not forgive. The massacres of their young. The entrapment of their race. They could not forgive.

So they will burn Dragoncliff to the ground. They will kill all who stand in their way. And then, in the end, they will build a home for themselves in the northern half of Nirandel. The people of the Frozen Mountains will be free to travel south to Al'Kalesh and the deserts beyond. The people of the islands will be left alone.

It is the... best... I could do. The only way I could find to save the worlds.

Most likely, the Ashwraith rebellion will succeed in this timeline. Most likely, they will take over southern Nirandel and Al'Kalesh. Kaden should be safe. But of course, I cannot be sure.

The Mask of Nir will not work again. As the Valarata said it could only be used once. I did what I had to do to make sure the worlds would survive. It may not have been the best course, but it was the one I could be sure of.

Now, perhaps you understand who I am.

And perhaps, just a little, you understand more of who *you* are.

———

HER STORY IS A FANTASTICAL ONE, beyond the realm of reality, beyond my comprehension. And yet, it must be real, for she has my face, and as she shares more with me, about nights of eating 'pasgetti with the kids, about sharing her secret with Blake, I realize she has my memories as well. This cannot be. And yet it is.

"If you are me from the future," I ask, "then does what happen to me effect you? If I am hurt are you hurt? If I die do you die?"

She shakes her head. "No. Not as far as I know. Once I traveled back in time, you and I became two completely separate individuals."

I see the Mask of Nir laying between us. Such a simple, plain thing, and yet so powerful. It tugs at my memory. I feel like I have seen it before, on another person, in another place, but I don't know why I think such things.

I tell the Outcast, the Red Queen, the other *me*, my own version of events, the way they differed from her own. Fighting dragons past the Wall. Finding the woman in the cave. She listens patiently, carefully, clutching her legs close to her chest and pressing her chin against her knees.

When I am finished, I ask the question pestering my mind. "What about Kara?"

The Outcast sighs. "She cannot be saved. It is impossible. Pike cannot be defeated."

"But there must be a way."

She scoffs. "Do you think I fought with all my strength when I faced Kaden in the cave? When I challenged your group past the Wall? That was but a splinter of my power. I had to be careful simply not to kill you all. And yet, I could not defeat the son of Nir."

I frown. "I have seen Kaden fight Pike. He held his own."

"Pike was holding back. He doesn't like killing unless it is necessary. Besides, he cares for Kaden. As Orcael, he trained him, raised Kaden since he was a boy. He does not wish him dead."

I cannot abandon Kara. I will not. I need more information. "What of the Dragoneyes Squad? They are at the fortress, probably defending it right now. Can they be saved?"

The Outcast shrugs. "It is possible, I suppose. I don't believe they will willingly surrender the Cliff, but perhaps they can be guided away from the battle. Or maybe you can just knock them out, take them somewhere safe." She speaks so casually about the people I have come to call friends, family even.

"Do you care nothing for them?" I ask, my voice harsh.

"I did... once... but to be honest," she sighs. "To be honest I can barely remember their faces. My memory isn't perfect, and they have faded away in my mind. I know they were good friends. I know they were kind. But they were *not* a priority."

I see her in a new way now. No longer is she just the Outcast. Now, I see a broken woman, one who lost everything when she lost Kara, when she lost Kaden. And over a millennium of a lonely, solitary existence, somewhere along the way she stopped caring. She decided to save the Nine Worlds, but forgot about her friends. She decided to save billions of people, but forgot about the individuals among them. About the people who make life worth living. Somewhere, in a distant future of ash and death and solitude, the Outcast forgot how to be human.

I stand, leaving her sitting alone in the dust. My voice is low and quiet as I speak. "You may have abandoned Kara, but I have not. I will go to the Palace of Storms. I will go the Dream that Cannot be Dreamt. And I will save my daughter." I turn away from her. "You can come with me. Perhaps together we will stand a chance. But I will fight alone if I must, and if I die, I will die knowing I did not abandon those I love."

I am halfway out the door, when she finally speaks. "I will take you to the palace," murmurs the Outcast, still clutching her legs. "I will do this one thing and nothing more. But first, I must show you something."

SHE TAKES MY HAND, and where once we were at the top of the city, now we are at the bottom. Hatchlings swarm around us, playing with each other in the sand, nipping at each other's scales and breathing flame into the air. When I realize exactly where we are, I turn around, and see the largest dragon I have ever seen.

She is the size a mountain, curled up in a ball, her head resting on her tail and legs. Her green scales shimmer in the sun like a deposit of precious emeralds, while her giant white eyes shine like the moons. Her breath is so powerful it warps the very air around her. Her heartbeat is so loud, I feel it instead of my own.

I gaze deep into one of her giant eyes, mesmerized by her sheer beauty and strength. And then I hear it.

Adragasa.

Adragasa.

Adragasa.

I hear her name in my mind, just as Kaden heard Umi many years ago.

The Outcasts walks up behind me. "The reason dragons can kill Twin Spirits, is because they are masters of Sanctuary. They can destroy an Ashlord in their *dream,* in what feels like an instant to us. They too have their own Sanctuaries, more vast and beautiful than we can imagine. I want you to experience hers."

I step forward trepidly. "Is she okay with me doing so?"

"She is. Within her Sanctuary, you are no threat to her. Her dream is different than our own. It is why we can slay dragons without entering their Sanctuaries, but it is also why we cannot enter their Sanctuaries as easily. It took me years to discover this. First, I learned about Pike, and how he possessed a Sanctuary. Then I found out other dragons possess one as well. They use them differently than we do, as a way to communicate, to share feelings and ideas. It is how they sometimes seems to act as one. It is how I have spoken with them, given them orders over vast distances and without a word. I want you to *see* Adragasa's Sanctuary, because it is the only way to truly know a dragon."

I nod and step forward, reaching out with my hand. I place my palm gently against the massive dragon's tail, and close my eyes, focusing as Kaden and Phoenix taught me to do, reaching out with my Spirit. Slowly, I feel myself leave my body, and I awaken in a new world.

Thousands of images, thousands of places, flash before me. Fields of grass that stretch out as far as the eye can see. An ocean with waves the size of mountains. A forest with trees that weave into the shapes of dragons. A sky full of stars. A hundred skies. A planet. Thousands of planets. A galaxy. Millions of galaxies. The world, all the worlds, before me.

Is it not, I realize, something my mind is made to comprehend. This place, this dream, is beyond me, beyond humanity. It is a place infinitely larger than I can imagine, infinitely more complex that I can navigate. All I can do is attempt to soak up even the slightest detail, the slightest glimpse of euphoria and unending wonder that far surpasses my own paltry existence.

One scene appears with more clarity than the others. A crooked mountain, a cave within its depth. A dark chamber. A dozen stones piled in the shadows.

I see it again and again.

The crooked mountain.

The crooked mountain.

The crooked mountain.

And then I appear in a world of gray, standing on a slab of stone, as Adragasa, her skin glowing a pale blue, her body ethereal and majestic, towers over me. *Save us,* she says.

And then the visions fade, and I slam back into my body, falling backwards and opening my eyes.

The Outcast catches me, keeps me from crashing into the dust as she holds me.

"I saw..." I whisper. "I saw... everything."

The Outcast, a reflection of myself, nods. "Then perhaps now you understand that dragons deserve to live," she says.

Her voice is soft, and calming, as if it is my own voice. "And now, I will take you to the Palace of Storms. Now, I will take you to the Dream that Cannot be Dreamt."

I see her then, so much myself, and I realize I am on the same path she once traveled. When my friends sought to help me find Pike, I turned them away, because my task was my own. It was *my* burden. And I see how soon, or perhaps in years, I will turn them away again and again. I will turn Kaden away, because his goal is not mine. And one day, I will be alone. I will have found the solitude the Outcast found, and lost everything I hold dear.

I will *not* become her.

I will make a change now. Because I am not alone. I never was. And it is time I stop pushing away those who seek to help me. We can do this. Stop Pike. Stop the Sundering. If we work together.

I look up at my own withered reflection, "No," I say. "First, you will take me to my friends."

44

SUNDERING

We appear on the tallest tower of the Cliff, the wind raging against us, whipping at our hair and robes. Fire streaks across the sky. The horizon burns. Roars and cries and screams fill the air. Below us, the battle has begun.

A dozen small dragons swarm the fortress, attempting to set the ballistae on fire, avoiding bolts aimed at their skulls. My friends, the Dragoneyes squadron, have divided into two groups, each doing their part to fight the battle. Bix, Landon, and Mabel remain on the ground, manning the largest ballista at the Cliff. They use barrier talismans to protect their flanks and rear, leaving only a small place of vulnerability in the front, from which they fire bolt after bolt. One hits a dragon in the wing, and the beast smashes into the tower beside us, tearing it down as it falls to the earth, bones and muscles crushed.

My friends cheer as Bix single handily loads a new bolt twice his height into the war machine. He wears his Spirit armor, having transmuted most of his skin into a hard emerald shell. To his side, stands Landon, having also transmuted most of his body, not for armor, but for speed. His skin is covered in auburn fur, his legs twisted into a form allowing for great agility. When Bix lands another shot, and a dragon falls to the earth, wing crippled, but still very much alive and dangerous, Landon lunges outside the protection of his barrier talisman, moving in a blur, and rams his giant white lance into the dragon's eye, killing it in one blow. Before he can be targeted by a flame strike, the Ashknight retreats back to the ballista, ready for another opportunity.

Mabel wears her Spirit armor as well, skin gray and rough and sturdy like a shark's. But unlike her allies, she presses the offensive using talismans, flicking coins marked with the disintegrate glyph far into the sky with her enhanced strength. When one hits a dragon in the belly, the scales began to peel away, melting and burning, as the beast's blood turns into an acid-like substance, killing it from within.

Three dragons down. Nine remaining.

Here, the other half of Dragoneyes squad seizes initiative. They have chosen a different approach, taking to the skies. Raven glides through the air on wings dark as night, slicing at a dragon's throat with her transmuted black sickle. Her aim is true, and she rips open the beast's neck, turning her weapon crimson.

Zev zips beside her on translucent wings, tossing a disintegrate talisman at one of the smaller dragons. The beast evades, then crashes into Zev, knocking him down. He recovers mid fall, zooming back up to join the battle. Zev was never particularly gifted at slaying dragons, and the beasts seem to notice his weakness. Four of them surround him. But as they open their mouths to breath fire, a blazing comet streaks through the sky.

Phoenix, in her Spirit armor, body aflame, wings of crimson, dashes at the closest of the four dragons. Before it can react, she smashes into its side, and bursts out the other end, having burned a hole straight through the serpent's body. It collapses before it even realizes what happened, guts spilling from it's carved out belly.

The second dragon tries to spin out of the way, but it is too slow, and Phoenix hits it in the neck, decapitating it. This is one of the strongest Ashlords in her element. A weapon honed over centuries to slay monsters. She targets the third dragon, and the beast, having learned from its fallen comrades, manages to evade her assault, only to be struck by a ballista bolt in the eye.

The final dragon turns and flees.

It regroups with the five remaining dragons on the other side of the Cliff, who fight against Gray squad, or at least what is left of them. I only see Tara and Clive, Ashknights I don't know well, but admire. They were new to their rank, however, newer than us, and it appears they were unprepared.

This slaying of six dragons happens in under half a minute.

The battle is going better than I expected. But these are smaller dragons. What happens when a colossus shows up? Or something larger, like Adragasa?

"I..." The Outcast's voice shakes. "I cannot take sides in this battle."

I nod, understanding her position. She has spent years creating an alliance with the dragons. I don't expect her to break it for me. "Very well. Meet us below then, once I rally everyone together."

I don't wait for her to respond as I jump off the tower, transmuting my Spirit armor and silver wings, and dive toward the remaining six dragons. I descend like a falling star against a dark, smoke filled sky, gaining momentum with each second, my enhanced senses the only reason I can still see. I toss two disintegrate talismans at the dragons to my sides, hitting both in the back of the head, turning their blood into acid. As they writhe in pain, I transmute my hand into a claw and smash into the beast below me, shattering its skull with one blow.

Only two dragons remain. I focus on the one before me, but realize I have lost track of the other one. Then something hits me from the side. Hard. Sharp teeth in a jaw capable of crushing bone bite down on my arm, and blood sprays the air. My blood. I scream, my entire body on fire. I try to pull away, but the dragon has me locked in its mouth. I use my free hand, my claw, to hit it in the nose. I don't have momentum this time, so the attack doesn't break bone, but it does do damage. The dragon doesn't let go as we fall through the sky, spiraling down, so I hit it again and again, until its jaw goes slack.

I tear my arm free from its teeth, and see that my Spirit armor is shattered on my left side, the pale skin below cut up and bloody.

I flap my wings to stop my fall, but it doesn't work. One is broken, I realize, the bones snapped by the dragon. The ground rushes up quickly toward me. I do the only thing I can think of, and toss a wind talisman at the earth below. As soon as the coin hits bottom, an unnaturally powerful gust of wind erupts from the ground. It pushes against my body, catches my wings, and slows my descent. I still fall, but not as quickly, and when I hit the side of the Asylum and tumble off the roof, I don't break any bones. Just get a lot of bruises.

Only one dragon remains. I see it hovering above me, until a red comet strikes it through the side, ending its life.

Then they land around me. Landon, Mabel, Zev, Bix, Phoenix, and Raven. My friends. My family.

Each of them grabs a part of my body and helps me stand, and Mabel places a regenerate talisman on my arm, helping it heal faster. "Thought you were looking for your daughter," she says, raising an eyebrow.

"I was," I say, breathing quickly. "I am. But I need your help to find her. If you don't want to come with me, if you wish to stay and protect the Cliff, I understand. But if—"

"Stop your yapping," says Landon, clasping my good shoulder. "Like we said before, we will follow you anywhere, Silverwing."

The other Ashknights exclaim their agreement.

I turn to Phoenix. "What about you, Ashlord?"

She looks toward the horizon at the burning forest along the river, at the silhouettes growing larger in the distance. "More of them are on their way. And they'll be bigger this time." She gestures at the dead dragons around us. "This was just a scouting party, a way to gauge our strength, and still we lost half of Gray squad." There is no sadness in her voice, no mourning. There will be time for that later. Her face is hardened by battle. "We're getting tired. Our talismans are running low. Our bolts are almost gone. Maybe we can survive another wave. But not two. I say..." she looks at each of, eyes serious. "We abandon the Cliff."

They don't know about the deal the Outcast made with the dragons and, because it would be difficult to explain, I'm glad Phoenix makes the decision to leave Dragoncliff on her own.

"However..." the Ashlord adds. "I cannot go with you, Sky. My mission is to fight the dragons. I cannot do it head on, that is clear, but I can fight from the forests, the shadows. I can take them out one by one. I will not force the rest of you to join me, however. The world may very well be ending, and you should decide how to spend your last moments."

I understand her decision, and so I say my next words carefully. "If my plan succeeds, we can end the Sundering."

Phoenix frowns, face skeptical. "What do you propose?"

"First, we need to evacuate the north," I say. "Everyone needs to head south of Al'Kalesh." Once, this would have seemed a ridiculous proposition, to move hundreds of thousands of people out of their homes. But now, as the countryside burns and the air blackens with smoke, no one challenges the idea.

Phoenix gestures at Gray squad. "Tara. Clive. Deliver this message to every remaining village or city north of Al'Kalesh. Dragoncliff has fallen. They must head south." The two Ashknights nod and run to grab horses at the stable. They could fly instead of ride, but they would tire after three or four villages. This mission will take them weeks, maybe months to complete, yet they do not hesitate, do not pause over the dead bodies of their comrades. Those deaths would mean little if they were to surrender now, and so they carry on steadfastly, performing the duty they spent years training for.

My own mission will end much sooner. The moons are already appearing in the sky. There are only a few hours left until the sacrifice is made.

"Second," I continue, "We must travel to Al'Kalesh and find Kaden and Enzo."

Mabel scowls. "Enzo is in the Asylum." I can tell his loss is still tender in her heart.

"He is not," confirms Raven. "You will see."

Landon sighs. "Even if Enzo *is* there, it will take weeks to get to Al'Kalesh."

It will not, but I don't argue yet, as they began to discuss amongst themselves. I use my commanding voice to snap them back to attention. "Listen to me," I say. "I know how to repair the Wall." This is only partially true, but it will have to be enough, and it grabs their attention like nothing else. "The man I have been seeking, the man called Pike, is the key. The children he takes are for a sacrifice. A sacrifice that is supposed to restore the Wall of Light. However, this time it will not work. The only sacrifice that will do... is Pike himself." I glance up at the tower with the Outcast, hoping she cannot hear me. She would not approve of my plan, if she knew the whole of it.

"So we find this Pike then," says Bix, "and kill him."

"We enter his Sanctuary," I clarify. "The Dream that Cannot be Dreamt. And there we make the sacrifice."

Bix nods approvingly.

The others don't look as convinced. Not even Raven, though she heard what Illian had to say.

"Even if this is true," says Phoenix, "Pike is said to be undefeatable."

"He can best any of us alone, that is true," I say. "But together we *can* win." The words are a lie, but they are all I have.

Landon rubs his chin, then nods. "Like I said, Silverwing, I'm with you."

"As am I," says Mabel.

Bix puts a fist over his chest. "I will follow you anywhere, Sky of the Knightly clan."

Zev shrugs. "Your plan sounds highly implausible, but I suppose it's the best we have."

"I..." begins Phoenix. "I don't understand how you know this... but... I trust you. I will follow you."

I grin at her, then turn to Raven.

"You are all fools," she says quietly, her voice venom, her body stiff and full of rage. "He will kill you. Kill all of you."

"Not if we work together," I say calmly. "Not if we—"

"You cannot defeat him." Her eyes turn glossy. "I will not watch you die. I will not."

I had almost the entire group convinced, but now I see doubt begin to creep back into them. And then I see how small they all look, like children playing at a game far beyond them, when all they want to do is go home, to rest in their bed, to sleep and feel safe.

"I know you are scared, Raven," I say softly. "We all are. But we have a chance to end the suffering. Not just for us, but for everyone. We *can* end the Sundering."

"Fine," she says. Something about the way she says it makes me not believe her, but I don't have time to argue now.

I turn back to the rest of the group. "Bix. I need you to find the stash of dragonstone in the fortress and grab as much as you can." He grins widely.

Phoenix raises an eyebrow. "Dragonstone? Why?"

I smile as if to say *forgive me.* "There is something you should know."

And then I tell her I am High Dragon, but I don't think she believes me. The rest of the squad confirms my story, but all Phoenix does is shrug. "It seems the world makes no sense anymore," she mumbles.

I gesture to the group. "Everyone else, grab as many talismans as you can find. Nir knows, we'll need them."

They disperse, returning moments later. Bix returns last, carrying a giant steel chest over his shoulder. He drops it to the ground and plops it open, revealing what seems a hundred blue stone. "Will this do?" he asks smugly.

I nod. "There's something I haven't told you yet." I pause making eye contact with each of them. "Something you will not understand, but for all our sakes you must trust me anyway." I grit my teeth, then wave my hand over my head as a signal. "I'm working with the Outcast."

45

SYLUS

The Red Queen dives from the tower and lands at my side, her crimson hair wild in the wind. She wears her white mask once again, to help avoid confusion.

Phoenix summons her Spirit armor instantly, body covered in flame, her eyes fierce and vengeful.

I jump between her and the Outcast. "She is not our enemy," I say.

"She killed Alec," spits the Ashlord.

"She had her reasons," I say. "Alec was a traitor. Working for the man who stole my daughter."

Phoenix's fire dims, but she doesn't drop her armor, eyes fixed on the Outcast.

"She is no threat to us," I add. "Isn't that right?"

"I am no danger to you," replies the Outcast, her voice distorted by the Mask of Nir. "I can get you to Al'Kalesh. Pike will most likely be there to defend the palace from the Ashwraith rising."

Phoenix scowls. "How do you know about the Ashwraiths?" She glares at me. "Did you tell her?"

"No," I say. "But does it even matter? Look around? The world is on fire. And it's not as if their existence will be a secret much longer."

Phoenix bites her lip, still fuming with anger.

Landon clears his throat, then scratches at his blond hair. "Um... care to explain the Ashwraith rising?"

I turn to him. "Ashwraiths are real. Corrupted Twin Spirits who have regained control of their bodies. For millennium they have lived in hiding underground, and now seek to take Al'Kalesh for themselves. Got it?"

"Um... sure?" He looks as confused as the rest of my friends, all except Raven and Phoenix, but I have no time for more details at the moment.

"Listen," I say, playing squad leader once again, pulling them in with my voice. "Right now, we need to get to Al'Kalesh as quickly as possible, and the Outcast is the way. I leave to stop the Sundering. Anyone who is coming with me, grab onto the woman in the mask." I clasp the Red Queen's shoulder. Slowly, the others follow, grabbing onto her shoulders, arms, and hips, Bix once again holding the chest of dragonstone. Raven is the last to join us, still angry and afraid. Once we are all touching the Outcast, she bows her head, and as a thunder of dragons blots out the sun, we disappear from the center of Dragoncliff and appear at the very heart of Al'Kalesh.

We stand in the plaza where I watched nine bodies burn on pyres three years ago. Now, the city that is ablaze. Fires rage into the sky, consuming the tallest and most splendid manors—the homes of nobles, of the Emperor's strongest supporters.

It does not take long to see what caused them.

A black dragon, as large as three of the ones we just fought, glides through the dark sky, spewing flame. But this is no creature of the Ashlands. This is Kaden. *No*, I realize. This is Darkflame. This is the side of him that lives with death.

Below him, men and women flee screaming and yelling, clutching babes and precious belongings to their chests. Darkflame does not target them, leaving them be. In fact, his efforts seem focused on forcing an evacuation, nothing more.

The clash of steel echoes to my right, where a group of Al'Kalesh soldiers clad in white and red fight in the streets against a mob wielding obsidian swords. The Ashwraiths. They are here. They have come. And though they are not as well armed as the guards, they are highly skilled from lifetimes of training, and they overtake their enemy with ease.

"Whose side are we on again?" asks Landon quizzically.

"The Ashwraiths." *I think.*

The Outcast steps back from the group, turning away. "I have done as I promised. I have brought you to Al'Kalesh. Now, I must go."

"Thank you," I say, "I understand." But I don't. Because even though she denies it, I know, if she truly is me, she still cares for the squad, even if she has forgotten. She will regret not helping more when the time comes.

The Outcast nods. Then vanishes. And I focus on the mission.

The moons are high. Time runs low. There is no sign of Pike yet, but he will come. He is convinced the sacrifice will work, the Sundering will end, that life and civilization will go on. He will wish to protect the city he has cultivated for centuries.

"Follow me," I say, as I dash toward the fires. Toward Darkflame.

Something blocks my way.

He stands in the middle of the street, his arms and torso bloody, his chest heaving with effort. He turns his bald head up, staring at me with two empty black sockets.

"Have you come to kill me?" Sylus asks.

I shake my head. "My quarrel is not with you."

"Liar," he hisses, spitting out blood. "You are with him. With the Darkflame. You wish to kill the Emperor, may he never burn."

He is not wrong, and I realize there is no way to avoid this conflict. Kaden prayed I would never have to face a Shadow in combat, but not all prayers are answered.

The rest of my group catches up, halting at my side, waiting for instruction. Sylus notices them, but he does not seem fazed. He tastes the air with his forked tongue, and then, like a coiled viper ready to strike, he unleashes himself.

He moves faster than any being I have ever seen, with the exception of Pike, closing the distance in an instant, weaving between us, slicing at our throats with his claws. I avoid his first strike, but the others are not so lucky. Zev gets hit in the thigh, Mable across the forearm, Landon in the shoulder, and though they wear transmuted Spirit armor, it is not enough, and the claws cut through their protection, tearing open their flesh. Phoenix, the most skilled of us, takes the offensive, summoning a flaming whip into her hand and swinging at the Shadow's knees. He evades with ease, jumping up and twisting in the air, cutting Phoenix across the shoulder as he lands, then smashes into her with his body, sending her to the ground.

I understand then why Kaden warned me. Why he told me to never fight a Shadow. I faced off against Sylus before, but it never led to battle, I assumed because he was worried about fighting me and the squad. I was wrong. He never feared losing. He wanted to avoid a spectacle, a showing of death, because, most likely, it would not please his master. But now there is nothing to avoid. Now he is free to fight at his best, and his best is too strong for us.

Sylus tears our group apart, cutting through joints, breaking our armor. He is so fast there's no time to reach for our talismans. I try to strike at him from behind with my claw, but he turns as if he saw me coming with ease and trips me with his foot. It is his dragonstone, his Flesh Imbuing, it allows him to see not with his eyes, but with something else, with his Spirit.

I roll out of the way just as he slams his hand into the ground where my head was a moment ago. Bix jumps at the Shadow from behind, trying to body slam him, but Sylus dashes out of the way, striking out with his spiked tail as he does, cutting Bix across the side. It is a shallow cut, but it bleeds, and as Bix lands, the Shadow strikes at him again. The giant Twin Spirit throws up his transmuted arms as a shield, and unlike the rest of his armor, they hold, the emerald shell hardest around his wrists.

Raven swings her sickle at the Shadow's knees, but he leaps up just in time and kicks her in the chest, sending her flying.

We will not win this fight using regular methods, so I look for the stash of dragonstone Bix left on the ground near a building and run toward it while Sylus is distracted. I am almost there when the Shadow tackles me from behind, pinning me on the ground. He raises his hand, about to cut me open, but Raven dives down from above, slicing with her sickle, her eyes red and glossy.

Her maneuver is fast, but dangerous. She will save me, but she puts herself at risk. Sylus must know this, because he smiles as he turns away from me and leaps up into the air to meet Raven. She is already mid-flight. There is nothing she can do, at least not quickly, to change her direction. She cannot evade the Shadow.

They meet in the air. With one claw, Sylus knocks aside her sickle, and with the other he strikes at her throat. He can kill her, I am certain, because he is some form of Twin Spirit, enhanced with dragonstone and Flesh Imbuing, and once he cuts her open, she will die. He may have to enter her Sanctuary, or he may not. Either way he will defeat her. He is better. Faster. Stronger.

He slices at her throat, claws inches away from her neck, nothing anyone else can do to stop him. And then...

Then the air between them shimmers.

And the Outcast appears.

There isn't enough room between Raven and Sylus to block the attack. So she doesn't. She just hovers there, head right in front of Raven, as Sylus cuts through her neck instead. Red liquid pours from her throat, and she makes a gurgling sound behind the mask, as her body begins to spasm. She is dying. But she has done what she set out to do. Because though she could not block Sylus's attack, she could strike. And by her waist, she holds her sword, and it pierces the Shadow's belly, cutting him through.

When he realizes what has happened, his smile fades, and the three of them collapse in a heap. The Shadow clutches at his wound, his gut spilling out, leaking red, but before he can stand, Raven jumps on top of him, cutting his stomach once. Twice. Then, when he slows, she swings at his neck, severing it after three strikes. The decapitated head tumbles to the side, tongue still tasting at the air. And then it goes still, and Sylus the Shadow is dead.

I run over to the Outcast and grab her hand as she spasms on the ground, the life leaving her.

She *returned*.

Though she said she could not remember the squad, no longer cared for them, no longer called them a *priority*, she gave her life for Raven. For the others.

And I realize, somewhere she had been watching, from a building or tower perhaps, for how else did she know what Sylus was about to do. Not only did she come back.

She never left.

At some point, she remembered what it was to be human. And for that I will forever be grateful.

Darklfame—Kaden—roars from somewhere in the distance, and I remember I must go, I must finish the mission.

I start to stand, but the Outcast grabs my hand, pulling me closer, throat gurgling. She is trying to say something, but she cannot, neck torn open. But somehow, *somehow*, she reaches out to my Spirit.

There is something... she says.

There is something you should know about Ka...

Her words trail off unfinished. Her hand goes limp. And I realize the Outcast is dead.

What did she mean? What was she trying to say?

Something about Kaden?

I can't worry about it now, and I have no time for guesses, though still I wonder what could have been if she had stayed with us from the beginning, if she had fought in earnest. In the end, I will never know, but I will remember her for what she did, for the lives she saved.

I study the sword in her hand. It is covered in hundreds of glyphs. Some I recognize: Density, to make the steel unbreakable. Weight, to make the blade lighter. But the other glyphs I do not know, have never seen before, and I wonder how much knowledge died with the woman before me.

Her weapon can still be of use, however, so I take off her belt and scabbard and tie it around my waist, and I take her sword for my own. Then I leave her body behind as I stand and run down the street, my friends following. I yell toward the sky. "Kaden. I know where Kara is!"

46

PALACE OF STORMS

E
ventually Darklfame hears me over the burning buildings and dying screams, and he dives toward the ground, shedding his scales and turning to Kaden once again.

His body becomes human, but he retains his black Spirit armor as he lands before us, eyes frantic. "What are you doing here?" he asks.

"I know how to find Pike," I say quickly. "He is the Emperor. Titus is one of the faces he wears."

I hear a few gasps behind me, the information new to all of my squad, but I don't go into more details.

Kaden clenches his jaw. "Then the fight for Al'Kalesh will be an even more difficult battle than I imagined."

"Come with us," I say grabbing his hand. "We can storm the palace together. We can find Kara."

He sighs. "The palace... the palace is impenetrable."

"What do you mean?" I ask.

"It is guarded by at least thirty Shadows, far more than I thought. I had no idea the Emperor had created so many. The records spoke of only nine."

Phoenix walks up beside us. "So what was your plan?"

"We would take the city but leave the palace," says Kaden. "Then we would starve them out, or perhaps come up with something quicker. But if the Emperor is Pike..."

"It will not work," I finish. "I have a way," I add, my mind spinning.

Kaden looks at me, then Phoenix, then the steel chest Bix carries on his shoulder. "What is your plan?" he asks.

"I will—"

A battalion of soldiers turn the corner. When they see us, they halt in their tracks, but there is at least twenty of them, and only eight of us, so after a moment they raise their swords and charge.

I clutch my offhand, the one injured by the dragon, and find it mostly healed as I prepare to battle. The soldiers are nearly upon us, their white capes drifting in the wind, when something crashes into the building next to them, breaking its foundation and causing it to collapse on top of the warriors. The stone crushes their bodies, trapping them under piles of rubble. An enormous elephant charges past the debris, and when I see its rider, I smile.

Enzo sits atop his Spirit, clad in gray armor, carrying a bow. He notches an arrow and shoots at one of the soldiers stuck under a beam of wood, putting him out of his misery.

Mabel runs forward, tears in her eyes as she leaps into the sky and lands next to Enzo, embracing him and whispering into his ear.

Everyone is together again. We are *nine* again.

I stand before my friends, and speak over the sounds of chaos. "The Dragoneyes Squadron is whole once more. Now, we will breach the Palace of Storms and kill the Emperor. Here's how we're going to do it."

FIVE MINUTES after I have explained my plan, Bix, Landon, Enzo and Mabel rush up the hill toward the Palace of Storms, clad in Spirit armor, weapons at the ready.

The rest of our group—Kaden, Phoenix, Raven, Zev and I—take

to the skies. We could all fly ourselves, but instead we ride on top of Kaden's dragon form, because he blends in with the night sky, and because he also carries the heavy steel chest full of dragonstone.

The Palace of Storms stands amongst the clouds, above the soot and smoke filling the city. Its walls are a pale blue in the moonlight, its golden dome roof is dark. I see the Shadows crouching on top of towers and ledges and window sills. I count thirty six in all, but more could be hidden within the structure. Each of them is different somehow, either because of their tattoos or their horns or the length of their spikes. Some are woman, I realize, though their chests are as bare as the mens'. They are all individuals, people, or at least they were before they gave themselves to the Emperor. To Pike.

I feel no pity for what I am about to do. For the deaths I am about to cause, as I flip open the chest and grab two fistfuls of dragonstone, then dive into the sky.

Below me, the Shadows notice our ground assault and leap into the open to strike them down, but before they can attack, Landon and Mabel toss out a dozen barrier talismans on all sides. The Shadows slam against the golden shields, their claws cracking the barriers but not breaking them completely. The talismans will not hold long, but they don't have to, because now the thirty six Shadows are all gathered in one contained location.

They *sense* me as I near them, a few turning their heads in my direction, but it does not matter. They are too late.

I squeeze my fists and shatter the dozens of dragonstone in my hands. Power unlike anything I have ever felt surges through me, as my skin turns ivory and my hair turns white, and a storm of lightning explodes from within me.

It strikes at the ground, hitting each of the Shadows and incinerating them instantly. I land in a crouch among the ash statues that remain of their bodies, then turn toward my squad. They are safe, protected by the barriers as I knew they would be, varying expressions of awe on their faces. I stare down at my hands, amazed as well by the power I held moments ago. The power of the High Dragons.

A wave of exhaustion overcomes me, but I am so full of adrenaline, it barely registers.

Then I hear a snap and see one of the barriers shatter into countless pieces. It barely held. I almost broke through a dozen shields. I tremble at the thought, thankful for my luck or my restraint or whatever it was that saved my friends.

Landon looks uneasy, staring at the barrier pieces fading into smoke, then he shrugs as if to say 'it is what it is.' He glances at me, then his mouth opens in an o, and before he can yell, I know what he sees. Nine Shadows emerge from the palace.

I thought this might happen, which is why Kaden, Zev, and Phoenix are still in the air. Mabel and Landon toss out three more barrier talismans for protection as I leap into the air, and Kaden dives to meet me. As his massive dragon body falls through the sky, Phoenix throws a small gray sack full of dragonstone from his back. I wish I could have kept a second reserve on me, but I don't know how to shatter only *some* of the dragonstone I am in contact with and not the rest, so this plan is the best alternative. I am about to catch the bag, when something grabs me by the ankle and yanks me down. I crash into the ground and my head spins from the impact.

A Shadow stands over me. She raises her claws, about to strike down. I try to roll away, but I'm not fast enough, still stunned by my fall.

The claws slash at my neck.

And Bix slams into the Shadow.

Somehow, he found a gap in the barrier and leaped out to save me. He pushes the Shadow back, holding her away from me, a vein pulsing in his neck from the strain. He did the one things that could protect me, but now he has left himself open.

I jump up to help, but I am not fast enough.

Bix is one. And the Shadows are nine.

They tear into him. Breaking his armor apart. Cutting at the soft flesh below. The giant Ashknight tries to fight them off, but his movements are sluggish compared to his assailants, and they easily evade his attacks while delivering more of their own.

They break him in an instant.

But as he falls to his knees, blood pouring from his mouth, the bag I failed to catch earlier lands beside me, and I grab the dragon-stone and *shatter*. Lightning explodes from my hand, arching before me, incinerating six of the Shadows. Then it turns into Umi and rips into the remaining three, tearing their bodies in half, ripping off their limbs, breaking them apart.

The Shadows die.

And I rush to Bix's side checking his wounds as Mabel runs up with me, tossing regenerate talismans onto her friend. His flesh begins to knit together, but there are more wounds than I can count and everything is covered in blood. Bix trembles, his jaw chattering, his eyes glazing over. "Stay with me, friend," I murmur, grabbing his hand. "Stay with me." The talismans will work. They must work.

Bix hisses in pain, and then his body begins to calm, and his eyes gain focus, and he smiles. "I am not done yet, Sky of the Knightly clan. Not yet."

I gasp with happiness, clutching his head in my hands and grinning. The rest of our group lands on the ground, Kaden transmuting back to human form as they surround Bix and me, watching for more Shadows as the large Ashknight recovers.

None of us look up.

And in our foolishness, we do not see the attack.

It comes like a soft rain. So hard to detect. So innocent at first. And like rain, I feel it before anything else. A slight breeze. A slight force from above.

I glance up.

And there I see the last Shadow.

He falls overhead, only a few feet away. He must have been waiting on a tower or at a window while I killed his comrades. And when he saw us distracted, overjoyed by our victory, he dived, silent as a breeze in his decent.

I try to *blink* away, but I cannot; it is a fitful talent over which I have no mastery, and I am too drained after my use of dragonstone.

I know I will not escape this. I know this is the end. But my friends will outlive me. They may yet succeed where I have failed. I close my eyes, accepting my fate, and then I hear his roar.

"No!" booms Bix as he pushes me out of the way, taking my place, standing where I just stood.

And the Shadow crashes into him, slicing open his belly.

I scream.

Raven jumps on the Shadow and tears into him with her sickle, yelling and crying and howling. This is no Sylus; he dies quickly, but still she keeps hacking away at him, until there is nothing recognizable left of his corpse.

Bix falls.

I try to catch him, but he is too big, and all I can do is slow his descent to the cold earth. He lies on the ground, body shaking, guts spilling open. Mabel places a regenerate talisman on the wound, but the gash is too large to heal. "More," I yell.

"Sky—"

"More."

"It won't matter," Mabel cries.

It will matter. It must matter. I grab her bag and lay three more regenerate talismans on my friend's stomach. "You will heal," I say. "Just give it time."

He meets my gaze, his eyes shaking. "No, Sky of the Knightly clan. I do not think I will." His words are staccato, his breath rapid. He looks down at his stomach, and gasps as tears begin to pour down his face. "Is this... is this an honorable death?" he asks, voice pleading.

"It is," I say, holding his hand tighter. "Your people will sing songs about you for generations to come. They will carve your deeds into the halls of ice and whisper your name upon the frozen winds. They will remember you, Bix of the Dragoneyes."

Zev falls to his knees beside us, and I see him cry for the first time.

"Do not weep, friend," says Bix. "I go to the world beyond, where I will once again see the face of my father, and feel the warm embrace of my mother. I go to be with my people, to hear them share their tales and this time share my own. Once, I lived in shame of who I was, but then I met you, and I learned to embrace all that I am. I thank you for that, friends." His words are cut short by a cry of pain, but it does not deter him. He squeezes my hand. "I will tell your stories in the world beyond, but I know they are not finished yet. And one day, you will have to tell me the endings. But I like a long and happy tale, so do not rush to greet me."

He gazes at each of us then as his eyes begin to close. Zev chokes out a sob and grabs onto the Ashknight in panic.

"Do not weep, friends," says Bix. "For we will see each other again."

Life leaves him then, and the Spirit known as Gaf the Mighty materializes one last time, before fading into dust. His remains catch in the wind, swirling up to the sky, and land amongst the stars.

47

THE DREAM THAT CANNOT BE DREAMT

There is no time for mourning. No time for a burial. It is almost midnight, and we must press on. Kaden and Enzo pull open the massive golden gates of the Palace of Storms, and we enter a hall shrouded in darkness, large windows casting pale blue moonlight onto the floor. A giant statue of Nir stands at the end, large and magnificent. And at its base sits Pike.

The man I have sought for so many years. The man who stole my daughter and destroyed my family. The man who robbed me of happiness. He is alone, on one knee, back turned to us, as if praying to the statue of his father.

Now, I will fulfill the promise I made three years ago. Now, I will save my daughter. I clench the new handful of dragonstone in my hand, and I *shatter*.

It doesn't work.

Because, I realize, I am no longer in my body. I am drifting away. And I appear in my Sanctuary. Dressed in white, feet bare, hands empty of dragonstone. I still wear the Outcast's sword, however. This should be impossible, and I wonder if one of the unfamiliar glyphs allows the sword to travel into the Spirit world.

Pike stands across from me amidst a sea of grass that is too real and beautiful. Two graves rise to our side. A silver tree sways in the warm breeze.

He summoned me here, I realize, like he did before when he poisoned me. I assume he wants to talk, but I don't let my guard down.

"I have come for Kara," I say.

"Then you best turn back," he says. He does not speak of the bones and the blanket he left me, at the ruse he played. Perhaps he sees I am beyond that. Instead he says, "Kara must play her part, perhaps the most important part of all, to end the Sundering."

"The sacrifice won't work," I say.

He freezes. "How do you know of such things?" By his tone, I can tell he means not *how do you know about the future*, but *how do you know about the sacrifice*.

"Illian told me about the Pyre of Souls," I say.

"Illian... it cannot be... she is Corrupted..."

"She found a way to regain control."

He shakes his head in disbelief at first, then chuckles madly. "If anyone could, it would have been her. She was, *is*, I suppose, truly, the greatest Twin Spirit of this world. And she was a good friend, until she betrayed me."

I snicker. "I recall the story differently. I recall you left her for dead."

He clenches his jaw. "There was no other choice. She wanted us to abandon the duty Nir himself had given us. She read some fable that my sacrifice would end the dragons, and she became obsessed with the idea, convinced my death was necessary. But it could not be true. Nir himself ordered me to sustain the Wall of Light, to continue the cycle. And though I never knew my father well, I knew he did not wish me dead. Illian was wrong. I tried to tell her so, but she would not listen. She insisted I give myself to the Pyre, said she would throw me in herself if I did not. And so, for the good of Nirandel, for the good of the Nine Words and beyond, I did what I had to do. I trapped her beyond the Wall. It broke me to do so, don't you see? But we all have our duty."

There are two sides to every story. And this one is so ancient and lost, there is no way I will ever discern the whole truth. I cannot sway him with the past, but perhaps I can sway him with the future.

"Each Sundering, the Wall of Light demands a stronger sacrifice, does it not?" I ask.

He nods. "Well, yes. The Wall of Light was created by Nir's magic, but his magic fades. It requires more and more Spirit to remain alight."

"Then is it not possible that this sacrifice will not be enough?"

He pauses, considering, and a flash of panic fills his eyes. "No. She is strong. Strong enough." He talks more to himself than me, and the more he talks the more the panic fades. "Yes. It will work. She is the strongest I have ever trained. The strongest there ever was. If she had more time, she could exceed us all."

"The sacrifice will *not* be enough," I say again fiercely. "The Outcast told me herself. She had the mask."

"The mask..." his face lights up at the mention, and I see Orcael in him once more. What good friends we had become, until I learned the truth. "It's real, then? I knew it. Could it truly be only used once?"

I nod. "Only once, as the Valarata said."

He smiles, but then his face turns angry. "And she used it for... what? To return here? To try and stop me? She... she could have gone anywhere. To the time of Nir and Val and the Elder Dragons. To the time before even then. She could have learned the secrets of the past. She could have preserved the knowledge that is lost to us, kept it safe so that perhaps we could benefit from it."

"I know you would have done so," I say, remembering our talks and studies in the library. "But she was more concerned with the future than the past." I step forward, my voice hard. "If you go through with the sacrifice, it will fail, and the Wall will fade, and the cycle you have fought so desperately to continue will end. Dragons will spread over Nirandel, perhaps even beyond, turning all to ash. Your father's sacrifice would have been for nothing."

His eyes twitch at my last words, and I know the mention of his father hits him harder than any physical wound. He has always sought Nir's approval, even when Nir was dead, perhaps even more so then. I could see it, in the way he spoke of the Elder Dragon as Orcael. At the time, I thought it an odd curiosity, a childhood fantasy, but now I understand the deep roots of his obsession. His father was the greatest being in all the Nine Worlds, and yet, he had never cared to know his son. And the son wondered why. Why was he not good enough? Not worthy enough? And there was no answer. And all the son could do was try to impress his father, try to become worthy of his name. He tries still. A millennium later, the son seeks to honor the father.

"If..." Pike says softly. "If what you say is true, then what do you propose? That I cast myself upon the Pyre as Illian wanted?"

He already had the chance—many times over as each Sundering came and went. He will not give up his life, this I know. So I propose the only other option.

"Sacrifice me," I say, stepping forward. "Take me to the Dream that Cannot be Dreamt, and I will walk into the Pyre of Souls. I am High Dragon. My Spirit is stronger than Kara's. She will break the cycle, but I will make the Wall shine another hundred thousand years."

Pike does not respond right away, considering, a sadness in his eyes. "But you are..." he chokes on the words. "You are my daughter. I will not lose you again."

And now we come to this truth. How different it is to the both of us. "I have no father," I say. "And my mother was not your wife, Elliana. My mother was Laura Knightly. The woman who clothed me, fed me, told me stories at bedtime and held me close as I trembled from nightmares. The woman who gave her life to be my mother."

Pike scowls, hands trembling. "Laura was but your mother's hand-maid. The two of them conspired to keep you away from me. They had no right. If I had known you were my daughter, I would never have... " He grits his teeth. "I would never have taken Kara from you. They made fools of us both."

He makes no apology. Takes no responsibility for his own actions. He is a man blinded by his own vision of the world.

"If you care at all for me," I say, "then you will sacrifice me instead of Kara." I beg. It is all I have left. "Let me save my daughter. Let me do this one thing for her. Do not take her from me as your child was taken from you."

My eyes fill with tears, because I do not know what to do if he doesn't listen. I do not know how to defeat him. And so I plead once more, "Sacrifice me."

He says nothing. Shows no hint as to his feelings, his face empty, eyes hollow, as if he has become a shell of a man. And perhaps he has. Perhaps being confronted by the memory of his dead wife and the daughter he never knew he had has broken him.

The air cools and the orange and purple sky of my Sanctuary grows darker. It is not because time has passed. It is because I am at my end.

"Very well," says Pike, voice cold and quiet. "I will take you to the Dream that Cannot be Dreamt. I will take you to my Sanctuary. But you will have to speak to Kara alone. She has accepted her fate. Only you may be able to convince her otherwise." He holds up his hand, and the center of his palm begins to wither away. The sky blackens, crumpling like paper, burning away, and ash falls from the sky. The grass turns yellow, then black, then gray. The silver tree catches fire and leaves nothing but a charred corpse. The stone graves turn to dust in the wind. All fades away.

And I enter the Dream that Cannot be Dreamt.

PIKE IS GONE, and I stand alone in his dream. In this quiet and lifeless place where the world is gray and the sky pitch black. Where there are no stars and no moons, and yet somehow there is light.

This is nothing like the infinite dream of Adragasa. This place is small, tiny even, just an island covered in ash floating in a sea of darkness.

This world must be much like the one the Outcast walked, after everything burned away around her.

Except, I am not alone.

A shadow stands at the edge of the island before a beam of white light that shoots up so high into the sky you cannot see its end. The Pyre of Souls.

I walk forward, feeling the soft ash beneath my feet as I approach the dark figure. She stands facing the light, her back to me, wearing nothing but a white dress. Her long black hair falls down her back. Her body is small, delicate, but there is strength there as well.

Tears pour down my cheeks. A sob escapes me. My entire body shakes and my legs crumple beneath me and I fall onto my knees. I had given up on this moment, given up on any chance of seeing my little girl again. She is not little anymore, however. She has grown. And how I wish I could have seen her grow. How I wish I could have been there to watch her learn and become all she could be.

My voice is a broken thing. "Kara?"

She turns.

And I see a face I know better than any other. The face I have called friend. The face I have loved.

"Raven?"

48

RAVEN

My body breaks as I realize the truth. "You were with me the whole time..." I murmur. Ever since I arrived at Dragoncliff, she was by my side. And I did not recognize her. I did not *see* her. The similarities I dismissed as coincidence, if I even gave them any thought. But now I see so clearly. The dark eyes that would look up at me as I held her close to my chest. The smile that would warm my day as I told her favorite stories. My little girl. Kara. Raven. They are one in the same.

She speaks softly, and I hear her voice like never before, the voice I wished to hear for years as I imagined what Kara would sound like as she grew older. It is beautiful and gentle and strong all at once. It is the soft whisper of the wind. The warm caress of the sun. It is the patient, distant hum of the storm.

"Before we give ourselves to the light, we are all permitted one Gift," she says. "My Gift was you." Her lips curl in a half-smile. "When I learned you had arrived at Dragoncliff, I asked to spend my last few years with you. I wanted to know you. Your voice. Your eyes. Your soul." She blinks, eyes glossy. "At first, I hated you. For letting me go. For ending your search. I know you had no choice, but I hated you all the same. But..." her voice brightens. "Then I got to know you.

Your kindness. Your strength. The way you cared for those you loved. The way you cared for *me*. You never let me be small. Instead you let me be everything. Sad and spiteful and angry and happy and mean and friendly, and you cared for me all the same. You taught me what it meant to be a friend, to be a family. And I could hate you no longer. I love you, Sky." Her voice breaks. "I love you."

With her last words, something changes inside her, and tears stream down her cheeks, and I can see they are of both sorrow and joy.

I find the strength within my limbs once more, and I run toward her, and I grab her in a hug and I hold her close like I will never let go.

She hugs me back, laughing through her tears.

I kiss her cheek. Her head. I clutch her hair in my hand. "How?" I ask. "How could you be... When I arrived at Dragoncliff, you should still have been a small child."

She wipes her eyes, calming her sobs. "I traveled to Nirandel before you. And though I cannot remember this, Pike told me he carried me between multiple worlds as a child, and so I aged faster than you for a time. I think I am older than Kyle now." We both chuckle. "So many times I wanted to tell you who I was... but I didn't want you to lose me twice. But now, I am glad you know. I am glad we have this moment.

I pull away to see her face. "What do you prefer now, Kara or Raven?"

"Raven," she says quickly. Then softly she adds. "But it would be nice... to hear you call me Kara one last time."

I hug her once more and whisper in her ear. "I love you, Kara. I am so sorry I let you go. I am so sorry I failed you."

She pulls away this time. "It's okay," she says. "You made these last few years worth living." Then, she lets go of me and steps back toward the light. "It is time. I must go. Do not mourn me, for I will be in the world beyond. I will see Bix there, and I will tell him this story. I think he will be most happy to hear it."

I grab her by the shoulders, startling her. "No, Raven. The sacrifice will not work. That is why I am here."

She shakes her head. "I have to try. If I don't, you and Zev and Landon and Mabel and Kaden and Phoenix will die. I will not watch you die." Her body trembles.

I hold her tighter and look upon her face one last time. I memorize the lines there, the twist of her lip, the curve of her jaw, the arc of her nose, the shape of her eyes. "There is another way. Goodbye, Kara." Then I push her to the side and dash forward into the light.

49

KARA

She grabs me from behind and pulls me back and throws me into the ash. Her face is full of rage. "I will not watch you die!"

"There is no other way," I plead. "I am the only one who can relight the Wall."

"No," she says, and I fear she is about to jump into the light, but instead she walks forward, past me, into the center of the dream. She falls to her knees and sticks her hands into the ground and she screams and the very earth and sky begin to shake. "I am in your dream," she roars. "I am in your Sanctuary. If I tear apart this world, I will tear apart your body. So come. Come and face me, Son of Nir. I am Raven of the Dragoneyes clan. I am Kara. And I am your slave no longer."

50

SON OF NIR

A roar fills the sky. I have heard its kind before, from Adragasa, but this is even louder and more powerful. And then he is there. Above us.

Majestic and terrible in his form.

The Son of Nir.

Dark blue scales shimmer in the black sky. Sapphire wings thunder through the air. A tail, longer than the span of this ashen island, swipes across the land. This is a creature too marvelous and dangerous for this world. A creature unmatched. A titan amongst giants. The largest dragon I have ever seen, and the son of a god.

His roar is a thousand roars. His voice is a thousand voices. "This is my domain, child," he growls. "And you will fulfill your duty, willingly or not."

Raven yells again, shaking the dream once more, and the great dragon recoils. Whatever she is doing, she is hurting his Sanctuary, hurting *him*. And something shifts, the barrier Pike had up to keep my friends away weakens, and as the air shimmers, they begin to appear. Zev. Landon. Mabel. Enzo. Phoenix. Kaden.

They are here. We are together once more.

For a moment, they are confused, but when they see the mighty dragon above, they understand. They transmute their Spirit armor and, without exchanging any words, the nine of us form a circle and prepare for battle.

The dragon opens its massive jaws and fires down blue flame. We scatter to avoid the blast as the inferno strikes down beside me, the heat melting my silver armor even from a distance. I leap backwards, out of harm's way, and take flight with my wings toward Pike. But even as I glide toward the massive dragon, another figure emerges from the blue blaze. A man, his skin pale and thin, his body covered in red stone, leaps from the fire, his ragged black cloak drifting behind him, as he swings a scythe through the air. It is Pike. His human form. Somehow, he is in two places at once. And then I remember, this is his Sanctuary. He can do things here that are impossible in the real world.

The human Pike dashes forward, and he is even faster than I remember. When he cuts through my friends, the sound of his scythe tearing through flesh is barely audible. It is such a quiet, simple thing. And yet it turns the air red. It brings my friends to their knees.

First, Pike strikes at Landon. He cuts through his Achilles tendons, as he once did to me, and sends my friend falling to the ground. Before Landon has even hit the ash, Pike is upon Mabel. With two swings, he cuts off both her arms, then glides toward Enzo and slashes him across the waist. Next, he cuts off Phoenix's hands, then Zev's feet. But when he tries to strike at Raven, a sword clashes against his scythe.

Kaden blocks Pike's advance, just as he did for me three years ago. He seems the only one fast enough to fight the Son of Nir.

Even I, a High Dragon, am too far away and too slow to help. I need dragonstone, but this a Sanctuary; there will be no dragonstone here. So as Pike twists to strike at Kaden from the side, I do the only thing I can think of, and beckon my Spirit to appear between them.

Umi heeds my call and materializes in front of Pike, biting down on his shoulder. For once, Pike cannot evade an attack, because there was no way for him to see it coming, and my silver dragon tears into his collarbone. Pike tries to pull away, but my Spirit has him pinned, Umi's jaw a vice around his arm. Kaden seizes the advantage, and drives his sword into Pike's gut. Once. Twice. Three times.

He's about to strike at Pike's head when a massive tale swings past them, hitting Kaden in the side and sending him flying. Pike tosses his scythe into his free hand and cuts down on Umi's neck, and my Spirit has no choice but to let go of his shoulder and pull back. Pike smiles, the black blood oozing from his shoulder and stomach doing little stop him as he leaps across the island to strike at Kaden while he is down.

I beckon Umi toward the Ashlord. Usually, I would be too slow, but Pike has a lot of distance to cover, and he moves slower due to his injuries, and Umi reaches Kaden first, blocking the scythe midair with his claws.

Pike growls, with both of his bodies at once, and another beam of blue flame strikes down at me from above, but Pike's dragon form isn't as fast as his human one, and I fly out of the way. I realize then, we are targeting the wrong enemy. "Kaden. Raven. Focus on the dragon!"

They nod and transmute to become airborne. Zev, gritting his teeth, body shaking, follows them too. His feet have not yet regenerated, but he doesn't need them to fly. I don't know how he can focus through the pain, but he does, and the four us strike at the mighty dragon above.

We can't use talismans here, because it's a Sanctuary, so we must make do with our beckoning and transmuting. Raven cuts at the colossal serpent's feet with her sickle. Kaden transforms into Darkflame, body growing black scales and red wings, but his dragon is only a quarter the size of Pike's. I beckon Umi to his side, and together they battle the Son of Nir.

One dragon that of darkness.

One dragon that of light.

They swirl around the sky, using their superior agility to tear into the larger dragon's flesh. He tries to incinerate them with his fire, but they glide behind his head, managing to stay behind him as he thrashes about with tooth and claw. He is too slow. They are too fast.

Umi and Darkflame tear him apart.

They bite down on major arteries. Cut through his wings. And when once, long ago, Kaden and Umi stood as enemies, they now stand as allies. Their Spirits entwined.

And even the mighty Son of Nir cannot defeat them. With wings full of holes, he begins to fall. And then small Zev, who was never great at slaying dragons, charges through the sky and tears into the great dragon's eye. He rips it out. Then cuts into the brain.

And the titan dragon dies.

What remains of Pike, the hollow man below, trembles at the sight. He sits in a pool of his own black blood, staring with frantic eyes as his Sanctuary begins to fade away. As the black sky turns brighter. As the wind starts to blow the ash away.

"I will not let the light fade," he whispers. And then he jumps and skeletal wings sprout from his back. Before any of us can react, he grabs Raven by the waist and dives down. Toward the Pyre of Souls.

Kaden is the only one fast enough to catch them, but he is too far away, high above in the gray sky. I beckon Umi toward Pike, summoning my Spirit out of thin air, but Pike twists out of the way each time, anticipating my attacks. Raven strikes at his back with her sickle, but he is unfazed by the blows, as if he feels no pain. She cuts off his wings, but it does not matter, because now they are only fall-ing. She tries to cut off his arms, but he bites down on her hand, breaking it, and she screams. Soon they will be at the Pyre.

And my little girl, my Raven, my Kara, will die for nothing.

I understand then why the Outcast did what she did. Why she gave her life for Raven. She knew Raven was Kara. It is what she was trying to tell me before she died. And now, I know what I must do. And I know it will work. Because it must work. Because I have dedi-cated my life to Raven, to Kara, and I will not fail her again.

I draw the sword at my side.

And I *blink*.

I appear between Raven and Pike, tearing them apart. The Son of

Nir howls and digs his nails into my daughter, and so I slice upwards with my sword and cut off his arms. Then I twist us around, lift up both my legs, and kick Pike in the chest. He flies forward. Into the Pyre of Souls.

And he burns.

51

THE CYCLE ENDS

The Pyre of Souls glows bright and the man within screams and writhes as his body burns to ash. The Dream that Cannot be Dreamt fades away.

And we fall back into our bodies within the Palace of Storms.

Behind us, the Wall of Light flashes in the distance, burning so brightly we can see it from Al'Kalesh. Then the light explodes outward, covering all of Nirandel.

I feel it as it happens.

The mass death of all the dragons.

Their souls burning out, their bodies turning to ash.

I fall to my knees as a cry of pain is torn from my lungs.

I hear Adragasa's cry in my mind, in my heart and soul, as she watches her children die around her, before succumbing to the light herself.

She is the last to die.

With her, the age of light ends.

And a new age begins.

52

TWO WORLDS

The Ashwraith rising succeeds, and the people who once hid underground for millennium become the rulers of Nirandel.

Illian takes the throne and enacts new laws and regulations as the city of Al'Kalesh is rebuilt after what becomes known as The Ascension.

Any man, woman, or child, who does not wish to be ruled by the Ashwraiths is given nine months to leave for a land once mysterious and dangerous, and thus the exodus to the Ashlands begins.

Hundreds of people pass the through the gates of the Wall of Light, which burns brighter than ever, and head toward the city of Na'Razim. There Naoki and Makoto help them settle in amongst the Worshipers of the Wall and begin a new society. Naoki works with cheers and smiles, but I heard they wept for days after Adragasa and her children burned at the center of the city.

I too wept in the quiet of night. For after my time at Na'Razim I began to see dragons as more than monsters. They were beautiful, majestic, intelligent creatures deserving of so much more than they ever received. And sometimes, secretly, I wish that the Wall of Light had faded away and that somehow we had found a way to live together in peace.

After the Ascension, the Dragoneyes Squadron transports the body of one of their own, the man called Bix, to the north and buries him at the base of the Frozen Mountains as his people sing the song of his deeds and call him *Agrala*: hero, in their tongue.

They bury one more body as well. The one called Outcast by some, Red Queen by others.

And then, once they have mourned and said their goodbyes, they too travel for the Ashlands.

I SIT on a cart pulled by two Boxen, beside Massani and Etu and their children. We ran into them on the way south, and they offered us a ride amongst their caravan. Raven sits with the children, telling them the story of she and I slayed the Son of Nir. They gasp, and ooo, and aw, and after the tale is finished, they teach her how to play a game of symbols. There is a joy in Raven that was not there before the Ascension, and I am glad she has found a new kind of happiness.

I pet Ashpaw, who sits on my lap, purring. He was safe at Dragoneyes Manor during the Sundering, and now rides with us along with the Keeper and his protege, little Appleseed.

Zev, Landon, Mabel, and Enzo sit in the other carts. Phoenix stayed behind in Al'Kalesh to aid Illian and her new regime. She had, after all, known about the Ashwraiths for many years. I am not surprised she wishes to see them thrive. Illian named her a general, and from I understand, she leads forces to quell any uprising committed to the old Emperor.

Kaden stayed behind as well. For he is the son of Illian, the first born Ashwraith, and their prince.

We parted on good terms, for we will see each other again, but it was still hard to say goodbye. The Ashwraiths intend to begin trade and maintain good relations with the people of the Ashlands. Kaden will serve as diplomatic representative of his people. And I, it was decided by others, will represent the people within the Wall of Light.

When we arrive at the gates, I see that they have been altered. No longer can they only be opened from the outside; Levers to unlock the passage have been built on the inside as well. We travel past the gate, and for a moment my body tenses, preparing itself for danger, but then I remember the danger is gone, and my body relaxes, and for the first time I enjoy the beauty of the Ashlands.

Vast plains spread beyond the horizon covered in patches of emerald grass, and long rivers stretch throughout the land, because water can and always has passed through the light of the Wall. Towering mountains loom in the distance, and I grow excited as I realize this land is yet to be discovered. Yet to be mapped.

So when we arrive at Na'Razim, I announce that I will lead an expedition to explore the Ashlands and locate regions suitable for new cities. Naoki argues with me to stay, because they believe a High Dragon should rule the people, and after much thought, I agree to a leadership position, if I can create a council to be elected by the populace who will manage daily affairs. Naoki, after much grumbling, agrees to my proposition, because what else can they do?

Raven offers to join me on my expeditions, but the rest of the squad remain in Na'Razim and begin a new School of Ash. Though the dragons are gone, Spirits remain, and there must always be Ashknights and Ashlords to find the Broken Ones of the world and guide them. The practice of Charred however, is dissolved, and slowly Naoki begins training as well, unlocking powers once forbidden to them.

At first it is whispered that the the Dragoneyes Squad are the last remaining Ashknights still alive after the Ascension. But that assumption is quickly proven false as Ashknights and Ashlords and Ashlings who survived the Sundering find their way to Na'Razim, Tara and Clive of Gray Squad among them. The Charred too, hundreds of them, find their way to the city, and are surprised when their wristbands are removed. Some of them weep. Some of them shout in joy.

Landon and Zev become the head teachers of the new school, their friendship growing even stronger as they argue over new policies and teaching methods. Enzo and Mabel help from time to time, but they seek out a more private life. One in which they can make a home together and perhaps one day even have children.

Raven and I begin our expeditions, traveling the vast Ashlands for months at a time. We map rivers and mountains and give them names. The first mountain we found we called Bix the Honorable.

And one day, as the sun begins to set, and we are tired from a day of traveling, I cross over a hill and see a familiar sight in the distance. A mountain crooked and weathered by time. And then I remember Adragasa's dream.

The crooked mountain.

The crooked mountain.

The crooked mountain.

Save us.

I run all night until I reach my goal, finding the dark cavern I saw in my vision. Raven and I crawl deep into the bowels of the mountain. We discover old glyphs and words carved into the walls. Tales from the ancient days of Nir. And then, far below the surface, in the heart of the crooked mountain, we find a cavern with nine stone eggs.

Somehow, nine dragon eggs survived the Ascension. I suspect it is because of how deeply buried they were underground. Raven theorizes the glyphs carved into the walls may have given them protection. Adragasa knew of the eggs. Showed them to me. I suppose she must have prepared for the possible threat of extinction to her race. Why she decided to show *me* the location of her precious children, I will never know. Maybe because of the blood bond we shared.

We transport six of the eggs with us to Na'Razim, leaving three behind in case they are ever needed again. After the eggs are given proper warmth, they begin to hatch. Four are female. Two are male. They are not the intelligent dragons of old. They are the newer breed the Outcast told me of. But they are full of love and wonder and joy at being alive.

The people of Na'Razim consider them their greatest treasure. And it isn't long before the babies grow into drakes. They develop personal bonds with certain individuals. One takes a special interest in Raven, and she names the dragon Bix.

One day, as I work on the design for a dragon saddle, I hear news of the Ashwraith emissary. He was not supposed to arrive for another month however, and I rush out to greet him and find out why he is here so early.

Kaden stands at the entrance to the city. When he sees me, his face lights up and he wraps me in a hug.

"Is something wrong?" I ask, pulling away to see his face.

His eyes are glossy. "No," he says. "Things are just as they should be. I have renounced my position as Prince of the Ashwraiths, and now I come here, seeking a new life, if you will have me?"

I am overjoyed at the news. But... "Your people?"

"I have given my life to the Cliff," he says. "I have given my life to the Ashwraiths and their freedom. And now, with the battles over, perhaps I can have some freedom of my own. To make my own life. With you."

I smile and grab his face in my hands, leaning into him until our lips touch. We linger there at the entrance for quite sometime until we reluctantly pull away to find somewhere more private. It isn't until many hours later that we head back into the city, holding hands.

In the coming days, Kaden takes a keen interest in the drakes. He helps find them the best food, the safest places to roam. He nurtures them and loves them as they grow. I think it is his way of atoning for the many dragons he killed as an Ashlord, and I see him happier than ever before.

And then, many months later, Raven comes to me with peace and determination in her eyes. And she says, "I'm ready to go back."

53

HOME

Fear. Trepidation. Excitement. It all builds in me as Raven and I stand by the fountain in a world that used to be home and now seems so very foreign. It smells different here. Worse. I scrunch up my nose and look at Raven, who is taking it all in without giving any hint as to what she's thinking.

"You don't remember any of this, I imagine," I say. "You were just a baby."

She looks over at me, her face softening. "I remember you. And I remember my brothers."

She never told me this, that she remembered us. She knew who I was when we met because of Pike. At least, that's what I always assumed.

But this. I had no idea. And my heart breaks again for the little girl I lost, but I can't help feeling proud of the woman she's become. With or without me.

I reach for her hand, and she slips hers into it. "Are you ready to see them?" I ask.

She nods.

I pull out a cell phone and American currency—retrieved from a local cache Kaden told me about—and schedule an Uber. When our car arrives, I give the address I have never forgotten, and then I stare out the window and try to imagine what my life would have been like if I hadn't gone with Kaden that day.

I look at Raven, and I know it's not a choice I could have made. She'd be dead right now if I hadn't gone. So much would be different.

The Uber driver drops us off at the curb, and I hand him some cash. Once he's gone, Raven and I look at the house. And then we approach the door and I knock.

It takes a moment, but we hear someone running to the door, and then it opens.

At first, I think we have the wrong house, or that they've moved, which is a possibility I'd considered but couldn't face. But then the tall man at the door cocks his head in a way so familiar I have to bite my tongue to stifle a cry.

"Kyle?"

"Yes. Do I know you?" He looks more closely at me and his face pales and then hardens.

He recognizes me. I see the moment it happens. The moment his hurt and pain turns to anger.

"What do you want?" he asks.

He's a young man now, grown beyond what my memory can hold. He stands tall, shoulders broad, towering over me.

But within this man's body, I see the child I left so many years ago. And I hold out my pinky, tears filling my eyes. His face collapses and he holds out his. We link them together as I say, "I promised I'd come back and that I'd tell you everything once I understood it."

He nods, his eyes glossy now too. "Where have you been?" His voice cracks.

"It's a long story. You going to invite me in? I've brought someone who really wants to meet you."

BLAKE CAME home within ten minutes of getting the call, and he pulled me into a bear hug and cried into my shoulder. When he saw Raven, he went speechless. It took us long into the night to tell the story. To explain why Kara was older than them now, when she was the baby. To explain why I was gone for most of their lives. To explain what all of it had meant.

Caleb was quiet most of the night and only now raises his hand to speak.

"You don't have to raise your hand," I say. "You can just talk."

"Did you miss us?"

That's his only question. Did I miss them.

Tears stream down my face and I nod. "With all my heart, I did. With all my heart."

And then there are hugs, and more stories, and more hugs, and more tears, and this lasts many days. And then weeks. And then months.

And then.

Then.

It is time to go home.

Because this is no longer our home, mine and Raven's. This is where we are from, but no longer where we belong.

And in those goodbyes, there are hugs and stories and tears and more hugs and stories and tears.

No one makes any promises, because we can't be assured we can keep them.

Save one.

That we will hold each other in our hearts forever.

Before I leave, I give each of them a necklace I had carved before we left.

Kyle looks down at his. "A dragon." He looks up. "Is this real? Like, really real?"

I look at Raven, and she nods, and I connect to Spirit. When I hold out my palm, Umi appears.

Caleb screeches. Kyle gasps and Blake drops his jaw in awe.

"This is Umi. He's a part of me, and I of him. Umi, this is my family."

"Way to bury the lead," Blake says, as my baby dragon takes turn perching on everyone's hands.

We leave with happy tears and happier memories.

We leave knowing we kept our promise.

We came back.

One last time.

EPILOGUE

Twenty years later

A GENTLE BREEZE carries the scent of dragon's breath as the three moons shine brightly in the night sky. The stars are dazzling this early in the morning, and I wonder at the vastness of it all. I pull my robe more tightly around my body as Umi perches on my shoulder, purring gently in my ear. Wind pulls at my long loose hair, whipping it through the air, and the little dragon bats at it with his wings.

My thoughts buzz through my mind like angry bees, and I breathe in the cool air and try to let the stillness of the night seep into me.

When I hear his footsteps approach, I smile. Even after all these years, he makes my heart dance.

"Another dream?" Kaden's voice is deep and seductive, still laced with sleep.

"Yes," I say, my eyes still glued to the horizon. In the distance, moonbeams catch on a dragon's scales as it soars through the stars.

"Nir is out there, somewhere. Not on this world, I think. But out there, waiting for me to find him. To free him. To bring him home."

Kaden's arm slip around my waist and I lean my head against his chest, snuggling into his warmth, into the comfort of him.

Umi, disrupted from his spot on my shoulder, flies off and lands on Ashpaw's back, who followed Kaden to the balcony. The two play with each other, and we watch for a moment, amused by their antics and kinship after all these years. As Ashpaw rolls to his back, I see the gentle red pulse in his chest that has kept him alive long past his mortal life expectancy. His reward for saving the lives of our twin children when they were babies.

"You'll find him," Kaden says, pulling me back to my swirling thoughts. "The diggers continue to excavate the underground caves. Each clue brings us closer."

He's not wrong, but it's been years. So many years.

I turn in his arms and look up at the chiseled face of the man I have loved most of my life. "Who would I even be without you?" I ask.

He leans down to kiss my forehead. "You would still be the most magnificent woman in all the Nine Worlds," he says.

His lips dip lower to find mine, when a crash and raised voices disrupt our moment. "What the... "

The door to our bedroom suite slams open and a fierce woman dressed in black storms in followed by two bedraggled guards—a man and woman—who look at us apologetically.

"We tried to keep her out," the man says.

The woman rolls her eyes. "Sky, who are these dragon-bait?"

I laugh and leave the embrace of my husband to join Raven and the guards. "They're new," I say. "From Lacrasha. Landon sent them. He wasn't impressed with our personal retinue last time he was here, so he insisted on sending his personally trained guards."

Raven smiles at that news, and her features soften instantly. She turns to them. "Apologies. I didn't recognize you and didn't know you were sent by Landon."

They grunt, but still look unhappy as they glance at me for

instructions on what to do next. "We're okay here," I tell them. "Raven is family and welcome any time."

They both nod and return to their guard duties outside our suites.

I turn to the woman who was part daughter, part sister and is now my best friend. "What couldn't wait until the sun rose at least?" I ask, though my grin belies my gruff tone.

"I knew you'd be awake." She raises an eyebrow. "The dreams are getting stronger aren't they?"

I nod. There's a spark in her dark eyes, and though she's harder to read than most since her time with Pike, I can read her. I know she's got news. "Tell me."

Kaden stands by my side, and reaches for my hand.

"We've found something."

Umi perks up at this, and flies to land on Kaden's shoulder.

Those are the words Kaden and I have been waiting to hear for twenty years.

Twenty years since we took our people into the Ashlands after the Sundering.

Twenty years since we found that first cluster of dragon eggs and knew there was hope. That we hadn't destroyed them all. That we could rebuild. That we could start anew with a better vision for living in companionship with them.

We've nurtured them. Trained them. Integrated them into our communities.

These dragons aren't what they once were. They no longer feed on Spirit. They no longer hunt humans. They have become allies. Friends.

Nir's vision has been fulfilled, and now, I need to find Nir. To save him. To bring him home.

And so I continued to look. To search. To scour the earth for clues. He comes to me in my dreams, as he did so long ago. But his messages are harder and harder to decipher. We are running out of time. If the dreams stop, if that connection is lost, I may never find him and reunite him with his children, his world, his legacy.

"What did you find?" Kaden asks, his voice urgent, as my heart skips erratically in my chest.

"Come see for yourselves," Raven says, a sly grin on her face. "Sky's the only one who will know for sure. Nico and Nova are meeting us at the stables."

Raven leaves us to dress, and though there is much I wish to say to Kaden, I don't know the right words.

Because if this is what we've been looking for, it means everything will change.

"Are you ready for this?" he asks as we finish dressing.

"Can anyone ever be ready for what comes next?" I ask.

"Security is mostly a superstition," Kaden quotes. "It does not exist in nature, nor do the children of men as a whole experience it. Avoiding danger is no safer in the long run than outright exposure. Life is either a daring adventure, or nothing." He raises and eyebrow and I laugh.

"I have no idea," I say. This has been a game of ours since we met. He quotes someone and waits to see if I can correctly identify who originated it.

He frowns melodramatically. "You have to at least guess, or it's no fun."

"At least tell me which world it's from," I say.

He sighs. "Gai."

I shrug. "Um, Benjamin Franklin?"

"Helen Keller," he says with a wink.

We stand by the door of our quarters and I look around at the comforts we've surrounded ourselves with. The opulence. The luxury. A huge four-poster bed with silk and satin sheets. Hand carved furniture made from the trees of Ash Forest. A blazing fire to keep the chill out. Books that line the walls, even though we have a fully stocked library in the east wing of the castle. A life we walk in and out of each day. How much longer will this be ours? I wonder.

Kaden tugs at my hand and we make haste through the castle that was built into the cliffs with the help of the dragons.

Horses are readied for us when we arrive at the stables. Nico and Nova are there, and our eyes meet.

"Do you think this could be it?" Nova asks, her long dark hair braided into twists on her head. She has her father's blue eyes, but my face.

Nico is the opposite, with my eyes and his father's features.

Our miracle twins, born into a world still recovering from the war and the Sundering. Born as powerful Twin Spirits, with High Dragon blood flowing through them. They now lead the Council of the Ashlands, with Kaden and I as advisors and figure heads. Handing them the royal crowns freed us up to pursue our quest of finding Nir and discovering if any other Elder Dragons remain.

Kaden and I each have our own motivations for this. For me, it's to reconnect with my blood. To find and free Nir—who is my grandfather. For Kaden... it's a bit more complicated. He feels guilt for how much dragon blood is on his hands. For living blindly in a world that used dragons as resources. Now, he wants to make amends. To set things right.

"It has to be," I say, answering Nova's question. "Nir is waiting."

Raven is already mounted and waits for us to join her before heading to the caves.

By the time we arrive, the sun is already casting golden hues into the night, sending the moons and her children, the stars, back to sleep, as the stories go.

There's a general hum of anticipation and excitement amongst the workers, who are waiting for us.

They bow deeply as we approach, and I hasten them to relax. "We need not stand on ceremony today. Show us what you've discovered."

Raven has been lead on the cave excavations since the Sundering. She has been as committed as myself to finding the instructions Nir left for us.

We light torches and enter the caves, the light dancing off the walls as we move cautiously through them.

I want to run, to hurry everyone along, but I know we must proceed carefully and quietly, lest we cause a cave-in.

There are drawings on the walls as we enter the deeper levels of the cave, and though initially they resemble others we've found, they soon start to change. A shiver runs up my spine as new images appear. New writing in the ancient High Dracos.

I run my hand along the words, the power of them shimmering up my arm and into my body.

And then we turn and step into a cavernous space with a clear pool of water in the center. I look to the walls for clues and see drawings and writings, but Raven shakes her head. "That's not what we brought you here for," she says.

"Then what?" I ask, confused.

She points to the pool of water. "Look."

I step to the edge and look down. The water is still, like glass, and I peer into it. The bottom is a flat silver stone with gold flecks that shimmer. There are engravings on the stone surrounding a large golden dragonstone in the shape of a star.

A thrum of power pulses through me, and Umi appears perched on my shoulder. I rub his chin and smile. "What do you think, little guy? Is this it?"

Umi chirps and flaps his wings, then dives into the pool, splashing everyone with water. I turn to Kaden. "I'm going in," I say, though I know he already knows this.

I strip off the top layer of my robes and pull off my boots. When I'm left with just my binder and underwear, I dive in.

The water is shockingly cold and steals my breath. It's deeper than it appears, the water making the bottom look closer than it is.

As I swim deeper, the pressure around me changes, and my lungs feel tight, my head fuzzy.

Water that was previously still now churns like a whirlpool. I can no longer see where I'm going. Everything is a frothy white, blinding me, and obscuring which way is down and which is up.

I reach my hand out, trying to get a sense of my position, when I feel something cold and smooth against my palm.

The whiteness turns to black, and I'm no longer underwater, but rather floating through a velvet dark sky full of diamond stars.

"You have come at last," a great voice says.

"I've been looking for you," I say, recognizing the voice as Nir, the Elder Dragon who set so much of my life's course.

"And now you have found me. Or the echo of me. The memory. Whether I still exist or not, who can say?"

"What do you mean?" I ask. The voice seems to come from everything, even within me.

"Layered illusions are still just illusions," he says, clarifying nothing.

The stars begin to pulse together, their brightness amplifying as millions of them fuse into one and a shape begins to form out of the nothing.

The shape of a dragon. The shape of a man.

And then the shape explodes, blinding me, piercing into my soul, sending me shooting through space and time and history and the future and all that ever was and is and could be.

My brain aches. My body feels ready to burst from the pressure.

And something within me cracks. Pain shoots through me until there is nothing left but the pain.

Pain and darkness.

I gasp. Water ejects from my throat like burning bile and I choke and gag as someone slaps my back.

I'm rolled onto my side on cold stone. My clothes are soaked through. Umi sits inches from my face, staring at me. When my eyes open, he shrieks and jumps up and down, his wings flapping.

"Thank the gods," Kaden says.

I struggle to sit up, but he has to help me. He is also wet. Our children are bent on knees near us, as is Raven. "What happened?" I ask.

"You were drowning," Nova says, her voice full of worry. "You sank to the bottom and didn't come back up. Then the water went white and started bubbling." Her eyes glance to Umi. "He flew out of the water in a panic, and dad jumped in before anyone could do anything."

I look up at Kaden. "Thanks for saving me. Again."

"I owed you one," he says.

He and I have saved each other's lives more times than I can count over the years. Seems we aren't done yet.

I smile, unable to contain my excitement. "I know where Nir is," I say.

Raven smiles.

Our kids share a look, and I can tell they are less enthused. "You'll be leaving then, won't you?" Nico asks.

Kaden nods. "We've always known this would be the course, should we find what we need. This is a quest we must take."

Nova nods. "I wish it wasn't so, but I understand."

We spend the rest of the day packing. The kitchen is notified and prepares travel food for us while we spend time with Nova and Nico and Raven.

We leave at sunrise the next morning. We will travel to Dorshire and use the pools there to leave this world. As I suspected, Nir isn't on this world. He's been trapped on a less hospitable world, but I know how to find him and free him.

At least I think I do. Nir dreams are fuzzy creatures, prone to misinterpretation.

Nova wipes a tear from her eyes and hugs me again. "Be safe. Don't be stupid."

I laugh at that. "Would your father or I ever do anything stupid?"

She and her brother exchange a look that makes Kaden snort.

There is a pause, as we all realize it is time to say goodbye. For how long, none of us know.

There are tears, more hugs, kisses and more tears.

I have imagined going on this quest for years.

I just never imagined the leaving part. The saying goodbye to my children, my friends, my life...

"Goodbye is just another way of saying hello to a new adventure," Kaden says.

Nova cocks her head. "Buddha?"

I laugh. "I think your father just made that one up himself."

Kaden winks at me. "It's only fair I get to add something quotable into the lexicon I've stolen from all these years."

Nico laughs. "Fair, indeed, father. Fair, indeed. You will be remembered. And quoted."

Umi chirps and grows bigger and bigger, until he is large enough to easily carry two adult humans. Kaden and I mount the great dragon, and then...

We fly.

ALSO BY KARPOV KINRADE

Visit KarpovKinrade.com for more books and music

THE NAUGHTY LIVE LONGER
(standalone psychological thriller/suspense)

VAMPIRE GIRL SERIES
(complete fantasy romance)

Vampire Girl

Vampire Girl 2: Midnight Star

Vampire Girl 3: Silver Flame

Vampire Girl 4: Moonlight Prince

THE NIGHTFALL CHRONICLES
(dystopian fantasy/science fiction)

Court of Nightfall

Weeper of Blood

House of Ravens

Night of Nyx

Song of Kai

THE FORBIDDEN TRILOGY

(complete sci fi thriller romance)

Forbidden Mind

Forbidden Fire

Forbidden Life

ABOUT THE AUTHOR

Call us Karpov Kinrade. We're the husband and wife team behind *Of Dreams and Dragons* and *Vampire Girl*. And we want to say... Thank you for reading it. We worked hard on these characters and this world, and we're thrilled to share this story with so many readers. Thank you so much for joining us on this journey. We are sad to see it end. If you are interested in our other work, sign up for the Karpov Kinrade newsletter at KarpovKinrade.com and get all that and more!

And if you have a moment, please consider leaving a review for any of our books you've read and enjoyed. Reviews help inform new readers and expose the series to a wider range of people. Every single review matters. Every single review is important.

And visit KarpovKinrade.com for more great books to read. If you're looking for something new and exciting, check out *Court of Nightfall*. It's an epic adventure full of suspense, love, betrayal, friendship, and twists and turns that will leave you breathless.